In common with her heroine, Ann Granger has worked in British embassies in various parts of the world. She met her husband, who was also working for the British Embassy, in Prague and together they received postings to places as far apart as Munich and Lusaka. They are now permanently based in Bicester, near Oxford. Ann is currently working on her tenth Mitchell and Markby novel.

A Touch Of Mortality

Ann Granger

headline

First published in 1996
by HEADLINE BOOK PUBLISHING

First published in paperback in 1995
by HEADLINE BOOK PUBLISHING

15

ISBN 978-0-7472-5186-6

Typeset by Avon Dataset Ltd, Bidford-on-Avon, Warks

Printed and bound in Great Britain by
Clays Ltd, St Ives plc

HEADLINE BOOK PUBLISHING
A division of Hodder Headline PLC
338 Euston Road
London NW1 3BH

I should like to thank all those who have helped and encouraged me during the writing of this book (and, indeed, of all my books). My husband, John, my editor Anne Williams, my agent Carole Blake, my friends and all those readers who have written to me about the books or whom I've had the opportunity to meet in person. With regard to this book in particular, I'd like to thank Messenger's auction rooms of Bicester, for inviting me on to their premises, and the manager and staff of the Chipping Norton postal sorting office for allowing me to bother them at five a.m. of a chilly morn!

Chapter One

'There'll be frost again tomorrow, just like there was this morning. A chap in the pub said so,' Libby's Uncle Denis had announced the previous evening at the family table.

'They're a mine of information, these men you keep meeting in pubs!' muttered Mrs Hancock, setting down the teapot with unnecessary force.

Libby had hastened to head off family acrimony. 'The frost had turned everything white this morning. Just like a snowfall.'

Mopping up this piece of information as easily as he was mopping up gravy with a lump of bread, Uncle Denis had flowed on. 'That'll have given the bookies a nasty turn! Every year, you know, people put bets on it snowing for Christmas.' He stirred his tea noisily and added as a generous afterthought, 'But nasty for you, Lib. Driving on those country roads.'

'I'm better off in the van than the people who have the town walks and deliver on foot,' Libby had said, hoping that by replying she would stop him clattering his spoon against his teacup.

Uncle Denis, as usual, rolled over her comment. His conversations were always conducted for his own benefit.

'Yes, the bookies will get a fright, no mistake!'

He chortled, slurping up tea at the same time, so that he had to put the cup down, coughing. The tips of his moustache, which had been trapped, trickled moisture, and he looked more than usually like a walrus on an iceflow.

His sister and niece both winced. Mrs Hancock said tartly,

1

'Well, you'd know how bookies' minds work if anyone does!' In a different voice she added, 'You'll have to wrap up warm, Libby, if it does keep cold like this. I wish you had a job indoors all the time. I worry about you in the winter, turning out on the dark mornings and everything.'

She gave Denis a meaningful look, indicating it would be nice if he had a job of any sort.

Uncle Denis's acquaintance with the betting fraternity was of long duration. Some years ago it had led to his wife divorcing him. Finding himself temporarily without a roof, he had come to stay with his married sister: 'As a stop-gap, until I find a place of my own.'

The stop-gap had already lasted two years when Libby's father died. Uncle Denis had then nobly volunteered to go on living with them so that he could look after his widowed sister and her little girl.

The little girl was now twenty-four and Uncle Denis was still in residence. They'd become inured to the sight of his bald head, florid features, drooping moustache and flabby paunch. To say nothing of his fondness for personal jewellery and unsuitably youthful leather bomber jackets. They didn't ask where he got his money. Frankly, neither of them wanted to know. He didn't work. His social benefits, apart from erratic amounts paid to his sister for his keep, went into the pockets of bookmakers and publicans. Occasionally he was, in his own term, 'flush' and then he was embarrassingly generous. Nags romping home first past the post would account for this, of course, but somehow Libby didn't think so. Despite assiduously studying form in the sporting press, Uncle Denis didn't appear to have an eye for a winner.

She mused about all these things as she drove the little red post office van carefully along the B road towards the hamlet of Castle Darcy. It would be nice to be rid of Uncle Denis. Plotting ingenious means of *getting* rid of him had harmlessly occupied Libby's mind on many occasions as she made the twenty-five-mile round trip delivering mail to outlying communities. No Denis. It would give her mother a chance to make new friends. Herself, she'd no longer have to dread the way he always embarrassed her in front of hers. And they'd both be spared his table manners.

Uncle Denis's meteorological predictions had proved right. This morning had seen a second hard frost. In sheltered spots where it hadn't melted away from yesterday, a thick white layer had built up, transforming the bare winter countryside. The first sun's rays revealed the silvery lace of spiders' webs veiling the bare twigs of wayside bushes. The outstretched white fingers of oaks and horse chestnuts lining the road glittered like the tinsel branches of Christmas trees in a seasonally dressed store window.

In Libby's fancy the house roofs and gables became the iced gingerbread dwelling of Hansel and Gretel's witch. Right down to bare damp patches in the area of chimneystacks marking the location of early morning fires below. The witch preparing to cook little children. But only in pantomime.

'She isn't real, children!' A voice echoed down the years in Libby's head. Wailing infants in the audience paused in their terror, hesitating, wondering whether to believe the good fairy.

'She isn't real!' promised a chorus of accompanying parents and aunts.

But she looked real. Oh my, yes, thought Libby. A man in drag, of course. She knew that now. A man who, in his own clothes, probably resembled Uncle Denis. But what a witch he made! With the tangled grey hair, striped stockings and pointed hat. But, in the end, Hansel pushed the witch into her own oven. Hansel's death would have been murder, but the witch's was justice. How we wanted her dead, Libby remembered. How we wanted the threat destroyed! In the end, everything turned out right.

'Christmassy!' said Libby aloud and felt happy.

The council lorry had been along the day before and gritted the road; usually these minor roads were forgotten and turned into

3

something resembling the Cresta Run. Libby was duly grateful. The council had shown itself less efficient with all year round maintenance of the road surface itself. The van bumped its way over small holes and cracks past the first dwellings and came to a halt before a pair of low-roofed cottages set back from the roadside behind long front gardens.

Libby switched off the engine, pulled on the woolly gloves her mother had insisted she bring, and opened the door. Her breath formed vapour clouds on the chill crisp air which seeped in. There was no one about. Most people were still only having breakfast, she thought.

Few households got up at crack of dawn as theirs did. Her job required rising early. People expected their letters to arrive with the breakfast bacon and eggs. Mrs Hancock was a light sleeper and glad to get up to see her daughter off to work, although Libby had repeatedly begged her not to bother. But there was another reason why Mrs Hancock was in the kitchen before dawn.

Uncle Denis, thank goodness, found four in the morning an ungodly hour to rise and slumbered on heedlessly. The shared early morning cups of tea and toast in the warm kitchen were treasured by Libby and her mother. The absence of Denis was never mentioned, any more than his presence was. But occasionally, a faint snore from the bedroom above would permeate down and they'd exchange furtive grins.

Libby leaned across to the front passenger seat where she'd deposited the little stack of mail for Castle Darcy. She had put the items for these cottages on the top of the pile. One of them, a package addressed to the right-hand cottage, had been sent by recorded delivery and required a signature. There was another package secured by an elastic band to a couple of envelopes, which was intended for the left-hand cottage. Libby took them both together with her clipboard and got out of the van.

Her sturdy footwear bruised spikes of frosted grass *en route* to the first gate. As she made her way up the path to the door she

4

heard a faint bleat from somewhere behind the cottage. She wondered whether Mr Bodicote was out back with his goats and she'd have to make her way round there to get the required signature. She'd been making the postal deliveries for two years now and knew quite a few of her regulars. She rapped on his door.

A curtain twitched at the window. After a moment, a doorchain rattled and a minimal crack appeared. A thin, elderly face pressed against it, showing only one eye and a corner of wrinkled mouth above a whiskery chin.

'Post!' called Libby, adding less obviously, 'I need a signature, Mr Bodicote.'

'What for?' The question was issued in a fierce voice.

'Recorded delivery. This package.' She held it up and then waggled the clipboard.

The withered lips moved again as an eyelid drooped suspiciously above the visible eye. 'Who's it from? Does it say?'

Libby sighed and turned the package over. 'A Mrs Sutton.'

'Ah, that's my niece, Maureen.' The chain was released and the door opened fully. Mr Bodicote was revealed.

He must have been a tall man once, but age had shrunk him. The habit which height had given him, of stooping beneath low lintels, hadn't been lost. He hunched now as he moved forward, although it was no longer necessary. He was wearing an ancient jacket stretched over two woolly pullovers and, to be on the safe side, a tweed cap. None of the clothing disguised how thin he was. He stretched out covetous scaly talons, tipped with yellowed nails.

The witch! An echo of her earlier daydreaming returned with a frightening suddenness. Libby's heart gave a leap. Then she grinned sheepishly at the old man.

'That'll be her Christmas present for me.' Bodicote sounded much more amiable. 'She never forgets me, Maureen. She's a good girl. And she always posts early for Christmas, just like they tell you to.'

'Wish everyone did!' said Libby, holding out the clipboard and maintaining the package out of his reach. 'Sign here, please, and print your name underneath in capitals.'

'I'll have to go and get my glasses.' Disappointed at the delay, he padded away into some unseen region. He was gone a few minutes during which Libby stamped her feet and became aware that her post office issue navy jacket wasn't as warm as she'd thought it was. She could see down the cottage's narrow hall straight through into the kitchen at the back. She could make out an ancient stove and, on it, a pan bubbling. A huge pan, too big to prepare any human meal! The witch, the witch . . . A strange bran and vegetable odour wafted down the hall to Libby's nostrils.

'The goats!' she muttered. 'He's boiling up mash for the goats. Pull yourself together, Lib! You'll be seeing goblins next!'

'Here we are.' Mr Bodicote was back, fixing his spectacles. The tortoiseshell frames were mended with pink sticking plaster. He studied the clipboard and wrote his name carefully. His handwriting was surprisingly clear. He'd learned to write when children were made to practise 'hooks'. Age had made him a little shaky, but the copperplate letters were still beautifully formed.

'You'll have to excuse me, my dear,' he went on. 'Having the door locked up like it in broad daylight. I never thought I'd have to do it, but I've got enemies.'

Mr Bodicote had been pronouncing unlikely statements ever since Libby had been bringing the post.

'I heard the goats as I came up the path,' said Libby, over-looking the latest eccentric claim. She exchanged the package for her clipboard. 'Cold for them outside this morning.'

He was shocked. 'They're not out of doors, not today!' He whisked the package from her. 'Except for the old billy, Jasper. He starts kicking the door if I don't let him out first thing. I had to put a bolt on the outside of his house. Any kind of latch within his reach, old Jasper can undo. But I haven't let the nannies out. This cold weather don't suit them. They need looking after, do goats, if you want a good yield. I keep 'em in and make sure they got plenty of feed. But the old billy raises merry hell if I don't let him out in the paddock, come rain or shine.'

He leaned forward. 'I got to keep a close eye on them. Folk have tried to poison them, you know.'

'Surely not!' said Libby, knowing that she shouldn't let herself be drawn into this. She had a whole round to get through, several villages. More likely, if the goats had been ill it was because they had nibbled laurel or some other unsuitable plant.

Mr Bodicote was fortunately distracted, peering at the address on his parcel. 'Maureen sent it,' he repeated. 'And always by the recorded delivery to make sure I get it!' With that, he closed the door in her face. She heard the chain rattle.

Libby retraced her steps, automatically following the imprint left on the crust of frost by her approach. The poor old chap was getting pottier. Such a shame. She crunched down the path to the second cottage, slipping the elastic band from the bundle as she went and checking the address on the two envelopes.

There were clear indications of a different lifestyle here. An adjacent barn appeared to have been turned into a two-car garage. Also an extension had been built on to the side of the cottage itself. The addition was modern, single-storey, flat-roofed and spoilt the symmetry of the old building. The builders had left behind a pile of rubble, planks and general debris which was stacked to the rear of the barn-garage, in an angle formed by the garden hedge. The rubbish heap was covered with a white layer just like everything else. Libby glanced at it with mild disapproval. She was thinking how untidy it normally looked, without its frosted blanket, and wondering whether it would stay like that till spring. She rang the bell.

Inside the cottage, Sally Caswell was tightening the top on a vacuum flask of hot coffee. She looked out of the kitchen window as she did, and noticed that old Bodicote had let out one of the goats, the big brown and white one with the curved horns. Despite repeated requests to the old man to put the animal on a running tether, it was roaming loose about its paddock. She hoped it didn't eat its way through the party hedge and into their garden. Not again. Liam would go mad if it happened again. He'd already threatened to put the matter into the hands of their solicitors and she really thought he would.

Only two days ago that same billy-goat had got through the hedge by dislodging a sheet of corrugated iron from one of the patched areas. It had wandered right up to the new extension where Liam had his study and peered in the window. Poor Liam had looked up from the screen to see a bearded, horned face only inches away, watching him intently from the slit pupils of chalky-blue eyes.

'Enough to give anyone the screaming habdabs!' he'd said afterwards. At the time, he'd let out a yell like a man possessed, rushed outside, picked up a lump of rock from the pile of unused hardcore left by the builders and shied it at the beast.

Unfortunately, old Mr Bodicote had seen him do it and a very nasty scene had ensued. It was at the end of that exchange that Liam had threatened his elderly neighbour with the law.

Unrepentant and unbowed, Mr Bodicote had merely observed that, 'Town folk like you and your missus have got no business in the country! You wants to go back to London, you do!'

A chance would be a fine thing! thought Sally, a little sourly.

Going back to London or its environs had ceased to be an option, not only with the sale of their tiny Fulham terraced house, but with the other sale of Aunt Emily's rambling mock Tudor Englefield Green villa. Sally had inherited the villa on Emily's death some eighteen months before and was sorry now that they'd sold it. But Liam had been keen to get rid of it. They'd received a fair offer which, so Liam argued, they'd be foolish to turn down. The villa was in urgent need of structural repairs and modernisation. The present property market meant that they mightn't get another offer soon. It had been nice, of course, to get the money, but Sally had grown up in that house. It had been a place where she'd been secure, loved and happy. She felt now that Liam had rushed her into selling.

But it was over and done and there was no use moping about it. Holding the flask, Sally set out for the study, but before she got there, the doorbell rang.

'Morning, Mrs Caswell!' said Libby, handing over the package and the two envelopes. 'This looks to have more postage on it than it needs. Someone's guessed instead of taking it to the post office to be weighed. Always best to take things along to the post office and get it right. Might save yourself some money!'

Sally took the padded mailbag indicated and the letters. She didn't recognise the printed handwriting on the package. She had herself sometimes popped things into a postbox with extra postage to be on the safe side, when she hadn't been able to get to the nearest sub post office, which was at Cherton.

'You haven't seen Mr Bodicote this morning, have you?' she asked Libby. Receiving an affirmative, Sally added nervously, 'What sort of mood is he in?'

'All right!' said Libby. 'Quite cheerful. No odder than usual.'

Sally proceeded on her way to the study, the vacuum flask clasped against her breast as she studied the post.

Liam was seated at his computer, glaring at the monitor.

'I've brought your coffee,' she said. 'It's very frosty out there again and a good job you didn't go to Norwich yesterday. I've just heard on the radio there's freezing fog on the East Coast. At least we haven't got that. Just think, if you'd been driving back today!'

'I didn't *not* go to Norwich because of the weather,' Liam mumbled, punching at the keyboard. 'I didn't go because Jefferson rang up and said he had to reschedule everything. The Russians have been delayed. So there wasn't much point.'

'Good job you hadn't set out, then. I mean, ringing up here at the last minute like that!' She held out the post. 'These look like

9

Christmas cards. It's only the first week in December. I haven't even bought mine. The package is addressed just "Caswell". I suppose it's for you. I'm not expecting anything. London postmark.'

'I can't be bothered with it now!' he said tetchily.

Oh dear, she thought. What's put him in a bad mood? Because he couldn't go off for his scientific beano in Norwich, I suppose. She kept her tone resolutely bright. 'Shall I leave it here? By the flask?'

'No!' He spun round. 'Take it away! I said, I can't be bothered with it! I thought I heard a goat! Has he let them out again?'

'Well, yes,' she admitted. 'But only one of them.' Hesitantly, she went on, 'I suppose he is entitled to let them out into his own paddock.'

'But not into my garden!' said her husband through gritted teeth.

It occurred to her that she could have corrected him. It was her garden, actually. She'd bought this cottage. But she said, 'He did patch up the hedge again.'

'Yes! He patched it with an old bedstead this time! Now it looks bloody awful, worse than the iron sheeting, and the goats will only eat through somewhere else!'

'Shall I pour your coffee?' she asked placatingly.

'No! Leave it there! I'll pour it out when I'm ready!'

'Some sort of problem?' She tried to sound sympathetic.

He grunted. 'I'll have to go to Oxford, to the lab, tomorrow. Might even go later on today. We'll have to reschedule everything to do with the Russians' visit.' He glanced at the vacuum flask. 'Just leave it there. And take away the post. Deal with it yourself.'

'But it's a video.' She held out the package. 'Although it's a bit on the heavy side for a videotape. But it says so, on the front. Did you order a video?'

'No! It'll be some moronic Christmas present! And I'm not going to stop what I'm doing and run a video right now, am I? Take it away!'

She accepted rejection. It was the easiest thing to do when he was in this mood. 'All right. I'm just going to make my hot drink and then I'm driving into work. I'll be back late-ish. It's preview day for tomorrow's sale. I want to talk to Austin about Aunt Emily's things, too. He did say he'd come out and give me a valuation this week but with the sale I suppose he's been too busy.'

He grunted and hunched over his computer.

'Oh, and Meredith said she'd call by the saleroom. She wants to take a look. I told her we had some rather nice Victorian wine glasses. She may put in a sealed bid. And then we might have a bit of lunch together.'

Liam clutched his head. 'For Chrissake! Will you just go and do whatever you want to do and leave me in peace?'

She went back to the kitchen and switched on the kettle to make up her own flask to take into work with her. Her round snub-nosed face was uncharacteristically despondent. She was a healthily attractive young woman. Her flyaway fair hair was secured by an Alice band and she was comfortably dressed in pleated skirt and sweater over a shirt, with thick winter tights and flat shoes. Country lifestyle suited her. She had been instrumental in persuading Liam that the cottage would be ideal. He could concentrate on writing the book, for which purpose he'd arranged to spend only part of his working week at the lab and the rest at home. She, in her spare time, could garden.

But it hadn't really worked out. Liam couldn't get on with the country. It bothered him. The goats were an example. She didn't really mind the goats, although it was true old Bodicote did nothing to prevent them straying into the Caswells' garden. She suspected it was part of a systematic harassment designed to drive away his new neighbours. She'd thought once that the old man quite liked *her*, if not Liam. But then there'd been that unfortunate matter of the turnips.

'Thank God I've got a job to go to!' Sally thought. Immediately she felt guilty. She loved her husband but some days he was impossible. What with Liam hating the cottage and nothing having worked out as hoped, little wonder she'd been suffering from stress. Getting away, going in to Bamford to her job had kept her sane.

She got other occasional breaks when Liam went over to Norwich. Despite being preoccupied with the book, he still kept an eye on the exchange student programme run by his Oxford research laboratory and one engaged on similar work in Norfolk. Now events had interfered with his latest trip, probably causing the bad temper, and depriving her of what she'd come to view almost as Liam-free breaks.

She moved across to a worktop on which stood a row of stoppered glazed pottery jars, each carefully labelled. She didn't drink coffee or ordinary tea, but had a liking for herbal tea. Here in the country she could make her own. In the summer she used suitable fresh leaves or flowerheads picked in her garden, poured on boiling water and let the whole mix steep, finally adding a good tablespoon of honey and straining off the resultant brew. Also in summer, she dried racks of leaves in her airing cupboard so that in winter she still had a supply, although the tea lacked the flavour of fresh ingredients. You had to know what you were doing, of course, and be careful only to pick the plants suitable for tea-making.

Liam disapproved of her home-blended teas. But then, Liam seemed to disapprove of most things she did. 'You don't know what you're drinking!' he sometimes said. To which she would reply, 'Yes, I do. I know better than you do!'

On days when she went into Bamford to her part-time job, she took along her 'tea' in a flask, leaving Liam his flask of coffee. She now set about preparing her own brew and, while the kettle heated, sat at the table to open the two envelopes. As expected, they contained early Christmas cards. She must remember to buy a couple of packs whilst she was in Bamford today. She turned her attention to the package.

It was the popular sort of padded mailbag, and addressed simply in printed capitals CASWELL. The word VIDEO was also printed on by hand. She had no idea who'd sent it. There was no indication apart from the central London postmark. She picked it up; gave it an experimental shake. The kettle began to hiss. She glanced at it, then back at the package in her hand, hesitating. The kettle gave a loud click. Sally put down the padded mailbag, got up and started towards the worktop where the kettle stood.

Crump! Behind her came an explosion similar to those she recalled from childhood when the unswept chimneys of coal fires caught alight. What began as a throaty snarl finished as a triumphant rending noise, as if some penned creature had burst loose. It was accompanied by a pressure in her ears. A balled fist hit her in the middle of the spine and pitched her forward to strike her head on the cupboard edge. A bright flash lit up the gloomy winter kitchen. Things were happening all around and all at once, yet she was conscious of each, distinctly. Plates crashed down from a shelf. Small pieces of debris whizzed through the air, one sheering through the window sending shattered shards of glass tinkling down, some outside and some inside the room. Smoke rolled up from the area of the table, hiding it from view. It filled the kitchen and was accompanied by an acrid stench of melted plastic and scorched wood varnish.

Bewildered and temporarily disorientated, she lay slumped across a worktop, her fingers still clutching the handle of the electric kettle. Miraculously it had remained upright, saving her from being badly scalded. The burning odour increased. Smoke got into her lungs making her cough and retch. She released the kettle and pressed her hands to her mouth and nose. She saw, and for some reason it distressed her more than anything else, that the dried herbs had spilled from the pottery jar. As she watched, the jar itself rolled over the edge of the worktop and crashed on to the floor, breaking into half a dozen pieces, ruined. Through it all she heard her husband's voice. It came from the kitchen door.

'What the dickens have you done now? Am I going to get no peace at all?'

Sally pushed herself upright and turned, leaning against the worktop for support. A trickle of blood ran down her forehead, along the bridge of her nose and dripped scarlet spots on her sweater. Through the smoke she could see his outline in the doorway.

Spluttering, she denied the accusation. 'I didn't do anything.'

'What's happened here?' He was moving forward, towards the table, his hand outstretched.

She came to life, jerking herself away from the worktop and lurching forward. 'Don't! Don't touch it!'

He stopped at the shrill note of panic in her voice and stared down at the pine table in a perplexed way.

'The package . . .' she croaked. 'It was the package . . .'

'What package?'

That was Liam for you. When he was writing, nothing else registered at all. But perhaps he could be forgiven the question because there was little left of the package. Only where it had lain, a dreadful, sinister burned circle.

She lost her temper in fear, anger and bewilderment. 'The one supposed to contain a video! I showed it to you not ten minutes ago! For crying out loud, forget that wretched book for a while! It wasn't a video at all! It was a letter-bomb, don't you understand? Those animal rights' extremists sent you a letter-bomb! The ones who broke into your lab last year! It must be them!'

He opened his mouth and she was sure he was going to say, 'Rubbish!' But he couldn't deny that the centre of the table was burned black and there were scraps of smouldering paper and broken plastic and wire lying around.

He seemed to become aware of her appearance. 'You all right?'

'I think so. I banged my head.' She touched her forehead

14

gingerly. 'I was so lucky. Liam! I was going to open it. I even *shook* it, for heaven's sake! The kettle switched itself off and I got up. Otherwise I'd—' She fell silent.

He stood with his hands hanging loosely by his sides, his face with the boyish features which always made him look younger than his thirty-eight years, twisted in puzzled disbelief.

'It couldn't be,' he said without any conviction.

'It was! Whoever sent it could have blinded you, Liam! You could have been horribly disfigured! We've got to call the police!'

Chapter Two

Meredith Mitchell had been on sickness leave from her Foreign Office desk for the past two weeks, following a particularly virulent attack of influenza which had struck her down in mid-November. She hadn't suffered from flu for years and had forgotten just how devastating it could be. There was no question of returning to work yet. Needless to say, she hadn't sought the preventive jabs earlier in the year.

'Not,' said Dr Pringle kindly, 'that it would have made much difference in your case. This is a new flu-type. Every few years we get one.'

Stay in bed, drink gallons of liquids and sweat it out had been his advice. He'd scribbled out a prescription to alleviate the head and joint aches and that pretty well had been that.

She'd followed his advice, being able to do little else. From her pillows she'd memorised the cracks in the ceiling and formed inchoate plans to get up there and do something about them. There were cobwebs up there too, dangling in the corners and undulating in the draughts. Another thing to do something about. She had grown, during her bed-bound sickness, to dislike the ceiling intensely. It was a memo-pad of domestic chores. No inspirational ideas sprang from it. No encouragement to deep reflections on the Meaning of Life. No ghostly finger obligingly sketched out any portent. No *Mene, Mene, Tekel, Upharsin*. Just a cracked Victorian ceiling and, probably, some very dodgy wiring in the electric light, all prodding her conscience just when she was least able to resist their nagging.

The final straw had been Mrs Harmer's cooking. Mrs Harmer was housekeeper to their vicar, James Holland. James, being currently out of town, had kindly 'loaned' Mrs Harmer to the invalid and, again, Meredith had been too debilitated to resist.

This meant that Mrs Harmer had arrived at eight every morning, slammed the front door and clumped in winter boots down the narrow hall to the kitchen, bawling, 'It's all right, Miss Mitchell, it's only me!'

She had then brewed tea and made porridge for Meredith's breakfast.

'A good breakfast sets you up for the day. Especially if a body is picking at food like you are. At least you know you've got something solid in your stomach.'

The porridge was solid, all right, probably just the thing for plastering up those cracks on the ceiling. But it was edible and by far the best item on Mrs Harmer's invalid menu. The menu had been worse than all the symptoms of flu put together.

Not for Mrs H. the latest notions on nutrition. 'Fads!' she called them scornfully. If you were ill, according to Mrs Harmer, what you needed was plenty of plainly cooked fish. It was good for the brain. Rice pudding was also good for you, it seemed. Poached eggs, horribly underdone and glassy, sitting on soggy toast were excellent. Not so, boiled eggs. 'Binding!' said Mrs Harmer mysteriously.

Coffee was deemed bad for the nerves. 'Oxo!' declared Mrs Harmer, plonking down huge mugs of this nourishing beef extract brew.

During Mrs Harmer's well-meant ministrations, the house stank of boiled cod, baked milky rice and Oxo. One positive result from all this was that it encouraged one to get better as soon as possible. When the day came that Mrs Harmer could be dispatched to the vicarage, Meredith had ungratefully felt like cheering.

Now the symptoms had subsided. But they'd left behind a disconcerting weakness in the legs and, unsurprisingly in the wake of all that plain fish and beef extract, a disinclination to eat. Nevertheless, today Meredith was up and about early. Sally Caswell, who worked at Bailey and Bailey, the local auctioneers, had told her that among items to be inspected during today's preview of tomorrow's auction was a set of Victorian wine glasses.

'Just the sort of thing you said you wanted, Meredith.'

It was true, she had mentioned Victorian glassware some time ago, and Sally had promised to keep a look-out. Generally, Meredith's cramped end-of-terrace cottage did not lend itself to the accumulation of antiques. Her sole foray to date in that direction had been the acquisition of a Welsh dresser and the adventures attendant on that had perhaps put her off adding to it. But today she was going along to take a look and, afterwards, have a bite of lunch with Sally. Not that the appetite was back yet, but a bowl of soup or something would be nice.

Meredith clattered down the stairs to the kitchen, feeling quite cheerful. She ran water into the kettle and peered through the kitchen window at her backyard. It looked cold out there, but bright. Something moved, catching her eye, a shadow in the far corner behind the disused coal-bunker, where the frost still lay up. It was the cat.

The cat was a stray and had been around for about two weeks, on and off. Its general condition was skinny and battle-scarred but it was a young animal, a tabby. She liked tabbies.

It might have been around longer and Meredith, away at the office all day, hadn't noticed it. It was only during the enforced sick leave that she'd become aware of it. She didn't know whether it had been abandoned and was seeking out a new and comfortable home, or whether it was genuinely wild, but she suspected that it had been turned out by an uncaring owner. It was nervous. It didn't respond to friendly overtures. But she didn't like to see any animal so thin. Mrs Harmer having obligingly stocked the freezer with frozen fishsteaks, Meredith had taken to cooking them up and feeding them, piece by piece, to the cat. This could only be done at a distance because it refused to come near or let her approach, even tempted by the smell of cod. She had to leave the scene. When she returned, the food would be gone. It was an excellent way of getting rid of the fish without wasting it. The cat was definitely a Good Cause.

Meredith took a plastic tub of previously cooked cod from the fridge, opened the back door and stepped out into a biting wind. She scraped the fish on to a saucer and called the cat. But it disobligingly scuttled back over the wall. Meredith retreated, leaving the fish. Presumably, as before, it would come back. Not only that cat, but every other cat in the neighbourhood.

Half an hour later saw her driving into the car park of the town's auction rooms. She locked her car and made her way across the irregularly shaped yard towards the open doors of a rambling building of weathered stone. The place showed signs that it might once have been a livery stable. But now above the oak lintel was a sign – itself probably two generations old at least – which read:

BAILEY AND BAILEY
Valuers and Auctioneers
House Clearances
Antique furniture and memorabilia

A poster tacked on a notice board on the wall announced the forthcoming Christmas Auction Sale. Preparations were clearly underway. Passage into the auction rooms was blocked by a bow-fronted walnut chest-of-drawers. On her side of it, outside the building, stood a stocky man in a baize apron, arms akimbo. At the further side of it, inside the building, and only his head and chest visible, was a pale youth wearing a baseball cap.

'We'll have to turn it sideways on, Ronnie!' said the stocky
man.

'Take the drawers out,' opined Baseball Cap.

'No need to, just run this bit of rope round it, the drawers won't
fall out.'

'For Pete's sake!' cried a voice from somewhere inside, 'Take
the drawers out! And mind the corners! That's an early Victorian
piece!'

'Don't you worry yourself, Mr Bailey,' rumbled the first man.
'You leave it to me and Ronnie.'

The walnut chest began to rock as it was heaved 'sideways on'.

'Right! Lift your end, Ted!' cried Baseball Cap.

'Watch the drawers!' howled the unseen owner of the voice
within the building.

'We're putting a rope round her!' shouted back Baseball Cap.

'Not you, dear!' he added to Meredith, who stood by as an
interested observer. He winked and took off his cap long enough
to scratch his head. When he did, it could be seen that he was
older than his first appearance suggested. The wearing of the cap
was less a youthful fashion fad than to disguise thinning hair.

The piece of furniture, secured, was inched through the gap
and Meredith followed it inside.

She found herself in a large, low room. She blinked and when
her eyes had become adjusted to the dim light, saw that stacked
around her was all manner of furniture, bric-à-brac, pictures,
books and mysterious boxes with unidentified contents. Ronnie
and Ted had set down their burden on the further side of the room
and it was being examined anxiously by the owner of the third
voice.

He was a tall, thin man, whose gold-rimmed spectacles and
collar-length greying hair lent him an academic appearance. He
wore a Prince of Wales check suit of old-fashioned cut and, in
contrast, a rather jazzy bow tie. Meredith knew this to be Austin
Bailey and that he was, despite the legend over the door, the only

21

Bailey at present connected with the business. Clearly he was occupied for the moment.

She left him peering at the chest and made her way through the jumble of furniture, past trestle tables of china and glass, casting an occasional curious glance at begrimed oil paintings and damp-spotted prints, and finally into a tiny office at the rear of the room.

The office was empty. She had expected to find Sally Caswell in it. But she supposed Sally had stepped out for a moment, though the little sanctum had an abandoned air to it that suggested no one had been there that morning. No sign of any personal belongings, no coat hanging on its hook, not even Sally's vacuum flask. The computer was switched off and cold. It was very odd.

There were two stacks of printed sheets on the desk. Meredith took a leaflet from the first pile.

Like the poster outside, it announced the CHRISTMAS AUCTION SALE and went on to list items of special interest from furniture and books to garden statuary. It included the walnut chest she had just seen manhandled into place. She turned over the next page. All the items to be auctioned the following day were numbered off in lots. She ran a finger down the page until she found the glasses that had interested her. Lot 124. Six Victorian wine glasses. She went back into the main room.

Austin Bailey was now alone, mopping his forehead with a large spotted handkerchief. Apparently the chest-of-drawers had suffered no harm. Ronnie and Ted had departed on other business. Austin looked up and saw her.

'Oh, Meredith! So sorry, didn't see you. How are you?' He tucked the handkerchief in his pocket and held out his distinctly dusty hand. He suddenly became aware of its state and withdrew it before she could grasp it.

'Sorry!' he said, 'Been moving stuff around.'

'Everything here now?' She indicated their surroundings. It

hardly seemed there would be room for anything else.

'I think so. I was expecting a set of chairs. . .' He frowned. 'The woman said she could get them over here today. I told her if she wanted them in the sale. . .' He fixed Meredith with a stern eye. 'They are listed in that!'

She realized he meant the catalogue in her hand. 'I was rather interested in the wine glasses,' she said. 'Where are they?'

He led her past a large Benares brass gong on a stand to a table laden with all manner of glassware and odd items associated with drink. Pewter tankards, stoneware jugs, a pair of Bavarian beermugs with lids, a wooden wine cooler.

Two or three people had come in and were wandering around looking at items, including a bearded man in a sheepskin coat who was examining a small writing desk with the air of an expert fault-finder. Austin Bailey cast him a wary glance.

'Got a green form?' Austin asked Meredith absently. 'You can write in a bid on a green form today and you needn't come and bid tomorrow. Unless you want to come and see the fun. You might be outbid in the actual auction, that's the risk. Ten per cent buyer's premium, don't forget.'

'I'll take one before I go. I actually hoped to see Sally. Isn't she here today?'

The sheepskin-coated man had moved on to look at a dining table. The other people, a husband and wife, were gazing doubt-fully at one of the paintings, nymphs in a glade, yellowed with old varnish and encased in an ornate carved frame.

'It's a bit big for the lounge, Frank,' said the wife.

'Show up better, then, wouldn't it?' said Frank.

'I don't know as I want naked women hanging over my fireplace, Frank. It's not nice, somehow.'

'That's art,' said Frank, the connoisseur.

Austin Bailey sighed. He rubbed his dusty palms together and gazed down at them in puzzled manner as if wondering why the dirt still hadn't shifted.

23

'Sally and I'd arranged to have lunch together,' Meredith persisted. 'So I expected to meet her here.'

'Oh, dear.' Austin's worried expression became more marked. 'I don't think she'll be coming in today. It's a nuisance because of all this . . . It's viewing until half past four this afternoon and we need everyone we can get. The public wandering in and out, you see. We need as many bodies on the floor as we can muster.'

She understood his security problem and said so, before prompting again, 'Sally?'

'Oh, yes. She phoned. That is, she didn't, but her husband did. About half an hour ago. It seems they had a bit of trouble at the cottage this morning.'

'Oh?' That sounded ominous, especially if it had been Liam who'd phoned and not Sally herself. Liam didn't normally concern himself with domestic matters. Nor had Sally contacted Meredith, despite their lunch date, and Sally was meticulous in that sort of courtesy.

'I think they had a gas explosion or something,' said Austin Bailey vaguely. He stared down at his hands again. 'I'll have to go and wash these. Excuse me, won't you?'

'Austin!' Meredith dodged the brass gong, a seated stone greyhound and a knobbly, awkward piece of furniture designed to accommodate an Edwardian family's coats, hats, umbrellas and walking sticks. 'A gas explosion? Is anyone hurt? I mean, how bad an explosion?'

Whole houses had been demolished by explosions from leaking gas appliances or fractured pipes before now.

'No one's hurt. Only shocked, you know. Sally got a fright, poor dear. But she's all right.' Austin assured her earnestly. 'I asked Liam. It was in the kitchen. Liam wasn't precise. I suppose they'll have to wait until the Gas Board gets there and sorts it out.'

Austin dived into Sally's office which they were just passing and emerged with a green form from the second of two piles of papers on the desk. 'Here, write your bid on this and leave it with me – or if I'm not around, with Ronnie or Ted – No, no, madam! Don't leave it there!' He hurried away to deal with an emergency.

She hadn't inquired about a reserve price on the glasses. She scribbled the maximum she was prepared to pay, put the lot number, her name, address and phone number, and handed the folded sheet to Ronnie who had just returned. Austin and Ted were gazing at a virulently hued painting of the bridges of Paris, held up by a large lady.

'You sell paintings for people, don't you?' demanded the would-be vendor.

'In principle, yes,' said Austin, gazing at the picture with some dismay.

'I've got to go.' Meredith said to Ronnie, since Austin was clearly occupied, 'Would you mind giving this to Mr Bailey? Thanks. You, er, you haven't heard anything about Mrs Caswell this morning, have you?' She pressed the green form into Ronnie's hand.

'Kitchen cooker!' said Ronnie, taking the green sheet and opening it. He pushed the baseball cap to the back of his head and studied what she'd written. Viewed even closer and capless, he now appeared around fifty.

'Is that not enough?' she asked anxiously. 'Or too much? I don't know the reserve.'

'You never know,' he said. 'Depends if anyone else wants 'em. Should think it's about right.'

'You're sure it was the kitchen cooker?' That did sound serious.

'Either that or the boiler,' said Ronnie.

Ted had abandoned Austin and the large lady. He appeared carrying a cardboard box containing what looked like assorted china ornaments.

'Mrs Caswell?' he puffed. 'Bathroom geyser, wasn't it? Here, that woman's brought them chairs. Where're we going to put them?'

It was clear, if she wanted to know what happened at the

Caswells' cottage that morning, she had to drive out there herself. Meredith went out and got back in her car. She just hoped everyone was safe and sound.

It wasn't cooker, boiler nor even geyser.

'It was a letter-bomb!' Sally Caswell whispered.

'Hell's teeth!' Meredith said and afterwards wondered she hadn't said anything stronger.

She had, however, been expecting something dramatic. The first thing she'd seen as she drove up to the cottage earlier was a police car parked outside the door and another further down the lane. A white van, which she'd first taken for a Gas Board vehicle, was seen, when she got out of the car, to be marked ominously BOMB DISPOSAL UNIT. A small gathering of villagers hung about at a safe distance, whispering together.

Alarmed, Meredith had hurried to the gate to find her way barred by a police officer. But, just at that moment, Liam had appeared in the doorway and at his insistence she'd been allowed to enter.

Liam had his reason for wanting her there. 'Sally's in a state,' he said. 'See what you can do, Meredith, can't you?'

She'd found Sally Caswell sitting on a sofa in the tiny drawing room before an electric fire. An injury to her forehead had been administered to in a makeshift fashion with a strip of plaster. She was gripping a glass of brandy whilst Liam mooched about scowling in the background. From the kitchen came the sound of voices and movement.

'The police!' she went on in the same low voice. 'And explosive experts. Forensics as well. Everyone! They're taking away all the bits of debris. There wasn't much left of the package. But I think they can tell what sort of explosive was used from the way it – it exploded.' She gestured wildly. The brandy slopped in the balloon glass. 'They took photographs of the t-table and k-kitchen . . . '

'Are you sure you're all right, Sally?' Meredith asked in concern. She glanced at Liam as she spoke, but Liam was brooding darkly on his own problems.

Sally croaked, 'I'm fine, honestly. Liam stuck on a plaster dressing for me. It had stopped bleeding. I was really lucky. There was broken glass everywhere. I do still feel a bit shaky and for some reason, I'm so cold.' She shivered.

'That's shock,' Meredith said. 'Try and take it easy. Have they been asking questions?'

'They tried. I wasn't much use to them. I really couldn't tell them anything. It was so sudden and I'd turned away just before – It was a package just like any other, except that it was addressed simply "Caswell". Liam was busy so I opened it.'

Hearing his name, Liam announced loudly, 'I don't know how I'm expected to get any work done today with that lot swarming over the place!'

Meredith pushed back a hank of dark brown hair which had fallen over her face and glared at him in some exasperation. She had known the Caswells for some years. There had been a gap in the acquaintance during the years Meredith had spent abroad as a British consul. Now back in England for good (unless the FO relented which it showed no sign of doing) they had all met up again.

Meredith liked Sally very much. Liam, she had always found irritating. In the wake of today's events, he was annoying her more than usual. Even allowing for shock, it was difficult to drum up sympathy for him. His wife could have been seriously hurt. Blinded or burned. But all that seemed to worry him was that it was holding up his work!

'I did ask Liam to call you, Meredith,' Sally's voice was marginally louder. 'But he forgot in all the fuss. I'm so sorry I stood you up over lunch.'

'Don't worry about it. I'm not greatly into lunching these days, anyway. I called at the auction rooms and saw Austin. He seemed to think it was a gas explosion. I was expecting to find the cottage reduced to rubble!'

Sally began to show increased signs of agitation. 'I ought to go in to work! It's the sale tomorrow!'

'Nonsense! Austin doesn't expect it. Everything is under control there. Just relax.'

'We've got to wait here, anyway,' Liam Caswell growled. 'Some other policeman is coming, someone more senior. I suppose we're going to be pestered for days by coppers!' He strode out.

'The book's going badly,' Sally explained. But Meredith noticed that as soon as Liam left the room, his wife's manner relaxed and her voice steadied. 'Poor Liam, this really is the last thing he needed. Nothing's gone right lately. The country doesn't suit him at all. I thought it would be quiet and he could work undisturbed. We both did. But he really needs to be nearer the laboratory. He has to drive miles all the way to Oxford, every time he wants to check on something. Add to that other upsets. It's been getting him down. You'll have to excuse his manner. He doesn't intend to be unfriendly.'

'I understand.' Liam's manner, as far as Meredith could tell, was only marginally more abrupt than it usually was.

Sally held up the brandy glass. 'Would you like a drink? Sorry for not asking before, rotten hostess today!'

'No thanks. Do you want another?'

'Daren't. Got to try and keep a clear head for this super-intendent who's coming over. Normally I never touch the booze. Gives me hiccups.'

'From Bamford?' As far as Meredith was aware, nowadays there was no one above the rank of inspector at Bamford, not since Alan had moved on.

Sally was unwise enough to shake her head, winced, touched the plaster and said, 'No, from regional police headquarters apparently.'

A quiver ran up Meredith's spine. Surely it wouldn't prove to be Alan? But what if it did? He wouldn't be pleased to see her here. He'd trot out that lecture again, the one on not interfering in police matters. But she was entitled to be here, she was Sally's friend.

'Did they say his name?' she asked as casually as she could.

'No, don't think so. I hope Liam isn't rude to him. I've told Liam, we've got to tell him everything.'

Meredith leaned forward, 'You mentioned other upsets just now. What kind?'

Sally looked miserable. 'Difficulties with a neighbour. And other nasty things through the post. Not exploding parcels or anything like that, just letters. I didn't know about them. Liam only told me just now, after the – the explosion. Apparently he's had some very offensive mail. He kept it from me so as not to upset me. Someone seems to have got it in for poor old Liam.'

The names of people offended by Liam Caswell over the years probably numbered legion, thought Meredith. But to have offended someone to the extent that whoever it was sent a letter-bomb, indicated a grudge provoked by something beyond Liam's ordinary rudeness.

'I suppose it's all to do with the beagles,' Sally said obscurely.

There was sound of another car drawing up outside and the slam of a door. Footsteps crunched up the path and someone could be heard talking in the kitchen. Then Liam's voice was heard. He came back into the sitting room, another figure discernible behind him.

'This is the chap from the regional squad.' Liam announced the visitor with a distinct lack of grace. 'Superintendent Maltby.'

A lanky, fair-haired figure in a Barbour moved out from Caswell's shadow and into the room.

'Markby,' he corrected. 'Good afternoon, Mrs Caswell.'

His gaze moved to the other woman. An eyebrow twitched and the look in his blue eyes sharpened. 'Meredith?'

'Hullo, Alan,' she said.

29

Chapter Three

Meredith did offer to leave, but it was Sally who said, 'I want Meredith to stay. She calms me down.'

Alan had accepted that pretty well in the circumstances. The last of the forensic team had quitted the cottage with numerous plastic binbags of rubbish and now the four of them sat round in the quiet which had fallen over the scene. Meredith had made them all tea, bringing the kettle of water into the room and plugging it into a free point. Sally was clearly nervous again and Liam's brooding figure stretched out in a chintz armchair wasn't encouraging.

'Do you need further attention to that bump on your forehead, Mrs Caswell?' Alan asked.

'Liam took a look at it and patched it up,' Sally repeated the assurance that she'd made to Meredith earlier. 'I was really lucky.'

Meredith reflected, with a touch of embarrassment, that one always tended to forget that Liam was a qualified medical practitioner, even though – or perhaps because – for years now his work had been in research, spent amongst test-tubes, not with people.

However, having seen the chaos in the kitchen for herself when she fetched the water, she took issue with Sally's last remark. 'It was more than luck! It was a miracle! Whoever sent it, it was a wicked thing to do!'

Liam muttered and sank deeper in his chair. Markby gave him a questioning glance but Liam didn't elucidate.

'You feel up to talking to me?' Markby asked Sally. He emphasised 'you' very slightly.

'Yes, but I can't tell you much. It was a just a package.'

'Addressed to you both, I understand.' Again a glance at Liam who ignored it.

Sally nodded, winced again, and said hurriedly, 'There was no Mr and Mrs. Only our name and the address and the word "video" in capitals.'

'Were you expecting a videotape to come through the post?'

'No. But Liam thought it might be a Christmas present.'

'How about the handwriting?'

'It was just hand-printed. I didn't recognise it. It had a London postmark, I think central. I put it on the table and was just going to open it—' Her voice faltered. 'Then the kettle boiled and I got up.' Eyes cast down she finished in an almost inaudible mumble. 'That's when the package exploded. They've taken away what was left of it.'

Markby turned to Liam Caswell. 'How about you, Dr Caswell? Did you see the handwriting?'

Liam, obliged at last to join in the conversation, shook his head and replied briefly. 'No.'

'And you have no idea who might have sent it?'

Fiercely, Liam repeated, 'No!'

'The animal activists, Liam,' protested his wife.

He glared at her. 'Obviously! Anyone could work that out! But *who* they are, the police will have to find out that one, won't they?'

An awkward silence fell on the room. Meredith, her eyes on Alan, could see that he was sizing up Liam and working out how to tackle an uncooperative subject.

'You understand, Dr Caswell, that I'm from the regional force. We were informed because, as I understand, such a group of activists targeted your laboratory last year. We're naturally concerned that the more violent wing of the animal rights' movement may be starting a new campaign hereabouts. They may be posting devices to other people engaged in your line of work. We shall be warning others to look out. But as you appear to be the first for some time to be targeted in this way, we want to know if that's chance or if there's some reason why you were singled out to be first recipient.'

Liam said wearily, 'They're yobs. They don't have reasons.'

Alan asked in a way Meredith thought admirably courteous, 'But you've used animals in your research work, haven't you?'

The courtesy was lost on Liam who again snapped, 'Not for some considerable time!'

Alan's voice was quiet but persistent. 'But perhaps there's been some other change in your work recently which has attracted renewed interest from some group? Have you begun some new project of any sort? Something to which someone objected?'

Liam fidgeted and mumbled, 'I got some letters. Just junk. Practical jokes.'

Alan said sharply, 'A letter-bomb is no joke, Dr Caswell! What were these other letters about?'

'They were from those people!' Sally said loudly. 'Those who tried to take the beagles from the laboratory last year.'

Liam drew a deep breath and hauled himself out of his chair. He took up a position on the rug before the fire and with his hands behind his back, declared, 'All right, I'll tell you. But I warn you, it won't help. I've received a few anonymous letters. Poison pen, I suppose you'd call them.'

'You reported this?'

'No, of course not! I chucked them away.'

'You weren't distressed in any way? You didn't want to find out who had sent them?'

'I told you!' Liam raised his voice. 'I took them as a practical joke. All right, a sick practical joke – but the work of a weirdo somewhere. I didn't take them seriously.'

It was clear that Alan was having difficulty keeping the courteous tone. Meredith saw him direct an exasperated look at

Liam before he turned back to Sally. 'You saw these letters?'

'No. Liam only told me about them today, after – after the explosion. I must have seen them arrive . . . I mean, I must have seen the envelopes. But if I did, they didn't look different from ordinary mail. Most of our mail is addressed to Liam. I only know they contained horrible, mischievous letters because Liam told me today, as I said. I was horrified. He'd said not a word about it because he didn't want to frighten me. But after what happened here today, he thought I ought to know. I said he ought to have told the police at the time, when he received them. He ought to have told me at the time, not kept it to himself. But he just threw them away.'

Markby returned his attention to Caswell. Liam's manner which had been somewhat professorial since getting to his feet, had abruptly become deflated and was now sullen. He avoided the superintendent's gaze.

'I wish you had informed the police, Dr Caswell. We might have been able to trace the sender and possibly, though we can't be sure, prevent today's incident! Am I to understand that these letters had to do with laboratory animals?'

'Look, have I been talking to myself or what?' Liam snapped. 'We did use some beagles about a year ago. They didn't come to any harm! We had a controlled breeding programme and the animals were excellently cared for! As I've tried to tell you, we haven't used animals since. I can't help it if lunatics out there think we do! They ought to check their facts first!'

If his account of the life led by the beagles was received with some scepticism by the two visitors, he didn't appear to notice it.

Sally frowned and winced, touching the plaster on her brow. 'They can't know much about us at all. I mean, Liam should have been away in Norwich today. It's only because there was a last-minute delay he didn't go. They must just know Liam's name from that business last year when the lab was raided, and somehow they've got hold of our home address, which is scary.'

'In Norwich, Dr Caswell?'

'It's a joint project,' Liam told him. 'Since the opening up of eastern Europe, there are a number of similar programmes. We take a steady stream of post-graduate students from the old eastern block. We send people across there. Before the changes in Europe, doing something like that meant endless quibbling and bureaucracy. We wouldn't always get the people we thought best, rather the ones they chose to send. They were nervous who came from our side. Now we just do a straight swap. It's been very beneficial. But look, it's got absolutely nothing to do with this!'

'I see. Usually, Dr Caswell, in a case like this, whoever has sent the abusive mail has signed it with the name of the group concerned. They want the publicity. Was there any indication who might have sent these letters?'

'No.' Liam took refuge in a monosyllable again.

'Postmark?'

'Can't recall. London, I think.'

'Anything unusual about the lettering?'

'No. Look, I get a lot of post from London.'

'And what, exactly, were they about?'

Forced at last to provide detail, deep emotion, as opposed to simple bad temper, entered Liam's voice. It quivered with passion. 'They made stupid and inaccurate insinuations about my book. Ignorant and insulting criticisms!' His words tailed away in a splutter.

'Book?' Markby prompted.

Liam, regretting perhaps having revealed the depth to which he'd been wounded by the anonymous accuser, said stiffly, 'I'm at present engaged in putting my research notes in order, writing them up for publication. I happen to think it'll be an important book and contribute to worldwide knowledge of the subject. I'm sorry if that sounds conceited. It happens to be true.' A snarl crossed his bearded face. 'Most people in this village seem to assume I'm writing a novel!'

Markby steepled his fingers and pressed them against his chin. 'How many people know about this book? Do you know of any resentment against your work in other quarters? I've heard that academic rivalries can give rise to strong passions.'

'If you think one of my academic colleagues is jealous enough to send me stupid letters and exploding videos, forget it!' Liam shouted. He saw his wife's agonised expression and went on more calmly, 'Look, Superintendent, I don't mean to be offensive, but this letter-bomb business is the last straw. What am I supposed to do? Barricade myself in against every crackpot in the country? Refuse to accept any mail in case it blows up? Go into hiding altogether and change my name? Of course not! That would be ridiculous. I just have to ignore it. It's all I can do.'

'Unfortunately, Dr Caswell, one can't ignore letter-bombs.'

'Cranks!' shouted Liam. 'I won't dignify their activities by according them serious consideration!'

This remark was received in silence. Eventually Markby said in a curious voice, 'Dr Caswell, as a police officer, I am obliged to look at this incident as very serious indeed. I don't wish to alarm, but whilst most of the people who make up these parcels only intend to frighten the recipient, a letter-bomb is a very dangerous thing and in the right circumstances can certainly kill.'

Sally Caswell gasped and whispered, 'How can they be so *sick*?'

Meredith put an arm round her shoulders and grimaced at Alan.

Markby met her gaze and held it. 'I'm sorry to distress Mrs Caswell, but you, Dr Caswell . . .' he turned from Meredith to Liam again, 'shouldn't be taking this lightly.'

Liam reddened. 'I'm not taking it lightly. I'm just saying I can't do anything about it! Can *you*?' He glared at his visitor.

'We'll do our best.' Markby glanced round the little room. 'Leaving aside your medical work, is there any other reason you can think of which might be behind this? Have you made any enemies? At any time, even years ago, for any reason?'

'Local people don't like us much,' Sally said with sadness in her voice. 'I don't know why. I can't say we've really been terribly happy here. It's such a shame. I love this cottage.'

Sympathetically, Markby told her, 'It takes time to be accepted in small communities. You have to tread carefully. They'll come around.'

'Old Bodicote won't!' said Liam. 'He lives next door here.' He pointed at the wall. 'Vindictive old blighter! He lets his goats through into our garden.'

'Not on purpose, Liam!' his wife protested. 'They eat through the hedge!'

'He could tether them on long ropes, couldn't he? Or put chainlink fencing along? Not him. I've told him, and I mean it, that the next time it happens I'll be seeing my solicitor about it!'

The winter evening had drawn in as they talked. In semi-darkness in the light from the electric fire, the room had grown very warm and stuffy. Meredith's head had begun to ache and the all-to-familiar 'flu weakness swept over her. She leaned back and tried to fight it off. This isn't the time to buckle! she told herself sternly. She saw Alan glance her way and forced herself to sit up and look perky. But she suspected she didn't fool him.

Sally got up and switched on the main light-switch and they all blinked in the sudden yellow glare. The distraction was welcome to Meredith, but without warning, there came another.

From the kitchen came first the scrape of a footstep, followed by a clatter as something was knocked over.

'I thought the police had left?' Sally stared at them. 'I suppose the back door must still be open.'

Markby got up and made for the door of the room. But before he reached it, it swung open.

'Talk of the devil!' snapped Liam, jerking upright and gripping the chair-arms. 'Would you credit it? It's Bodicote! Just bloody walked in! Helped himself!'

It didn't surprise Meredith that the old man had wandered through the unlocked kitchen door of a neighbour's house. It was old-fashioned country usage. Nor did he look particularly devilish to her, but he did look a little reptilian. His head was small, on a long, thin, wrinkled neck. Tortoise-like, he moved it from side to side, surveying them. His arms dangled by his sides, skinny wrists and knotty hands protruding from too-short jacket sleeves.

'I come in through the back door!' he rasped.

'I wish you'd knocked, Mr Bodicote,' Sally told him. 'You gave us – you gave me – quite a start.'

'I called out!' he retorted defensively. 'But you never answered. I heard you talking, so I come in.'

'What do you want?' Liam asked disagreeably. 'We're busy!'

'I come to see what's going on. Police chap came round earlier and asked a lot of daft questions. I thought he'd come back. But they packed up their van and drove off a little while back. Left me sitting there not knowing what I'm supposed to do. So I reckoned you'd know.'

That sounded reasonable enough.

'I'm sorry for the disturbance,' Sally said.

Bodicote received her apology ungraciously. 'Never heard such a racket in my life, and going on all day long! Starts off this morning, blooming great bang what made all the ornaments rattle on my mantelshelf! Glass breaking. Then cars and police and people trampling back and forth! A policeman comes to my house and makes off with Maureen's Christmas present! Won't say what he wants it for! Am I going to get it back, that's what I want to know!' He glared at Markby.

'This was always a quiet village before *they* came!' His tortoise head turned and thrust forward in challenge towards Liam. 'As for threatening me with the law, Mr or Dr or whatever-you-are Caswell, *I'll* have that on *you*! Making a disturbance like it!'

'Mr Bodicote,' Alan stepped forward as peacemaker. 'I'm Superintendent Markby. Perhaps I could come round and have a word with you before I leave Castle Darcy? Say in about twenty minutes' time? I'll explain what's happened.'

Bodicote raised a veined hand and pointed trembling at Liam. 'A copper? Well, arrest him! That feller there! He chucked a lump of brick at my billy! Valuable animal, he is! I should have had the RSPCA on him! I will do, if he goes chucking bricks at my goats again!'

Liam's bearded face had turned purple with fury. Meredith waited for him to explode with rage. But before he could, his wife acted.

Sally Caswell rushed forward and, in an uncharacteristic outburst, shook her fist under the astonished Bodicote's nose.

'You horrid, hateful old man! Liam said you let your smelly goats through the hedge on purpose and I believe him! You did it to be mean and horrid to us! You want us to leave! We've done nothing to you! We've tried to be nice and friendly and neighbourly. Yes, neighbourly! And you've been downright unpleasant from day one! More than that, you've been aggressive! I bet you had something to do with those foul letters! You're just a thoroughly nasty old mischief-maker and I wish you were dead!'

And with that she burst into tears.

Chapter Four

'I oughtn't to have said it!' Sally pressed a paper tissue against her eyes. When she took it away, smudged purple eye-shadow and black mascara had created the illusion of a splendid couple of shiners on her distraught features.

They'd all gathered round her, even Liam, startled by his wife's vehemence out of his customery self-absorption. Mr Bodicote, equally taken aback by the reaction he'd provoked from the normally placid Mrs Caswell, had retreated to his own home with a certain amount of alacrity.

'Don't worry,' Meredith urged. 'We all say things like that from time to time. You're upset.'

'I know I'm upset. It's been such a dreadful day and it was the last straw when he threatened to call the RSPCA about the goat! I *like* animals and so does Liam! That's why it's so silly for people to write letters accusing Liam of doing horrid things to the beagles in the lab! But Bodicote doesn't keep his goats fenced in properly. The other day one got right up to the house and Liam threw a stone at it. He didn't mean to hit it, did you, Liam?'

'I missed,' said Liam.

'But you weren't *really* trying to hit it, were you? I know you weren't. Old Mr Bodicote was so cross. He didn't understand. And he did give me such a shock wandering in just now like that. But I still shouldn't have said what I said. I wanted to hurt him. Saying I wished he was dead was an awful thing to say to a very old person, but I said it because I wanted to hurt him. It sort of surged up out of some pit of the subconscious as the worst thing I *could* say to him!'

'We all do it under stress,' Meredith repeated. 'We say things we don't mean and upset people.'

'I think,' Alan Markby said, 'that perhaps Mrs Caswell's had enough for one day. I'll call again tomorrow if I may, or someone else will. We'll need to talk to you in more detail about these anonymous letters, Dr Caswell. You might look round and see if by chance you haven't kept one. Threw it in a wastepaper bin, perhaps? Try and remember anything you can. Were they typed or hand-written or composed of cut-out newsprint? What kind of paper was it? Cheap, ruled, plain, typing paper, quality letterpad? And the envelopes. Brown business envelopes? White letter ones? Oblong, square? Self-sealing?'

'For crying out loud!' Liam shouted. 'I can't be expected to remember all that! They were bits of newsprint stuck on a sheet, apart from the envelope which was – um – printed by hand. The envelopes were just envelopes!'

'We can identify the newspaper used from the typeface and paper. And try to remember the exact wording and write it down for us.'

Liam groaned but remorselessly Markby went on, 'Try and recall the postmarks. Any kind of clue, even the tiniest.'

'Why have I got to go through all this when I know – and you know – who sent them?' Liam's voice rang round the little sitting room. 'It's that animal rights lot. The ones who broke in last year and tried to get the beagle cages open! They'd have got a helluva shock if they had managed to get the animals out, I can tell you! They give nasty bites!'

I hope they bit you! thought Meredith, but managed not to say it aloud.

'It's possible, although the group which targeted your laboratory last year is by no means the only group around.'

Alan, while speaking, was studying Liam thoughtfully. 'I

wasn't involved at the time, and I haven't as yet had a chance to study the file. Dr Caswell, you've expressed a great deal of anger, but your attitude appears to me somewhat inconsistent. Last year your laboratory was attacked. Recently, you received abusive mail but told no one. At the very least, you must have realised that it meant – as your wife pointed out just now – that one of these groups has your home address. Now today you received an explosive device which injured your wife. It's imperative we find the culprit as soon as possible. But we must have your cooperation. To put it bluntly, our conversation has been akin to drawing teeth!'

Liam said dismissively, 'The break-in at the lab was a year ago! I had forgotten about it by the time I received the letters.'

'Forgot?' Alan's voice echoed disbelief.

'I put it out of my mind!' Liam exploded. 'Those people want to worry me, right? So the best way to deal with them is to ignore them! If I allowed myself to be thrown off course by every delinquent in a ski-mask who thinks he has the right to smash expensive lab equipment and wreck experiments set up over months, I wouldn't have achieved half of what I have—'

Belatedly, he added, 'Not only I, but the whole team working on the project.'

The stilted manner in which he referred to his fellow scientists, told them more, Meredith felt, about Liam's attitude to others, than anything else. She saw a flicker of a sardonic smile on Alan's face and realised he thought the same.

'We'll talk to your fellow workers. One or more of them may also have received hate mail. And may have kept it!' This time Alan couldn't keep all the sarcasm from his voice.

Liam flushed, but much to his obvious relief, the superintendent had risen to his feet and showed signs of leaving.

'I hope if you receive any more mail, that you'll get in touch at once and keep everything!'

'Yes, all right!' Liam muttered.

'Try and get a good night's sleep, Mrs Caswell.' Alan's voice was milder. 'And if a headache persists, or you feel any distress, call your doctor.'

He looked across at Meredith. 'I'll just go next door and have a quick word with Bodicote. Are you staying here?'

'I'll be leaving soon.'

'I'll probably be about twenty minutes next door.'

She read the sub-text. 'Fine.'

Markby made his way to the cottage next door. The curtains were tightly drawn but the room behind them was lit. He knocked loudly and called, 'It's the superintendent, Mr Bodicote.'

A light was switched on in the tiny hall, glowing through the dirty transom glass above the door. Shuffling footsteps approached. A chain rattled. Bodicote's face appeared at the gap.

'Oh, 'tis you . . .' He unchained the door and unwillingly allowed the superintendent inside. 'You just wait a moment there.'

As Markby watched, the old man rechained the door and hobbled with surprising speed back into the living room, closing the door and isolating Markby in the narrow hall.

He looked down it, grimacing. The carpet was threadbare. Various items of shabby outer wear hung on an array of hooks at the foot of the rickety stairway. At the far end of the hall, a door stood ajar giving a dim glimpse of an untidy kitchen. Among the many odours drifting about could be distinguished that of fried onions and something which smelled like boiled mash. It indicated Bodicote prepared his own and the goats' feed in the same place and very likely at the same time. It wouldn't surprise Markby if he didn't use the same pans. A tough constitution and the fact that he'd always done so probably preserved him from food poisoning.

The old fellow was taking his time. Markby strained his ears.

He thought he heard a rustling as of paper. Then some noise which sounded like a drawer sliding closed, followed by a faint click as of a turning key. After a moment, Mr Bodicote returned.

'You can come in now.'

'Thank you.' Markby stepped into the tiny room.

Though this room corresponded to the one he'd just left next door, the overall first impression was quite different. No repainting had been done for some years and the open fire smoking in the hearth had covered wallpaper and paintwork with a tawny film. The air was stuffy, though marginally better smelling than out in the hall, at least no stink of mash.

Markby sniffed. There was another smell. He was sensitive to odours but he couldn't place it. Though faint, it suggested that at full strength it would be pungent. An acrid smell which made him think of horses. Horses were animals, as were goats. Very likely the smell of the goats got everywhere, carried in here on the old man's clothing.

He looked round for a chair. All the furniture was sagging yet it was otherwise a comfortable little place. The tidiest area in it was the top of an oak dining table which was swept clear.

Markby's curious gaze examined further. Every shelf or other space where an ornament or item of practical use could stand was filled. A sideboard was covered in photographs, many sepia and of venerable age. A well-corseted young woman in a large hat and tailored suit draped with a feather boa might be the old man's mother. Movement took his attention. A little key swung in the lock of the top left-hand drawer, telling its own tale. It didn't take much detective work to deduce that Bodicote had been looking at or working at something spread out upon the table, something he hadn't wished Markby to see. Whatever it was had been hastily scooped up and locked away in the drawer. He was sure the old man had checked around to see nothing else had been left out for a visitor to discover. But what had he to hide?

The superintendent asked, 'May I sit down?'

Bodicote indicated that he could and they took facing chairs either side of the hearth. The coals spat and yellow flames sprang up. Markby felt an odd moment of nostalgia. When he'd been a child, visits to elderly people had always seemed like this. Small, stuffy, overcrowded rooms, flickering flames in a hearth reflected off brass fenders, all manner of china ornaments and occasionally an ancient dog or equally aged cat. Bodicote apparently didn't keep animals indoors.

'So, what's all the fuss about, then?' Bodicote sat with his hands on his knees. The knuckles, swollen by rheumatism, pushed up through paperthin skin like a miniature mountain range. But the hands still looked as if they had strength enough in them, a working man's hands.

Markby wasn't so easily drawn. 'I understand an officer called on you earlier to explain there'd been a mishap in Mrs Caswell's kitchen.'

'He did. And asked me if I'd had any post delivered today. As it happens, my niece, Maureen, had sent me my Christmas present. And he took it away!' Bodicote's voice rose indignantly. 'That young copper! He asked me if I'd opened it already and when I said no, he took it away!'

'Just a precaution. I'm sure you'll get it back when it's been examined, Mr Bodicote. You will know by now that a suspected letter-bomb went off next door.'

'Exploding parcels!' said Bodicote with great disdain. 'Before those Caswells come here, we never had exploding parcels in Castle Darcy!'

'I understood you to say just now, next door, that you heard the explosion.'

Bodicote muttered grumpily, 'Darn near made me jump out of my skin, I can tell you!'

'But you didn't go round to the cottage at once to see what had happened, or if anyone was hurt or needed help? You weren't curious? You left it until just a little while ago to make inquiries?'

'I'll tell you what I did,' Bodicote fixed him with faded and unfriendly eyes. 'I went down to see if Jasper was all right.'

'Jasper?' The Caswells hadn't mentioned anyone called Jasper.

'My billy. I'd turned him out in the paddock. He's a valuable beast and that feller Caswell tried to harm him before! Throwing rocks at him, like I told you!'

The billy-goat. It seemed the billy was going to be part and parcel of the inquiries whether Markby liked it or not. 'What time was this, Mr Bodicote, did you notice?'

'It was around breakfast-time and I'd not long turned out the billy. I didn't turn out the nannies on account of the cold weather. You've got to cherish goats. Not like some folk think. But Jasper don't like to be shut in all day. If you wants to know when exactly I can't tell you by the clock. But I can tell you it was just after the postlady come. Very nice young girl, she is. About quarter of an hour or twenty minutes after she came to my door, not more, that's when I heard the racket and the breaking glass.'

'So, you went down to see the billy-goat was unharmed and then what did you do?'

Bodicote fidgeted. He took his hands from his knees, stooped and picked up a brass poker and rattled it in the hearth. Coals fell in on one another, crackling and spitting. 'Make yourself handy,' he said. 'Just pick up the tongs and put a couple of lumps on the fire, from the scuttle there, by your foot.'

Markby did as he was bid. When he sat back again. Bodicote had composed himself, his hands loosely clasped. He hadn't had long but the manoeuvre had given him time enough to marshal his story in his head as he wanted it. So Markby realised. He was annoyed to think the old man had seized the initiative so easily.

'I saw the billy was all right and I started to walk to my back door again. Then I thought, better go and see what's up next door. But I wasn't sure how I'd be received. You saw the welcome I got just now! Abuse thrown at my head! There's a place in the hedge where I patched up a hole. I used an old brass bedhead. It makes a sort of gate, if you know what I mean. I just pulled it back and slipped through and walked up to the back of their cottage across their bit of garden. I could see the kitchen window broken and smoke coming out.'

Bodicote paused. 'I couldn't see in. It was dark in there. I went along to the new place they built on alongside. I looked through the window there and I saw all his papers and things on a desk. He wasn't there. That machine of his was switched on, with writing all over a screen, like a telly. Then I heard him shouting at her and she was shouting at him.'

'Where were they?'

'As far as I could tell, in the kitchen, only I couldn't see on account of the smoke. They must have been all right, to be yelling at each other like it. Then, while I stood there, he come back into his little study place. He didn't see me at the window. He lit himself a cigarette which struck me as being rum, because I thought it might've been the gas. You don't go lighting up cigarettes with gas leaking, do you? But then, when I saw him do that, I realised it couldn't be the gas and that was a relief, I can tell you! Because if it had been, I might've had to clear out of my place, too, until it got fixed.'

The old man was both observant and sharp, Markby thought. He was proving a better witness than might have been hoped. Provided, of course, that he was telling the truth.

'Then he went over to that telly sort of affair . . .'

'The computer?' Markby asked.

'That's what they call 'em. He sat down and started tapping on the keys.'

Markby looked startled. 'He started working again? With smoke in the kitchen, glass broken, his wife upset?'

Bodicote thought about it. 'Maybe it was important to him to finish something? You do what's important to you first, don't you? Like I ran down to see if old Jasper was safe. Caswell went back and mucked about with whatever he was doing on his computer-machine.'

Possibly Liam had been saving important data to disk. Markby nevertheless found himself shocked that Liam's work had still been uppermost in his mind at such a time. Or was Bodicote, in his country way, putting his finger on a basic fact of human psychology?

A memory stirred in Markby's brain and he was distracted enough to chase after the line until he found it and murmured aloud, 'A married woman grabs at her baby; an unmarried one reaches for her jewel-box.'

Bodicote's grin returned. 'Sherlock Holmes!' he said unexpectedly. '*A Scandal in Bohemia*. I don't like that one so much. *The Sign of Four*, that's my favourite.'

It seemed the old man had a way of turning the tables on his visitor. 'You like a good book, then, Mr Bodicote?'

'Ah,' said Bodicote with satisfaction. 'I like a *good* yarn. But they don't write no good 'uns now, not like the books people used to read when I was a youngster. Sexton Blake, they were good stories. And Dr Fu Manchu, they were another! That feller next door reckons he writes books. I bet he don't never write anything near as good as *The Thirty-Nine Steps* or *The Riddle of the Sands*! I got 'em all over there in my bookcase!'

He nodded towards the far side of the room where Markby could see, in the shadows and half-hidden by an armchair, a set of shelves crammed with venerable volumes.

Markby would dearly have liked to get up and go over there to examine them, but he dragged his mind back to the matter in hand.

'Actually, I understand Dr Caswell's book is non-fiction. To do with his work. You didn't know about that?'

'He don't do no work!' said Bodicote. 'He's there all day long, tapping away at that machine. His wife goes off in her car to work most days. Not always. Part-timer I suppose.'

'So you've no idea what kind of work Dr Caswell is engaged in?'

'I told you, he does none! Calls himself doctor, though! He's got no patients, then, if he's a doctor.'

'He's not that sort of a doctor.'

'What other sort is there?' Bodicote stared belligerently at his visitor.

Either Bodicote really didn't know what Liam Caswell's profession was, or he wasn't going to let on.

'You don't like Dr Caswell?'

'No.' Bodicote's faded gaze fixed his visitor. 'But there's no law says I've got to like the feller, is there?'

Markby abandoned that line of questioning for something nearer to the old man's heart.

'I believe there has been some dispute with your neighbours about the goats,' he began.

Bodicote cleared his throat. 'On their part, maybe. Not on mine. Not to begin with. I was here first, wasn't I? Me and the goats. The old woman who lived in that cottage before these new folk, she didn't mind the goats. I was civil to them Caswells when they moved in. Not but what it wasn't wasted on him who's a surly devil. And as to my going round there to ask if they were all right, I hope you've noted that neither of *them* came round *here* to tell me what happened and see if I was all right, eh?'

Markby was inclined to agree with Bodicote. 'Surly devil' wasn't an unjust description of Liam Caswell from what little he'd seen of the man.

'Dr Caswell claims the animals have broken through the fence and into his garden.'

'Once or twice,' Bodicote conceded grudgingly. 'Goats are wanderers. It's their nature. They did no harm. Ate a bit of grass and nibbled a few leaves. It's not as though he's got a top-notch garden! I never saw him doing any gardening! His missus does it all. And it isn't my fault if she grows a lot of stuff goats like.'

'What sort of stuff?' Markby asked him.

'Kitchen bits, herbs and that. She makes tea with 'em, so she

50

told me. Mint and comfrey and the like. She's got a bit of soft fruit growing, blackcurrants, but she don't tend 'em and they won't crop proper. Now blackcurrant leaves you can make a nice tea with. My mother used to use them.'

'You get along better with Mrs Caswell, then?'

'Better than with him, aye. But lately she's got nearly as bad as he is! Not but what she's a bonny lass for all that.' Bodicote nodded.

Markby suppressed a smile. 'It's never occurred to you to, say, play a trick or two on Liam Caswell, to get your own back?'

Bodicote's eyelids flicked rapidly over his faded eyes so that Markby, as others had been, was reminded of some kind of reptile, a lizard on a rock. 'Why'd I do something so daft? I'm not a child to be playing tricks. I'll tell the cruelty people on him, if he goes chucking rocks at my goats again, that's what I'll do, phone up the RSPCA. That'll fix him.' Bodicote leaned forward.

'You care about animals, Mr Bodicote? Don't like to think they're mistreated?'

'Course I care about them! Kept animals of one sort or another all my life!' Bodicote's gnarled fingers tightened on his kneecaps. 'He's been threatening me, you know. Says he'll set his lawyers on me. Can he do that?'

'If you're allowing the animals to stray and they're causing damage, he might have a grievance in law.'

'And what about the damage he's done to me? To my animals?' Bodicote's voice grew louder. He pointed a forefinger at his visitor. 'What about that, eh?'

'So far you've claimed he threw a stone once. He admits it. It was a reaction. He says he didn't mean to hit the animal, only frighten it away. Not everyone is as used to handling animals as you, Mr Bodicote, especially livestock like goats.'

A dull flush crept over the folds of loose skin around the old man's throat and into his wrinkled face. His chin wobbled and his pale eyes sparked with a new life. 'Didn't mean no harm! Didn't

51

he? What about when they tried to poison them, eh? What about when they tried to poison my goats?' In his agitation spittle escaped his mouth and dribbled down his chin.

'Now, Mr Bodicote,' Markby said peaceably. 'I'm sure you don't really mean that.'

'Don't I?' Bodicote snapped and saliva sprayed everywhere. 'Then what about those turnips?'

Markby stepped outside the cottage, into the blackness of a country night, and looked up at the sky. It was clear of cloud, dominated by an almost white moon, and sprinkled over with glittering points marking the stars. He could make out the constellations easily. Possibly there'd be another frost tonight. He took a breath of clean cold air, filling his lungs after the stuffy interior behind him, and walked towards the road.

He could see Meredith's car and the dim outline of her head as she sat in it waiting for him. She let down the window as he approached.

He stooped to speak to her. 'Thanks for hanging on. Sorry to be so long. How are you?'

'I'm fine. I wish I thought Sally was. Honestly, sometimes I could wring Liam's neck! It's not that he doesn't care about her, but that for an intelligent man, he can act awfully thick! He doesn't think anything matters but his work!'

'Was he always like that? You knew them before, some years back, didn't you?'

'Yes. He was always a bit like it, but not so bad as he's become as he's got older.'

Alan put a hand on the window rim. 'Look, I was wondering, if you're free tonight, whether we could have a spot of dinner later on.'

She looked a little doubtful, perhaps surprised that he appeared to have dismissed the new case from his mind so quickly. He was forced to add apologetically, 'You see, you know

the Caswells and I'd like to have a word with you about them.
Business rather than pleasure!'

That wasn't, he supposed, very polite.

She was silent for a moment but her hesitation wasn't on that
account. 'I don't like to gossip about friends. And I don't know
about dinner. I'm not eating much at the moment.'

'Look, it's not gossip! Someone has made a murderous attack,
apparently intended for Liam Caswell, which nearly got his wife
instead. At the moment Caswell isn't offering any help. I've got
to talk to anyone at all who might be able to throw some light on
this. You do know you can talk to me in confidence, I hope?'

He couldn't help sounding a little sharp. She raised an
eyebrow.

'Yes, I know that! But surely the animal rights extremists who
targeted Liam's laboratories are responsible?'

'I'll look into that, don't worry. But my impression of Caswell
is that he's the sort of person who's likely to have more than one
set of enemies! Correct me if I'm wrong, that's all I'm saying.'

She tapped her fingers on the steering wheel. 'No, you're not
wrong. But it's not as simple as you might think. Where do you
want us to meet?'

'Do you fancy Indian? We could eat at the little Kashmiri
place where we've been a couple of times. It'll be quiet there mid-
week.'

In Meredith's stomach, reduced to inertia by Mrs Harmer's
bland cuisine, the idea of spices and curry sparked a genuine pang
of hunger.

She nodded in the shadows. 'Great. See you there at seven-
fifteen?'

He was already at the restaurant when Meredith arrived later. It
was only a small place, papered with crimson flock wallpaper and
with subdued Indian music tinkling in the background. Its
intimacy meant that she saw him as soon as she walked in.

Despite it being some time since their last visit, she was recognised and enthusiastically welcomed by the owner.

She sat down opposite Alan and smiled at him a little uncertainly. Walking here through town, she'd had time to think about things and her doubts had returned.

Police work, as she'd discovered before, didn't take account of people's feelings. Her own feelings at the moment were a jumble of contradictions. She was glad that Sally wasn't seriously hurt; but appalled that the incident had taken place at all. She was pleased that Alan wanted to share his problem with her; and dreaded that it would finish with an argument.

The truth was that, although she loved him – and she did love him, despite an awareness that her love for him was not as straightforward as his for her – he became a different person when he 'wore his police hat'. That other Alan could seem a frightening stranger. It had happened before that they'd found themselves in the situation of two persons standing either side of a divide, stretching out hands to one another and unable to touch fingers. At the same time, confusingly, the cases in which he became involved had often fascinated her and led to her becoming involved herself. That was something that had frequently exasperated Alan.

But this time he was asking her to come and talk about what had happened. The trouble was, talking to him in his official capacity, about friends like Liam and Sally, felt an awful lot like ratting on someone. Accordingly, she'd thought out what she wanted to say. Now she sat up straight and fixed him with a businesslike stare.

'So, the regional force is handling this?'

He grimaced. 'This could be just the first of a series of attacks on random targets. Supposing it's the work of extremists, the first thing is to find out just who. Most organisations aiming to improve the lot of animals are open in their methods. They try to keep within the law and, when they don't, it's generally a matter of public order. There may be a scuffle on a picket line or rough-house when emotions run high and tempers flare. It gets on to the evening newscast and the organisers aren't too displeased with the publicity. The police aren't happy but I, for one, much prefer that to what happened today. Any cause attracts its undesirables. There are renegades in the animal welfare movement as in any other. Their methods are nasty and their true aims obscure. A letter-bomb is about as nasty as you can get.'

He broke off with an apologetic smile. 'I haven't asked you to dinner just to talk about this case. We haven't seen much of each other lately.'

'I've had flu.'

'I know that. I called round with flowers and sympathy, but a dragon in a pinny opened the door and wouldn't let me in.'

'Mrs Harmer. She's James Holland's housekeeper. He nobly sent her round to take care of me.'

'Thought I recognised her. One way of the church taking care of its parishioners, I suppose!'

Meredith protested, 'I did phone and thank you for the flowers the next day!'

'And told me to stay away!'

'With best intentions!'

They both laughed. 'So,' he said. 'How are you feeling now?'

'Much better, honestly. Right as a trivet, as the saying goes.' She suspected he didn't believe her. His blue eyes were concerned, still searching her face critically, looking for lingering traces of the effects of the flu.

But all he said was, 'Good. Ahmed recommends the spiced vegetable samosa starter.'

'Fine by me!' Meredith told him heartily. But she hadn't got away with it so easily.

Without warning, he returned to the subject of her recent indisposition. 'Tell me if you aren't feeling up to talking. Are you sure you're all right? What you need is a tonic. When I was a kid, we were always being dosed with stuff from a bottle when we'd been laid up. It was supposed to fix you up in no time.'

'I don't suppose you can get that sort of tonic these days. There was probably stuff in it a pharmacist wouldn't be allowed to dispense now!' She leaned across the table and touched his hand briefly. 'I'm all right! I felt a bit headachy in Sally's place, but I only needed some air.'

He would have caught her hand, but she slipped it free. 'I am worried about Sally. I realise how dangerous that bomb was today, even if Liam doesn't. And I really am feeling quite all right.'

There was an interruption as they were asked if they wished to order and also, what they wished to drink.

When they'd placed their orders and the barman had brought the drinks, Meredith went on, 'It's been a while, as you say. Tell me what's been happening on your side of the fence.'

'Police work, what else?' He grinned at her, his fair hair falling forward in the way she knew so well and which always provoked in her the corniest of reactions.

'You probably don't want to hear about it. But you remember Pearce who was my sergeant in Bamford? He's passed his exams and made inspector. Even better, he's joined us over at Regional HQ. I'm hoping we'll be working together on this Caswell business.'

That brought them back to business. 'I have to confess, it still feels odd, talking about friends,' Meredith admitted, fiddling with the corner of her napkin.

'It may help save their lives.'

Put like that, there was no possible further objection. Meredith sipped her gin and tonic and wondered how she ought to begin. She was saved by the arrival of the samosas. There was another break in conversation. She prolonged it by asking, 'Glad you've got Pearce back. I know you always liked working with him.' He mumbled assent but wasn't drawn. She took a deep breath. 'Right! What do you want me to tell you about the Caswells?'

'Anything which might give a lead. All I know is that a letter-bomb has been delivered to their home early today. Correction, Caswell also sprang anonymous letters on me. So anonymous he can't tell me a thing about them.' Alan spoke the last words with some ferocity.

The samosa hit Meredith's stomach with a mini-explosion of taste. Though delicious, after so much bland food lately, it was too much to take. She put down her fork. 'Surely people who write poison pen letters go out of their way to hide any clues?'

'It wasn't ordinary poison pen mail. Or, we suppose it wasn't. It seems, from what Caswell remembers about the content, that it was from someone who knew about this book, his work. That suggests animal rights activists. But they like the recipient to know he's been targeted and usually sign their offensive mail – not with their names, naturally – but with the name of some action group. Usually some group no one has heard of and which might be new – or an old group using a new name. Publicity and instilling fear is the name of the game with them. As for the package—' He pushed away his empty plate. 'We may get a phone call tomorrow, claiming responsibility.'

He hesitated. 'It was fairly powerful. I had a brief word with the explosives boys. They expressed surprise. When pressure groups send letter-bombs they usually intend to frighten and warn, as I say. Some of the packages are fakes, don't explode at all. They're rigged up to look as if they're meant to be bombs, but contain messages, cards of condolence et cetera. There's little point in including those if no one gets to read them! This one was designed to explode and indicates a willingness to do serious harm. Even to kill.'

Meredith had paled. 'It's vicious. The product of a sick mind. It has to be! They couldn't even be sure Liam would open it. Wasn't he supposed to be in Norwich or somewhere? As it happens, he was there, but as bad luck had it, poor Sally opened it. What's Sally ever done to harm anyone?'

'You sound as if you wouldn't have been too sorry if Liam had opened it!' he teased.

'I don't care for him much,' she confessed. 'One put up with Liam for the sake of Sally. Sally is a sweet person. That's what makes it so stupid.'

'The people we're dealing with, a mistake as regards victim from time to time doesn't put them off. Unfortunate casualties in a greater cause, as far as they're concerned.' He hissed in annoyance. 'I wish Caswell had kept those anonymous letters. There may have been some warning in them that he should watch out for more dangerous mail. He seems unbelievably off-hand about them!'

'That doesn't surprise me as much as it does you!' she told him. 'Liam's absolutely wrapped up in his work. For him, it's so self-evident that it's important, I really don't think he can take in the fact that anyone could possibly object to it in any way.'

'Caswell must have a general impression how people feel,' Alan said sharply. 'He was at pains to tell us his animals hadn't suffered, I noticed! Surely anyone whose work involves laboratory animals is well aware how much emotion that generates? To be honest, I wonder myself about the mind of a person who uses animals in that way. I know scientists say advances in medicine have been only possible using laboratory animals but I'm inclined to question that. However, what *I* think isn't what dictates my actions in this. I'm a policeman and supposed to uphold the law. The law's been broken here in a more than obvious way!'

He'd acquired a dogged tone. She recognised that, too. Despite their differences of opinion about his police work, there was no one, Meredith thought now, whom she'd rather have on this case, involving as it did, an old friend of hers. The realisation disposed of her reluctance to impart information about Liam.

'Sally told me that nowadays Liam's completely obsessed with the book he's writing. He's always been tunnel-visioned.'

'How did you first meet them?'

The waiter was back to whisk away the plates. Ahmed bustled up and regarded Meredith's almost untouched samosas with dismay. 'Something is wrong?'

'No, I'm sorry. It's delicious but I'm not very hungry.' She smiled apologetically. 'I'm just getting over influenza. My appetite's not very good.'

'The flu!' said Ahmed knowledgeably. 'My wife's mother also . . .'

He walked away shaking his head. Meredith folded her hands on the tablecloth and said ruefully, 'Poor Ahmed. I didn't mean to insult his food! As for when I got to know the Caswells, it was a long time ago.'

A plate of Naan bread appeared in front of them.

'It was when I first joined the Foreign Service and I was working in London. I had a flat in Holland Park, on the first floor of a nice old house. Normally the rent would have been beyond my means but it belonged to a colleague. He was overseas on a posting for a year or two and wanted someone who needed a short-term let. It suited him to let another government employee have it, at a reasonable rate.'

A savoury pungent aroma announced the arrival of rich lamb curry. There was another pause in the conversation.

'Liam and Sally lived in the ground-floor flat. They'd not long been married. Liam had qualified as a doctor and was working at one of the London hospitals, but he wanted to get into research. Gosh, this is hot!' Wishing to compensate for her neglect of the samosas, Meredith had taken an unwary, large mouthful of the curry.

'Like it hot,' said Alan indistinctly. 'This flat, wasn't it also a bit out of the usual league for an impecunious young doctor?'

'Oh, but Sally has money. That's not to say Liam hasn't – hadn't. I don't know his financial situation at that time. But Sally's family was wealthy.' She paused. 'I really am going to have to have some water.'

'Drinking water makes it worse.'

'I can't help that. Do ask if they've got a bottle of Evian before I start breathing flames.'

The water arrived by the hand of a grinning waiter. Meredith drank deeply. 'Ah! That's better! Both Sally and I grew up as the only child of elderly parents,' she went on. 'When we found out we had that in common we got on really well. She told me about her family. Her situation was a bit different from mine in that her mother died when she was tiny and her father was quite desolate. He had no intention of remarrying, but he wanted his little daughter to have a permanent female to whom she could relate, a mother-substitute. So he sold up and moved in with his sister. Aunt Emily was even older. She'd never married and was still living in the family home – Sally's grandparents' house. It was a big place in Surrey and there was plenty of room for Sally and her father.'

'Desirable property,' he observed.

'I told you, they were wealthy. Later Sally's father died and she carried on living with Aunt Emily. She was very fond of the old lady and they got on well but there was a heck of a generation gap. I think that's partly why Sally married very young, only nineteen. The aunt didn't object because Liam was a handsome young doctor who had what were usually called "prospects" by Emily's generation.'

'I presume Liam had managed to be polite to auntie?'

'He isn't rude to everyone!' Meredith found herself defending Liam, which put her in a false position. She put down knife and fork to gesticulate. 'It's like this, going back to Holland Park days, he and Sally appeared very happy and he was civil enough – to me, anyway. But, you see, Liam is a genius. Don't pull that face! He started as one of those gifted kids who become brilliant students, marked out for a special career from the beginning. If he became conceited, it's not surprising.'

'Some of the most gifted people I've met,' Alan said

pugnaciously, 'have also been some of the most modest!'

'Liam's not modest. It would be nice if he was, but he never has been. He's always been told he was special, from a very early age. He just believes he's different. Everyone has always told him so. In some cases, that sort of thing is balanced by a naturally pleasant disposition. That, I'm sorry to say, is something Liam doesn't have.'

'So he goes around treading on toes and behaving like a lout?'

It was clear Alan had taken a dislike to Liam. Since he was going to be protecting Caswell, that was probably a pity. But entirely Liam's fault, Meredith reflected.

'Let me put it this way,' she said. 'Some of us are civil to others because we have nice natures.'

'Present company,' said Alan politely.

She ploughed on determinedly. 'Some of us are polite because we hope others will be polite to us, in return. A way of getting along in society.'

'Do as you would be done by.'

'Exactly. But someone like Liam doesn't have to worry if people like him or not. He has an exceptional gift. The normal social rules don't apply to him. Or that's how he sees it.'

'Are you seriously saying he can go round offending anyone he wishes?' Alan sounded genuinely amazed and was staring at her.

'No! Of course not! I'm trying to explain the man to you! If he's upset people, he's never had to worry about it. A lot of people would say he's eccentric. Or that his behaviour is a mark of brilliance. I don't say I agree. To be frank, he drives me barmy! Although I repeat, he's normally fairly polite to *me*. But I also know that over the years, his arrogance has got worse and it isn't tempered by extreme youth any more. People overlook behaviour in young people that they don't forgive in older ones. Fact of life. Liam can be high-handed and he doesn't like opposition.'

Meredith gave a grin. 'Liam's career has been punctuated by flaming rows with just about everyone: colleagues, government departments, editors of professional journals, taxi-drivers, you name it! Even all those years ago in Holland Park, there was a dust-up about parking in front of the house. The other person concerned was willing to compromise but Liam decided to be awkward.'

'He's fallen out with his neighbour in Castle Darcy, too, hasn't he?' Alan pointed out.

'The old man, Bodicote?' Meredith thought that over. 'Do you think he might send anonymous letters?' She considered this, then shook her head. 'He wouldn't send a letter-bomb, surely?'

'I admit it's unlikely he'd concoct an explosive device. But write an abusive letter? Yes, he might. Almost anyone might. Bad blood between neighbours has led to really nasty acts before now. And we can't just assume the same person sent the letters *and* today's explosive package.'

Alan smiled. 'Funny old boy, Bodicote. A bit of a surprise, really. I quoted Conan Doyle to him and he picked it up straight away. He's a great reader of what he calls decent yarns. He seemed to think Liam was writing a novel.'

'Liam said something about that, didn't he? That villagers assume he's a novelist. Doesn't sound as if Bodicote knows anything about Liam's work, then.'

'Or isn't admitting it.'

The waiter had returned for their finished plates. Neither wanted anything more to eat and they settled for coffee. Another pair of hands deposited hot towels in little china dishes before them.

'You know,' said Meredith, picking up her towel and disinterring it from its hygienic wrapper, 'I love the food here but always have to wash my hair when I get home. The smell of the curry seems to linger.'

'Smells do linger . . .' Alan seemed to have drifted off into some reminiscence. Realising she was looking at him, he apologised. 'Sorry, just thinking. Old Bodicote's sitting room had a funny sort of smell lingering in it. It made me think of horses.'

'He keeps goats.'

'I know. I don't mean it was a strong horsey smell. Just a sort of smell you'd associate with being around horses.'

'Liniment? Country people rub odd preparations into their stiff joints. Saddle soap? Old Bodicote cleaning his boots with it?'

'That's more like it. It reminded me of a tack room. Leather saddles.' He shrugged. 'Mind you, that whole cottage of his is redolent of just about everything under the sun!'

Coffee arrived with a dish of mint chocolates.

'I don't know whether it has anything at all to do with the Caswells,' Alan said slowly. 'I'm certainly not accusing Bodicote of writing the letters as yet. But the old fellow is up to something. All the signs are there.'

'Old people are secretive. Probably counting his money. Keeps his savings under the bed.'

'Hope not,' said Alan, unwrapping a mint. 'Very dangerous thing to do!'

Outside the restaurant the town streets gleamed eerily under the yellow glow of the lamps. Few people were about.

'I didn't bring my car,' Alan said, 'I knew I'd be having a drink. I'll walk you home. Although the wind's chill. We'll take a taxi.'

She slipped her arm through his. 'I'd rather walk. I've been cooped up for a couple of weeks.'

They set off down the street, their shadows lengthening before them as they moved away from the lamplight, disparate forms, linked together.

Chapter Five

Meredith awoke, rolled over, and fumbled for the clock at her bedside. She saw with a groan that she'd overslept. It was sale day. She had planned to go and bid for the glassware and she wanted to find out how Sally Caswell was this morning. It was nearly nine and she had intended to phone Sally at the cottage before her friend left for the auction rooms, if leave she did.

Meredith sat up and swung her legs to the floor, fingers reaching for the robe thrown over a nearby chair. Her legs still felt a little wobbly when she stood up. Cursing the flu's obstinate legacy, she padded downstairs to the telephone and punched out the Caswell's number.

Liam answered. 'She's just about to leave. Sal!' In answer to his shout, a distant female voice could be heard.

'Ought she to go? Is she all right?' Meredith asked in concern.

Liam didn't reply. There was an exchange of voices at the further end of the line and then Sally herself came, breathless, to the phone.

'Meredith? I'm just leaving. You're coming along to see the fun today, aren't you? Bidding for your Victorian glasses? I'll see you there!'

'Hang on!' Meredith urged down the phone. 'Are you sure about this?'

'Positive. I can't let Austin down on sale day. It will be very busy. I'm fine, really.'

Meredith thought she detected an echo in Sally's voice akin to the one in her own when she assured Alan the flu was all in the past.

'Austin can surely get in someone else?'

'Hey,' said Sally, 'it's my job we're talking about here! I don't want to put the idea into Austin's head that I'm replaceable!'

Meredith set down the phone, hitched the robe round her shoulders and rang Alan. She explained that Sally meant to go in to work. 'It's not a good idea, Alan. Can't you give her a call and talk her out of it? She must still be very shocked and she had a nasty crack on the head.'

He was irritatingly non-committal. It was up to Sally, after all, was the burden of his argument. Meredith put the phone down again, this time with some force.

She went upstairs and turned on the shower.

When these terraced cottages had been built, bathrooms had not been considered necessary. There'd been a brick privy in the yard. (Still there but used as a shed.) Otherwise people washed in the kitchen or in a basin in the bedroom. To create a modern bathroom had meant sacrificing one of the three bedrooms. None of the bedrooms was large and the least of them little more than a boxroom. Lack of space had meant only the smallest of bathtubs had been installed in it.

This had been the situation when Meredith bought the little house but she'd soon got fed up with sitting in the mini-tub with her knees under her chin. It had also been old and badly stained. The answer had been to gut the bathroom, remove the antiquated fittings and replace the bath with a roomy shower.

The shower set Meredith's skin tingling. As she was rubbing herself down vigorously afterwards, there was a movement at the frosted glass window over the washbasin which wasn't a reflection.

'It's that cat again,' she murmured.

She went to push open the sash window, letting out the steam and letting in a whistle of cold draught. The cat, crouched on the wide stone ledge, peered under the open window frame, wide yellow eyes alert, body tensed ready to make a leap to the wall below.

'Hullo, Tiger,' she greeted it. 'You *are* a Peeping Tom!'

It opened its pink mouth and returned a soft squawk to this corny joke.

Meredith was encouraged to reach out to push up the window a little further. But the movement alarmed the cat. Like a tumbler, it leapt, twisting and turning in the air, to land with ease on the broad brick wall dividing her backyard from next door's. For a split second it paused to look up, inviting admiration at its cleverness. But as she leaned out, it slithered over the wall and dropped down on the further side.

Meredith retreated from the knife-edge thrust of the icy air. She pulled down the window, wrapping her towel more firmly around herself.

She hadn't time to worry about the cat. Sally took precedence. At least, at the saleroom, she'd be able to keep an eye on her friend.

The friend in question had replaced the receiver in the cottage, following Meredith's call, and made her way thoughtfully to the kitchen.

It was all very well joking with Meredith about it, Sally thought. She didn't feel cheery, fine or even part-way reasonable. But she had to get out of this cottage. She held out her hands and studied them. Reasonably steady. She ought to be able to get through a day at Bailey and Bailey's without completely cracking up. She supposed Liam would be all right here alone. Perhaps she ought to stay and keep him company? On the other hand, he would be working on the book.

She set about preparing the two vacuum flasks as usual. Although 'usual' could never be quite the same. Now, whenever she switched on the kettle, she heard in her head the echo of the explosion, followed by the clatter and crash of crockery. Sally twitched. She was not going to let this get to her.

Liam was at his computer, working. 'Coffee!' she said, putting down the vacuum flask.

He glanced up. 'You're going in to work, then? Do you think it's wise?'

'It will take my mind off things. You'll be all right here?'

'Sure. Wouldn't be surprised if the coppers don't come back in their size twelve boots and start tramping around the place. I hope that Markby fellow doesn't come, but he probably will. He threatened to. Or send his minions. Don't know which will be worse.'

'Alan? Didn't you like him? He's Meredith's friend. I thought he was rather nice.'

'You would.' Liam struck the keyboard with unnecessary force. 'I found him an arrogant, supercilious blighter.'

'Perhaps if the police come, they'll expect to see me,' Sally said, worried.

'They can find you at Bailey's, can't they?'

Clearly, he was in a mood. All the more reason to go into work. The qualms she'd had about leaving him here alone were effectively squashed.

Sally ran up the narrow staircase and into the main bedroom. To dignify the room with the title 'main' was estate-agent-speak. It was the larger of the two bedrooms the cottage possessed. Since the other was minuscule, 'larger' meant 'average-sized'. The ceiling slanted, reducing space still further and the tiny dormer-windows were set in narrow embrasures. Like Meredith, Sally was finding it difficult to accommodate her lifestyle into a space which originally had housed a family with several children. Such was progress.

There was little room for furniture and most of the floor space was taken up with the double pine bed. The dressing table was out of style with the room, but here because Sally liked it. It had been one of Aunt Emily's pieces, a thirties-designed extravaganza with triple oval mirrors atop and a row of tiny drawers, inlaid with mother-of-pearl, below. The surface was polished walnut veneer.

Sally always felt, when she sat before it, rather like one of those goddesses of the silver screen, a Hollywood Great of the days of glamour. She ought to wear a satin négligée trimmed with swansdown and the surface of the dressing table should be covered with cut-glass perfume sprays and huge powder puffs. As it was, Sally never sat before it in anything other than a towelling bathrobe and its surface carried only basic make-up items and a jumble of things which oughtn't to be here at all: letters and scribbled memos; paperclips and elastic bands. Nor could her face and figure be described as glamorous. Still, anyone could dream.

Not, however, this morning. No time for fantasy worlds. The bed hadn't been made. If she left it like this, it would still be in its unmade state when she got back. It wouldn't occur to Liam to tidy it.

Sally pulled the duvet straight and punched the pillows. Thumping them made her feel better.

So much for the bed. If only every problem could be dealt with so easily, with simple application of brute force! She understood why people, faced with no other way out of a dilemma, were tempted to see violence as the answer. Biff, biff, biff! She stopped, struck by guilt. It didn't justify those who'd sent the letter-bomb. They had no excuse for what they'd done. But that was ugly real-life violence, not vicarious fantasy violence. Just as real life was a towelling robe and not a diaphanous négligée.

The exercise had caused her to work up a sweat and when she peered in the oval mirror of the dressing table, her face had a healthy glow. She dabbed powder on her nose to remove the shine and applied a thin coating of lipstick to her mouth. Pressing her lips together and studying the result, she decided that, though an improvement, it could be better.

Her hand strayed towards one of the tiny drawers which held

recent impulse-purchases of mascara and eyebrow pencil. 'For whom am I doing this?' she asked herself. 'For Austin?'

If so, she oughtn't to be. She withdrew her hand. But she remained before the dressing table, staring down at the little row of drawers. Unwillingly, as if propelled by some outside force, she stretched out her fingers again, but this time to a drawer on the extreme left which contained miscellaneous small items belonging to Liam.

It was his personal drawer but she knew what was in there. He thought she didn't. She hadn't told him of her discovery. He'd lose his temper, wanting to know why she was rummaging in his drawer, anyway? She'd discovered it by chance about a month ago. She'd bought a new shirt-blouse with turned-back cuffs and had thought that a pair of men's cufflinks might look smart. Liam didn't normally use such things except on formal occasions but he had two or three pairs. Seeking them, in the little morocco-leather case which held them, she'd found the tie-pin.

Sally slid open the drawer and took out the box. The tie-pin was still there. She unfolded the tissue wrapping and it lay in her palm, still attached to its plush mount. It was gold, no question of it, but a horrid thing, designed like a snake with a ruby eye.

She ran the tip of her finger along its sinuous body, allowing herself the pleasure of criticising it. 'Flashy', that was the word. There was also satisfaction in knowing about it, when Liam thought she didn't. She returned it to its place.

Sally hurried back down the stair, unhooking her jacket as she passed the rack in the hall, and putting her head round the study door as she struggled to thrust her arms through the jacket's sleeves.

'I'll be back around four,' she promised.

Liam, sitting at his computer, his back to her, muttered, 'I'll see you then.' He didn't turn, but tapped the keyboard and script rolled across the monitor.

She wanted to tell him he might have the courtesy to look at her. She even took a step forward and reached out her hand before thinking, what am I about to do? Hurl the keyboard to the floor? Smash the screen? Such tantrums weren't in her nature.

Her hand dropped back by her side. The anger, subdued, was pushed back into her subconscious, like a wild animal returned to a cage.

Liam was not even aware of her movement. She muttered 'Goodbye!' and scurried out.

Dave Pearce's elevation to inspector weighed heavily on his shoulders, (encased today in a brand-new jacket). Since joining the force, Pearce had never lacked ambition. First to make it into CID and then to continue upward and onward. Just how far up and on, he hadn't been sure. He was privately worried that lack of extensive formal education and a hint of country accent might put a halt to his rise beyond a certain point.

'All bloody graduates these days!' he'd informed his new wife, Tessa. 'I mean, what chance do I stand against the university boys?'

But he'd assiduously burned the midnight oil and passed his exams, and here he was, detective-inspector. Tessa had immediately insisted on the new jacket. The other Mrs Pearce, Dave's mother, had visited, phoned or (in the case of a cousin in Australia) written to every acquaintance she had to spread the glad news of her son's success. Dave suspected that, had the elder Mrs Pearce been able to persuade the vicar, she'd have arranged for the church bells to be rung to announce the tidings to the countryside at large.

Now that it had come, his promotion, he had to deal with it. Put up or shut up, as the saying went. He couldn't let down Tessa nor the dowager Mrs Pearce. Their faith in him was absolute. He couldn't let himself down, though his faith in himself was by no means so complete. He couldn't let down his old guv'nor and mentor from Bamford, Chief Inspector, now Superintendent,

Markby, with whom Pearce found himself again working. He was pleased (secretly delighted, in fact) to be back on Markby's team. But it added to that invisible burden. Above all, he hadn't to fail in Markby's eyes.

This morning it was extremely cold but without the frost. Instead it was dank, with overcast skies and a promise of rain or even sleet. A clamminess infested the atmosphere which crept through the weave of Pearce's new jacket and even seemed to lend a damp feel to the papers he'd placed on Markby's desk.

The grey skies added to Pearce's sombre mood. He picked up his polystyrene cup of coffee, coaxed from a dispenser in the corridor on his way to Markby's office, sipped and burned his tongue. He muttered, 'Shit!'

'What's that?' The superintendent, shuffling irritably among the forensic reports, didn't look up.

Pearce said hastily, 'Prescott's checking out that raid at Caswell's lab last year. I asked him to bring along the file as soon as he's located it.'

'Good.' Markby swept the sheets of paper into a heap, picked it up, tapped it on the desk to knock it into shape and then placed it foursquare on the desk. Satisfied at last it was tidy, he rested his forearms on top of it, hands clasped.

'Expert opinion is that the package was an amateur effort, for all its effectiveness. Certainly it was unstable which was why it went off as it did. The explosive itself was probably old, perhaps badly stored. The bomber's supplier for his material may have been a stranger in a pub. It might have gone off at any time, long before it reached the Caswells. Might even have gone off in the maker's own face.'

Pearce nodded, grimacing, but not because of the carelessness of the bomber. The coffee tasted awful, bitter but without flavour. It might be better to drink it very hot, at the risk of scalding. 'If whoever sent it hadn't done it before,' he observed, 'he mightn't realise it was so powerful.'

Markby hunched his shoulders. 'True. Or perhaps he just didn't *care*. That could indicate someone particularly fanatical. Perhaps a group we haven't come across before. There are several small do-it-yourself outfits in the animal rights movement generally. It might consist of just one man, or a couple of people, one of whom has just sufficient knowledge to rig an explosive device but not enough to make a professional job of it.'

Pearce nodded, staring into the coffee tub. A dark stain was forming on the top of the coffee, reminiscent of oil seeping up from a submerged wreck.

Markby slapped the desk. Pearce jumped. The coffee slopped and he hastily held it away from the new jacket. 'Sir?'

'The senders are obviously totally irresponsible and may well strike again, having failed this time!' Markby emphasised the words, obviously aware of some inattention on the part of his listener. 'Warnings are being sent to all research establishments engaged on work involving animals and leading experts in the field put on their guard. They – whoever they are – may not strike here next. Having diverted us to one target, they may now seek out another. That doesn't mean Caswell and his wife are in the clear. I've asked someone to go out to Castle Darcy and show them both how to check their cars for booby-traps. That could be the next thing they try.'

His voice tailed away and he turned his head to stare out at the leaden sky. 'Dirty business and we're in for some dirty weather. Pity. At least the frost made the place look attractive.'

'Anyone rung to ask how Mrs Caswell is today?' Pearce was anxious to prove his mind was on business.

'Meredith rang early this morning. I mean, Miss Mitchell. You remember?' Markby turned questioning eyes on him.

Pearce cheered up and grinned. 'Course I do! I mean, yes, I remember the lady.'

Markby treated him to a suspicious look. He was well aware that when he'd been at Bamford, his underlings had run a book on when he and Meredith would announce their engagement. It hadn't happened. She liked things between them just the way they were. He hadn't given up hope of persuading her one day to think about a change in their situation, though he'd resigned himself to a long wait.

'Meredith knows Mrs Caswell from way back.' He spoke briskly. 'After she rang Castle Darcy, she rang me. Meredith's worried. It seems Sally Caswell intends to go to work today. She works at Bailey and Bailey, the auctioneers. It's a sale day and she feels she ought to be there. Meredith hoped I'd step in and dissuade her. I didn't because, between you and me, I'm glad she's there rather than in that isolated village. At least I know where she is and that she's safe. It only leaves me with Dr Caswell to worry about for a few hours.' He glanced at his wristwatch. 'She'll be at Bailey's now.'

Pearce's coffee had cooled. Bravely ignoring the dark stain on the surface, he drank it down, wincing.

'You don't look as if you enjoyed that,' Markby observed. 'Why don't you bring in a flask? Several people do.'

'I'll get used to it,' Pearce said nobly. 'We can't guard Dr Caswell night and day.'

'No. He'll have to take all possible precautions himself. I've told him to get in touch the moment anything odd happens and especially if he receives any more mail, anonymous or not, which is about his work. I hope he does.' Markby let out his breath in a hiss of annoyance. 'He's an awkward type. He receives threats and doesn't report them. Doesn't like being bothered with questions. Doesn't like policemen. Doesn't like anything interfering with his work!'

Pearce said slowly, 'To be honest, sir, I don't much care for the idea of people messing about with dumb animals in laboratories. I like animals. We've got a new puppy at home. I'd hate to think of someone, well, cutting it about or giving it diseases on purpose.'

'So do I, so do most of us. But Caswell's work is perfectly legal and according to him, his animals didn't suffer. We've only his word for that, I know. But the point is, whatever we feel about it, we have to try and find who is sending bombs through the Royal Mail. There's never any excuse for that!'

A tap at the door heralded Sergeant Prescott. His entrance was mildly dramatic, owing to a magnificent black eye which marred his youthful looks.

'Still in the rugby team, I see,' Markby remarked. 'Good match, last Saturday, was it?'

'Yessir. We thrashed Bamford Town!' Prescott touched the purple flesh with pride and added, 'It was a bit of a roughhouse but no one stretchered off. All walking wounded.'

'Don't break any bones,' Markby begged him. 'That's all I ask. We're short-handed enough as it is! Is that the file on the animal liberation gang?'

Prescott hastened to put it on the desk. 'The ringleader was a bloke called Michael Whelan. When he was picked up for the raid on the lab, he'd already got form. He got another six months for the raid. He must be out by now. There's an address for him. He lives out at Cherton, the Spring Farm estate.'

Markby and Pearce groaned in unison. Pearce added, 'Wouldn't he just?'

'Glad you're happy about it!' Markby told them both. 'Because you're going over there to interview him! If he served a gaol sentence after the raid on Caswell's lab, he may bear a personal grudge against Caswell, quite aside from anything to do with the animals.'

'Right!' Pearce got to his feet and dropped the empty polystyrene tub into the wastepaper basket. He resolved to stop somewhere *en route* to Whelan and get a proper cup of coffee!

'Better not go alone.' Markby nodded at Prescott. 'Take our sporting hero with you! That shiner might impress Whelan!' He slapped the file on the desk. 'As for me, I think I'll go and talk to Miss Libby Hancock.'

They both looked baffled.

'Miss Hancock,' Markby explained. 'delivers the post to Castle Darcy. Someone's got to talk to her. It'll save an officer a job if I go, and do me good to get out of this office!'

'He hasn't changed,' said Pearce unwarily to Prescott as they set off to find Whelan.

Prescott gave him a curious glance. 'The superintendent? You know him of old, don't you? That's what someone said.'

'Markby? He was my chief at Bamford.' Pearce grinned at the memory. 'He always hated being stuck at a desk! He loves being out and about talking to people!'

'I sometimes think,' said Prescott, 'I wouldn't mind a desk job. On mornings like this, anyway. I can't say I'm keen to go and talk to a bunch of villains in Spring Farm.'

'We've only got to check out Whelan and it shouldn't take us long.' Pearce had something else on his mind. 'Before we go there, do you know anywhere around here which does a decent cup of coffee?'

When Markby arrived at Bamford postal sorting office, most of its employees were out on the various 'walks'. The hectic reception and sorting of overnight mailbags was long completed. However, a recent delivery must just have taken place because a fresh stack had been emptied on to the tipping table and busy hands were picking it over.

The manager emerged from his office and shook Markby's hand. 'Libby? She came in this morning but I had to send her home. She was in no state to take the van out. This has given her a terrible shock. Given us all a hell of a shock! Sort of thing can happen to any of us. Libby's a friendly sort of girl, knows a lot of the people she delivers to. The idea that she personally handed the Caswell woman the package, well, you know. Nasty. Left us short-handed this morning.' He glanced wryly around the sorting room.

'You haven't had any similar incidents recently, say within the last six months? Any suspicious packages taken your eye?'

The manager shook his head. 'Not here. If anything happens elsewhere, we get an opsflash. We stick it up on the board here.' He led Markby to a corkboard by the entrance. A small printed notice was affixed. It gave details of the previous day's package to the Caswells and warned staff to look out for further mail addressed to Castle Darcy.

'Got our own opsflash today!' said the manager with a grim smile.

'What do you do if you get a suspicious package?'

'Take it out to the yard and drop it in the bomb box, then phone your lot. What else can we do?' The manager gazed moodily at the opsflash. 'Ruddy maniacs! Don't give a damn whether a postal worker gets his hands blown off!'

Libby Hancock lived in a neat red-brick terraced house. The brass letterbox was burnished bright. Crisp lace curtains decorously draped sparkling windows. The door was opened by a worried-looking, middle-aged woman in a hand-knitted pullover and polyester slacks.

'Oh, police!' she said flustered. 'Come in, won't you? I don't know what Libby can tell you. She's that upset. You won't go frightening her, will you?' She peered at Markby, seeking reassurance.

A door at the far end of the narrow passage opened before he could answer. A balding, moustachioed man emerged and bore down on them.

'Boys in blue?' he demanded loudly. 'Oh, plainclothes, eh? CID job!' He tapped the side of his nose and winked at Markby, as if they shared some secret.

'This is my brother,' said Mrs Hancock in a flat voice. 'He's come to have a word with Libby, Denis.'

Denis sidled up to Markby. 'Bring back the cat!' he advised hoarsely. In case Markby should misinterpret this as a request to seek out a missing moggy, he added, 'Flogging! That's what's needed!' Undeniable relish entered his voice. 'Bring back the birch! Joy-riders, football hooligans, bombers, the lot!'

'All right, Denis!' said Mrs Hancock, showing signs of spirit. 'He doesn't want to hear your views!'

'Yes, he does!' argued Denis. 'I'm a member of the public. They want to know what the public thinks, do the coppers. They like to know Joe Public is behind them. That's why you get all them programmes on the telly, like *Crimewatch*. If it wasn't for the public helping, the coppers wouldn't catch half the crooks!'

'Quite,' said Markby, edging past Denis in the narrow confines of the hallway. 'Er, your daughter, Mrs Hancock?'

'String 'em up!' continued Denis, undeterred. 'Bring back hanging! Corporal punishment and—' He paused, hunting the word. 'And the other sort! Capital punishment, that's it! Corporal and capital punishment. An eye for an eye and a tooth for a tooth! That's in the Bible,' he concluded piously.

'Take no notice,' said Mrs Hancock to Markby. 'He goes on a bit. He means well. In here!'

Libby Hancock sat in the neat front room by a coal fire. A pair of budgerigars, one blue and the other green, hopped about a nearby cage. As the stranger entered, they set up a loud chirrup of alarm.

'They'll settle in a minute,' said Mrs Hancock. 'The gentleman wants a word, Libby. Police officer.'

'Hullo, Libby,' said Markby.

'Hullo,' she returned almost inaudibly.

'I'll fetch in a cup of tea,' said Mrs Hancock. She went out and could be heard in lively conversation with her brother.

'Did you meet Uncle Denis?' Libby asked.

Markby smiled. 'Yes. Does he live here?'

She gave a faint smile in return. ''Fraid so. He's all right in his way. He'll probably go out soon. Down the bookies. It'll be quieter when he's gone.'

Her voice lingered wistfully on the last phrase and he wondered whether she meant Denis's departure in a permanent sense. He studied her. She was a sturdy young woman and although off work today still wore her uniform navy-blue sweater, skirt, dark stockings and strong lace-up shoes. But she had gone into work this morning to be sent home. Markby told her he'd stopped by the sorting office.

'I would've stayed!' she said, becoming agitated. 'I don't like letting people down. Someone will have to do my round after he's done his and people will get their mail late!'

'They'll understand. You don't mind if we talk about yesterday?'

She shook her head. 'No. But I can't tell you anything helpful. I still can't believe it.' Her voice dropped to a whisper again.

'Mind out the way, Denis!' came Mrs Hancock's exasperated voice outside the door.

'Just opening the door for you, Mary!' protested Denis.

Mrs Hancock entered with teacups on a tray and a plate of biscuits. She set it down while Denis hovered hopefully in the background. Mrs Hancock retreated, pushing her brother forcefully ahead of her and the door closed.

The budgerigars had settled down. One pecked at a spray of millet and the other balanced on its little swing. Markby reflected that Denis was doubtless living very comfortably in this cosy little home. He wondered if the lodger-relative did any kind of job.

'I went into work yesterday as usual,' Libby was saying. 'I got there just before five.'

Five o'clock on a chilly winter morning. While Denis was probably still abed, thought Markby, his niece was out in the frosty dawn, making her way to work. Irritation rose in his throat. He picked up a cup of tea and handed it to the girl.

She took it absently. 'There wasn't much post for Castle Darcy. But there were a couple of packages, one of them a padded mailbag for the Caswells. It was a bit heavy and whoever had sent it had put on extra postage. I remember saying to Mrs Caswell, that really it's best to get things weighed.'

She looked up in sudden agitation. 'I should have thought – I should have known then that something was wrong with it! It's one of the things we're told to look for, a package like that where someone had obviously not wanted to hand it over at a post office counter and had just stuffed it into a postbox.' She heaved a sigh. 'But it's coming up to Christmas, you see. And people do things like that around Christmas. They want to get a Christmas present off and they haven't time to take it in, so they just stick on as many stamps as they've got in the house and hope it'll be enough. I just thought – so stupid of me—'

'All right,' Markby told her soothingly. 'As you say, it's coming up to Christmas and there are a lot of packages going through the post, a lot of them wrongly labelled or packed.'

She looked at him gratefully. 'I put it on the front seat beside me. Castle Darcy's not my first call, though. I go to Cherton first. There's always more for Cherton because of all the housing estates there. Not that I do them all. I take half and someone else takes the other half. After I finished Cherton, that's when I put Castle Darcy's mail on the front seat.'

All in all, from sorting office to delivery, she'd handled the package several times and each handling had been potentially lethal. Markby reached for his own tea, frowning.

Libby's brow was also furrowed, in recollection. 'The other package was for Mr Bodicote, recorded delivery. He had to sign for it. I had to wait while he unchained the door and then while he went and got his glasses. He is a funny old man. He keeps goats.'

'Yes,' Markby smiled. 'I met Mr Bodicote and heard about Jasper.'

She dimpled. 'He's very proud of Jasper. He lets him out first thing every morning. If he's late, Jasper nearly kicks the door of his little hut down! Let's see, there were some letters and – and the package for the Caswells.' She looked up anxiously. 'She is all right, Mrs Caswell?'

'She's fine!' Markby assured her. 'I believe she's gone to work today.'

'I've been so worried. She's such a nice person. It's so awful!' Libby's voice trembled. 'And I do feel so responsible!'

'Drink your tea!' he advised. Her concern seemed to be entirely for Sally Caswell. He wondered whether shock had temporally obscured the fact that she could herself so easily have been the victim.

She took a sip of tea. 'I handed it over and got back in the van and drove on. I didn't hear any – any noise, nothing like breaking glass or an explosion. I only learned about it much later when I got back. I go off shift around twelve-thirty. Just as I was going, the news came in. I couldn't believe it. I still can't. Who would want to hurt either Dr or Mrs Caswell?' She gazed at her visitor, her large pale blue eyes distraught.

'You say there wasn't much post for Castle Darcy? Apart from Bodicote and the Caswells, was there any other mail for the village?'

Hate mail of any sort, as Markby knew, was sometimes aimed at a community, rather than any one individual. More than one person received letters. The explosive package was special. The anonymous letters might not be related to it. They couldn't just assume so.

'Mrs Goodhusband!' Libby said firmly. 'Mrs Goodhusband at The Tithe Barn. That's the name of her house. It's a lovely big house. She always has lots of letters. Apart from that, there were a couple of single items for other village people. Nothing unusual. A lot of Mrs Goodhusband's mail was in brown envelopes, business type.'

She was a good witness, Libby Hancock, Markby thought. Although shocked, she had good recall and she volunteered everything she could and let him sort it through. She didn't preselect as some witnesses did, telling the police only what they, the witness, thought of interest.

'Will you be able to find who sent it?' Libby asked him.

He drew a breath. 'Well, we think, although we don't know, that Dr Caswell may have been targeted by animal rights extremists because of some work he did last year, in his laboratory. Keep an eye open for any mail addressed to him. But try not to worry. With a little luck, we'll catch up with whoever sent the package before too long.'

She smiled at him uncertainly.

Mrs Hancock was in the passage, waiting by the door to show him out. 'I've shut Denis in the kitchen,' she said, as if her brother had been a disruptive pet. 'I told him not to come out until you'd gone. He's like a big kid, you know. You mustn't mind him.'

Markby reflected that he hadn't to mind Denis, since he hadn't to share a roof with him. He felt sorry for these two women, who did.

Mrs Hancock's view of what had happened hadn't missed the implication for her daughter. She fixed him with a direct look. 'It could've been my Libby, couldn't it? That wicked thing could have gone off in her hands!'

'Yes, it could, but it didn't,' Markby soothed her.

'I don't normally take any notice of Denis's ideas about the hanging and that,' she told him. 'But when something like this happens, to your own, it makes you think a bit, doesn't it?'

Chapter Six

Spring Farm estate was a notorious spot, a run-down council estate at Cherton. Cherton itself had once – long ago – been quite an attractive village. There were still a few old people, marooned in the handful of original cottages, who remembered it so. Sadly for them, and the village as a whole, the place had early been designated as a dormitory area for surrounding towns. It still was, and estates were still being built, although now a move upmarket was taking place and the new houses were smart and expensive.

Not so Spring Farm, which represented the first wave of development, on farmland from which it took its name. Built of prefabricated units, the houses had not been intended as permanent. The manufacturers had suggested a natural life-span of twenty years. Forty years on, the deteriorating flats and semi-detached homes of Spring Farm appeared ghosts from that distant time.

Respectable council tenants had long ago been channelled elsewhere into newer housing. The problem families, by tacit agreement, were allocated the crumbling dwellings of Spring Farm. Over recent years, when so much of the better stock of council housing had been sold off under privatisation schemes, Spring Farm remained untouched and obstinately unprivatised. No one wanted to buy any of its homes. No housing association saw in it a good investment. Its tenants passed through in as disorganised a fashion as befitted their surroundings. Most moved out as soon as they could. When they departed, the council boarded up the dwellings and left them empty to decay even faster.

In theory, the whole area was due for demolition and redevelopment. But the money had run out for such brave schemes, as money had a habit of doing. Slowly and inevitably, Spring Farm had become a village of the Damned. A hard-core population remained, drifting about its ugly, weed- and rubbish-infested pavements by day and screeching round its eerie streets in stolen cars by night. The cars were generally stolen from the new executive housing at the other end of Cherton and it wasn't uncommon to find a burnt-out wreck smouldering in the dawn light. Hardly anyone in Spring Farm had a job. Most were behind with the rent. Quite a few had served prison terms.

Pearce and Sergeant Prescott sat in the car opposite the low-rise block of flats where Michael Whelan lived. They sipped at coffee bought *en route* as they discussed how to go about their call. Their eyes flickered watchfully over the cup rims, taking in every detail of the scene. The police were not welcome in Spring Farm.

The block comprised six flats, three to either side of the central main entry. Whelan lived in the bottom floor right. The bottom floor left was boarded up, sprayed with graffiti and apparently abandoned. Whelan's flat had dirty lace curtains at the windows so that no one could look in. One window was cracked and mended with carpet tape. It was pushed open a few inches and the grimy gauze drape caught up on what looked like a tap. This was presumably the kitchen. A lidless dustbin stood outside and directly beneath. It suggested that Whelan, when he had rubbish to dispose of, simply opened the window and dropped it into the waiting bin.

'What a dump!' said Prescott, placing his empty polystyrene tub in the well of the car.

Dave Pearce grunted agreement. 'Let's get it over with!'

They got out. The slam of the car doors echoed around the

deserted street. If anyone was watching, and it was almost certain that several pairs of eyes were, they did so surreptitiously. The inhabitants were well acquainted with the law in all its forms. Plainclothes and unmarked cars didn't deceive them, they would have sussed out the callers at once. Some were probably hastily hiding suspect microwaves and television sets.

Things got even less attractive the nearer the two police officers got to the building. In the hallway a lingering odour of urine permeated the stale air. Crushed cigarette packets, empty soft drink and lager cans, and crumpled pieces of aluminium foil lay strewn about. Prescott pointed silently to these last.

Before Pearce could comment, heels tapped on the slogan-bedaubed stair and a young woman carrying a baby appeared at the turn of the stairwell above them. She was thin, straggly-haired and mean-faced. She wore leggings, high-heeled shoes, a baggy mauve sweater and was smoking. The child perched in her arm was about a year old. She and the baby were equally in need of a bath and clean clothes. The mother stared down at them. Her free hand hung by her side, smoke spiralling up from the cigarette smouldering between her fingers.

'Who d'you want?' she asked belligerently.

'Michael Whelan,' Pearce told her.

She looked relieved but put the cigarette to her lips in an attempt to hide the expression.

'Ain't seen him for a week,' she said. 'He mightn't be there. Why don't you try down the pub?'

Initially she'd clearly been worried they were seeking someone else. Now their visit no longer bothered her directly. Whelan was nothing to her. All the same, she created a token delay so that if Whelan had seen the police approach, he'd have time to hide or destroy anything he thought he should. The inhabitants of Spring Farm stood by one another against officialdom, even though they were otherwise split into warring factions.

'But he still lives here?'

The smoke from the cigarette drifted into the baby's face. It put up its little fists in a pathetic attempt to protect its eyes and whimpered.

She joggled her arm to quieten the infant but didn't remove the cause of its distress.

'That smoke's going in the kid's eyes!' snapped Prescott, annoyed.

She looked surprised. 'Oh, yeah . . .' She waved her hand, still with the cigarette smouldering, to dispel the smoke and only spread it further.

'He lives here, Whelan?' Pearce persisted.

'Suppose so. He did. He's a quiet sod. Haven't seen him for a week. What d'ya want him for?'

The two officers exchanged glances and by mutual consent turned away from her. Pearce rang the doorbell. Then he knocked loudly, to make sure. The girl with the baby remained where she was, watching.

After a moment they heard someone come to the door. There was a fit of coughing. A voice asked, 'Who is it?'

'Police!' Prescott called loudly.

A chain rattled. The door opened just wide enough to admit them and a voice hollowly invited them to come in, then, if they wanted.

The tiny hall was dark and smelly. The man's outline, silhouetted in the kitchen doorway, was disconcerting, a stick-like Lowry figure.

'Michael Whelan?' Prescott asked.

The stick figure moved, as awkward as a marionette, joints askew. 'Come in the kitchen.' The voice, like the body from which it issued, was reedy and lustreless.

The kitchen was filthy, unwashed dishes in the sink, grease-spotted tiles on the walls and a table still cluttered with the remains of breakfast.

'Want to sit down?' Whelan pointed listlessly at two plastic chairs.

'We'll stand,' said Prescott, giving the chairs a distasteful glance. He held out his identification. 'Sergeant Prescott and this is Inspector Pearce.'

Pearce gave an automatic tug to the new jacket. He was only human. Being introduced as 'inspector' still gave him a glow of satisfaction.

Whelan glanced at the card but didn't appear interested. 'What do you want?'

Pearce took over. 'Only a word. Have you been ill, Mr Whelan?' He was genuinely curious. In the kitchen light, Whelan could be seen to be almost skeletal. His hair, lank and receding, was brushed back from a domed forehead glistening with beads of sweat. His sunken eyes burned above drawn cheeks and almost lipless mouth. At one corner of the mouth was a sore. He put out the tip of his tongue and manoeuvred it so that it touched the blemish, of which he was evidently self-conscious.

'I'm clean,' he mumbled. 'I've done nothing.'

'Didn't say you had,' said Pearce conversationally. He glanced round. On the wall was a calendar, showing a picture of a mare and foal in a field. 'Still interested in animal welfare?'

'I care about animals!' Whelan became agitated. 'But I've got nothing to do with the action group. Not any more.'

'You're referring to the group which raided the laboratory last year?'

'I did my time,' Whelan repeated, 'I'm clean. I've done nothing. I don't have anything to do with the group any more.'

He moved towards the sink, a gaunt figure in jeans which had slipped at the waist to rest precariously on his bony hips. His faded tee-shirt hung loose around his ribs and his inner arms were patched with livid bruises.

'You remember the names of any of the scientists who worked at that lab?' Pearce asked him.

Whelan turned his head to stare at him, then away. 'No.'

'How about Caswell? Dr Liam Caswell? Remember him?'

Whelan shook his head. 'Don't remember any of them. I don't remember . . .' He paused. 'Names and things, they slip my mind.' For a second an expression of bewilderment which almost, but not quite, became panic, crossed his face. The watching officers saw Whelan push away the frightening truth which lurked somewhere in his confused mind.

'See any of your old mates in the action group, as you call it?' Prescott took up the questioning. 'I'm not asking if you take part in any of their activities. Do you ever see them to have a pint, talk over old times?'

As the sergeant spoke, Pearce's gaze was drawn again, unwillingly, to those dark patches of mottled flesh on Whelan's arms. When he'd first joined the force, his introduction to sudden death had come in gruesome form, by way of a body discovered by schoolchildren, part-buried in woodland. It had been there some time and putrefaction had been well advanced. Pearce, as a young constable, had looked down at it and wondered, in a way which had surprised himself, at the many curious colours of the decomposing flesh. Wondered, that was, until the smell of it took over and he'd turned aside to throw up.

It had been embarrassing but the sergeant in charge at the time had pointed out cheerily, a copper got used to it.

And he had got used to it. Up to a point. Occasionally something brought back a memory of that thing in the woods, the strange sweet sickly smell of it and all the colours, the greens, yellows, purplish-blacks . . . colours very like those emerging on Whelan's arms in a kind of hideous portent of what was to come.

Whelan was speaking and Pearce forced his attention to return from the distant past to the present and this squalid kitchen.

'I don't have anything to do with the group any more.' The words came out as if Prescott's question had pressed a button activating a recorded message. The tone was dead. 'They don't come near me.' The voice was firmer. Whelan's dark eyes, feverish bright, turned to Pearce. 'My cover's blown, see?'

Pearce saw. Whelan was too well known now to the authorities and had served time in prison. At the first whiff of trouble, the police were on Whelan's doorstep. His old acquaintances had dropped him. He was too dangerous to have around now. He was on his own.

'All right,' Pearce said. 'Thanks for your help. We may call back.' He hesitated as he and Prescott made towards the door. 'Do you need medical help of any kind? Social services to call round?'

'You can keep those buggers away!' Whelan said briefly with the first flicker of energy since remarking that he still cared about animals.

'All right. But there are centres where they help you—' Pearce faltered. Prescott gave him a curious glance. Pearce ploughed on, 'There are substitutes—'

He wasn't allowed to finish.

'I'm all right,' Whelan's flat tones contrasted oddly with the flickering light in his eyes. 'I've got a touch of 'flu.' He shivered as if to prove it. 'Be all right when it goes. There's a lot of it about.' He pushed his head forward anxiously and gave a nervous smile.

'What do you reckon?' Prescott asked when they were back in the car. 'What do you think he's using? Heroin? How long's he been shooting up? Nothing in his file says he was a druggie at the time of his arrest.'

Pearce shrugged. He was conscious, as in that far-off time when he'd thrown up by the side of a decomposing body, that he'd let himself down. By way of compensation his tone now was uncompromisingly hard-boiled.

'He might have picked up the habit in prison.'

'We ought to try and find out where he's getting the stuff,' Prescott offered.

Dave Pearce gave him a disgusted glance. 'Look around you!

You can buy anything in this place! Who're we going to ask? Whelan? That woman with the kid? The neighbours? Think they're going to tell you? Or do you think we can stake the place out and watch for packets changing hands? They can smell the Old Bill coming a mile off round here!'

There was a silence. 'How long d'you give him?' Prescott asked, switching on the ignition. The engine leapt into life.

'Who knows? A year? A few months? Even less if he's sharing needles. Dying on his feet. He's past caring about Caswell or anything else. Let's go.' Pearce's voice gained ferocity. 'Let's get out of this hellhole!'

Meredith had arrived at the auction rooms. The dull day hadn't deterred potential bidders. A large crowd had already gathered, many clutching catalogues. Some had already armed themselves with the obligatory numbered cards. Even more lots had appeared since the previous day. The sale, the more robust and less desirable part of it, now spilled into the yard. Rusty farm implements jostled empty picture frames, boxes of mixed crockery and stacks of stained volumes by once popular novelists now long passed into obscurity.

Meredith, rubbing chilled fingers, edged into the salerooms out of the wind. There, people were taking a last good look at the numbered lots. Austin Bailey wasn't to be seen but a rostrum had been set up at one end of the room, bearing a reading desk and decorously draped with a green cloth. Ted, in his apron, stood by the wall between a long case clock and a linen-press and watched the crowd with sharply appreciative gaze.

'Hullo,' he greeted Meredith. 'You may have to pay a bit more for your glasses. The dealers are here. That chap—' He nodded towards the far side of the room where a burly man wearing a tweed hat picked over the china and glassware. 'He buys a lot of glassware, Victorian and Edwardian stuff. He's got a coupla antique shops.'

But Meredith's attention had been attracted by a glimpse of another figure, an unexpected presence. Beyond the collection of glass and china, Bodicote stooped over a spread of old books on a battered pine kitchen table. His tortoise-head strained forward to decipher the lettering on the spines through spectacles perched on the very end of his nose.

'Excuse me,' Meredith murmured to Ted. She made her way to the book table and approached Bodicote unseen.

'Good morning, Mr Bodicote!' she said brightly.

Bodicote froze. He turned slowly and peered at her over the top of his spectacles without returning the greeting. He wore an ancient gabardine raincoat which hung in folds almost to his ankles and had either been made for someone larger or been purchased when Bodicote had been a heavier man. In style it recalled grainy black and white footage of the soviet hierarchy in the 1950s. Its age, signalled by its immensely wide lapels, almost qualified it to be in the sale. No two buttons on it were alike.

Bodicote placed her at last. 'You're that woman as was visiting Mrs Caswell last night.'

'That's right. Everything all right today, Mr Bodicote?'

'I suppose it is. *I'm* all right,' Bodicote added meaningfully. 'If you wants Mrs Caswell, she's in the back office there.' He nodded down the room. 'You want to ask her yourself if *she's* all right.'

'Yes, I mean to.'

Meredith looked down at the pine table. 'You're interested in these books, are you? Going to bid?'

Bodicote's head turned slowly on his long thin neck in the direction she indicated. 'I like a good yarn,' he said. 'But they don't write them no more, not like they did.'

'There are some books outside, novels,' she suggested.

'Seen 'em!' said Bodicote dismissively. He moved away and began leafing through a stack of yellowing motoring magazines.

Meredith picked up the topmost leatherbound volume of those on the table. It was entitled *The Clergyman's Vade Mecum*.

Opening it, she saw that it was published in 1790 and, just inside the cover, spikily inscribed in black ink, 'The Rev. J. F. Farrar 1797'.

The pages were crêpe-like to the touch with uneven hand-set print. Meredith raised the volume nearer her nose and breathed in. The odours of old paper, animal-based glue, dust and printer's ink entered her nostrils. But more besides. Tantalising hints of everything which had been in the vicinity of this book during two hundred years. Coal fires, candlewax, snuff, mulled wine, camphor. She could smell the eighteenth century, preserved between the covers of a country parson's sermon crib.

She closed it gently and replaced it. The other books were of equally worthy subject matter. All were bound in scuffed leather binding, some spines cracking, titles stamped in gilt. Moral guidance for the many, but if Bodicote wanted a 'good yarn', he wouldn't find it here.

Meredith left the table and made her way towards the back office in search of Sally Caswell.

The office was small and Sally, invisible behind a crowd of would-be bidders, anxious to be provided with a number before the sale began. Meredith waited patiently until the scrum thinned and departed, clutching cards, and then put her head round the door and called, 'Hi!'

'Meredith!' Sally looked up from her table and gave a grin of delight. 'Glad you made it! Got your card?'

'Not yet. How's it going?' Meredith eyed her friend with some concern. Sally's forehead still wore a large plaster.

Sally handed her a white card, perforated mid-way. 'It's going fine! Fill in the bottom half with your name and phone number and give it back to me. Keep the top half with the number and wave it at Austin if you want to bid. If he doesn't see you, shout.'

As Meredith scribbled on the card, Sally went on, 'It was a shock yesterday, but I've made up my mind to get over it. I owe it to Liam. We weren't hurt, neither Liam nor I, and that's the most important thing! Liam's refusing to let it frighten him and is carrying on with his book as usual. So I'm carrying on as usual, too. We'll stick together on this!' She nodded determinedly.

That was all very well, Meredith thought, and thoroughly British. But there were other considerations than Liam's book! Not that Liam was likely to think so. Still, as Alan had said earlier on the phone, it was in the end up to Sally herself. Meredith handed her the completed card. 'Bodicote is out in the saleroom. Has he taken a card?'

'Yes, he did.' Sally grimaced. 'He always comes to sales.'

Meredith showed her surprise. 'What does he buy?'

'Job lots of books and bits of china, mostly. He picks up odd items of ironmongery. Lord knows what he does with it. But country people are like that. They find a use for things the rest of us would just see as junk. Well, they find *misuses* for good things which would horrify us! I don't dare tell Austin this. But Bodicote has a really nice big Victorian *jardinière* outside his back door. Glazed pot with birds and flowers on it. And do you know what he uses it for? He puts some sort of dried food he feeds the goats in it.'

They were disturbed by the clanging of a handbell.

'Sale's beginning!' Sally said. 'Outside first. Are you going out or waiting in here? It's a bit nippy out there.'

Meredith hesitated. 'I'll take a look.'

Sally picked up her vacuum flask. 'I'm going to have a drink of my tea while I've got the chance. Come back and join me.'

Outside Austin Bailey had appeared. His appearance, in fact, was eye-catching, with a touch of the evangelist about it. He stood on a wooden box, well wrapped up against the wind in a heavy jacket and with a yellow woollen scarf wound round his neck. The ends of the scarf, and its wearer's hair, fluttered in the breeze. Austin's face was alight with enthusiasm. He clapped his hands together, waved his printed list of lots and bawled, 'Good morning, everyone!'

Then, with a briskness born partly of long experience and partly out of recognition that none of them wanted to hang about out here in the cold, he was off.

The first lots went quickly. But it was obvious they would be out here some little while. Without warning, a trembling assailed Meredith's knees, a return of the weakness which had become familiar since the flu. It would be better, she realised, to wait inside until the outside bidding was over. She slipped away.

Sally was alone in the office, doing as she'd said she would, grabbing a hot drink while she had the chance.

'Thought you'd be back! Too cold out there and he'll be at least twenty minutes. Here, have a cup of this. It's my special brew! Garden herbs and honey.'

Sally unscrewed the flask and poured out a cup of a treacly-looking beverage which she handed Meredith.

Meredith took it, cupping her hands round it for warmth and subsiding on to a chair. 'It is cold out there! I think I'm feeling it more too, since the wretched flu.'

Sally eyed her. 'You look a bit pale. Did you try the chamomile tea I recommended?'

'I did, honestly. But I found I could only drink so much of it. What's this? Something similar?'

'Not really. It's my own concoction.'

Meredith sipped the tea. At first she could only taste the honey. But following on that, came a brackish taste which, to be honest, she didn't much like.

'It takes a bit of getting used to,' Sally, watching her, said.

'Don't think my tastebuds are doing it justice.' Meredith took a last heroic swallow and put down the cup.

The sound of Austin Bailey's voice was heard through the open door. Sally cocked her head.

'He'll be finished outside in about ten minutes. Get yourself a chair in the main room before the mob arrives in about five minutes. The canny ones start drifting in then. The successful bidders will be in here soon, paying.'

She cleared flask and cups away from her desk. Meredith realised that Sally was politely clearing the decks of her visitor too, before business became brisk in the tiny office. But she had something she wanted to get off her chest before she went into the saleroom.

'Alan and I went for an Indian meal last night, after we left your place,' she began.

Sally, tapping at the keyboard, only nodded.

'This is a bit embarrassing,' Meredith persisted.

Sally turned her head. 'Why? What did you do? Tip your curry all over the floor?' She grinned.

'No, we had a talk.'

Sally abandoned her keyboard. 'About our explosive package?'

'Not directly. Alan doesn't gossip about his work. But he did want to talk about you and Liam. He asked me how I met you both and, well, if Liam had any enemies I knew of. Of course, I don't know whether Liam has and it's not my business, anyway. But I had to tell Alan that I knew Liam has had a few spats along the way.' She accompanied her words with a rueful look.

Sally was silent for a moment. 'That's all right,' she said at last. 'I appreciate your telling me. I know Liam does fall out with people. But it isn't always his fault!' Her voice rose indignantly. 'Things just seem to happen sometimes. Liam gets caught up in the middle of it.'

Meredith picked at the corner of her numbered card. 'Alan told me as we walked home that Bodicote seemed upset about the goats. He's old, we both realise that, and he probably gets overwrought. But he seemed to think someone had tried to poison them. He said something about turnips. Do you know what he meant?'

Sally threw both hands in the air. 'Oh, the wretched turnips! That's a perfect example of what I was saying. That things just seem to happen around Liam. Only really, what happened that time, happened to *me*. It was *my* doing!'

She heaved a deep sigh of exasperation. 'I don't know anything about goats, Meredith. That's how it all came about. I didn't mean any *harm*. You see, someone called into the auctioneers here one day to see Austin and brought a bag full of turnips. I don't mean to sell. Bailey and Bailey aren't greengrocers. It was someone who knew Austin. He'd grown a load of these vegetables and he wanted to get rid of them. Well, Austin couldn't use them all so he gave me some. But to be truthful, I don't like turnips much and neither does Liam.

'I brought them home to Castle Darcy, wondering what on earth I could do with them. I didn't like just to throw them out. It seemed so wasteful. They were very good turnips, as turnips go! Then I looked out of the window and saw Bodicote's goats in their paddock. I thought, Right! The perfect use for the turnips! Goats eat anything. When they get into our garden they eat my plants! They eat their way through the hedge to get there. So I walked round to Bodicote's place with my bag of turnips and knocked on his door. But he was out. I thought, I'll just tip the turnips into the field and let the goats nibble at them. And I did. All the goats trotted up and seemed to like the turnips and started munching away, as happy as anything. I went back home feeling very pleased with myself. As if I'd done my good deed for the day. Only I hadn't.'

Sally buried her head in her hands. 'Oh, Meredith, you can't imagine the fuss! Old Bodicote suddenly appeared about an hour later, absolutely purple with rage. I thought he was going to have some kind of a fit! He could hardly speak! It seemed the goats had finished nearly all the turnips when he got home and he arrived just in time to see them gobbling up the last few scraps. Someone passing by the cottage, apparently, had seen me with my bag of goat-goodies and had told him I was the culprit – I mean, I'd put the turnips out.'

'And goats shouldn't have turnips to eat, is that it?' Meredith asked, puzzled.

'So it appears. Turnips taint their milk. They don't make the animals ill, just ruin the milk yield until the food has worked its way through the animal's system. I was very sorry, I tried to tell Bodicote so, but he wouldn't listen! He acted as though I'd done it on purpose! He had to throw their milk away until it came right again. It was all an awful muddle. I had to pay him for the ruined milk. A cheese manufacturer buys it from him. Liam said I shouldn't because I hadn't acted out of malice. But I was truly sorry and I felt so badly about it, I wanted to do something to make it up. Bodicote has never forgiven me – or Liam. It's so stupid! Why should I do something like that on purpose?' Sally finished in an aggrieved tone.

'You wouldn't. He's probably one of those people who sees bad intentions everywhere,' Meredith consoled her. 'Old people sometimes grow very suspicious.'

Sally gave a snort of disgust. 'Well, tell Alan – or I'll tell him. I am the phantom goat-poisoner!' She declared the last dramatically and struck her breast.

'Alan thought it was probably something like you've said. He doesn't think you go about poisoning anything!' Meredith got to her feet. 'Thanks for the tea. I may see you later. I'll go and grab myself a chair. I think people are coming indoors.'

Out in the saleroom, several chairs were already occupied and the rest being taken fast. Meredith sat down on the nearest and looked around for Bodicote. But she couldn't see him. Perhaps he'd got what he wanted from the goods on sale outside.

Austin hurried in. He'd divested himself of his thick coat and yellow scarf. He climbed on his rostrum and from evangelist now took on the appearance of a political orator.

'Right, ladies and gentlemen!' He smoothed back his long hair. 'We'll proceed to lot 31. Two prints in Japanese style.'

Ted stepped forward and, using a long thin rod, indicated the two pictures hanging on the wall to the right of the rostrum.

'Am I bid five?' asked Austin hopefully.

Meredith settled down and waited for the turn of the glassware. The warmth imparted by Sally's herbal drink had worn off and she was beginning to feel chilled again. As she waited, the lots were sold at what, it seemed to her, was an ever-slower pace. Her head began to ache. She turned the sheet of her catalogue. The glasses she wanted were at lot 124 and they'd only got as far as lot 61. She glanced along the row and saw the man in the tweed hat sitting nearby. He was bidding already for something else. He held up his number in a brisk, no-nonsense way. He also seemed to be paying quite large sums of money. If he wanted the glasses, he'd outbid her for sure.

Suddenly, Meredith no longer wanted to wait here. She was cold, her head ached, pains were running up and down her spine. She got up between lots and slipped out.

Outside she felt better, but decided to go home. It would take her about twenty minutes to walk there. She set out as briskly as she could.

She had not gone far when she realised that she was walking crookedly. She was getting funny looks from passers-by. Perhaps they thought she was drunk! She made an effort to straighten her progress, keeping to the buildings' side of the pavement.

A horn blared and someone shouted. She had nearly stepped off the pavement in front of a car.

''Ere!' said a kindly, concerned voice. 'You want to watch out, dear!'

'Yes . . .' she muttered. 'I didn't see . . .'

'You all right, dear?' She was vaguely aware of a worried face peering into hers. A hand touched her elbow.

'Yes, yes, I'm fine. I've had a bit of flu . . .'

'Nasty, the flu! You want to go on home, dear, and stay indoors.'

She mumbled something to the effect that she meant to do that. The face receded. The shock had at least jolted her out of the fog which had descended on her senses. Concentrating desperately, she continued homeward, counting off the landmarks as she passed them.

She finally stumbled into her own terraced cottage, sweating and dizzy. Pushing the door shut, she crawled up the stairs and into the bathroom where she threw up in the handbasin, retching with a violence which strained the muscles of her diaphragm. When she at last staggered away, head thumping and feeling iller than in the worst days of her flu, it was all she could do to make the bedroom. There she collapsed fully dressed on the duvet and remained there miserably all afternoon.

Chapter Seven

Alan Markby stood by the telephone in his hallway. It was a little after eight in the morning and he was about to leave for work. He was debating whether to call Meredith before he left.

It was an early hour to call anyone. But she hadn't been in touch for a few days, not since phoning him the morning after the Caswell letter-bomb about Sally. Markby himself had tried phoning Meredith that evening and again the following morning, but to no avail. He didn't know whether she wasn't at home, possibly in London, or – and this was the worry at the back of his mind – she was there, but unable for some reason to come to the telephone.

He had not thought she looked at all well, the last time he'd seen her. Admittedly she'd been upset on Sally's account. But there'd been a distinct lack of the usual sparkle. The flu was taking its time to clear up.

His hand closed on the receiver. It would do no harm to call. He'd let it ring just six times. Perhaps ten times, to give her a chance to get downstairs. He lifted the receiver and, with his free hand, punched out the numbers.

She answered on the ninth ring, just as he was deciding that drastic action was called for and he'd better dash round there.

'Hullo? Alan! Was it you calling recently? Someone's been ringing but I've been a bit under the weather. I really couldn't take calls. I phoned the office to arrange extra sick leave.'

Markby cursed to himself. He should have gone round and seen what was wrong.

'No point in your calling round. Nothing you could do. I've been back to see Dr Pringle. He thinks I must have been harbouring some secondary virus. Anyhow, I'm better today. Honestly!'

'I'll come round this evening.' He said this so as to brook no argument.

'Yes, do.' She sounded relieved. 'I'm absolutely fed-up and I could do with some company!'

'I'll be there around seven!' he promised. 'I'll bring in something to eat. Chinese, fish and chips, Indian, pizza, name it!'

'My tum's not back to normal. Something I can eat a small piece of and you can have a reasonable meal. Pizza would be fine. Not pepperoni!' she added, as an afterthought. 'I've got plenty of wine here. Yes, do come, we'll crack a bottle.' As he was about to put down the receiver, she called. 'Alan! Hang on! You couldn't bring in a tin of catfood, could you?'

'Catfood? What for? You're not developing strange eating habits, are you?'

'Very funny. There's a stray cat hanging around. I've been feeding it Mrs Harmer's fish. But I thought perhaps I ought to vary its diet and the smell of cooking fish lingers in the kitchen.'

'Watch it,' he advised. 'You'll end up a cat-owner.'

'I think he's too independent. But I rather like cats. This one isn't friendly but he is thin. Buy a decent brand. Cheap catfood smells awful.'

She hung up before he could inquire where she'd become an expert on tinned catfood.

'Morning, Mrs Caswell!' said Libby. 'Everything all right today?'

'Everything's fine, thanks.' Sally held out her hand for the post. 'How about you? I am so sorry about what happened.'

'Not your fault!' said Libby. 'Only letters today, but I thought I'd hand them over in person, not just put them through the letterbox. I wanted to ask how you were.'

'I'm absolutely fine. And you, got over the shock?'

Libby grimaced. 'More or less. My mum's still worrying about it. And my Uncle Denis is still going on a bit.' She paused. 'But he's always going on about something, so it's no different from usual.'

She waved cheerily as she got back in her van and rattled off towards Castle Darcy's other scattered dwellings.

Sally made her way to the kitchen. 'That's such a nice girl,' she said, as she entered.

The kitchen had been restored to working order after a fashion. Gas and electricity engineers had called and checked the safety of appliances. The scorched table, damaged beyond reasonable repair, had been removed. In its place had come a make-do model, one from Bailey's salerooms which no one had bought. Not surprisingly, in Sally's view. It had a horrid bright red plastic surface which made it appear as if something had been butchered on it. She had covered this with a blue cloth. The broken windows had been reglazed. But elsewhere woodwork was still scored by flying glass, and damaged sections of the fitted units had to be replaced. When it was all done, then it would have to be entirely redecorated. That meant getting someone in, or Sally doing it herself. It was no use asking Liam. Liam didn't do things about the house with paint or tools.

Sally had got over the appearance of the kitchen, turning a blind eye to the evidence. She was still sorry about the loss of a set of decorative Christmas plates which she'd collected assiduously over the years since their marriage. The blast had sent the lot crashing to the floor. Likewise, china on the open shelves of her kitchen dresser had been reduced to a pile of fragments.

But it was no use grieving over it. Life meant more, she told herself, than possession of things. Things were replaceable. People weren't. Yet there was a not-to-be ignored symbolism in all those smashed plates, each representing a year of her marriage to Liam.

She put that thought firmly aside. But one thing she still hadn't quite got under control was her reaction to the sound of the morning's post coming up the path, and in that respect she'd lied to Libby about everything being fine. Her heart beat faster at the sound of the post office van and that sick, tight feeling assailed the pit of her stomach. It was only nerves. But she'd been physically sick the last two mornings, just after getting up.

She wasn't pregnant, she was sure of that. They had tried for a baby when they'd first been married. No baby had come along and subsequent investigation had revealed no baby would come. Liam hadn't seemed to mind. But the knowledge lurked at the back of Sally's mind, growing, as the years went by, into a sad acceptance.

Anyone else might have tried IVF or adoption. But Liam had never suggested they remedy their childless state. She knew, in her heart, Liam didn't want children. Children were demanding and noisy and cost money. That's what he'd said at the time, when the doctors had warned them they faced a childless marriage. Far too many kids being born nowadays, anyway, Liam had added.

That wasn't how she'd felt about it. But Liam didn't know how she felt about it. She'd never told him and he'd never asked. But that day, the doctor had told them the bleak truth, had been among the blackest of her life. For a long time she'd been fascinated by the sight of any baby in a pram or pushchair. Every young woman seemed to have one. Country towns were like that. They didn't have too many career women around here. They had young mums, some of them very young and some, it seemed to Sally, incredibly careless with regard to the infants they lugged around with them. They were treated like an inconvenient appendage, an overweight shopping-bag, to be parked in shop doorways and left on benches.

She'd learned to disguise the longing, to push it away deep down inside her. To look away from the babies. To avoid the exit gates of the primary school at half past three when the children rushed out and the parents scooped them up, bundled them into waiting cars and drove off, home to children's television and child-friendly food and bedtime battles. Not for her, for Sally. Not ever. Instead, Liam had become her child, a spoilt overgrown infant, demanding and ungrateful, trading on her love, breaking her heart. But forgiven, always forgiven. For what was the alternative? Nothing but emptiness.

So if sickness hadn't been of the morning variety, it had surely been because she feared the arrival of the post. Psychosomatic and unnecessary. Today it was just letters. No suspect fat packages. Thank God, she thought!

'All for you,' she said, handing the letters to her husband. No matter how many times she told herself it wouldn't, couldn't, happen again – that the mail sorting office was on the look-out for anything suspicious; that the senders had tried it once and it hadn't worked so they wouldn't try again – never, ever again, would she open any post not clearly addressed to her alone. Not because she'd prefer it to happen to Liam! She was afraid to, simple as that.

Liam, scraping muesli from his bowl, grunted and took the sheaf of mail. She felt a twinge of annoyance that he didn't say 'thank you'. Lots of little things were annoying her about Liam lately. Perhaps they'd annoyed her for years. Perhaps, she thought, since the explosion I've become better at facing reality. He really doesn't have any manners. If he weren't a highly educated man, let's face it, he'd be a lout. She didn't have to put up with this. She didn't. The worm, after so many years, was turning! Or seriously thinking about it.

But she did put up with it one more time. She went to the stove. 'Ready for your eggs?'

Again he didn't reply but she didn't expect it. He'd finished his cereal. She began to spoon scrambled eggs on to two plates. A burst of profanity from her husband caused her to stop and turn, startled, saucepan in hand.

'Bloody cheek!' He held out some sheets of paper. 'Flaming nutcases!' His hand was trembling and his face red with rage.

The sick feeling returned, wrenching Sally's stomach and sending a wave of nausea over her. 'You mean – more of those letters?'

No, no, please no! begged a voice in her head. It had to be a mistake!

'One of 'em. Threatening and illiterate. Well, two of them, if you count this one.' He waved the sheet of letter paper in the air. 'Except that this one isn't anonymous. It's from that crazy woman. What's her name, Goodhusband. Lives up the other end of the village in that rambling great house. No threats, just sanctimonious middle-class moralising.'

'Yvonne?'

Sally pulled herself together. She put down the saucepan and transferred the two plates of eggs to the table. Seating herself opposite Liam, she shook out her napkin and asked, 'Well?'

'What? Oh, here, look. This is the cut-and-paste job.'

He handed over one of the letters. The paper was cheap, ruled, torn roughly from a pad so that the top edge was uneven. The words were cut from a newspaper and glued on. No signature.

WE WILL GET YOU NEXT TIME

The nausea was replaced by anger. 'How dare they?' she exclaimed. 'How dare they persecute us?' She looked up. 'You'll give this to the police?' It wasn't really a question. He'd give this one to the police or she would. No arguing. It had gone far enough. Far too far.

A glance at her husband's face told her that he thought so, too. Liam's eyes blazed now. In a bearded face, undue attention is drawn to the eyes, Sally'd noticed before: if Liam were to shave off his beard, she'd often thought, it might be easier to argue with him. But for the first time, she was aware that, within the thick brown brush of his facial hair, his mouth trembled, and probably his chin.

'It's scared him!' she thought. 'The letter's scared him!' She felt a curious thrill, almost of satisfaction, which quite shocked her.

He was nodding agreement. 'Yes, all right. I'll ring that superintendent fellow, Markby. Supercilious blighter. Take the sneer off his face. Acting as if he didn't believe me last time!'

'Of course he believed you! What did you say the other letter was? From Yvonne Goodhusband?'

Liam handed over the remaining sheets in silence. As she took them, a printed folder fell out. On the front of it was a poorly reproduced photograph of some chickens, wedged uncomfortably in a tiny cage. They were a picture of misery. The one nearest the camera appeared to have been part-plucked alive.

Sally let it lie on the table and read the letter. It was on expensive notepaper, with an embossed address at the top. The handwriting was even, flowing, decided.

Dear Dr Caswell,
I was, as you can imagine, extremely distressed to learn of your recent bad experience. I do hope that your wife is quite recovered.

As you know, I am myself very interested in animal welfare, and together with like-minded friends, have formed a pressure group. I must stress that neither I, nor any member of our group, would ever consider violence in any form. I am strongly against the methods of groups such as those which targeted your home with an explosive package.

The hope and belief of myself and my group is that reason and sound argument will eventually prevail. I'm sure, if people only took time to think, they would see that so much is wrong in our attitude towards fellow creatures which are unable to speak for themselves. I was very sorry to learn that you have been using animals in your laboratory. I hope that I can call at some convenient time and we can discuss this matter?

In the meantime, I have taken the liberty of enclosing one of our leaflets as a sample of the information we distribute.

Yours very sincerely,

Yvonne Goodhusband

'The woman's loony,' said Liam. 'And if she thinks I'm going to let her lecture me in my own home, she's got another think coming! I'm going to send this letter with the other one to Markby. As far as I'm concerned, it constitutes harassment.'

'I wouldn't like to upset Yvonne,' Sally protested. 'I'm sure she didn't intend to be offensive. She's been one of the few people to welcome me to the village. Because someone takes up a good cause – ' she met Liam's scowl and amended this to ' – what they consider a good cause, it doesn't mean they're crazy. Yvonne's a bit of a stickler for conventions in lots of ways. I've been to a couple of her coffee mornings and they were positively formal!'

'Now you see what hob-nobbing with her leads to,' said Liam unkindly.

Sally picked up the leaflet. The featherless chicken stared out between bars at her, accusing, reproachful. She looked at her plate of scrambled eggs.

'I bought our eggs at the supermarket in Bamford. I think they may have come from that battery chicken place down the road. Do you know the one I mean?'

'Know it? I can smell it every time the wind blows from that direction!'

'Do you think—'

Liam leaned forward. 'No, I don't! You're going to ask, are all the birds at the place down the road crowded into tiny cages, pulling one another's feathers out with what remains of their clipped beaks, aren't you? These places are checked by the Ministry inspectors. They have to meet standards.'

'Yes, I realise that. But these pictures were taken *somewhere*. And how many inspectors does the government employ? I bet not enough.'

Sally's eye was drawn to the leaflet again. 'I think I'll start buying free-range eggs. They only cost a little more. After all, I don't buy so many. It won't make much difference to my grocery bill.'

'Please yourself,' said Liam. 'Go and join Ma Goodhusband's action group, while you're about it, why don't you?'

Sally had been reading the leaflet. Suddenly she slammed it down on the table. The crockery jumped and rattled. Liam looked startled.

'Don't!' she said. 'Don't patronise me! I may not be a scientific genius but I am as entitled to my opinions and my feelings as the next person – certainly as entitled as you are to yours!'

There was a silence. 'All right,' he said. 'I was only joking. What's the matter with you? Is it that bang on the head you got the other day? You ought to go and see Pringle.'

'I sometimes think,' Sally heard herself say, 'that I ought to go and see a good divorce lawyer!'

She jumped up from the table and the now unwanted breakfast and stormed out into the garden.

She hadn't got a coat and it was cold out there. But she didn't want to go back indoors, not just yet. It wasn't Liam's fault, she told herself, the residue of her loyalty still prompting her conscience. He had so many things to worry him and it made him brusque. But in her heart she knew that what had begun as a conscious willingness to indulge Liam in his abruptness and self-centred attitude to life, had slowly turned into a continual fabrication of excuses for him.

'And why the hell should I?' she muttered aloud. 'We all have

109

worries. I have worries. A bomb went off nearly in my face the other day. I'm physically sick when the post arrives. Austin wants—' This last was pushed aside.

The crisp air absorbed her words. Sally folded her arms, hugging herself, and walked slowly down the path to the very bottom of the garden. It was a good long way, terminating in an untidy area of unproductive apple trees, gnarled and dying. Cottage gardens were generous, designed to allow a labourer's family to be sufficient in vegetables and soft fruits and keep a few chickens or a pig. Down here, besides the trees, were equally neglected gooseberry and blackcurrant bushes. She ought to do something about it all, get herself more organised. The trees could be replaced, the bushes too. Just think of all that free fruit, she thought. The jams and jellies, the chutneys, apple tarts, fruit flans . . .

But gardening took time and what with one thing and another, the building of the extension, her job at Bailey and Bailey's – and Liam.

Her grievance returned.

'I don't take out my worries on other people,' she said to the bare-twigged blackcurrant bushes. 'So why should Liam think he can? Tell me that!'

'Mrs Caswell!'

Sally gave a squeak and jumped. The voice issued, as if in reply, from the blackcurrant bushes. But then she realised that, to be more precise, it came from the middle of the hedge behind the bushes, the one between this property and Bodicote's. It was Bodicote's voice, too, but she couldn't see him.

The hedge shook. It was hawthorn. Leafless now in winter, it was nevertheless an impenetrable tangle of twisted branches and sharp spikes, rooted in a low bank. It and the bank made a barrier standing altogether some five feet or so high. If it had been properly maintained over the years, even Bodicote's goats would have found themselves foiled by it.

But it hadn't been maintained and in places was broken by bare patches where it had died, been broken down or rooted out. Here Bodicote – because it was his hedge, his property border – had blocked up the holes with whatever came to hand, with more success in some spots than in others.

He was on the other side and making his way towards the nearest gap, half-heartedly blocked with a crinkled sheet of corrugated iron. He appeared suddenly, or the top half of him, over the wavy iron sheeting. He was wearing his usual grubby cap and a thick donkey-jacket besides, together with a plaid muffler.

'Oh, good morning, Mr Bodicote,' Sally said without enthusiasm.

'I've been keeping an eye open for you,' he said. 'Looking out to see when you was in your garden. Only you've not been out here much.'

'It's the wrong weather for gardening.' She hesitated. 'What did you want? You could have come round.'

He looked shifty. 'Best not. On account of him.' He nodded towards the extension and obviously meant Liam. He was probably right. Avoiding Liam was the best thing to do these days. Only she couldn't do it.

'I got something for you,' the old man was saying.

'For me? What's that?'

He was tugging at the corrugated iron sheet and dragged it out a little. 'Can squeeze through there, can you? Come on up to the house. It's in the kitchen.'

She didn't know what it was, couldn't guess, and frankly, didn't care. But if it delayed returning to her own kitchen and Liam, it would be five minutes well spent. Sally squeezed through the gap and followed Bodicote along the hedge towards his back door.

'You wants to put a coat on, cold day like this,' he observed. 'You'll catch your death, walking about in just that thin pullover you got there.'

The goats had been let out today and were wandering around the place, browsing on what they could find. He'd put some hay out for them, too, and the big brown one with the horns, the billy, the one she didn't like much, was eating that. He raised his head and fixed her with a malicious look.

'You don't want to mind old Jasper,' said Bodicote, divining her thoughts. 'He's got a deal of mischief in him, but no malice. Just keep your eye on him. He's knows if you're watching and then he don't get up to none of his tricks!'

They'd reached the end of the hawthorn hedge and reached a strip of mixed shrubs, mostly bare of leaves now, but one or two with a few green leaves still attached. It was at this point that the goats had eaten through during the summer. Here was the old bedhead with which their owner had patched the largest area of damage. Bodicote turned left and cut across the grass towards his door. Sally followed dutifully behind.

She'd been in his kitchen before and knew what to expect but the smell still made her gag.

'I've been boiling up mash,' said Bodicote. 'Now then, where did I put it?'

'The mash?' Had he taken into his head she wanted some of the horrible stuff?

He was hunting in a cupboard. She waited, looking about her, noting the ancient gas-cooker which seemed so rusted away and generally wonky it was a wonder that it didn't explode. And the table, a good one basically. Austin would be able to sell that table. A dealer would buy it and do it up and sell on for a good profit. It was certainly Edwardian if not Victorian. But it was encrusted with grime, scratched and scored. One leg had met with an accident, splitting it lengthwise and had been bound round with string by way of repair. Lord knew when the place had last been painted. Sally's kitchen, even in its damaged state, was *Homes and Gardens* stuff compared with this. Her gaze rose to take in a high, cobwebby shelf, laden with odds and ends of china. A

Staffordshire cream jug in the shape of a kneeling cow. My God, she thought, those things are collectable. What else has he got, hidden away in this place?

Bodicote emerged from his cupboard, holding a margarine tub with a lid on which, from the look of it, was on its way to becoming an antique among margarine tubs.

'I've been thinking.' Bodicote stood staring at her earnestly. 'You're not a bad sort of woman.'

'Thanks,' she said drily before she could stop herself.

He took it at face value. 'No, 'tis true. I'm really sorry for what happened the other day, you getting such a fright. All the glass blown out your windows and the rest of it.'

He was apologising! Sally said impetuously, 'I was very rude to you then, Mr Bodicote. When you came into the cottage. It was because you startled me. I didn't mean it.'

'No matter.' He held out the margarine tub. 'Thought you might like some of this.'

What on earth could it hold? And did she really want to know? It was possible, of course, that he'd just gone batty. She'd heard that could happen after years of eccentricity. One day, complete madness. All thread of reality lost.

Seeing she was looking at the tub doubtfully, he chuckled and pulled the lid off. Inside was a mix of dried leaves very similar to one of her own herbal mixes.

'I know you do like the tea from stuff in the garden. So did my old mother. I don't mind a cup myself from time to time. I dried this little lot off back in the autumn. It's all from my garden out there. Thought you might like to try it.'

'Oh, thank you.' She took it, embarrassed both at his kindness and at her own unflattering thoughts. 'I – I'm sorry about everything, Mr Bodicote. The goats and – and that business of the turnips.'

Bodicote looked grim for a moment, then rallied. 'Well, it's water under the bridge, any road.'

They parted on this mixed metaphor. Sally took the gift back to her kitchen where she found Liam rinsing his breakfast plates. He glanced at her as she came in.

'Saw you gossiping. You went through the hedge into Bodicote's. Did the old blighter block it up again properly?'

'I expect so. Look, he gave me some herbal tea. I think he wanted to make amends.'

Liam wiped his hands on a towel. 'You oughtn't to fall for that, encourage him! Next thing you know, he'll be up to some piece of devilry or other. Dealing with the enemy puts you in a false position.'

She put the margarine tub by her pots of herbs. 'Say what you like. I think it was kind of the old fellow. I don't consider him my enemy. I'll try out his tea one day. It's a mix his mother used to make.'

'Grotesque!' growled Liam and stomped off to his study.

'Don't forget to call the police about those letters!' she called after him.

Markby had arrived at regional HQ still in his good mood. As he walked towards his office, a door opened and Dave Pearce erupted into the corridor, jacketless, tie-loosened, sleeves rolled up and holding a half-eaten bacon sandwich.

'Thought I heard you, sir!' His voice was indistinct. He must just have taken a bite out of the sandwich, presumably his breakfast. 'Caswell's just been on the phone. He's had some letters.'

'Plural?'

Pearce swallowed. 'One an anonymous cut-and-paste job, newsprint. The usual sort of thing. The other is a regular signed letter from someone living in Castle Darcy. A woman called Goodhusband.'

'Goodhusband?' Markby hunted through recent memory. 'I've heard that name. Ah yes, Libby delivered post to her on the morning of the Caswell package.'

'It seems she runs an animal welfare pressure group. Nothing violent. They distribute leaflets and write to the press, demonstrate sometimes in an orderly fashion. Only one complaint has ever been lodged against them, by some chicken farm or other which they picketed. It got into the press and brought the farm bad publicity. Those places are sensitive.'

'We can check that out. Try the office of the *Bamford Gazette*. That sort of dispute usually makes the local news. So, I assume Caswell already knew her, before the letter arrived this morning? Since she lives in his village.'

Pearce looked unsure. 'He seems to be a bit of a hermit in that cottage. Put it this way, he knows about her now and he's furious! Because of the publicity over the letter-bomb, she's learned about his animal experiments. Now she wants to talk to him. Wouldn't give much for her chances.'

'Did you tell him to keep the envelope of the cut-and-paste job?' Markby demanded.

'Yes, sure. He's bringing the whole lot in.'

'When he does,' Markby said softly, 'I'd like to see him.'

Liam Caswell arrived around eleven that morning. He took the letters and their envelopes from his document case and placed the cut-and-paste one on Markby's desk with exaggerated care.

'There you are, all right?'

'We'll get this anonymous one over to the experts right away,' Markby picked it up. It was similar to hundreds of others he'd seen. 'There is another one, I'm told, regular and signed?'

Liam hesitated. 'Yes, it's from a madwoman in our village. Here!' He pushed it forward.

Markby glanced through it. 'It seems reasonable enough to me, Dr Caswell. Not mad, certainly.'

Liam flushed. He leaned forward slightly in his chair, his hands gripping the case on his lap. 'I want it put on record that I don't like your attitude!'

Markby raised his eyebrows. 'If you have a complaint, we'll be happy to look into it. There is, of course, a recognised procedure if you're seriously displeased.'

Liam emitted a snarl. 'That's what I mean. Your attitude. It's not what you do, or say, it's the way you say it. You act as if I'd done something wrong!'

'A policeman must sometimes act as devil's advocate, Dr Caswell. I have to ask questions.'

'If I thought you were just doing your job,' Liam retorted nastily, 'I'd accept that. But my distinct impression is that you're not doing your job! Anyone reasonably competent would have nailed the blighter who sent that package by now!'

The public always assumed the police could work miracles, Markby reflected. But it was routine which brought results, hours of painstaking inquiries, sifting through paperwork, comparing notes. And routine took time. He tried to explain this to Liam.

'A team of officers went to your laboratories, Dr Caswell, and interviewed everyone there. All were asked whether they'd received any abusive or anonymous mail or threats of any kind. They were warned what to look for, and how to behave if it happened. No one reported having been threatened and no one has come forward since to report anything. The details of the attack have been circulated all over the country to see if a similar incident has occurred elsewhere. *Modus operandi* often points to a particular criminal or, in this case, organisation. Known animal rights' activists are being checked in this area and elsewhere. So far nothing's come back to us. It takes time.'

'I don't believe this,' Liam's eyes rolled alarmingly. 'What I take all that to mean is that unless someone else gets blown to kingdom come, you're prepared to sit back and just let things potter along on the off-chance you get a break! What does it matter, for crying out loud, if no one else at the lab got any foul letters or a bomb shoved through their front door? *I did!* Isn't that enough? What do you want, a massacre? I'm expendable, is that it? Just one more boffin.'

Markby's anger spilled over. 'I did not say anything of the sort, Dr Caswell! I personally take as an insult any suggestion that my officers aren't trying their best! I've got everyone I can spare on this! I appreciate that you're upset but, frankly, it doesn't give you the right to come in here and make unfounded accusations!'

Liam rose to his feet, shaking. 'I'll make any accusation I want! I'm the one being hunted down by maniacs! I'm a tax-payer. I employ you, I pay your salary! And I want to know what you're going to do about it!' His voice quivered. His face had gained an unnatural pallor and the impression was of a man under intolerable pressure.

Markby had regained his self-control. He regretted the out-burst as he always did. But he was still filled with a deep yearning to dot Caswell on the chin. He spoke now with grim formality.

'I told you, we'll get this letter over to forensics.' He indicated the newsprint collage.

'What about that woman Goodhusband? Because she puts her name to her letters and is so damn civilised about it, doesn't mean she isn't just as much a fanatic as all the others!'

'I shall call on Mrs Goodhusband,' Markby snapped. 'Personally!'

Liam's mouth twisted unpleasantly. 'Good luck to you!'

'He seems a bit rattled,' observed Pearce as Liam stomped out. 'Do you think it's finally got to him? He's just realised this business isn't just going to go away because he wants it to?'

'Rattled? Good,' muttered Markby. 'It's time someone shook him up a bit. He might even start cooperating if he gets scared enough.'

He picked up the letter again. The heavy cream paper was embossed with gold Gothic lettering. He doubted crass methods would achieve much with the writer of this missive. She was the sort to observe the social niceties.

'Tell someone to ring her and say I'll call this afternoon if it's convenient.'

'Seen the house,' said Pearce, as if to support his boss's reasoning. 'Posh.'

The Tithe Barn had probably once been just that. In essence the house was still basically barn-shaped and its thick stone walls were many hundred years old. It had been considerably altered and added to and was now an imposing residence. Unlikely, so Markby thought, one for someone given to making letter-bombs or cut-and-paste threatening letters. More often, in his experience, people who lived in such houses were the recipients of these items.

The five-barred gate was open, perhaps on his account. But as he turned into the drive he had to swerve to avoid a black cat with a white bib which crouched slap in the middle of the gravelled way. It didn't move and as the car passed by, watched with un-winking eyes, its stony stare suggesting it thought this visitor ought to have used some tradesman's entrance.

A little further on a second black and white cat strolled towards the car exhibiting similar suicidal habits. He avoided that one too, remarking to it through the window that it was fast using up its nine lives. Since the whole frontage appeared to be inhabited by felines who regarded motor vehicles as of no consequence, he decided to park and walk the remaining few yards.

He could see, now that he was out of the car, that the extensive garden was not well kept. It must once have been a delight. But the shrubbery had been allowed to run riot. Grass and weeds grew over what had been flowerbeds. Hedgerow plants had found their way in from the village lanes. Around the remains of an ornamental pond, various types of *umbelliferae* had rooted and though now blackened by frost, their tall stems and the shrivelled remains of their distinctive leaves and flowerheads could still be identified. It was all a sad sight.

His reverie was disturbed by a third cat, marmalade in hue, which shot out of the shrubbery and bounded across his path. He walked up to the front door, wondering what he'd find there.

'I'm very glad you were able to call, Superintendent,' Yvonne Goodhusband said, as if she had requested him to come and not the other way about.

He judged her in her mid-fifties, her well-groomed chestnut hair streaked with grey. He thought her a striking woman, not least because she wore what Markby was sure his mother would have called an afternoon dress. He couldn't recall when he'd last seen a woman so formally turned out at three-thirty in the afternoon. The dress was of pale blue woollen material, long-sleeved with gilt buttons at the wrist. It fitted snugly over the lady's well-rounded hips and the cross-over bodice neatly encased her equally shapely bosom on which was pinned a small gold brooch. She had good legs, too. She was, in fact, very easy on the eye and he tried not to stare.

'Would you like some tea?' she inquired graciously.

He declined the tea, although he was sorely tempted. Not because he was thirsty, but because he would have liked to observe the ceremony he was sure would be attached to this refreshment. Little embroidered napkins and bone china, he suspected. But he hadn't time for such things.

'You'll know why I'm here,' he began.

She interrupted. 'Of course I do. I appreciate your calling to make an appointment. Good manners are so rare nowadays. It led me to make a few telephone inquiries about you. I hope you don't mind? I like to be prepared.'

So did he, but he'd given her the chance to get ahead of him. So much for good manners. Next time, he made a note of it, call on her unexpectedly and hope to find her in her curlers!

'It seems we have a mutual acquaintance.'

Blast. 'Who?' Markby asked bluntly.

'Annabel Pultney,' Yvonne said. 'She tells me you are a cousin.'

Oh lawks, Belle Pultney, the terror of her local Persian cat society.

'Several times removed!' Markby said firmly. He was in trouble. He dug himself out of it with renewed vigour. 'I haven't seen her in years. She's still – er – judging at cat shows and so on?'

'No longer, she's had to give it up. The varicose veins, you know.'

'Er – yes.' He attempted to visualise this distant relative's legs which he'd never seen unclad with thick brown stockings. His memory conjured up accompanying stout brogues and tweeds. And a lot of cat fur. Wherever he'd sat in that house, he'd got up with his suit decorated with clinging white hairs. A good-hearted sort, though, Belle. Fond of a gin and tonic and a Panatella.

'She does manage to get up to London three or four times a year. We meet for lunch at Harvey Nichols. She tells me you're a very reasonable sort of chap so I hope we shall understand one another.'

'This letter!' said Markby forcefully, producing the document in question with a flourish. He really had to stop this blatant manipulation of the old-girl network. He wished now he'd sent Pearce.

He was to be interrupted yet again.

The door opened and a young man slouched in. Slender in build, he was nevertheless quite tall, with long curling fair hair framing a narrow face with aquiline nose and small full lips. This rather girlish look was negated by tattered denims, heavy boots, a washed-out black tee-shirt bearing the name of a Heavy Metal band, and a none too clean suede waistcoat. It was difficult to guess his exact age. He might have been early or late twenties. Older looking younger, Markby thought. It suddenly occurred to him that this might also be true of the mother. His first judgement of mid-fifties might be out by some half-dozen years.

'My son, Tristan,' Yvonne said.

'Hi!' said Tristan and flopped into an easy chair.

'Tristan gives me a hand,' said his mother fondly.

'Really?' Markby thought Tristan didn't appear to have the energy to lift a hand, much less lend one.

'He is publicity officer of our little committee,' Mrs Goodhusband went on. 'I am its chairperson. Our secretary is Beryl Linnacott. She's so sorry she couldn't be here today to meet you. She's had to go to Norfolk to be with her daughter. She's just had twins.'

The daughter, presumably, not Beryl. It occurred to Markby to wonder about Mr Goodhusband. He didn't seem to be in evidence at all, not even by way of a snapshot. Perhaps he'd been driven out by his wife's devotion to good causes, a modern Mr Jellaby.

'About the letter,' he began again with a touch of desperation.

'Quite.' She graciously acknowledged that after all this social chit-chat it was time for business. 'The Caswells are comparatively recent arrivals in our village. Sally seems a sweet girl. Her husband, I have to say, I have always found a morose sort of man. On the few occasions I've met him about the village, he has rejected any attempt at conversation. One tries to be welcoming to newcomers, but if they don't want it, one can't force oneself forward. Sally did come and have coffee here. She told us her husband was engaged in some research work of a scientific nature. But nothing—'

Yvonne's voice hardened. 'Nothing had prepared us – the committee – for the shocking revelation that Dr Caswell has in the past conducted experimental programmes involving animals! The committee was distressed to learn of it and we held an emergency meeting, didn't we, Tristan?'

Appealed to, Tristan said, 'Yeah.'

Markby studied him briefly. Mentally he was adding even more years to his initial impression. Despite the youthful garb and attitude, to say nothing of the flowing hair, this was a man of thirty to thirty-five. One of those, he suspected, locked in permanent adolescence preparing to be a forty-year-old teenager, and after that?

An image of Libby's Uncle Denis formed in Markby's head. Would Tristan finish as one of those lost figures with hair which grew longer at the back as it became thinner on the top, and too-tight jeans, who assiduously kept up with the latest jargon and fashions? A starfish stranded on a beach when the tide had gone out on his generation?

'Did you know about Dr Caswell's work? I mean, before the affair of the letter-bomb?' he asked.

Tristan met his gaze. 'Not that I recall. Don't think so, no.'

Yvonne took charge of the conversation again. 'Our committee is strongly against the use of animals in laboratory experiments, as I hope you are, Superintendent?'

'I don't like the idea,' Markby took her letter from his pocket. 'But I'm here because of this letter. Or rather, I'm here because Dr Caswell has been the recipient of several items of abusive mail.'

She raised her eyebrows. 'You consider my letter abusive?'

'Indeed, no! Don't misunderstand me. I'm looking at all letters received by Dr Caswell which are on the same topic, shall we say.'

Unexpectedly Tristan blurted, 'He hasn't had any other mail from us!' He sat upright in his chair. 'And we don't aim to splat people over the carpet, either! So you're not sticking that explosive doodah on us!'

'As Tristan says, we don't resort to violence,' said his mother in the manner of an interpreter.

'What do you do?' Markby asked candidly.

'We lobby. It is, I believe, the most effective way in the end. I believe in going to the top.' Mrs Goodhusband smiled thinly. 'Votes, Superintendent. Politicians worry very much about votes. The agricultural lobby is itself a strong one, we realise that. But the ordinary voter is ignored at his or her peril! Supermarkets, too, are customer-conscious. They provide what the customer wants. If we can persuade the customer to demand, for example, free-range eggs, then that is what the supermarket will stock.'

'And how do you go about lobbying and persuading? Just by letter? Like this one?' He waved the letter received by Liam at her.

'We produce several well-informed and illustrated pamphlets. I write regularly to members of Parliament, all parties, and to all our Euro-MPs. Beryl writes to the drug companies and to the manufacturers of cosmetics and hair-care products. Shampoo is sometimes tested on rabbits in unspeakable fashion. We have on occasion picketed but never—' She bent a steely gaze on him. 'Never in a disorderly fashion. Rowdyism puts people off. We want to win them over.'

'Mrs Goodhusband,' Markby said. 'Your aims appear to be above reproach and your methods equally so. You cannot, however, be unaware that some other groups, with aims similar to yours, adopt very different means.'

'They are nothing to do with us!' she snapped. 'And some of them, Superintendent, are perhaps not entirely frank about all their aims!'

She was no fool. She was, in fact, of a breed he'd met before, educated, articulate, well-organised and utterly determined. She wouldn't send cut-and-paste threatening mail nor explosive packages. Nor would Mrs Linnacott, recently become grandmother of twins. He was less sure about Tristan. Clearly that young fellow (whatever his actual age) was the apple of his mother's eye and it wouldn't do to suggest it.

He rose to take his leave, making his thanks.

'I'm glad it's been sorted out.' Yvonne smoothed the pale blue dress over her hips. 'I intend to call on Dr Caswell soon to explain our objections to his use of animals. I hope, probably in vain, that he will be as pleasant as you have been. I shall not give up! I find if one is both reasonable and determined, Superintendent, most people are eventually open to persuasion.'

As Markby was conjuring with the consequences of Mrs Goodhusband cornering Liam Caswell, without warning, Tristan came to life. He jumped out of his chair and went to a nearby desk. He returned proffering a stack of leaflets.

'Here, take some of these.'

Markby took them, feeling rather as he did when representatives of religious cults pushed such things at one in the street. He saw that the topmost one concerned battery chicken houses and was identical to the one sent to the Caswells.

Seeing that Markby was studying it, Tristan said a touch smugly, 'I designed it. I design them all.' He tossed back his long fair locks.

'Really?' Markby turned the leaflet over. 'How did you come by the photographs?'

Tristan's full lips twisted in what might have been intended either as a grin or a sneer. 'You're not expecting me to admit to breaking and entering? I came by them more or less legally. No hassles. You just have to be ingenious – and quick on your feet.'

His mother was growing restless, clearly disliking the turn of the conversation. She cast her son a look to silence him and then bent her imperious gaze on Markby. A diamond encrusted hand indicated the leaflet he held.

'Read it!' Yvonne commanded.

'Read this!' Markby dropped the pamphlet and its fellows on Pearce's desk. 'I don't think we need bother Mrs Goodhusband again. But you might check on her son, Tristan. Too much the mother's blue-eyed darling to be true.'

Pearce picked up the pamphlet with its sad photographs of imprisoned hens. 'Poor beggars,' he said. 'We kept chickens when I was a kid. They scratched around the yard. Clean up all the bugs and things, you know, chickens do. We'd never have kept them like this.' He looked up. 'What's she like then, this Mrs Goodhusband?'

'Boadicea in a tea-gown.'

'A what?'

'Never mind. But believe me, when the Yvonne Goodhusbands of this world devote their minds and energy to a cause, they generally carry off victory at the end of the day. And they don't need letter-bombs to do it!'

Chapter Eight

It was around seven when Alan Markby reached Meredith's modest end-of-terrace cottage in Station Road.

He got out of his car, bearing the box with the pizza and a supermarket carrier bag. She'd heard him. He saw her curtain twitch. The front door opened and she stood on the step, hugging her arms.

'You'll catch cold,' he said. 'Go indoors.'

'I'm all right. There's no need to fuss.'

It occurred to him she was feeling better! She was still on the step, peering past him into the darkness.

'You haven't seen the cat hanging around out there, have you? He hasn't been around for a couple of days. Because I was laid up again, I wasn't able to look out for him. He may have taken offence and left. It's very cold at night. Did you bring the catfood?'

'I brought a dozen tins in a box. It was cheaper that way. But now I've lugged it over here, you tell me the animal's vanished. Not, mind you, that I'm surprised. It was probably just a wandering tom, passing through. Here, I also brought some ice cream.' He handed her the carrier. 'You'd better pop it straight in your freezer. It's the one you like, rum and raisin.'

'He might come back,' she insisted, as she took the packages. 'Rum and raisin? Lovely, thanks.'

'The pizza's seafood. That OK?'

'It's fine. I only said not pepperoni because it's on the spicy side and I made a poor showing at Ahmed's the other evening.'

'I hope that wasn't what upset you.' Alan looked concerned.

She shook her head. 'No. Pringle thinks my resistance is low because of the flu and I was extra susceptible to any other bug around. Whatever it was, it really did knock me out for a couple of days.'

They were proceeding down the narrow hall. 'Actually,' she said over her shoulder, 'I'm pretty hungry now and looking forward to all this! Like to open the wine?'

'Not been eating?' Markby asked severely as he busied himself with the corkscrew.

She was stowing the ice cream in the freezer compartment of her fridge. 'You sound like a kindly aunt!'

Meredith sighed as she stacked the tins of catfood in her cupboard. She hoped the wretched animal had found shelter on this cold night.

'I went to Bailey and Bailey's sale. I told you about the Victorian glasses?'

'You did. Get them?'

'No. I left a sealed offer but someone outbid me on the day. I mean, he offered more and I wasn't there to offer again. I hadn't felt quite a hundred per cent before I went. But I started to feel much worse while I was there. Sally gave me some of her herbal tea. It was the final straw – no pun intended. I started to feel awful after that and couldn't wait for Austin to reach the glasses. I just came home here and took to my bed. But I'm all right now.'

They returned to her tiny sitting room with a glass of wine a-piece while the pizza reheated. Meredith curled up on the sofa before her electric fire. Alan stretched out in the nearby armchair and surveyed the room with pleasure at being here again and with being with her. She was wearing jeans and a baggy white knitted sweater which didn't disguise that she'd lost quite a bit of weight. She hadn't been able to get to the hairdresser either, and her hair had grown quite a bit, nearly reaching her shoulders. He rather liked it like that, longer, and said so.

'Makes me feel like a hippy.' She scratched the top of her head. 'I may keep it for a bit but I think it'll have to be chopped off eventually.'

The television set flickered in the corner, the sound turned down. It was showing Channel Four news.

'Bodicote was at the sale that day,' Meredith said. 'Sally explained to me about the goats and the turnips and why he made such a fuss.'

'Yes, she gave me a call about it after you'd mentioned it to her. I didn't think Bodicote had got it right.'

The television screen jumped to a new subject, a piece of film. Figures surged to and fro around a lorry, an animal transporter. People were displaying banners against live exports. It must be at one of the ports. Markby leaned forward. Then he jumped up, dashed to the set, and turned up the sound.

The newcaster's voice blared forth, echoing round the room, informing them that the scenes they were now seeing had taken place early that morning. Ignoring the noise, Alan jabbed a finger excitedly at the screen. 'See that? That chap there? Long hair, carrying a banner, look! That one!'

'I see him. Who is he? Must we have it so loud?' she asked plaintively.

'Sorry!' He turned the sound down marginally. The newscast had moved on to a fresh subject. Alan returned to his chair. 'I was talking to that chap this afternoon. Tristan Goodhusband. He lives out at Castle Darcy. I actually called on his mama, a formidable lady who organises an animal welfare pressure group. I thought young Tristan seemed pretty whacked. No wonder, if he was out at crack of dawn down at the quayside. He could only just have got back when I saw him.'

'Well, at least he wasn't arrested.'

'No. There were a lot of people there. He may have been cautioned.' Markby's gaze had grown thoughtful. 'I'll get Prescott to contact the local police at – where was it – Dover? In case he was one of those whose details were taken.'

A buzzing noise from the kitchen announced that the pizza was ready. A little later when they'd eaten and were finishing the last of the wine, Meredith asked, 'This chap Goodhusband, has he got anything to do with what happened to Liam and Sally?'

'Not that we know of, although Liam's had a letter from Yvonne Goodhusband, suggesting she call and discuss matters. He's had another anonymous one as well. Keep that to yourself. Although, when you see Sally, she may tell you. It got Liam pretty agitated.'

Alan couldn't disguise his satisfaction at this memory. 'As for Mrs Goodhusband, she turned out to be acquainted with a distant relative of mine. Mind you, someone like that knows people all over the place in every walk of life. It was a bit awkward, though.' He grimaced. 'I shall get a phone call from Annabel now, wanting to know why I took my police boots round to her chum Yvonne's place.'

'Pulling strings?' Meredith grinned at him.

'Not quite. Although Yvonne would do that if she thought it'd get her anywhere. I gather it's her preferred *modus operandi*. She calls it lobbying.' He put down his empty glass. 'I'm not going to talk shop. Usually you won't let me.'

Meredith looked serious. 'This time it concerns Sally and I am worried about her. I haven't seen her since the auction, so I didn't know about these new letters. I meant to ring up, but I didn't want to talk to Liam and the phone's in his study.' She paused. 'I ought to spare a thought for Liam, I suppose. He's the one the package-sender was after. Whoever it was, may try again. What do you think?'

Alan chased the last of the wine round the bottom of the glass.

'Yes, I think the sender will try again. But something different, since everyone is now watching out for packages. It may be a booby-trapped car, that's a favourite. Both Caswells have been told how to check their cars every morning. The cars are garaged overnight, not left outside, which is a help. They've had a new padlock put on the garage door.'

Alan tossed back the last mouthful of the wine. 'The word garage is a bit of a misnomer. It's a barn. Have you been in there?' When she shook her head, he went on, 'Plenty of room for both cars and a lot of old furniture.'

'Aunt Emily's.' Meredith uncoiled from her chair. 'Shall I fetch another bottle?'

'Please, no! I've got to drive home tonight!'

'You don't, actually,' she pointed out.

He smiled. 'Yes, sweetheart, I do. Wish I didn't. But I've got to be at work first thing and all bright-eyed et cetera.'

She was watching his face. 'You're worried too, aren't you?'

'Yes, I'm worried. No use pretending otherwise. No other part of the country has reported any similar incidents. That may be because the effect of the explosion was greater than the sender anticipated and whoever it is is thinking again. On the other hand, I'd have expected there to be other packages. These things are often sent out in batches. Then there were the letters. We don't even know if they're connected and Caswell being so bloody uncooperative doesn't help. Although getting another anonymous letter this morning has given him a fright, reminding him that they won't give up.'

'Until someone dies?' Meredith's newly long hair fell forward around her face.

'Yes, someone could die.' Alan sat up and added briskly, 'But not if I can prevent it! That's my job!'

'I'm glad it's you in charge,' she told him. 'I feel Sally's safer because of it – and Liam, too, of course!' She glanced at her watch. 'It's just on ten. Did you want to see ITV news in case they show that piece of film again?'

They watched it again but it had been cut down and the shots of Tristan had been edited out. The national news ran on to the end and the local news items followed.

'There's Wilver Park,' Meredith pointed.

Wilver Park was a minor stately home some fifteen miles down the road. They were shown a brief shot of the Palladian exterior and then taken inside to an oak-shelved library where a gloomy man stood indicating, for the benefit of the camera, ominous gaps on the shelves.

'Mostly first editions!' he was saying, adding with a note of wrath, 'Considerable ingenuity was used to disguise the thefts! In some cases, remaining books were spread out to be less tightly packed. But in others, old but worthless books were substituted. Here, for example . . .' He picked up a book. 'Here is an eighteenth-century book of very little value – not part of the library stock – which the thieves must have smuggled in and very cleverly substituted for an early English translation of Plutarch's *Lives.*'

The camera landed briefly on the book in his hand. Meredith leaned forward. 'How odd!'

'Nifty idea, I should have thought.'

'Oh drat, it's gone!' She sat back. 'The book he was showing the camera, the ringer, it was very like one I saw over at Bailey and Bailey's sale preview. *A Clergyman's Vade Mecum*, it was called.'

'Hundreds of books like that printed between 1700 and 1900. Those were the days of the great sermon, lasting hours. Good preachers filled churches. Being a clergyman must have been more like being a solo variety act in some ways. If a preacher wasn't particularly gifted, he looked it all up in a book.'

'Yes, I dare say. Hundreds of books like it about.' She sounded only partly convinced.

The camera moved to the interviewer, an earnest, eager young woman. 'It is not known exactly when the books were taken,' she informed them. 'Wilver Park was closed only at the end of last week for the winter after a busy season of visitors. It will not reopen to the public until spring. In the meantime, necessary maintenance and cleaning will be carried out and the general inventory checked. It was the start of this annual check, here in the library—'

The camera left her face to pan around the book-lined shelves and dwell briefly on a marble bust of Shakespeare on a desk.

Back to the girl with the mike. '—which led to the loss being discovered yesterday. That means the books could have been taken any time over the last months! It is not even known whether they were taken singly or in batches, or by how many thieves.'

Back to the gloomy man. 'Security will have to be increased, but we haven't the resources to take on more personnel. Possibly a surveillance camera might be an answer. Or access to some of the rooms may have to be limited on certain days.'

'Robbery to order,' said the earnest girl to camera, 'a problem for our days, has reached the world of antiques which, of any kind, have never been so vulnerable.' She obligingly gave them her name and reminded them that she spoke from Wilver Park house, before returning them to the studio.

A final shot of the library and then the exterior of the house and a few bars of Mozart faded in to the next news item.

'I don't know about antiques being more vulnerable than ever before,' Markby said. 'They were pretty vulnerable when the Pyramid tombs were raided by Carter and others, weren't they? But it's true the art theft squad is kept busy.'

'Shame,' said Meredith. 'Wonder what's happened to the books. There were plenty of other old books in Bailey's sale. I don't mean anything as interesting as the ones pinched from Wilver Park.'

'The salerooms will be asked to keep an eye open,' Alan said. 'But the books have probably been taken to order, as the presenter suggested. A collector somewhere.' He glanced at his wristwatch. 'I should be going.'

'So you said.' She raised a quizzical eyebrow.

'I did. But perhaps not yet, not for another hour.'

Tristan was unaware that he'd made the evening newscast. At the time it was beaming into the nation's homes, he was standing at the front gate of The Tithe Barn with a girl named Debbie Lee.

It was dark there beneath overhanging trees and surrounded by the shrubbery. There was a single street-light, a poor fitful thing. From time to time it uttered a depressed buzz. A bough, caught by the breeze, moved and allowed the yellow gleam to flicker over the couple. It made their faces look wan and since both wore dark clothes, they gave the impression of a pair of spectres lurking there.

Debbie was a local girl, aged sixteen, not especially pretty nor especially bright. Tristan didn't know whether he felt sorry for her or was simply exasperated by her. He was careful to show neither of these emotions, always treating Debbie with a show of restrained affection.

Debbie, for her part, thought Tristan the man of her dreams. She worked at the chicken farm, in the egg-packing plant next door to the units housing the layers.

She shivered in the cool night breeze and fumbled in her padded jacket for the envelope. 'I got it, Tris.' She had a lisp. His name came out as 'Trish', like a girl's.

Tristan, who hated this abbreviation of his name anyway, even without it being mangled and undergoing a sex-change, said, 'Well done, Debs.'

Debbie didn't mind what version of her name he used. Just to hear it on his lips was enough. To hear him say 'Well done' was bliss.

'I took an awful risk, Tris. It'd cost me my job if I was caught. I mean, I'm really lucky to have this job, near home. There's no work in the village except at the chicken place. My dad would have my hide if I got the sack.'

Tristan knew her father, the landlord of the local pub, and believed it. 'You won't get caught, Debs. Not a clever girl like you. And it's for the cause.'

'I don't do it for the cause,' she said simply. 'I do it for you.'

Tristan was embarrassed when he heard her say this. He had no qualms at using her. But her loyalty and devotion, so artlessly expressed, never failed to make him cringe. Luckily it was dark and she couldn't see it.

She had something else on her mind, however, tonight. 'Tris? I want to help you, but I don't want to do nothing which would close the place down.'

'It won't!' he told her shortly.

'I hope not.'

'I told you, it won't! It might make them sharpen up their act and stick to the regulations better than they do now.'

'That's all right, then. You see, people like you and your mum, marching up and down outside and posting leaflets through doors, you might put it out of business. But people like me, we need the jobs. And anyway, they're only birds.'

'They should be kept in humane conditions, even so!' Tristan snapped. 'And not turned into egg-producing machines!'

'I suppose so, Tris. I did ask when I started what happened to all them birds when they didn't need them any more. Someone told me they go for petfood. All them tins of chicken dinners for cats and dogs. They get worn out, those chickens, very quick. They're all egg-producers. They don't raise no table birds. They're thinking of starting up a unit, though, for the broilers. The boss says they'd have to extend and that means putting in for planning permission. It'd mean more jobs for the village.'

'Are they?' Tristan asked her eagerly. 'If you hear any more about that, Debs, let me know at once!'

Privately he was asking himself if his mother knew anyone on the planning committee. The outlines of a new leaflet formed in his head, this time against the introduction of broiler houses.

Noise, extra traffic on country roads, smell, destruction of greenbelt. Start a petition, he thought.

Aloud he added, 'And don't worry about the place closing down. We're not trying to do that, I promise.'

'Don't you want this, then?'

She was still holding out the envelope. Tristan took it and the reel of film it contained. 'We do appreciate this, Debs. I've tried to get in there and get pictures but it's damn difficult. What I really need is some proper film, not just snaps. I'd like to get in there with my camcorder.'

'I can't do that!' she wailed in alarm. 'They'd see me. Anyway, I'm no good operating one of those things, camcorders. I can't seem to get the hang of them.'

Tristan believed this, too, and hadn't the slightest intention of letting her anywhere near his expensive new equipment.

'Don't worry about it, Debs. Leave it to me.'

She was waiting expectantly, her face turned up to his in the moonlight. This was her price – that was how Tristan thought of it. Debbie thought of it as romance.

He drew a breath, seized her in his arms and kissed 'in a masterly way' as she liked to tell her friends at the egg-packing plant.

Usually, during this pleasurable experience, she sagged in his arms and muttered incoherent endearments. But tonight, without warning, she jumped away from him and squealed.

'What the hell—?' Tristan exploded.

'There!' she pointed behind him. 'Someone's watching us!'

'Oh God, not Mother?' Tristan gasped. He whirled round. Behind him the bushes rustled in the night air but were empty, as far as he could see. He glanced nervously towards the lights of the house, but no vengeful figure of his mother hove into view. Yvonne didn't approve of her son's relationship, such as it was, with Debbie.

'The girl has expectations, Tristan. You oughtn't to encourage them. You asked her to take those photographs and she could make things very difficult for us.'

Lately, Tristan had begun to suspect his mother was right. Debbie was talking of taking him home to meet her parents. Mr Lee had for many years been anchor-man of the pub's tug-o'-war team. Mrs Lee was a gravel-voiced bottle-blonde who had no difficulty making herself heard from one end of Castle Darcy to the other and had, when roused, an astonishing vocabulary.

'There's no one there,' Tristan said now in relief. 'You're imagining it. It was the breeze.'

'It wasn't!' she insisted. 'The trees moved and the light shone right over there and I saw eyes! And I heard breathing! Someone was in those bushes and watching us!'

Tristan edged to the bushes in question. He parted some sprays and peered into the darkness. Faintly, in the depths, he heard a rustle.

'All right!' he shouted. 'Come out of there!'

'It's not me dad, is it?' whimpered Debbie.

'I hope not!' Panic seized Tristan who renewed his efforts at a search. 'I know who you are!' he blustered. 'So you might as well show yourself!'

A louder rustle made them both jump. One of the cats ran out and scuttled away into the further darkness across the drive.

'A cat!' Tristan said in disgust. 'Honestly, just for a moment . . . It was just one of the cats, Debs.'

She was unconvinced. 'I saw eyes! Not low down, like a cat's would be. Higher up, a man's. I saw him over your shoulder.' A thought struck her. 'Could it have been—'

'If it was,' said Tristan, interrupting. 'I'll have a word with him when I see him next, frighten him off. But it was a cat. You'd better get on home, Debs. Your dad will be looking out for you.'

'You'll walk me home, won't you, Tris? You'll walk me to the pub? I'm scared.'

So was Tristan, but not of the dark. He was worried that people would see him with Debbie and it would reinforce whatever romantic tale she'd been telling her friends about him. But she'd got the film, as she'd promised, and she was his eyes and ears inside the egg-production complex.

'I'll walk with you to the car park. You'll be all right from there. The pub's lit. There will be people about. It's best if we're not seen together, because of your job. Someone might tell your boss. It'll blow your cover, Debs, and you might get the sack. We don't want that, do we?'

She took his hand gratefully – and tightly. She didn't release it until they reached the edge of the pub car park. He bid her a hasty goodnight, wondering whether the whole thing hadn't been a ploy on her part to get him to march through Castle Darcy with her hanging on his arm.

But before they parted, she whispered. 'I really saw someone, Tris. Honest.'

Meredith set out after breakfast the following morning for the salerooms. She was almost sure that Sally would be working there today. It was a nice morning, sunny and relatively mild. After so much cold and damp, it was pleasant.

She was walking down the narrow road towards Bailey and Bailey's front entrance, when she heard her name called.

Turning, she saw Dave Pearce. 'Hullo!' she said in surprise. 'What are you doing here, Inspector? I thought they'd got you over at Regional HQ.'

Pearce grinned. 'They let me out on my old patch occasionally. I'm on my way down to the *Bamford Gazette* office.' He lowered his voice conspiratorially. 'I could have sent my sergeant, but I thought I'd take the opportunity to nip home. We've just moved, Tess and I, to a new house. Not brand-new, but new to us. She's got busy decorating this morning.'

'Nice to see you, anyway. And congratulations on the promotion!'

'Never thought I'd get it,' Pearce said frankly.

'Why ever not? You deserve it.'

'Thanks.' He grinned again, reddening. 'But you know how it is. Everyone's got a university degree these days. Even in the police. Times are changing. I feel like a survivor from the past.' Pearce was in his early thirties. 'How are you keeping, then?'

'I'm fine. Getting over the 'flu, but OK now. You're working with Alan again. I know he's pleased about that.'

Pearce grew even redder. 'Is he? Well, I must say it's nice for me to be back with him again. Mind you, he doesn't change.' Pearce broke off and they both laughed. 'He's the best, though, you know,' Pearce went on. 'You can ask anyone. They'll tell you. The superintendent is the best.'

They parted, Meredith to Bailey and Bailey's and Pearce to the *Bamford Gazette*.

There was no one in the front office. Following the sound of voices, Meredith traversed the silent auction rooms, oddly empty in the wake of the recent sale. She found Sally and Austin, their heads together before the computer, earnestly discussing something on the screen.

They were too engrossed to have heard her approach. Meredith cleared her throat tactfully.

Both started and jumped round. Austin's hand went out and tapped the keyboard. The parallel blocks of figures on the screen were wiped away. Meredith didn't know whether to be amused or annoyed. She wasn't here to spy. Whatever they'd been discussing, it was unlikely it would have meant anything to her, in any case. She probably wouldn't even have looked at the screen. Now, of course, she was left wondering what it had been that she wasn't allowed to glimpse.

'Meredith!' Sally sounded delighted. 'I'm so pleased to see you!' She threw out her hands. 'And I feel so guilty. I should have come round but Austin and I have been so busy and I don't like to leave Liam alone at the cottage more than I have to.'

'It's all right, don't apologize. I haven't been in the mood for visits, but I'm fine now and obviously, so are you. No more alarms?'

'None.' Sally glanced at Austin. 'We were just planning ahead. We have to start thinking about the next sale already.'

'I saw the item on the news last night,' Meredith told them. 'About the books stolen from Wilver Park. You have to keep an eye open for that sort of thing, I suppose, Austin?'

Austin took off his spectacles, pulled out his spotted handkerchief and began to polish the lenses assiduously. 'We get the usual lists circulated round the antique trade. But we've never been affected. Touch wood.' Gravely he tapped his forehead.

'I think I'd recognise a rare book,' he went on. 'We do get old books here, but generally of modest value. People who've got real rarities take them to a specialist if they want to dispose of them. That's what I'd advise if one was brought in. They just wouldn't get the price here. Paintings too. Anything special I'd recommend they take up to London, to Christie's or Sothebys', Phillip's . . . the big auction houses.

'Now, maps or botanical illustrations. That's another matter. People sometimes cannibalise books for those and try to sell the pictures. Always a terrible tragedy. But if something really rare and valuable turned up here. I'd want to know who was selling and why, on what authority. Bailey and Bailey's got a reputation to keep up.'

He shrugged. 'If you're talking about other kinds of stolen goods, then I understand the favoured means of getting rid of anything hot nowadays is the car boot sale. Fake labels, pirated software, proceeds of opportunist burglaries. But not here, not us.'

'We do lose things,' Sally put in tentatively.

'Quite,' said Austin bitterly. 'People are more likely to pinch things from us than bring pinched things to us!'

Sally murmured, 'A couple of books disappeared from the last preview.'

Austin glanced round as if the missing volumes could be spotted from where he sat. 'They came in a crate of mixed books. We split them into several lots. Much of it was cheap, tattered stuff. The missing ones were a couple of volumes of Dickens, Victorian and in good condition, but not particularly valuable. Some people are on the look out for leather bindings. They strip them and make them up into ghastly false fronts for drinks and TV cabinets.' He shuddered. 'Anyhow, all those books together weren't expected to raise more than forty quid. In fact, if I recall, the soiled lots remained unsold.' He put away the handkerchief. 'Would you – er – care for some tea or coffee, Meredith?'

There was a hesitation in his voice which indicated he would rather she refused. Obviously she'd interrupted something.

'No, thanks. I've got some shopping to do. I really wanted to ask Sally if she'd like to meet for lunch?'

'Come back to Castle Darcy for lunch!' Sally invited her promptly. 'I'll be finished here just after twelve. Meet me here.'

Pearce had proceeded to the offices of the *Bamford Gazette*. They were in a low-lintelled old building and the cramped interior was a hive of activity. It was some time before Pearce was able to secure the undivided attention of the editor, Mo Calderwell.

'Right, Sergeant Pearce!' said Ms Calderwell at last, recognising her visitor.

Pearce cleared his throat and diffidently explained about his promotion.

'Gone up in the world, eh?' said Mo. 'We'll put it in the paper. Item of local interest. Still live locally, do you? Jeff! Fix us a cuppa, will you?'

A faint roar in the background indicated that Jeff was stuck on the phone and they could fix sodding coffee themselves.

'He'll be a coupla ticks,' said Mo serenely. 'He's chasing up

141

advertising subscribers.' She swivelled her chair and stretched out her Doc Martens. 'Keeping the show on the road, as you might say.'

Pearce admitted that he did still live in the locality.

'Got any interests, hobbies?' She was scribbling hieroglyphics on a notepad.

'Started to play a bit of golf,' Pearce said self-consciously. 'Um, got a new garden . . .'

'We'll send a photographer out and get a pic of you and your wife. Good public relations for the police. Human interest item for our readers. I was short of copy this week. Glad you came in.'

'I didn't come to be interviewed,' said Pearce, aghast that she seemed to think he'd come bent on self-publicity. 'I came to consult your records. It's an item about a demonstration by animal welfare activists outside a local battery chicken unit. About six months ago.'

'Back in the summer?' Mo squinted at him. 'Remember that. Hang on. She punched at the keyboard of her computer, peered at the screen, muttered, 'July!' and got up. 'This way!'

She led him into an even more cramped back room. 'July!' she said, pointing at a thick file on a shelf. 'OK? Shout if you can't find it!' She disappeared.

It took him little time to find the article and even less to read it through. But although it offered only basic information in text, there was a valuable accompanying picture. Pearce gave a grunt of satisfaction as he peered closely at it, taking out his notebook. The names of the demonstrators were obligingly given underneath and he jotted them down. They hadn't objected to being photographed or, presumably, named, but had lined up for the camera and were smiling and waving their banners brightly. Tristan Goodhusband was far left. His mother, Yvonne, mid-centre, was orchestrating her little band. The only person whose face was disguised was that of a demonstrator dressed up as a chicken. His – or her – identity was only given as 'A. Bird'. The chicken's head was uninhabited, fixed atop the body of the creature, which contained the – one hoped – human within. The effect was to give the beast increased height. Studying the photo with his nose practically on it, Pearce could make out a slit at the top of the bulbous body through which a pair of eyes peered anonymously. When in doubt, study the legs, especially ankles, he told himself. But Pearce was foiled again. The legs were shapeless in wrinkly woollen tights and gave no indication of sex.

Nevertheless well pleased, he went to find Mo. 'Could we have a copy of the picture?'

'Sure, get on to our photographer. Send it over soonest, OK?'

Pearce, as he'd told Meredith he intended, took the opportunity to call home.

As he'd also told Meredith, he and Tessa were in a new house, new, that was, to them. His promotion and Tessa's having also obtained a better paid job, had encouraged them to upgrade their housing situation, as current jargon had it, Move, in other words, into something slightly bigger than the tiny flat they'd had. They'd at first considered a brand-new house on an estate under construction on the outskirts of town. But, as Tessa pointed out, the rooms in those houses were so small that, frankly, they'd be very little better off.

There was, however, a semi-detached turn-of-the-century villa for sale. Run down, for sure. Needing complete rewiring, redecoration and an updated heating system. But it offered two large reception rooms, proper kitchen, three decent-sized bedrooms, just enough room to park the car at the side of the place (Pearce would have preferred a garage but you can't have everything), and even a garden. It was, the estate agent had said, eyeing this keen young couple, a 'family home'. Well, said Tessa, there was that to be considered, too. Not that they planned any children just yet. But in a year or two. Then they'd need the garden, and it was near a primary school, too.

So they'd bought. Then they'd started work on the place. It had immediately become clear that a lot more was involved than they'd naïvely imagined. An entire new kitchen and bathroom had to be installed before the place was even habitable, they'd known that from the start but the work had mopped up what little money they'd had left. So now everything was being done by themselves, by hand, on the cheap. Tessa, on a week's holiday, was spending it up a ladder with a paintbrush. Pearce felt guilty. Hence the visit home to see she was all right.

He took with him the unexpected tidings that the local press would be arriving at some point to photograph them both in their new surroundings.

'What?' shrieked Tessa, nearly falling off her ladder. 'Not today? I haven't even got the new curtains up in the lounge!'

The puppy, already excited by Pearce's arrival, was infected with the alarm and began rushing round in circles, perilously close to tins of paint, jars of soapy water and white spirit and other paraphernalia of redecorating. Tessa wasn't expert, but she was keen.

'I don't know, love,' admitted Pearce. 'I suppose fairly soon if it's going to be in the next issue of the local rag.'

'Everyone will see it!' howled his wife, echoed by the now demented puppy. 'Everyone we know!'

She leapt from her ladder and rushed into the bedroom to stare in a mirror. 'My hair!'

He left her feverishly stowing away paintpots and ladder, and preparing to clean every corner of the house.

'And no staying late at work tonight, Dave!' floated after him. 'I need you back here to move the furniture!'

Pearce started off back to regional HQ, regretting in many ways that he hadn't sent Prescott on the original errand, after all.

It wasn't strictly necessary for him to take a route via the Spring Farm estate, but somehow, he found himself doing that.

144

There was no immediate need, he knew, to visit Michael Whelan again. As he'd already reported back to Markby, his opinion was that they could cross Whelan off the list as far as explosive packages went. But he hadn't been able to get that gaunt, pale figure out of his head. It wouldn't do any harm, he thought, just to call by and see how Whelan was getting along. After all, one never knew.

He drew up before the flat and got out, slamming the car door. The sound echoed round the treeless waste. Some boys kicking a ball around stopped to watch him, then whispered together. One of them set off at a run – to warn his parents, no doubt.

Pearce didn't like leaving the car here unattended, but at least he'd be able to see it from the flat. He went into the smelly familiar entrance and rang at the bell. No one came. He rang again. Nothing.

Fair enough, Whelan was out. Pearce wasn't going to hang around here nor leave the car any longer. Those kids were on the prowl. They'd strip windscreen wipers and anything else removable in seconds. He went outside and was about to get into the car when, from the corner of his eye, he saw the grimy net curtain move.

'Whelan!' he shouted. The curtain trembled. Pearce went to the window and tapped on it. After a moment, the net was drawn back and Whelan's unshaven face appeared, twitching nervously.

He pushed open the window a little way and asked, 'What do you want?'

'Inspector Pearce, remember me?'

'Yeah . . .' Whelan licked his lips. He still had the sore. 'I remember. I told you, I can't help you.'

'Can I come in and talk to you?'

'S'not convenient.'

There was a distinct sound of someone else moving in the room behind Whelan.

By now all of Pearce's instincts were on the alert. It was just possible that he'd interrupted something illicit. It might be drugs. If so, he ought to radio for back-up. On the other hand, by the time he'd done that, any evidence would have been spirited away.

'Let me in!' he ordered and went back to the front door. Technically he ought to get a warrant unless invited, but Whelan wasn't likely to lodge a complaint. Besides, Pearce could claim with some justification that he'd had reason to suppose something illegal was going on in there.

Whelan was opening the flat door as he arrived, slowly and with manifest reluctance. He looked as unhealthy as on the previous occasion, if not worse.

Pearce stepped briskly past him and walked into the sordid kitchen. Whelan and his visitor had been drinking beer out of cans. The two lager tins stood on the table by an ashtray of stubs, and a polystyrene box of the kind take-away food is packaged in. This one looked as if it had contained chips. An unpleasant red smear was presumably tomato sauce. A man, who had been sitting at the table, stood up. Pearce knew him at once. Not because they'd ever met, but because only a short time before he'd been looking at the same face in a newspaper picture.

'Mr Goodhusband, I presume?' he said politely.

'A copper,' said Tristan bitterly, 'and a humorist, too!' He stared belligerently at Pearce. 'What do you want? And how the hell do you know me?'

The ferocity of his tone took Pearce aback. The more so because Tristan Goodhusband, as described by Markby, had been a singularly laid-back figure. Pearce dealt with him now by ignoring him. He turned to Whelan.

'Perhaps we could have a word, Mr Whelan? In private.' He glanced back at Goodhusband.

Before Whelan could answer, Tristan had spoken for him. 'He's got nothing to say to you! And you don't have any right to come and badger him like this. Can't you let the poor bloke alone?'

'I don't know . . .' Whelan whispered.

'Just a five-minute chat, Mr Whelan.'

'You can get lost. You forced your way in here. Do you have any kind of warrant?' Tristan pushed forward, causing the kitchen chair to topple back and land with a crash on the greasy floor. 'Mick's done his time and his life's his own now.'

'Mr Goodhusband,' Pearce said with rising anger, 'would you stop interrupting me?'

'No. If you've got something against Mick, let's hear it. If you haven't, then you can clear out. This isn't a bloody police state!'

'You are obstructing me in my inquiries!' Pearce snapped.

'What inquiries?' Tristan's voice and look were insolent.

'Mr Whelan,' Pearce said. 'It might be easier if we took an unofficial ride down to the station. Nothing to worry about. But we might get some privacy there!'

'You don't have to accompany him, Mick.' Tristan instructed. He turned back to Pearce. 'He's entitled to have a friend with him if he wants. Someone with an interest in his welfare, right? If he wants me here, I stay. You want me here, don't you, Mick?'

The unfortunate Whelan uttered a croak.

'I can,' snarled Pearce, 'take anyone in and hold him for twenty-four hours if I think it necessary!' He emphasised the 'anyone' with a meaning look at his tormentor.

'And I,' said Tristan, 'will get a lawyer down there so fast, you won't have time to switch on the tape. But you haven't come to take anyone in, have you? This is a fishing expedition, right?'

As Pearce's face reddened, Tristan looked satisfied and nodded. 'I thought so. Right, Mick, you say nothing at all to this copper! If he takes you in, I'll see you get a lawyer. Then and only then, with your legal adviser present, can the inspector here, ask you anything! And remember, you've asked for your lawyer. Anything the copper might now get you to say before the legal eagle gets here, will be inadmissable evidence. Police and Criminal Evidence Act.'

'You seem to have studied a few lawbooks yourself!' Pearce snarled.

'Getting shirty, Inspector?' Tristan grinned evilly. 'Tut, tut! Don't like it if someone pushes the rulebook under your nose, eh?'

'Mr Whelan has not been cautioned,' Pearce said, breathing hard. 'He is not under arrest. This is a purely informal call. He's not in a police station but in his own home. Nothing is being recorded. There is no need for a lawyer – or for any dispute about admissable or inadmissable evidence.'

'That's right, his own home.' Tristan nodded. 'And I'm his guest, invited in here by him. Which is more than could be said of you.'

'Are you a frequent visitor here?' Pearce turned his questioning on Tristan, since it was a waste of time trying to talk to Whelan.

'What if I am? It's no concern of yours. I brought Mick over something to eat.' Tristan indicated the empty polystyrene carton. 'He's not been well. Hasn't been able to get out to the shops, right, Mick?'

'Had a touch of flu,' Whelan muttered hoarsely. 'It hangs about. Going though, getting better.' He gave Pearce a shame-faced look. He seemed embarrassed by Goodhusband's vehement defence of his interests.

'Shopping for him?' It was Pearce's turn to resort to sarcasm. 'A four-pack of lager and a take-away? That's not going to see him on very far, is it?'

Tristan's grin was positively triumphant. He walked to the grease-spotted fridge and silently opened the door. Inside could be seen cartons of soya milk, something in a foil tray which looked like a sort of nut loaf and gleaming dully through the plastic front of the vegetable compartment, the reds, greens and oranges of assorted salads.

A vegan, thought Pearce. Tessa's sister had a spell of that. All nuts, lentils and tofu. Fortunately it hadn't lasted long. It made sense, however, for Whelan to be averse to animal fats in any form.

He managed, with superhuman effort, not to swear aloud. He turned to Whelan. 'I'll call and see you some other time. As for you, Mr Goodhusband,' he glared at the other man. 'I'm sure we'll meet again!'

'Look forward to it, Inspector!' Tristan slammed the fridge door with a casual flip of his hand.

The car drew up before the cottage and Sally switched off the engine. 'I don't suppose Liam will have got any lunch so we'll have to wait a few minutes. I didn't have time to prepare anything before I left this morning. I went in to work early, just after eight.'

'Honestly,' Meredith said. 'We could have eaten in town.'

'No, it's all right. It won't take me a jiff. Oh, there is Liam.'

Liam had heard the car. The door of the cottage opened and he appeared, stared and then sauntered to the gate.

'Hullo, Meredith.' He sounded quite welcoming.

'Hullo,' she returned. 'Everything all right?'

He shrugged. 'As well as can be expected. No insulting letters in the post, at least. I didn't know you were coming back with Sal.'

'I'll get us something to eat. You've not eaten already, have you?' Sally asked him.

He shook his head. 'No, been working on the book. It's going a bit better.' So that was why he was in such a rare good mood, Meredith thought. Liam glanced at her. 'See you in a minute. I'll just go and back-up what I've got on disk this morning.'

'And I'll go and root through my fridge. Tell you what,' Sally pointed at the barn-garage. 'Why don't you take a look in the barn, Meredith? I've got what's left of Aunt Emily's things in there. We got rid of most and I picked out what I wanted to keep.

Austin was supposed to be coming out and giving me a valuation but he's not got round to it. I'll have to remind him and get the things in the next sale. But there might be something there of use to you. If so, you're welcome to have it.'

She was pulling open the door as she spoke. They went inside.

Meredith's eyes took a moment to adjust to the dim light. It was as Alan described it, a roomy place, more than adequate for the Caswells' two cars. The barn origins were clear in the rough stone walls. Above their heads, stout, rough-hewn rafters crossed the ceiling. At the far end were the small holes in the masonry which marked where mediaeval scaffolding had been dismantled when the original builders had finished their job. Liam's car stood at the front, by the door. Behind it was stacked a mixed lot of furniture, all kinds, dust-covered but obviously in good condition.

'Just a pity,' said Sally, 'that there wasn't a kitchen table amongst it! It's mostly chairs, sideboards, a couple of wardrobes, that sort of stuff. Old-fashioned and not much to anyone's taste now. But then, you might just see something. Take a good look. Don't worry about pulling stuff out. I'll see you indoors when you're ready.'

'Sure.' There was always something fascinating about being let loose on a pile of junk. Treasure-hunting, thought Meredith. She didn't really have much room at home for more furniture. But the chance to obtain, for example, a set of good oak dining-room chairs, wasn't to be passed up lightly. Or that dear little corner cupboard. Now she could just squeeze that in. She imagined it, snuggled into her living room. She pushed past other pieces to reach it, opened its door and stooped to look inside.

It was as she was like that, bent double with her head half in the cupboard, that she realised she wasn't alone. First of all, she heard the breathing, an odd snuffling breath. There followed a scrape of furniture pushed aside, tapping of feet and, even as she struggled to extricate herself and turn to confront the intruder – biff!

Meredith shot forward, propelled by an undignified and painful blow on the backside, and hit her head on the cupboard door.

'Oy!' she yelled. She scrambled out and up and whirled to face her assailant.

It was a billy-goat. A large brown animal with curved horns and an expression of undisguised glee on its hairy face. It lowered its head and made a butting gesture, as if to demonstrate what it had just done. Aren't I clever? it seemed to be asking.

'You wretched monster!' Meredith told it, rubbing her backside.

The billy took a step forward, reaching out its neck, snuffling.

'Don't you dare!' she threatened.

But she realised that it was not violent in the sense of being bad-tempered. It was playful. Her rear end, presented to the animal as it wandered through the open door, had been just too much to resist.

'You,' she said, 'must be Jasper.'

And he must have come through the hedge from Bodicote's. Neither Liam nor Sally could have spotted the intruder yet. When they did, there would be ructions, certainly on Liam's part.

'Come on, let's get you home.' She took hold of Jasper's leather collar. 'And just cooperate, quietly!'

Jasper seemed encouraged to think this was some kind of game. He trotted beside her amiably enough as she led him across the front of the cottage and down the far side, in order to avoid the kitchen.

She couldn't see either Liam or Sally but there was a faint sound of running tap water and the clang of a pot or kettle.

'Maa-a . . .' offered Jasper suddenly.

'Shush!' she ordered. He rolled a disconcerting chalky blue eyeball at her, with a slit of a pupil. There was something of the satyr about him and not just his goat's legs and wispy beard. There was a wickedness of expression and a knowingness which left one not quite sure what was going on in his head. He was also rather less than fragrant, she realised. When she got back, she wouldn't be surprised if Sally didn't guess what company she'd been keeping.

The gap through which he'd come had been stopped by an old brass bedhead. Such bedheads, she knew, were not without value. But Bodicote had put it to purely practical use. Unfortunately it had become dislodged and fallen flat to lie on the ground on Bodicote's side. Jasper had simply walked through. She couldn't see the other goats but there was a considerable litany of goat complaint coming from a long hut at the far end of Bodicote's land. The goat-house. The door was ajar but something prevented them from coming out. There was no sign of their owner.

Meredith grew curious. She released Jasper on his own turf and he cantered away. With some effort Meredith picked up the bedhead and rewedged it in the gap. Then she went up to Bodicote's kitchen door.

It was open. Meredith looked inside. No one and no sign of recent activity. She called his name but there was no answer.

He must, she supposed, be down at the goat-house. She began to walk down there. Jasper, seeing her, trotted over and kept her company. This, he'd evidently decided, was a friend.

The goat-house door, which opened outward, creaked to and fro in the breeze as she approached and her nostrils were assailed by a strong smell of the assembled nannies within. They sounded distressed. Meredith began to feel uneasy.

'Mr Bodicote?'

Jasper trotted ahead, rounding the swinging door and stopped to snuffle at something on the ground. He uttered another loud 'Maa-a!' and jumped back, kicking up his heels and skittering around the object.

It was then that Meredith saw the foot. Rather, she saw a stout mud-caked boot of old-fashioned design, with nail-studded sole. It was just visible under the creaking door, twisted sideways on the ground and emerging from a grubby corduroy trouser leg. She walked round the door and pushed aside Jasper, who had pranced up to her.

Bodicote sprawled on the trampled turf on his stomach, his head by the goat-house and his feet pointing back at his cottage. He was wearing a thick dark jacket. His cap had fallen off. His face was turned towards her, and rested against a sizable chunk of rubble. The uneven surface was smeared with a dark, sticky substance. Bodicote's visible eye was open and bulged up at her, filmed over. His thin cheek had collapsed inward like a crumpled sheet of parchment. His mouth was open wide in a grotesque yawn so that his long yellow teeth protruded like a rodent's. One of the old man's hands was flung out and the fingers had spread stiffly in onset of the rigor which had first affected eyelids and jaw muscles. It was as though he grasped at something, forever now beyond his reach.

The nannies, aware of a human presence, were bellowing their displeasure. They must be in need of milking. Jasper was standing nearby, watching Meredith intently. When she didn't move, transfixed with horror, the billy grew impatient. He moved forward and sniffed at the prostrate body of his owner.

Meredith was jerked into action. She grabbed at the billy's collar and hauled him away.

'Now now, old chap,' she said. 'He can't play with you now. He's dead, Jasper.'

Chapter Nine

Pearce put his head round Markby's door and found the superintendent glowering at a report held in one hand. In the other, Markby gripped one of the familiar polystyrene tubs which held the unidentifiable liquid disgorged by the machine in the corridor downstairs.

Pearce cleared his throat. The superintendent looked engrossed, even to the point of not noticing how awful the nameless brew was.

Markby looked up, blinked and saw Pearce in the doorway. 'Good, glad you're back. Any luck?'

'I've got a couple of things.' He searched for his notebook, found it and thumbed through to find his notes. 'I called in the office of the local rag and found that article. There was a picture of them all and Mo – the editor – is sending a copy over. All their names and faces are there except one, who's dressed up as a chicken—' Pearce grinned. 'And called A. Bird.'

'Let's see . . .' Markby put down the report and the coffee. He held his hand out for the notebook and quickly scanned the list of names. 'Ask someone to run 'em all through the computer.' He returned the notebook to its owner.

'I – ah – ' Pearce took pleasure in springing a surprise. 'I've met Tristan Goodhusband.'

Markby was gratifyingly startled. 'In person, where? At the *Gazette* offices?' He set down the tub.

'No, I called on Mick Whelan, just on the off-chance, and

there he, Goodhusband, was, likewise doing a spot of visiting.'

Pearce summarized the encounter. 'He's a stroppy blighter, Goodhusband. A bit like that Caswell character. I'd love to know why he's so thick with Whelan. As for the good Samaritan routine, fair enough, maybe.' Pearce gave Tristan grudging acknowledgement of a good deed. 'But why so pally in the first place? The Goodhusband group has nothing to do with the more violent activists. Or so Mrs G. told you, didn't she, sir? So why's her son hobnobbing with Whelan? And him just out of clink, too!' Pearce clicked his tongue disapprovingly. 'Tell you what, I bet young Tristan's mum doesn't know what kind of company he keeps.'

Markby was scowling, turning the news over in his mind. With evident regret, he put it mentally on one side.

'We'll follow it up later. It's intriguing, certainly. Here's the lab report on that cut-and-paste letter Caswell received.' Markby picked up the report he'd been reading, discovering, when he did, that he'd inadvertently set the polystyrene tub down on it, leaving a wet brown ring. He gave a grunt of annoyance and then shrugged.

'All the newsprint used would appear to have come from the *Daily Telegraph*. Not the sort of paper generally read by extreme action groups. That doesn't mean they didn't buy a copy – or used it in an attempt to put us off.'

'Bet they read the *Telegraph* at The Tithe Barn!' growled Pearce, the memory of his encounter with Tristan rankling.

Markby swept on, ignoring him. 'The glue is a common paperglue sold everywhere. The paper likewise. The envelope is more interesting. It's a brown business envelope of the sort sold in bulk by office stationers. Fifty or a hundred envelopes at a time. Not the kind you'd usually buy in your corner shop. The postmark is central London again, that could be in an attempt to put us off.'

'Have to wait and see if he gets another one,' Pearce observed. He wondered how Tessa was getting along. He hoped she didn't go quite overboard with tidying up. The chances were the *Gazette* photographer would only want a snap of them at the front door. Wait till the elder Mrs Pearce heard about it! She'd be buying up umpteen copies of the *Gazette* and posting them all over the place to friends and relatives.

Footsteps could be heard approaching rapidly. An urgent knock on the door was followed by Prescott erupting into the room. 'Sir!'

'Can it wait?' Markby interrupted. 'We're in the middle of something—'

'I think you'd want to know, sir. There's been a fatal accident – out at Castle Darcy!'

'What!' Both the superintendent and the inspector leapt to their feet, momentarily staring disaster in the face.

Dave Pearce gasped, 'Ruddy Caswell? You mean, they got him?'

He paled at the implication of this and all that would follow.

Prescott looked taken aback and then embarrassed as he realised the considerable consternation he'd caused was due to a misunderstanding over identity of the victim.

'No, not at that cottage. Next door. The old bloke, Bodicote. He had a fall or something and bashed his head. Dead as a dodo, I'm afraid. Already a stiff when he was found.'

Pearce uttered a gasp of relief, followed by a spurt of anger. 'For God's sake, why didn't you say so straight away? I thought we'd lost Caswell and there'd be hell to pay!'

'Sorry,' Prescott's face turned a deep red, clashing with the greenish-yellow which had developed around his bruised eye. 'I didn't mean it was a development in our case. It's actually only a local matter. Bamford are handling it, treating it as an accident. Sergeant Jones is in charge there. She thought you'd want to know, even though there's no sign of foul play, so she called through and asked me to tell you. She's out there now.'

'Get hold of her!' Markby exclaimed. 'Tell her not to let them move the body! I want to see it for myself!'

'Yessir. But she did stress there's nothing suspicious—'

'Move!' yelled his superintendent.

Prescott moved.

'Come on, Dave!' Markby said grimly. 'When bodies start dropping in this business for any reason, I want to see things first-hand!'

The sun was beginning to go down in the early winter evening when they reached Castle Darcy. Word had got around and several villagers stood watching from the side of the road opposite Bodicote's cottage. An ambulance waited at the gate, its driver and his partner indulging in a quiet cigarette.

Markby and Pearce nodded at them as they passed, and made their way towards a windswept chilly little group gathered around a sheeted form on the ground at the far end of the plot of land. From the open door of a long hut came a furious maa-ing and stamping of hooves. Even more angry bleats came from a large brown billy-goat. The animal was tethered to a clothes-post by what looked like the clothes-line. It didn't appreciate its activities being curtailed, nor the presence of so many strangers on its home turf. It rushed at the two newcomers, head lowered, but was brought up short by the tether. It bucked in rage.

'Hullo Jasper!' called Markby, identifying it as Meredith had.

'Who?' Pearce was unaware of the billy-goat's name.

Sergeant Jones was already advancing to meet them. 'Hullo there, Gwyneth,' Markby said. 'What have you got here?'

She smiled her welcome and attempted to push back a strand of curling fair hair which the breeze blew across her face.

'We were called just after one o'clock, sir. The doctor's been and certified him dead. He said he thought he'd been dead a few hours, probably since early morning.'

Jones indicated the ground at their feet. 'All the frost has left this ground as hard as iron and slippery. It's pretty cut up, as you can see, from the goats, and frozen in ruts. All in all, very tricky to negotiate. As I see it, the old man came down to see to the animals, slipped and hit his head on that lump of rock.' Jones pointed again.

The sheet over the body didn't quite cover the piece of rubble. The rock itself was composed of concrete in which small stones were embedded. Nor did the sheet disguise the dark stain on its rough surface.

Jones was still talking. 'Either that, or the billy-goat came up behind him and butted him so that he lost balance. It does that, apparently, the billy. We had to tie it up. It chased us all over the field!' She allowed herself a brief grin. 'We tried to drag it into that pen over there, but it dug in its hooves and wouldn't budge. Then Constable Whitmore had the bright idea of tying it to the clothes-post.'

'Where did the chunk of rubble come from?' Markby asked.

'It's a lump from a pile left over from foundations to an extension to the cottage next door.' Jones gestured, widely encompassing the paddock. 'There are pieces of it all over this field. It seems the next-door neighbour, a Dr Caswell, was in the habit of lobbing chunks of it at the goats. They kept getting into his garden.'

'You've had a word with him, then?'

'Yes.' Jones gave Markby an arch look. 'And with Miss Mitchell.'

'Meredith?' He was startled and couldn't disguise it.

'Yes, sir. She found the body.' Jones nodded at the cottage next door. 'She's still there, with the Caswells, if you want a word with her. I thought, as soon as I saw Miss Mitchell, that you'd want to know about it. She told me about the goat butting people. It butted her, apparently. Came up behind her while she was bending down looking at something, and sent her flying!'

'Did it?' Despite the sombre situation, Markby suppressed a grin.

'Yes – so it might have done the same thing to the old man, mightn't it?'

Pearce had been studying the layout of the ground. 'If that piece of stone got over here originally from next door by Caswell throwing it at a goat, all I can say is that it's a blooming big lump of rock for *anyone* to chuck about!' he observed. 'Caswell must be an Olympic class shot-putter to get it as far as this! We're about as far from the boundary fence as we can be here. I reckon no one could throw that more than six, seven feet, and that's without getting much elevation on it.' He glanced at the Caswell cottage and as he did, a light came on in the kitchen. It was already getting dark indoors.

'So I suppose that lets him out, I mean, as far as throwing it at a goat and hitting the old man instead goes.'

'I did consider that and discount it,' Jones said. 'As you say, it's too big a chunk to go throwing around.' She hesitated. 'Anyway, I asked him and he doesn't reckon he threw that bit, sir, not today, not ever. Much too big, as you say. The smaller pieces around the field, yes. He admits he shied a few of those at the goats. But although he agrees that piece must have come from his property, he doesn't offer any explanation other than that the old man pinched it and brought it here. He says the old man was apt to wander on and off his property, much as the goats did.'

'What would he want it for?' Pearce asked.

Jones smiled in triumph. 'See the door of the goat-house here?' She pointed. 'It opens outwards. It looks as if the old man had helped himself to a lump of the rubble, a big lump, in order to use it as a door stop here.'

'Makes sense, Gwyneth, certainly,' Markby agreed. He'd always had respect for Jones. She'd been a constable over at Bamford when he'd been there. She deserved to have made sergeant and to go further. He'd had a good team all round at Bamford. He missed them and those days still.

The goats in the hut were still stomping and the smell was getting stronger.

Pearce had noticed it too and observed. 'Those things are crapping all over the place in there. Someone's going to have to clean them out and generally look after them, like.'

'The door of the hut, that was open when you got here?'

Jones nodded.

Markby went to the door and glanced in. It was a roomy hut with a raised platform at one end. The nannies were penned behind a lattice, a movable, temporary structure. It looked home-made and would have enabled Bodicote to control the goats within the hut. But for that, he thought, they'd have got out of the door and strayed all over the place.

Seeing him, they'd stretched out their necks and were bleating in a cacophony of sound. He met the nearest baleful goat eye.

'All right, girls, won't be much longer. Someone will see to you,' he promised.

Markby went back to the others and asked Jones, 'Has any relative been informed?'

'Yes. A niece, a Mrs Sutton. She's on her way over.'

'Right,' Markby dropped on to his heels. 'Let's have a look at him.'

The sheet was turned back. Bodicote lay as Meredith had found him. His head was towards the door of the goat-house and his feet roughly pointing towards his cottage. Markby touched the outstretched hand. It wasn't as stiff as he'd anticipated. Experimentally, he tried to raise Bodicote's middle finger. It was awkward, wooden, but still movable. In the failing light, the features were grey-blue and shrivelled. He looked almost mummified.

'Take the sheet away completely,' Markby ordered.

It was removed and the entire body revealed. Markby studied it, noting the position of all the limbs, its distance from the goat-house and the surrounding earth.

'Anything been moved?'

'No, sir. The doctor had to touch him but he was clearly dead and it didn't involve actually turning him over or anything like that.'

'How about his clothing? Any of that disarranged?'

Gwyneth Jones shook her head, her eyes curious. 'Got something in mind, sir?'

'What?' Markby turned his head to look at her. 'Oh, no. Just checking. How about his cap? That was there when you first saw him?'

Jones looked at Bodicote's cap which lay near his head. 'Yes, sir. As far as I know – I mean, I haven't moved it.' She raised her voice and called to one of two constables nearby, 'Neither of you moved his cap, did you?'

They denied it.

'What's worrying you, sir?' Pearce asked quietly.

'Nothing. I like to get a clear picture. Talking of pictures, the photographer's been out and got shots of all this?'

Jones nodded.

Markby heaved a sigh. 'Fine, you can tell the meat-wagon to take him away. I just wanted to see it as it was.'

Jones asked hesitantly, doubt in her voice, 'It does look like an accident, sir, doesn't it? Have I missed something?'

Before Markby could reply there was a shout. They all looked up.

Striding across the ground towards them was a woman, accompanied by a constable. She was a tall and rangily built person, clad in drab work clothes, grubby jacket, slacks and gumboots. She looked as if she'd been called from the farm herself. She was, however, made up in a hit or miss way, rather as though she'd dispensed with the use of a mirror. Scarlet lipstick was applied lopsidedly and mascara smudged above her eyes in two uneven patches.

'Maureen Sutton!' she announced as she came up. 'What's this about Uncle Hector? I've had to drive thirty miles.' At that point she saw the shape on the ground. 'Is that him? Is that the old chap?' She sounded shaken.

'I'm very sorry, Mrs Sutton,' Gwyneth Jones said. 'We will require a formal identification, but that can be done later, at the morgue.'

'Might as well take a look now,' Mrs Sutton rallied. 'Get it over with. What happened? Heart attack?'

'We don't know exactly, Mrs Sutton. There will have to be a post-mortem. He may have slipped.'

The sheet was turned back. Mrs Sutton stared down silently. She nodded and the sheet was decorously replaced.

'Uncle Hector,' she said. She searched in her pocket and drew out a grimy square of linen with which she rubbed at her face, smearing the mascara and lipstick even more. 'Poor old bugger.'

'Mrs Sutton,' Markby said gently, 'we don't want to distress you with questions, but I wonder if you recognise that lump of rubble.'

She gestured at the door. 'He used it to prop that open.'

'So it's in its normal position?'

'The rock? Yes, I suppose so. What's the matter with those nannies?'

Mrs Sutton marched past them and into the goat-house. 'Bloody hell!' she was heard to exclaim in a disgusted tone. She reappeared. 'Couldn't you milk them?'

'We were more concerned with your uncle,' Sergeant Jones protested. 'And we're not goat experts.'

'You're not deaf, are you? Poor brutes are bellowing their guts out! How would you like it if your udder was bursting with milk and no one did anything about it?'

Jones reddened. The constable put his hand to his mouth. Pearce stared up at the sky.

'Well, I'll do it,' said Mrs Sutton. 'Since someone's got to.'

'Is it possible,' Markby asked her, 'for you or someone else to arrange for them to be taken care of for the immediate future?'

She stared at him. 'Gary – my son – will bring the trailer over tomorrow and move them over to our place.' She pointed at the sheeted shape. 'And how much longer are you going to leave my uncle lying there? It's not exactly decent, is it?'

Bodicote's body had been removed, watched by silent villagers. Pearce and Markby walked across the paddock, through Bodicote's scrap of garden, much mauled by goats, to the open kitchen door.

'There's an empty mug here, had tea in it.' Pearce was inspecting the draining board. 'It looks as if he got up and made a cuppa. Then went down, let out the billy, and was going to let out the nannies, got the door open, when he slipped, or the billy butted him. Or he had a heart attack perhaps and just dropped?'

Markby was nodding. 'Well, it's Gwyneth's problem. But we'll just go next door and have a word with the Caswells – and with Meredith, since she apparently found him.'

And how did that come about? he wondered.

Both Caswells and Meredith were in the Caswell kitchen, sitting round the table, fortifying themselves with a dram a-piece of malt whisky. A sizable dram, by the look of it. Each of them had a slightly squiffy look.

Apart from that, Meredith was looking pale but composed enough. Nevertheless, clear signs of relief appeared on her face as she saw him. She exclaimed, 'Oh, Alan! Thank goodness!' sounding, Markby thought, rather like a frontierswoman in a Western who has spotted the arrival of the cavalry just as the last box of ammunition has been broken open. Still, it was nice that she was pleased to see him, whatever the circumstances.

'There you are, Superintendent!' Liam hailed the newcomers after his own fashion. 'And the inspector, too? Everyone turns out for the old man!'

'Liam . . .' Sally whispered.

'All right, all right!' Liam waved a hand at his wife to calm her protest. 'I won't behave badly! I am sorry, really, for the old chap. It's no way to go.'

'What isn't?' Markby asked politely.

Liam gave him a suspicious look. 'What's this? Quiz time? I mean, dropping dead in your back garden – or in your goat-pen, whatever you care to call Bodicote's backyard.'

'Won't you both sit down?' Sally asked. 'I suppose you don't drink on duty?' She picked up the bottle of malt. 'I'm not a drinker ordinarily. But what with all that's happened recently, I think I'll finish up a candidate for AA!'

'Oh, I'm not on duty,' Markby told her amiably. 'Sergeant Jones from Bamford station is in charge of this matter.'

'In that case,' Sally got up. 'I'll fetch a couple more glasses. There's water in the jug. It's Scottish spring water, from a bottle, not plain old water from the tap.'

Pearce had cheered visibly. Markby settled himself in his chair.

'I just came over, with the inspector, to take a look. Naturally I was interested, since I interviewed the deceased recently in connection with your problem, Dr Caswell. It's contiguous to my inquiries, shall we say?'

Liam hummed the tune *If you want to know the time, ask a policeman!* Then he met his wife's eye and said, 'Sorry, I've had a couple of whiskies. After your Sergeant Jones came over and cross-examined us all. All this – anonymous mail, exploding letters, bodies in the backyard. It's got to my nerves, I'll admit. I was taking refuge in a spot of graveyard humour.'

Markby, knowing that police officers saved their sanity by doing likewise, was not unsympathetic. For once, Liam's manner was understandable and to be excused.

'You were here all morning, Dr Caswell, I understand? Thank you, Mrs Caswell.' Markby accepted a generous measure of whisky. Pearce did the same.

165

'All morning.' Liam nodded. 'We both of us made an early start today. Sal had got behind at the auction rooms and wanted to go in early. She brought me my flask of coffee as usual. I was already in my study, been there since six. I'm so behind with the book I've had to put in all the hours I can get.' He looked moody.

'Ah yes. You don't go and make yourself coffee. I remember. Yet it's only a step, surely, from your study to the kitchen here?' Markby asked him mildly.

Liam flushed. 'It's a disruption, if the book's going well. Having to break off, get up, go out and boil water. Easier just to unscrew the vacuum flask and pour out a cup if I want one. But, as it happens, this morning the book went so well, I didn't even bother with the coffee. The flask is still in my study, still full. Sally left around eight, didn't you, Sal? I just carried on working until I heard her car come back. That was just before one, say twelve-forty-five? I got up and looked out the window and saw that Meredith had come back with her to lunch. I went out to meet them. Prior to that I hadn't left my desk. No, not even to pee, Superintendent, in case you want to know that, too!'

'In all that time, you didn't hear the goats? They were kicking up quite a row when I got there.'

'I didn't. Not consciously, anyway. I was engrossed in my work. Also the windows are shut. Cold weather. Superintendent, I've already told that woman sergeant all this!' Liam's voice rose and became aggrieved.

Markby ignored the protest. 'There are windows on both sides of the extension, I noticed. Facing the road and facing the back of the property.'

Liam smiled thinly. 'Yes, but I didn't look out. Even if I had done so, I can't see Bodicote's goat-house. There's a fairly high hawthorn hedge growing on a low bank which divides the lower half of these two properties.'

'Mmn.' Markby finished his malt, rolling it appreciatively round his tongue. He turned to Sally. 'How about you, Mrs

Caswell? You didn't notice anything amiss when you left the cottage this morning?'

'On Bodicote's side of the fence? No, but I wouldn't. It was still quite dark. I didn't go round the back of the cottages. I went out of the front door to the garage, checked over my car as we were told to do—' Sally winced '—and drove into work. These cold dark mornings are so unpleasant, I don't think anyone takes much notice of anything. Liam had got up early to work on the book as he told you. I didn't feel like breakfast. I've been feeling queasy in the mornings. As Liam had said he didn't want to stop, once he got going on the book, I decided to give breakfast a miss and didn't make any. I know that's bad for you.' She sounded apologetic.

'I frequently don't have breakfast,' Markby told her, which was true. 'The lump of rubble on which Mr Bodicote appears to have struck his head, that came from your property, it seems?'

'Probably.' Liam took up the narrative. 'Go round the back of my garage and you'll see a whole pile of it. It went into the foundations of the extension.' Liam leaned forward. 'Look, I know I threw the odd bit of it at the goats. But only small bits. I didn't heave a great boulder! He must have come over here and helped himself to a piece at some time or other. He was like that. He wandered about, all over the village. He was eccentric. Dotty.'

It had been Markby's opinion that Bodicote had been remarkably in possession of his senses. But that, alas, was no longer here nor there. He turned to Meredith.

'You found him?' he asked sympathetically. It was a pity she'd had to be the one. But knowing her as he did, she'd cope. She had an ability to deal with the unexpected and keep her head which never failed to earn his admiration.

'Yes.' She sat up and tossed back her thick brown hair, her manner practical. 'I was in Sally's barn, looking at some furniture when the goat snuk up on me!' She looked aggrieved. 'Just for the purpose, I'd got my head stuck in a cupboard and I must have presented a wonderful target! It got me amidships and sent me flying! I know Liam—' She glanced at Caswell. '—doesn't like the goats getting through into this garden. So I thought I'd better take the goat home. I saw where it'd got through the hedge. I looked in Bodicote's kitchen. He wasn't there. I went down to the far end of his plot of land and – and found him.'

In a nutshell. Markby asked. 'Did you move him?'

'Of course I didn't, Alan!' She was indignant at the very suggestion.

'All right, I'm sorry. Had to ask. What did you do?'

'Raced back here and raised the alarm. Liam went down and took a look, didn't you, Liam?'

Liam grimaced. 'Yes. I didn't touch him. I came back and phoned the police and ambulance.'

Markby thought for a while. They all sat and watched him. At last he asked, 'The door of the goat-house, Meredith. Did you touch that, open it or shut it?'

'No, left it. It was open. The nannies were bleating. But I didn't have time for them.'

'But Jasper was loose!' Markby muttered to himself.

Sally spoke. 'He always let Jasper out first. Jasper has a house to himself, to one side of the main goat-house. A sort of little hut and pen. Bodicote was rather fond of the billy. It was a kind of pet. It used to kick up a fuss of a morning until he went down and let it out.' Her voice trembled. 'It's so sad. He was an awkward old man in some ways but harmless.'

Markby gestured, dismissing this. Harmless or not, Bodicote was dead. At the moment, he wanted to concentrate on Jasper. 'I didn't see any gap in the hedge where the animal could have got through.'

'Oh, there was!' Meredith replied quickly. 'It's up near this end of the back garden. It's blocked with an old bedhead. But that had fallen flat. I picked it up and wedged it back in again.'

'Completely flat?'

She looked puzzled. 'Yes. Just fallen out, on Bodicote's side. It was heavy. If it was dislodged by the billy-goat pushing at it, it would just collapse, I suppose.'

'I see.' Markby got up. 'Well, I'm very sorry you've got this to deal with now, Mrs Caswell – Dr Caswell. I understand Mrs Sutton, who is Bodicote's niece, will be making arrangements to remove the goats tomorrow.'

'Thank God!' Liam said.

Meredith was getting to her feet. 'Can you give me a lift back into Bamford? Will it be out of your way? I came out here in Sally's car.'

'I can run you home!' Sally said at once.

'I'll take you home.' Markby smiled at her. 'Got to drop Inspector Pearce off, anyway. Hope you won't find the press besieging your house, Dave!'

'Oh blimey!' said the stricken Pearce. 'I'd forgotten that!'

Tessa flew out of the front door as they drew up.

'Dave! Where on earth have you been? Oh, sorry, Superintendent, didn't see you there!' She stooped, peering into the car, allowing them to see that her normally loose-flowing hair was tortured and sprayed fast into some sort of topknot with corkscrew strands framing her face.

'Have they been?' Pearce asked, scrambling out.

'No, they rang to say the photographer's calling tomorrow morning, nine o'clock. I said we'd both be here. It will be all right, won't it, Superintendent? I mean, if Dave comes in to work a bit later? Only, the *Gazette*—'

'I've heard all about it, Tessa. Of course he must be here for the press! Goodnight!'

Markby drove on to Meredith's terraced home. 'Here we are. All right, are you, now?'

'I'm fine. It was a shock. I can't say he was a dear old man.

169

But he was a character. It's a great pity. I think Liam's upset too, only he doesn't know how to show it. I mean, to know the poor old chap was lying dead all morning, perhaps. What do you think happened?'

'Post-mortem will tell us.'

She had opened her door and swivelled to put one leg out of the car. Now she twisted back to face him. His face was shadowy in the street lighting. Meredith asked, 'It was an accident, wasn't it? Sergeant Jones seemed to think so.'

'Oh, I dare say. Sort of thing happens all the time. Domestic accidents account for any amount of injuries, some quite serious. People fall off ladders, down the stairs, trip over the dog . . .'

'Or goat. I hope it wasn't Jasper.' Meredith prepared once more to get out of the car. 'But he did creep up on me and butt me into that cupboard. He's playful. It would be awful, though, if he were responsible for the death of his owner. Mr Bodicote was rather proud of that goat.'

A voice echoed in Markby's head.

You do what's important to you first, don't you? Like I ran down to see if old Jasper was safe . . .

A wave of great sadness swept over Markby. Aloud he said softly, 'A married woman grabs at her baby; an unmarried one reaches for her jewel-box.'

'Alan?' Meredith was staring at him.

'Nothing,' he said.

'Are you coming indoors?'

He shook his head. 'No, get yourself an early night. You've had an upsetting day. I'll call you. Goodnight.'

Meredith watched him drive away, but didn't go indoors at once. She walked down the road looking over walls and under hedges, occasionally calling out, 'Puss!' and making the sort of noises people make to attract cats. She called up a couple of neighbourhood felines, but not the one she was looking for. When she'd checked the entire block, she went through the house and checked the backyard. She even collected a tin of catfood from the cupboard and stood outside tapping it with a spoon and calling, all to no avail.

Chilled and feeling slightly foolish, she went indoors. It was a disastrous day in every way. Bodicote dead. Sally upset again. No cat.

Alan had reached his own Victorian villa. The click of his key echoed in the empty hall. It was, as always, untidy, lonely, looking more like a place half-packed up for someone to move out than a place where someone lived. The chances of ever getting Meredith to move into it seemed pretty remote. She prized her independence and he respected it. But he envied Pearce.

As he settled down before his TV with a mug of coffee and a plate of hastily grilled sausages, he felt, as Meredith had done, that it had been a bad day. There was something evil at work out there, and he had failed so far to track it down.

As for Bodicote, that was probably just a sad accident which had occurred at a difficult moment.

'But I don't like coincidences around death!' he said obstinately aloud into the deserted space around him. 'I've been a copper too long!'

Perhaps he had, at that, and saw mysteries where none existed. He sawed furiously at a lump of sausage. Either it was tough or the knife was blunt. Nor could he remember whether the packet had claimed the contents to be pork, beef, or a mixture of the two. They didn't taste particularly like any of these. At least, he could presume it wasn't goat.

'Jasper,' he mused. 'You could tell us exactly what happened, I dare say. If you could speak.'

Chapter Ten

'And what brings you, Alan?' inquired Dr Fuller. 'No murder cases on the table at the moment, are there?'

Markby reflected grimly that when the pathologist said 'on the table' he meant it literally. Fuller's detached interest in cutting up bodies was something which elicited both admiration and repugnance from the superintendent. It was the regard due to someone who did a job one knew one couldn't do oneself, whatever the circumstances. Not that Markby was squeamish. He'd long got past that. It was that people, for him, remained people, even when dead. They didn't become mere anatomical specimens.

Perhaps – and he'd often wondered about this – his clinging to the belief in the innate humanity of a cadaver, was a way of clinging to a belief in the essential humanity of all mankind, however depraved. Each of us had to be more than a clever piece of biological engineering. This seemed to him self-evident. After all, he'd reasoned, as a policeman, what would be the purpose of inquiring into any death if the cessation of a life were only akin to a machine being switched off.

Fuller himself was apparently untroubled by metaphysics and relentlessly cheerful. But then, he had to be, thought Markby. If it ever got to him, he'd have to give the job up. He acknowledged Fuller's welcome, adding, 'No murder perhaps. But a body. An elderly man, Hector Bodicote. I thought that the autopsy might have been carried out by now.'

'Oh yes, head injury, right?' Fuller looked over his glasses. 'Want to see him?'

'No, thanks.' Not in the state Fuller would have left him. Although, in due course, the body would be patched together so that the relatives could have Bodicote laid out tidily in his coffin.

'It's not a murder inquiry,' Markby said. 'At least, not as far as I know. Nor is it strictly my concern. He was a peripheral witness to something I've been looking at. How about cause of death? There's a suggestion he might have slipped and hit his head. You'd go along with that?'

'Tsk, tsk!' Fuller smiled happily. 'Now when did I ever commit myself completely to any theory, eh?'

'Never that I can recall,' Markby admitted.

'I am not a detective!' announced Fuller. 'I'm a doctor whose patients are already dead. I can diagnose the damage which caused death, but not the circumstances in which they came by it, since I can't ask 'em about their symptoms, or how they came by their bumps and bruises. I'd inevitably be led into the realms of guesswork. Unless, of course, someone's obligingly left a dagger sticking out of their backs! Even then, one has to be careful not to be misled. But you know that.' Facetiously, and with an excruciating attempt at a Cockney accent, Fuller added, ''E was strangled, guv. Hit wiv a blunt instrument and stabbed – before he was shot!'

He looked apologetically at Markby. 'Only he wasn't, if you see what I mean. Wasn't poisoned, strangled or shot.'

'So, what was he?' Markby allowed impatience to show.

Fuller, unfazed, beckoned. 'Follow me!'

Markby followed him down the corridor. The smell of death lingered here together with mixed odours of various chemicals and disinfectants. He hated this place, always had.

Fuller's office was cluttered, warm and relatively sane in appearance. At least the charnel-house atmosphere was blessedly absent.

'Heard about our faith, have you?' Fuller asked jovially.

Markby hesitated. It was certainly some time since he'd seen Fuller and it was possible that the pathologist and his wife had become reborn spiritually in the meantime, but he hadn't heard of it.

'You remember Faith, don't you?' Fuller was pointing at a framed photograph of his formidable trio of daughters. 'On the left.'

Of course! He'd nearly put his foot in it there! Gratefully, Markby exclaimed, 'Yes, of course I do. Plays the violin.'

'Clarinet, old chap. Miranda plays the violin. You haven't been to one of our musical evenings for ages. I'll give you a call when we arrange the next.'

Markby mumbled thanks with a sinking heart. He wasn't blessed with a musical ear. It all sounded screechy and squeaky to him. Miranda on the violin especially . . .

'She's decided to take up medicine and has got a place at Oxford. It's a pity she couldn't have gone in for music, but making a living at it is difficult. Not that making a living out of any branch of medicine is very easy these days. However, Faith is thinking along the lines of medical research.'

Like Liam Caswell. It brought Markby back to the matter in hand.

'Bodicote . . .' he murmured.

'Got it.' Fuller had dived into a filing-cabinet and emerged with a folder. 'Only just put this in here. These are my preliminary notes. Someone's typed them up and should be sending down a nice clean copy to Bamford. I thought they were handling it?' Fuller peered over the tops of his spectacles.

'They are. I'm trespassing. But I'd like a copy of your final report, for my own interest.'

'By all means. I'll send one over to you. Where are we – ah, here we are. I remember, anyway. Carried out the autopsy last thing yesterday. Had to rush it a bit, we were going out to dinner.

But there were no problems. The old man was very fit for his age. No sign of heart disease. Joints beginning to stick. He'd sustained a severe blow to the head and it killed him. I can give you that in technical jargon, but it amounts to that. Severe fracture, shock, internal damage, a lot of bleeding into the brain.'

'So you'd go along with a fall out of doors, occasioning a blow to the head?'

'No reason to suppose not. What you've said is more or less what I concluded. I understand he was found with his head resting on a lump of concrete.'

'A chunk of rubble he'd used as a doorstop for his goat-house. You had a chance to match the wound and the rock in question?'

Fuller nodded. 'Yes. It was a good match.'

'He'd have died instantly?'

Fuller pursed his lips. 'Instantly? Yes, he may well have been killed outright. If not, he certainly died fairly quickly. It was a mortal blow, certainly. He'd have been unconscious and lying out there in the open, early in the day, hypothermia would have played a role. Post-mortem hypostasis suggests the body had lain undisturbed for some time after falling to the ground and the reddish colour of the affected area suggests cold conditions.'

'So a fall rendering unconscious, followed by a prolonged period lying on frozen ground.'

'That would be a safe diagnosis. I can't tell you exactly when he died. I never can. You know that. From the outward signs, I'd say he died early yesterday morning.'

Markby thought it over. 'Had he breakfasted?'

'No. Several hours since his last meal. Small quantity of milky liquid in the stomach. Had a cup of tea.'

'I touched his hand. It wasn't all that stiff. I'd have thought, being elderly and so on, dead for several hours, rigor would have been more advanced, especially in the extremities.'

'Oh, rigor.' Fuller shook his head. 'The cold might have played a part in delaying it. I had a body in here a few weeks back, found in cold conditions out in the open, been lying there two days, still as limp as a haddock.'

'There's absolutely nothing else you can tell me?'

Fuller scanned his notes. 'He'd been handling animals shortly before his death, or that would be my guess. Animal grease on his hands and animal hair under his fingernails. I sent the scrapings over to the lab but I'd expect them to confirm that.'

Fuller looked up. 'The smell, you know. I'm particularly sensitive to the odour of goats. I had an aunt used to keep the brutes. She made a particularly awful cheese from their milk. Although, they tell me, it's the latest fashion in eating fads and people pay the earth for it. But as soon as he came in, I thought to myself, hullo! Goats!'

Markby sighed. 'Fair enough.' He thought of Jasper. 'What colour goat hair – supposing you to be right and that's what it is?'

Fuller looked surprised. 'Er – white, mostly.'

The nannies. They were mostly white, Markby recollected. He'd check with the lab but Fuller, always careful not to commit himself, wouldn't have suggested goats if he hadn't been sure.

He brought out a photograph with which he'd armed himself before coming. 'This is the scene of the accident with the body in position as it was found. Perhaps you've already seen it.'

Fuller studied the photo. 'Ah, yes. It's what I'd expect. I don't see a problem, to be frank. Not unless you can be specific.' He peered over his spectacles. 'That's the best I can do for you.'

'Appreciate it. It's not my case, as I said. I'm just checking. I suppose someone from Bamford has been down here?'

'Sergeant Jones. She showed me the same picture. She seemed happy enough with a fall and a crack on the skull. I wasn't able to find any mysterious, unexplained bruises or anything like that. No punctures of the skin from needles, no strange substances in the body. A blow on the head is always dangerous and, at his age, unsurprisingly fatal. It's only in cartoons or the sort of action films where people get hit over the noggin with a bottle, that the victim gets up and walks away.' Fuller chuckled.

'Thank you, Malcolm, I'm obliged.' Markby rose to take his leave.

'Give you a call about the musical evening,' Fuller promised. Markby hoped he'd forget.

He returned to regional HQ to find that Pearce had arrived, fresh from his encounter with the photographer from the *Gazette*.

'Go all right?' Markby asked him.

'Bloomin' waste of time!' Pearce said in disgust. 'He turned up, drank a cup of coffee, took a snap of us on the front doorstep and buzzed off again. Tess was really disappointed. She'd worked herself into a frazzle getting the house in order.'

'That's the press for you!' Markby consoled him. 'It'll probably look quite good when the picture's printed up.'

Pearce didn't look convinced.

'This'll cheer you up,' Prescott appeared in the doorway. 'I got a print-out on Tristan Goodhusband as long as my arm. The bloke's a professional trouble-maker. Never had a regular job as far as anyone can tell. He just goes from one organised protest to another. He fills in the time between with meetings and distributing his pamphlets, either on behalf of his mother's group, which is harmless enough, or others not so above-board. He's a familiar in the magistrates' courts all over the country, breach of the peace, causing an obstruction, you know the sort of thing. Gets a fine which he can always pay. Mummy's loaded with loot. He's no fan of the police, forever accusing us of over-reacting, if not worse. He's one of those who lies down in the road in front of cattle transporters and has to be hauled away for his own safety. Whereupon he accuses the police of heavy-handed tactics!' Prescott looked aggrieved.

'Depends which side of the thin blue line you're on, I suppose,' Markby told him.

This comment clearly shocked Prescott to whom it must have smacked of heresy.

The superintendent nodded to the offended sergeant with a mollifying, 'Good work. See what you can run down on his friends and acquaintances.'

Prescott retreated. Pearce observed, 'Someone like that, who keeps getting himself picked up and charged with minor offences, probably isn't into clandestine bomb-making.' He sounded regretful. However Tristan felt about the police force, as far as Pearce was concerned, the dislike was mutual.

Markby dismissed Tristan for the time being. 'I've been following up the death of the old man. Even though it appears to be just an accident, one of those unfortunate but not unusual things. I've been down to the morgue. Fuller is content with a fall, striking the head on the lump of rubble.'

Pearce cast him a sidelong glance. 'But you're not happy about that, sir?'

Markby glanced at the clock on the wall. It was nearly twelve. 'Tell you what, Dave, I'll buy you a pint. That place of Fuller's leaves its smell in my nostrils.'

There was a pub not too far away which did a line in baked jacket potatoes at lunchtime. It being lunchtime, Markby and Pearce ordered a potato a-piece at the bar and settled themselves in a convenient corner with their pints. It was an old place. The fire roared cheerfully in the inglenook hearth and the horse brasses nailed along the oak beams gleamed. Warm and comfortable, Markby settled back and relaxed as Pearce expanded his account of Tessa's disappointment with regard to the press, something which was obviously going to dominate conversation in the Pearce household for some time to come.

'One prawn, one ham and cheese!' The two baked potatoes appeared before them.

'Thanks, Jenny.' Markby acknowledged her brisk delivery of

their lunch, even though she'd put them down the wrong way round.

He exchanged the prawn, which was Pearce's, for the cheese and ham, which was his. He liked seafood, but not in baked potatoes. It seemed to him a needless affectation. A baked spud was a rural dish, the labourer's hot lunch in days gone by. Where, this far inland, had a son of the soil been able to get himself prawns?

'So, sir,' said Pearce some minutes later when both potatoes were pretty well demolished. 'What's worrying you? Is it something about the old fellow, Bodicote?'

'Oh, Bodicote.' Markby drained his glass. 'Care for another?'

'My shout,' Pearce said. He returned shortly with the fresh pints. When he'd set them down, Markby began, 'This is just a chat over a pint, Dave. There's nothing to go on. It's just that I feel dissatisfied about it. You know the feeling?'

Pearce nodded. Sometimes it was all a police officer had to go on, that instinct which warned all was not well. It seldom let the experienced copper down. If Markby wasn't happy about Bodicote's death, Pearce was prepared to listen carefully.

'There's nothing,' Markby was saying, 'which can't be perfectly well explained. I'm nit-picking, as they say. Looking for little oddities which don't quite fit. But then, if everything did fit exactly, that would be suspect in its own way, wouldn't it? I mean, this world's full of imperfections. Every bit of evidence has its weak point. That's where defence lawyers earn their exorbitant fees. If everything's too perfect, then I start smelling a different sort of rat. The careful crook, checking every detail.'

'I've been thinking about it, too!' Pearce said unexpectedly. 'I don't like coincidences, either. I mean, the old man choosing just this time to fall over in his own field. How many times had he gone down there of a morning and let the goats out? Hundreds. Every day of the year for God knows how many years. And now . . .' Pearce sighed.

'Every day, regular as clockwork,' Markby muttered. 'A routine which never varied.'

A shout of laughter came from a group of young men at the further end of the bar. They were sharp-suited and pale of complexion. They appeared to be celebrating something.

'One or two of them are going to be over the limit!' Pearce said. He'd been keeping a wary eye on the group.

'His cap.'

'What?' Pearce put down his glass.

'The old man's cap.' Markby clenched his fist. 'See, this is Bodicote's head. Right? And this,' he placed his open hand flat over his fist, 'is his cap. Use your imagination. Bodicote comes a purler. Falls absolutely flat and hits his head. The cap falls off, thus . . .'

Markby turned his open hand over representing the cap, and let it drop on the table, palm uppermost. 'You see what I mean? I'd have expected his cap, in falling off, to have turned over and landed with the lining facing upwards. But it was lying with the lining downwards, on the turf.'

'Ah,' said Pearce doubtfully.

'Of course, you can say, and you'd be quite right, that I'm only supposing that it would fall off in that way. It could have landed the other way. It did, to all appearances.'

Pearce was silent, sipping his beer and thinking it over. 'Anything else?' he ventured. 'I mean, with respect, it's not much.'

'No, it isn't.' Markby agreed. 'How about this? The goat-house door was open. So why was he lying with his head towards the goat-house and his feet towards his cottage? That indicates he was walking from his cottage to the goat stable when he fell. But evidence suggests he'd already been in the goat-house. If he'd left it and fell, his head would have pointed the other way.'

'He went back to his kitchen for something and was returning to the goat-house,' objected Pearce.

Markby ploughed on determinedly. 'Fuller reckons, and we expect the lab will confirm it, that the old chap had been handling the goats. Grease on his hands and hairs beneath the fingernails. He'd been in the goat-house. They needed milking. Why suddenly break off?'

'He let Jasper out first,' said Pearce. 'The dirt on his hands came from Jasper.'

'White hairs, the nanny-goats.'

'Jasper's not all brown. He's got some white hair.' Pearce paused in playing devil's advocate to observe, 'Funny, you can't help talking about that goat as though it were a person.'

Markby put down his glass with such violence that the contents spilled. 'I talked with Bodicote. He was an eccentric, I agree, but a genuine one and despite what Caswell says, Bodicote was both sharp and literate. He liked to read Conan Doyle and could identify a quotation at the drop of a hat.'

'Bit of a joke, that,' Pearce observed. 'Drop of a hat. The old man's cap puzzling you and so on – sorry!' Hastily he added, 'What did you make of that beefy woman, that Mrs Sutton? Reckon she inherits? I mean, how much would the old boy be worth?'

'Land might be worth something. The cottage – renovated it would be highly desirable, I expect. But at the moment it's almost fit to be condemned. Just held together by the grime of ages. Other than that? What's the price of goats on the market?'

'Old blokes like Bodicote,' said Pearce wisely, 'keep their wealth in notes between the mattress and the bedsprings, or under a loose floorboard. They don't trust banks.' He paled. 'Hey! Did Gwyneth check that cottage to see if anyone had turned it over?'

'I think,' Markby looked ruefully at the spilt beer and signalled to the barmaid to bring a cloth, 'that I'll go over to Bamford and have a word with Sergeant Jones. In the meantime, Dave, how well do you know your Sherlock Holmes?'

'Seen the telly version.'

'Recognise this? . . . the curious incident of the dog in the night-time. *The dog did nothing in the night-time.* That was the curious incident . . .' Markby raised his eyebrows.

Pearce shook his head. 'Got me. I think I remember it but I couldn't tell you which story it's from.'

'*Silver Blaze*. Silver Blaze is a racehorse. What we've got here is a goat. Drink up. We're on tax-payers' time!'

'Dogs, horses, goats,' muttered Pearce into his glass. 'Bloomin' Noah's Ark!'

It was one thing to tell Pearce he meant to have an informal word with Jones, but quite another actually to carry out this apparently simple objective. So Alan Markby reflected as he drove to Bamford police station the following day.

He was a member of the regional squad and, so far at least, not involved with inquiries into the sudden death of Hector Bodicote. That was until now something which had happened by chance next door to the scene of an investigation in which he was involved. Jones wouldn't mind. She'd be happy to chat about it. But Jones wasn't in charge of Bamford station. Apparently an Inspector Winter now was.

Markby hadn't met Winter. All he knew was that Winter held the job which he himself had held for so many years, running Bamford. It filled him with a mild resentment towards Winter – but nothing, he suspected, so much as the resentment Winter might hold towards him. To Winter, if Markby wasn't very careful, it would look as if the former Bamford chief was returning to his old haunts to tell them how to run their business. In Winter's shoes, he wouldn't like it.

But he couldn't avoid Winter. Simple courtesy demanded he call on the inspector first and inform him that Markby intended talking to a sergeant on his staff concerning an incident Winter's team was investigating.

Winter turned out to be a terrier of a man. Not particularly tall for a police officer, his bullet head was crowned with bristling grey spikes. His small, sharp eyes were sunken in permanently puffed and scarred flesh, and his nose was battered flat. He was also almost completely square, having extraordinarily broad shoulders and a way of walking with his muscular arms held away from his sides like a gunfighter. To Markby, the suggestion was that a lack of stature – comparatively – had led Winter to compensate with a devotion to muscle-building exercises and brute-force sports. Markby judged him the sort of football player who left the imprint of his studs on his opponents.

Today, clearly, Winter considered this visitor from the regional squad to be the key player in the opposing team and meant Markby to leave, metaphorically, dotted with bootmarks.

'We're honoured!' He didn't trouble to hide the sarcasm. 'A visit from the regional force! Thought you were all busy chasing twenty-quid notes!'

This was a reference to a recent investigation into a forgery case they'd carried out.

Markby smiled thinly, choosing to share the humour of the greeting, such as it was. 'All cleared up as far as we're concerned – until it gets to court!'

Winter grunted. Anything could happen when cases got to court.

'I've already spoken to Sergeant Jones,' he said gruffly. 'I've had a look at her report. I've also been down to the morgue myself, since you expressed an interest. I've seen the stiff and spoken to the pathologist. Everything points to an accident. Cold frosty morning. Elderly man. Old-fashioned footwear. Slipped. Can't see what's bothering you – Sir.'

Markby looked wistfully round what had once been his office. There were no longer any plants, carefully nurtured in their pots along the windowsills. Winter hadn't replaced them with any other personal item. Not so much as a photograph of his dog. But wait, wrong! There was something. A small framed certificate awarding the honours to a youthful Winter in a long distant inter-force boxing championship. Oh dear.

It offered a bridge, however. Markby remarked on it.

Winter squared his shoulders even more so that he now looked as if he'd forgotten to take the coat-hanger out of his jacket. 'Fine discipline, boxing! Teaches self-defence while understanding your opponent. Quick mind, quick feet! Find his weakness!' Winter made an automatic feint with his fists, apparently unaware, and ducked his head.

Getting worse. Markby, in his mind, grouped Winter with Uncle Denis and probably a future Tristan Goodhusband, destined to be forever prisoners of their youth.

Markby plunged on and explained his reasons for wanting to talk to Jones about the circumstances of Bodicote's death. His reasons had sounded tenuous when he'd told Pearce. Now they sounded so thin that they appeared little more than a concocted excuse for his presence.

Winter clearly thought so, glaring at him. 'And you want to talk to Jones because of the position of the old man's cap?'

'Well, I—' Markby gestured. 'I had interviewed Bodicote with regard to the Caswell incident. So naturally, when the old man is found dead, I'm interested.'

Winter's head sank into his collar-bones, his neck collapsing like an Edwardian opera-hat. 'You've got reason to think Bodicote sent the poison pen letters or the explosive package?'

'It's possible the explosive device was posted in London,' Markby admitted. 'As was the only anonymous letter in our possession. We've no evidence yet Bodicote ever went up to London. He had animals to care for.'

'So where's the problem?' Winter was aggravatingly obstructive.

'I just want to run through a few things with Jones, if you've no objection!' Markby contrived a theatrically conspiratorial air. 'For all that the old man was a village resident of long standing, I can't just exclude him from my inquiries. There was a good deal of bad feeling between him and his neighbours. He may have got a bee in his bonnet, you know.'

'I understand,' Winter was impressed by the theatricals. 'Pity he's dead, then, isn't it? Nothing a corpse can tell you.'

'The inspector's been breathing down my neck,' said Jones gloomily. 'Ever since you said you were coming over here, Mr Markby. I haven't missed anything, have I, sir?'

'Shouldn't think so, Gwyneth. I just don't like sudden deaths occurring around a case I'm looking into. Did you talk to any of the villagers about Bodicote?'

She brightened. 'Several. He was obsessed with the goats. He took them to local agricultural shows and gave demonstrations of milking and general goat-care. But otherwise he never even went into the local pub for a drink on a Saturday. If it hadn't been for the goats, he'd have been a recluse. Or at least, that's the impression I got from everyone.'

'Long-time resident?'

She laughed. 'And how! He was born in Castle Darcy. His parents lived in that cottage. Although he was just on eighty when he died, I met a couple of very old gents who'd been to school with him, if you can imagine it! Do you know, they even remembered Mr Bodicote's parents? They were sort of unusual. I gather they'd kept the village shop for a while. His father was a local lay preacher and since he had the gift of the gab and knew a lot of long words, he was called on whenever anyone wanted someone to make a speech. Bodicote's mother was also well-educated for those days and *her* mother before her had been the first schoolmistress in Castle Darcy.'

This was going back to the 1880s or 1890s. Village memories were long. An image of a Victorian rural school formed itself in Markby's head, the schoolmistress in her long skirts teaching all ages, all grades, in one room, to help her, the brightest of her older pupils, pressed in to oversee the little ones.

'Once I got the old chaps talking about the Bodicotes, I couldn't get them to stop! In fact, I encouraged them to ramble on a bit because I got interested.' She shrugged. 'I wasted rather more time on them than I should, I suppose.'

'Nothing's wasted, Gywnny.'

So Bodicote's parents had been literate, numerate, and more bookish than most villagers. So much so that they'd become something of a legend in their own time and were still remembered by the old. Though there would have been little money for extras when Bodicote was a child, there would have been books in the house. Bodicote had early acquired his taste for 'good yarns'.

Good Lord! Markby thought suddenly. When Bodicote had started reading as a boy, Conan Doyle had still been alive and writing. As for Bodicote's mother, a bright young woman with a head for business, perhaps she'd used books to escape, at least in her mind, the confines of her village life. And what a wonderful pool of literary talent had been available to her for a shilling or so!

Markby remembered the bookcase in the corner of Bodicote's parlour, and the venerable examples of popular literature on its shelves. A tingle ran up his spine.

Gwyneth was still talking. 'Local people knew he was odd but they respected him for what they call his learning. It was the way they'd respected his parents before him. I can tell you, sir, talking to those old chaps was fascinating! Anyway, Bodicote was a loner, never let anyone into the cottage, other than perhaps just inside the kitchen if it was someone he knew very well. Lately he'd taken to chaining the front door and wanting to know who was outside before he opened up. But no one thought that was significant, only that he was getting odder as he got older.'

'Seems I was privileged to be invited in!' Markby remarked. Had Bodicote been afraid? Or had his caution been intended to protect something?

187

'Check the bookcase, Gwynny!' Markby said suddenly. 'In the parlour. A first edition, clean and in its original wrapper, is sought after by collectors and dealers. Individually not fetching vast sums, perhaps, but a whole bookcase of them might tempt someone! Check disturbed dust! Talk to Mrs Sutton! Make sure nothing's been taken!'

Chapter Eleven

Alan Markby, had he but known it, was not the only one to whom the estate of the late Hector Bodicote was a cause of concern, or about to become so.

Sally Caswell sat before the computer in her tiny office the following morning. Her mind was currently given to the temporal affairs of Bailey and Bailey. She frowned at the columns of figures on the screen and pulled a thick accounts ledger towards her and ran her finger down a page, pausing occasionally, to check the entry against the screen. When she reached the end of the sheet, she closed the ledger and leaned back in the chair, turning her head away from the flickering screen. You weren't supposed to work at these things for more than short periods of time. It did awful things to your eyesight and froze your joints.

The thought of such a thing made her get up and stretch. She was stiff, getting overweight with all this sitting about, and just a little bored. Of course, it didn't have to be like this, not if she went along with what Austin suggested. He had made it seem quite feasible. Then the job – indeed, life itself – would be much more interesting. It was tempting. But there was Liam. Sally sighed and sat down again. The problem was Liam. The problem, now she considered it, had always been Liam.

She rested her chin in her hands. It was stupid to think this way, because after all, the truth was—

Someone had come into the outer room and was walking towards the office door. It wasn't Austin, she knew his step, and although a decided tread, it wasn't heavy enough for either Ted or Ronnie. It wasn't a viewing day, either, so not a browser. Sally spun the chair to face the door and called out, 'Hullo? Can I help you?'

A figure filled the doorway and she recognised Mrs Sutton. Bodicote's niece looked much as she'd done the day of the old man's death, except that she didn't wear gumboots. Instead she wore down-at-heel cheap slip-ons and snagged tights beneath a skirt, the pleats of which had been badly laundered so that they had more or less flattened out. With this, Maureen Sutton wore a hand-knitted Guernsey pullover of mannish style. Her hair was unkempt and her make-up no better applied than the day before. Nevertheless, Sally had the impression that Mrs Sutton had done her best to make herself presentable. This was a business visit.

'Do sit down!' Sally invited her hastily, realising she'd been staring. 'How are you today? We're all so sorry about your uncle.'

Mrs Sutton sat gingerly on the designated chair, as if not sure that this was a good move.

'He was getting on,' she said brusquely. 'Couldn't last for ever.'

Sally was taken aback. The shock was two-fold. In the first place, it seemed an unkind and matter-of-fact dismissal of the old man. The second shock lay in Mrs Sutton's hands which the woman had folded on her lap as she spoke. The fingers were workworn and the nails untrimmed. But in honour of the visit, Mrs Sutton had donned her jewellery: a huge emerald cluster engagement ring, a veritable knuckle-duster of an eternity ring, her wedding ring, and sundry other rings, all inset with large, undoubtedly genuine, stones.

'I've seen all sorts in this saleroom,' Austin had once told Sally. 'Never let appearances lead you astray.'

Mrs Sutton wasn't poor, obviously, not sitting there with two or three thousand pounds on her fingers. Sally wondered whether the awful clothes were a deliberate attempt to mislead, or whether

Mrs Sutton just liked dressing in that bag-lady fashion.

'I've come about Uncle Hector's cottage,' she said loudly. Her manner was such as would brook no argument. 'I'm his executor, of the estate, you understand? Named in the will. You can check that with the lawyer. You'll see it's all right. So that's why I'm here.'

'But he only died—' Sally bit the words back.

Mrs Sutton wasn't troubled by tactlessness on Sally's part, nor, it appeared, by any finer feeling of her own. 'I know he's not buried yet. We've got to wait for the inquest and the coroner to issue a certificate. But that's all routine. The inquest is tomorrow and it won't take long to make arrangements afterwards. But there's other things got to be done sharpish, and I'm the one to do them!'

'What sort of things?' Sally asked in some trepidation.

Mrs Sutton's expression became grimmer. 'You don't know my family!'

'No,' admitted Sally thankfully.

'Grabbers and scroungers! You've got to keep one step ahead of them! That's why Uncle Hector made me executor. To stop them getting up to their tricks.'

'I see.' Sally didn't but Mrs Sutton had paused as if expecting a comment. She decided it was time to get to the reason for this increasingly unpleasant visit.

'So how exactly can Bailey and Bailey help you, Mrs Sutton?'

'You're valuers, aren't you?' the woman demanded. 'It says you are, outside over the door. I want you to go over to the cottage and value everything over fifty pounds.'

'For probate?' Sally was startled. 'Is that necessary? I think you ought to have a word with your solicitor, Mrs Sutton. Generally valuations are only called for when a considerable estate is left. A stately home or a private art collection.' She thought of the cowcreamer. 'I'm sure Mr Bodicote had his valuables, little ornaments and such. But I don't think they'll

191

interest the taxman. In fact, although please check with your solicitor, if Mr Bodicote has only left very little, the formalities can virtually be dispensed with.'

Mrs Sutton was shaking her head. 'It's not for probate. It's for me! To give me some ammunition when the guns start firing from the family's side! I want you to put a number on every item that's got a value over fifty pounds, and write down what it's worth. It won't take long. He's not got that much. But the furniture might fetch something. That old stuff does nowadays. Can't think why.'

'If it's antique and in good condition,' Sally stipulated hastily, lest Mrs Sutton be expecting unrealistic sums for furniture which was probably in the same sort of shape as Bodicote's kitchen table. Old, yes. Worth doing up, yes. Of interest to a dealer, very likely. But expensive – no, not in the sort of shape it was in.

Mrs Sutton said impatiently, 'It's so that when it comes to sorting things out, everyone will get his fair due. Uncle Hector, you see, left it to me to divide it all up. He gave a general sort of instruction. Everyone to have one item of his choice, and all that's left over, comes to me. The solicitor suggested I just let them all go in the cottage and pick out one item each. I told him, it'd be like the battle of Waterloo! They'd all be squabbling about the value of things. They'd be reckoning this one had got something worth more than the other one, do you know what I mean? Or that I persuaded them to take the rubbish and kept the good stuff for myself.'

'Sounds awful!' said Sally frankly.

Unexpectedly, her visitor grinned. 'It is awful. I told you. Terrible crowd they are. Uncle Hector couldn't stand them. It was only me he liked. Only me he trusted. But blood is blood. He wouldn't leave them out when it came to the will. But I'm in charge.'

It seemed an extraordinary idea, but the woman clearly meant it. 'I'm not sure we should – at least, not until after the inquest,' Sally protested.

'It's tomorrow, I told you, ten o'clock in the morning. You'll be there, will you? Coroner's verdict'll be accidental death, bound to be. He'll issue a certificate for burial. I'll bring the keys with me and give them to you after proceedings so you can go out there. I'll nip along to the funeral parlour and make the other arrangements. I can't hang about. I want someone to get there and value it all before *they* do, the family!'

The following day's inquest proceedings were blessedly brief but a highly unpleasant experience. Sally sat miserably listening to Meredith's evidence. She could only admire Meredith's competence and apparent *sang-froid* as she described the body. All that practical consular training, thought Sally. Nevertheless, it emerged as a pathetic scene as Meredith spoke of the bleating of the nannies inside their house, of her first sight of a hobnailed boot, of the old man's cap lying on the ground, and of the billy, dancing inquisitively around his dead owner.

Then it was the turn of herself and Liam. She had little to contribute but Liam gave a terse account of having been called by Meredith to the scene, viewing the body, returning to the cottage and calling the police and ambulance services.

Sally, listening to him, wished he could have managed to sound a little more sympathetic to the fate of their elderly neighbour.

The coroner summed up. It was a sad but not rare occurrence. Old people frequently fell and in this case it was possible that old-fashioned footwear on slippery ground had been a contributory factor. He gave his verdict of accidental death.

The Bodicote clan had gathered in a phalanx in the middle of the courtroom. Mrs Sutton sat expressionlessly, flanked by a pair of equally unattractive women who bore her a strong resemblance and were presumably her sisters. She'd brought along a taciturn middle-aged man and a surly youth. Husband and son, Sally assumed. The two unnamed women also had silent, unattractive menfolk. In much the same way as they'd arrived with various bags and packets of sandwiches which they had to be dissuaded from munching in the courtroom, they'd also brought a very old lady. This tiny bird of a woman, with wispy white hair under a felt hat, wore a grubby winter coat which reached to her ankles, leaving a glimpse of wrinkled lisle stockings and surgically adapted shoes. The beldame was deposited on a chair and ignored by the whole family.

Various other people had taken seats at the rear of the room but it was difficult to tell if they were relatives or interested villagers. The atmosphere was tense, less with grief, than with unexpressed rivalries. At the close of proceedings, Mrs Sutton advanced on Sally and pressed a bunch of keys into her hand.

'Soon as possible!' she rasped.

The others pressed forward, suspicion writ large on their faces.

'Who's she, then?' shrilled the ancient one.

'From the valuers, Gran!' howled Mrs Sutton into the old woman's ear. 'From Bailey and Bailey, you know who they are, don't you?'

'Rogues!' cried the old woman. 'Wally Bailey? He never got no one a decent price! He give me five miserable shillings for my mother's chiffonier! Rosewood, it were! With mirrors and all!'

'Not Wally,' yelled Mrs Sutton. 'He's dead and gone thirty years or more, Gran! It's his nephew there now, Austin, you remember?'

'Austin? What are you talking about, Maureen? Austin Bailey is Thelma's kid, wears glasses and always got a cold!'

'Ignore her,' said Mrs Sutton, breathing heavily. 'Take the keys and go, go on.'

'You're never going to let Wally Bailey pick and choose what we gets from Hector's place? Here, you ask him what become of that rosewood chiffonier!' The old lady was becoming dangerously distraught.

'Listen, don't you think—' Sally tried ineffectually to return the keys to Mrs Sutton, who merely pressed them back into her hand.

'Don't take no notice,' she advised again.

One of the other women said loudly, 'They oughtn't to be let in there all alone, they oughtn't. Looking through Uncle Hector's things! You ought to go with them, Maureen.'

'Brass drawer handles and bendy legs!' shrilled Gran.

'I've got things to do!' snapped Mrs Sutton. 'And I'm the executor of the will, right? So I decide what's what!'

With that she nodded to Sally and made off rapidly towards the exit.

The other family members gathered into a sullen conclave and glowered at Sally, suspecting they were to be done out of their due inheritance.

'Er – right,' Sally backed cautiously away. 'I'll – er – see to it, then. Nice to have – er – met you all.'

'And a knife drawer wiv green baize lining!' said Gran viciously.

Sally fled.

Later, when Sally recounted subsequent events to Meredith and Alan Markby over a glass of wine, she said, 'They were a dreadful family, and it didn't surprise me that Mrs Sutton wanted to be a step ahead of them!'

'Happens all the time,' said Alan. 'Nothing like a death to bring out the worst in a family.'

He had suffered his own irksome moment at the conclusion of the inquest when Inspector Winter had remarked, 'Can't all get exciting cases like you lot over at the regional squad with your bombs and paramilitary groups! Just a routine accidental death as I thought it was.'

Across the table from him now, Sally took a deep drink of her wine. 'All this,' she said, 'is turning me into a drinker.'

'Fine,' said Meredith, topping up her glass.

'So Austin and I went out to the cottage that afternoon,' Sally continued. 'Frankly, I also wanted it over and done with, so that we could give back the keys and forget it. At the same time, I can't say I wanted to go into the cottage, not given any choice. I didn't feel in the least bit like it. But then I reasoned that it was next door to me and I was going home, so it was a convenient moment in that way. Austin came along, of course, to do the actual valuations.'

The goats had been removed by the Suttons. Sally missed them more than she'd ever imagined possible. Liam was highly delighted to be rid of their sometimes smelly or noisy and always destructive presence. But Sally missed their knowing expressions as they peered at her over the hedge and Jasper especially, with the mischief in his pale eyes.

Bodicote's cottage had the look of a home abandoned. No smoke wreathed from its chimney into the crisp air. An empty, lost feel shrouded it. It made her nervous of approaching it down the uneven path. She felt an intruder, as if Bodicote's spirit still lurked about the place ready to drive off unwanted visitors.

'It seems indecent!' she said to Austin who was locking his car door outside the gate in the precise way he had with everything. 'He's not buried yet. Are you sure this is in order?'

'She's the executor, I checked.' Austin always checked. 'There are the usual formalities with the will, such as it is, but there's no reason why she can't start the valuation. Of course, she can't actually dispose of anything, that's something which has to wait for the will to be cleared, now she's set the legal moves going. Nor can we, or anyone else, remove anything. But we can go in and look it over. It might be wise on her part to get an independent view, especially if there's going to be any dispute. Though, for goodness sake, I can't for the life of me see why she's worrying. We're talking about an old boy who spent his life in this village and kept a few goats, not a country landowner with acres and an ancestral home! The cottage itself has possibilities, but will need complete renovation and you know how much that costs, having done up your place! There's a fair bit of ground. But the building boom's collapsed and I doubt any council now would give planning permission. Failing a new motorway going through—'

'Don't!' begged Sally. 'I've got troubles enough.'

'Just giving an example. There isn't any such plan, that's my point. The land is just a big garden. Ideally, if it were me, I'd knock the cottage down and build a new one. But, in the first place, it's not detached – it is very much attached to yours. In the second, it'll be listed, right?'

Sally nodded. 'Yes, we had awful problems getting planning permission for the extension and renovated kitchen. We had to promise not to move any original beams or partitions, and to put in windows which matched the originals.'

'See? As for the contents of the cottage, if the relatives think we're going to find anything of value, they're deluding themselves. Price everything over fifty pounds?' Austin snorted. 'Take us five minutes!' he chuckled.

'All right, Austin, if you're sure.'

He beamed kindly at her. 'Of course I am. Why not? Let's get in there and get out, that's my view.'

Sally shared it and said so.

Austin shrugged, the wind which tugged at Sally's full skirt, whipping up his long hair. 'Families!' he said. 'Nothing like a will to breed ill-will amongst your nearest and dearest!'

The attempt at humour didn't work. She felt just as bad. She handed the bunch of keys to Austin. She wasn't going to be the one to open the door. Liam, who'd come back with them, had disappeared into their own cottage. Back to his book, no doubt. She envied his detachment from this squalid little affair.

Austin unlocked the front door with the Yale key.

'New lock!' he observed. 'Looks as if the old chap had put new security in place.' He peered round it. 'New doorchain, too. And

197

a great big bolt at top and bottom. Didn't mean anyone to get by him, did he?'

'Poor old chap,' said Sally. 'I keep thinking about him. I keep wishing we'd been nicer to him.'

Austin smiled down at her. 'I'm sure you were nice to him, my dear. You couldn't be nasty to anyone!'

'Well, I was nasty to him. I told him I wished he was dead! Now he is dead. Three hundred years ago, I'd have been burnt as a witch. There are plenty of places, even in Europe, where locals would say I had the evil eye! I even feel as if I *did* bring it on him!' Sally shook her head. 'I'm not looking forward to this at all.'

'Don't worry,' Austin pushed the front door wide. 'It won't take long.'

'The smell in there was awful, Meredith. You can't imagine it. It always did smell. But being shut up for several days, it was worse. Old goat mash and old boots, principally. Together with that funny smell you sometimes get around old men. But there was something else, too. I couldn't quite name it. A leathery sort of smell.'

'Yes,' Alan said softly. 'I remember it in the sitting room.'

Sally glanced at him. 'The first surprise was in the sitting room.'

'Ah,' said Austin genially. 'We'll open a window first, I think! Not feeling iffy, are you, Sal? Whiffs a bit in here. Although it's cold enough without an added draught.'

'I don't feel sick. But do open the window. Better frozen than suffocated. He's got some very interesting bits of old china. I've seen them in the kitchen. He's got a cow-creamer . . .'

'We'll get there in due course. Let's have a look in here first. This is his best room and it's probably where the desirables are, the ones the Suttons and the Bodicotes are prepared to feud over!' He looked round. 'A bookcase! It might be interesting to see what the old gentleman read!'

Austin, having opened the window, had gone to the bookcase in the corner. The pale winter sunlight flooded through now that the curtain had been pulled right back, and played on the worn spines of the packed volumes. Austin had eased out the first book on the top row.

'Gawd . . .' he whispered and then fell silent.

'Austin?' Sally became alarmed.

He didn't reply. He was easing out – very, very carefully – the next.

'Sally?' His voice sounded muffled, suppressed excitement spilling out despite his best effort. 'Come and see this. It's John Buchan, *The Thirty-Nine Steps* in original wrapper. And here's *Greenmantle*. First edition. Well-read, but well cared for. Absolutely intact. And here's the old man's favourite reading, if Markby's right! Sherlock Holmes – hold on!'

Austin's voice expired in a squeak. 'This folder contains an 1887 copy of Beeton's Christmas Annual! It's the one with *A Study in Scarlet*, the first ever Sherlock Holmes' story! A collector's dream! Do you realise, one of these recently cleared £20,000 at auction in London! Yikes! There's a manuscript letter tucked inside this copy of *The White Company*. That's one of Conan Doyle's historical yarns. The letter's signed and apparently written by Conan Doyle himself! It's addressed to Miss Charlotte Edwards and going by the date, that must have been the old man's mother or grandmother! Probably grandmother. It looks as if Conan Doyle had quite a correspondence going with her because he refers to previous letters and congratulates her on her sterling work bringing literacy to country children! Good God! Do you think there are other manuscript letters around in the cottage?'

'Perhaps,' Sally suggested nervously, 'we ought to take a look at the other books first.'

'Yes, yes – look!' Words failed Austin at this point.

Together they took the books from their shelves and spread them on the table.

199

'Look at 'em!' Austin said faintly. 'Look at all those Agatha Christies. First editions, in wrappers, clean ... collector's delight!'

In a sort of litany he chanted, 'Graham Greene. D. H. Lawrence. Somerset Maugham. H. E. Bates. The Americans, too. Faulkner, Hemingway, Dashiell Hammett. All first or early editions! But Conan Doyle, everything the man wrote!' Austin's voice rose in wonder.

'There obviously was a tradition in old Bodicote's family of buying every new title hot off the press and, whenever possible, sending them to the authors with a request they sign them! And they did! They wrote back! There are five or six autographed letters, stuck inside the covers and probably dozens hidden elsewhere. The oldest by date are to Charlotte, addressed to her first as Miss Edwards at the schoolhouse and later to her as Mrs Purdy. The next lot are addressed to Alice Purdy and later to Alice Bodicote. That makes her Charlotte's daughter and Hector's mum. Finally the correspondence is with Hector. Grandmama started this hobby of corresponding with writers. Her daughter and grandson kept it up! And they were just villagers! Who would ever expect it?'

'Charlotte wasn't just a villager,' Sally said. 'Not if her first letters are addressed to the schoolhouse. She must have been the schoolmistress here.'

Austin ran a hand through his dishevelled hair. 'Tell you what!' he announced. 'We can check this out, but I reckon what happened was something like this. Before 1870 there were church schools, but Castle Darcy probably hadn't got one. The kids walked miles to, say, Cherton? Or they didn't go to school at all. Then Gladstone brought in the Board Schools, from 1870 on. Castle Darcy probably got a new-fangled Board School when such schools were popping up all over the place. Charlotte came here to be its teacher! The date would fit. Poor girl was probably bored to tears and took refuge in books and became a literary groupie, writing all those letters. Then she married a local man, Purdy, and stayed. But she still wrote the letters to her favourite authors and Alice, her daughter, did the same. As did Alice's son, Hector Bodicote.'

They stared at one another. Austin said in a strained voice, 'I think we ought to take a look upstairs.'

They climbed the narrow stair, Austin first, Sally following behind unwillingly.

The first tiny room was Bodicote's bedroom, monastic in its simplicity. Like a mediaeval hermit, Bodicote had built shelves above his head for his precious books.

'More of 'em,' Austin said dully. 'I'm getting blasé about this now, Sal.'

He was to eat his words when they opened the door of the other bedroom.

There was no furniture in it at all apart from crudely constructed shelving on the walls. Instead, books were stacked from floor to ceiling. They spilled out of ancient cardboard boxes. They were wrapped in lengths of cloth. They packed the shelves. They ranged from the antique to the modern. Some were worthless, some of value, some extremely rare.

'And all of 'em,' Austin said, his voice tending now to shrillness, 'stolen!'

'What?' Sally stared at him.

Austin spun round and threw out his hand, pointing at the haul. 'He was clearly nuts! Crazy, literally, about books! Grandma had started off the love of reading, Mama followed. By the time it got to young Hector, as he was when he started, the whole thing had got to be an obsession! What he couldn't buy, he pinched! Then he hid them up here! A lifetime's collection of purloined tomes! Look, look . . .' Austin snatched up a nearby volume. 'This has got the stamp of the Bodleian library in Oxford in it! How the devil did he get in there to pinch it? And here, these are his recent acquisitions! The stamp of Wilver House library and my gosh! The old blighter! Here are the two missing Dickens' volumes from our sale! The man was totally without a sense of *meum* and *tuum!*' Austin's voice cracked.

Sally whispered. 'He always came to sales. He used to buy odd bits of rubbish. He always wore that baggy old raincoat . . .'

It was difficult to breathe in there. The windows were tightly sealed. The air was thick with the musty odour of old paper and leather bindings.

She picked up a book at random. 'In Latin. He couldn't even read it.' Sally's face expressed her bewilderment. 'Why?'

'Why?' Austin replied hoarsely. He took out his handkerchief and mopped his brow. 'Because he was crazy!'

'But Austin,' she protested, 'we can't value these! I mean, how on earth do we tell which ones are pinched and which aren't? I know you can tell the ones with library stamps in them, like those Wilver Park ones. But the others? He could have been stealing them over a period of fifty years! We'll never find the owners!'

'Not our job!' Austin said firmly. 'Police job. In fact, it's a job the police should've done already! Didn't they check upstairs? Didn't they realise—' He spluttered and resumed, 'The only thing I know for certain, Sal, is that we've been set up, you and I!'

'Set up?' She blinked at him, distressed. 'How?'

'By that female Sutton! She wanted us to find these! That tale about having to get in and value before the family got here! Of course she wanted an outsider in here before anyone else! She didn't want to be the one to find all this!' Austin threw out his arms. 'She wanted us to find them! She'll swear blind, I bet you, that she knew nothing about any of it!'

'You think she knew?' Sally couldn't take it in.

'Of course she blasted knew – knows! The books downstairs on show, and possibly the ones in his bedroom, those are legitimate, bought and paid for. That's my guess. The rest, all of these, are stolen! Oh, how I wish I'd been there when she came to the office. I'd have smelled a rat. You weren't to know – don't be upset, Sal!'

Austin sounded alarmed, seeing horror and dismay mingled on her face. He put his hands on her shoulders. 'It wasn't your fault. You weren't to realise what she was up to. But I've been in this business years . . .'

Sally turned her face up to his. 'He was a thief! I was feeling so sorry for him! But he was a thief!' Her eyes filled with tears.

'Oh, Sal . . .' Austin said. And there, amongst the stacks of stolen books, he kissed her.

'That's what I could smell,' Alan Markby said. 'Old leather. I thought of horses. But what I was really thinking of was saddlery. Old devil. I did wonder whether he mightn't have penned the abusive letters to Liam, or some of them. The evening I called on him, he hid something in a drawer before I got into the room. But he was probably gloating over one of his stolen treasures. As for the police, I'm sorry to say they were negligent. I did direct Sergeant Jones to the bookcase and she sent a couple of constables to take a look at it.

'They interpreted their instructions literally. They were told to check if anything appeared to be missing. Since the cottage was stacked to the roof with things, they reported that no, on the contrary, everything appeared to be there! It never occurred to them that they'd stumbled on a lifetime's haul of stolen goods! They just thought he was a hoarder as some old people are. If they'd looked inside any of the books upstairs and seen the library stamps, they might have become suspicious, but they didn't. They thought the cottage and its contents a bit of a joke. I'm sure Winter is making sure neither of them is laughing now!

'Mrs Sutton – if she knew about the books upstairs – must have cursed the fact that the coppers didn't find the haul. She had no option but direct you to it, Sally. Off the record, I'm sure Austin's right. Mrs Sutton wanted someone else to find them.'

'I was cross at first,' Sally admitted. 'I thought what a dreadful old rogue. Then I began to be sorrier for him than I was before. He must have just loved books. He bought what he could, but he couldn't afford to buy everything, so he took. Years and years, collecting other people's books. There were public library books in there, you know. Common or garden cloth-bound public library editions. No value except to the libraries which had lost them. He just took anything and everything. There was a tri-lingual seventeenth-century Bible, Latin, Greek and Hebrew in parallel columns! He couldn't even read it! And yet, it's so sad. To think of him, all alone in there, poring over the books. Handling them, touching the bindings, and the pages, peering at the funny old print. Poor Mr Bodicote!'

But Alan Markby was smiling. 'What is it?' Meredith asked him.

'I was just thinking,' he said dreamily, 'of the unfortunate Winter who's got the job of sorting all this out!'

Chapter Twelve

'It's the last straw!' Liam slammed his document case down on the kitchen table. 'Now it turns out Bodicote was public enemy number one in the world of librarians and bookdealers! A kleptomaniac! I knew he was barmy.'

'My head aches,' Sally protested. 'I wish you wouldn't crash about like that.'

'Your head aches? My head feels as if it's going to explode! I can't work here, that's for sure! Country quiet? Peace?' He snorted. 'It'd be quieter in the middle of Piccadilly Circus. Would you believe the Arts and Antiques Squad sent a man down? There are distraught librarians from all over the country descending on Bamford police station to view the haul from that cottage! Not to mention journalists! It must be slow for news at the moment, if even the tabloids want a picture of Bodicote's lair! One even tried to interview me!'

He was marching up and down the kitchen, flinging out his hands to underline points, narrowly missing crockery and pots. He might have been lecturing to a class of students, she thought bitterly. Goodness knows, his voice was loud enough. They ought to be able to hear him at the other end of the village.

'They've cleared all the books out now,' Sally pressed her hands to her temples. 'Don't keep on so, Liam. All the librarians and the police and everyone else, they've all gone.'

'For how long?' Liam was unpersuaded. 'Until the next ridiculous bit of nonsense! I tell you, I *cannot* work here! I'm taking my notes into the lab this morning. I'll work in my office there. I might just as well have stayed there as take time off to work here!'

'You go back there every week anyway, at least once or twice,' Sally retorted with some spirit. 'So it isn't this business of Bodicote and the books which is driving you away!'

Liam paused with his case in his hand, turning in the doorway. 'Meaning just what?'

She couldn't be bothered to argue with him. A row first thing in the morning would only upset her for the rest of the day. She had to go into work. She needed to get her head together.

'Look, just go,' she said. 'I'll see you tonight.'

He stared at her. 'Take an aspirin.' He hesitated as if seeking to suggest some more efficacious remedy. Perhaps failing to think of one, he added. 'Drink some of that herbal brew of yours. You swear by it!'

She nodded. Liam hunched his shoulders and went out. Moments later she heard his car draw away.

Without him a calm fell over the kitchen as in the wake of a storm. She got up and went to the sink, turning on the hot tap to run over the breakfast dishes. Austin had urged her not to arrive at work before ten. Time to clean up a little here first.

Washing up proved therapeutic. She felt much more in control of things when the breakfast crockery was neatly ranged away and the work surfaces wiped down. Only the headache persisted, beating dully at her forehead. It was still only just before nine. She'd make a cup of tea before she left.

Sally's hand hovered above the neat row of pots containing her herbal infusions. Finally it descended with a certain reluctance on the battered margarine tub containing Bodicote's present.

'Poor old chap,' she murmured. She prised the lid free and lifted the tub to her nose. 'Phew!' It didn't smell very good. It had probably been shut up in this tub for months, since the summer. She gave it a shake. It was a mixture of some kind. She couldn't identify it all. Some of it looked like feverfew. Perhaps that would help her headache? She could at least try, just the once. She had kept the tea because just to throw it away seemed to insult the old man's memory. He'd given it to her as a kindly gesture. Well, why not try it?

The tea, brewed up, didn't taste all that good. Sally grimaced at the first sip. Determinedly she swallowed most of it, but reaching the dregs at the bottom of her mug, tipped them down the sink. *Pace* the shade of Mr Bodicote, she wouldn't make it again. She picked up the tub containing the remaining herbs and dropped it into the waste bin.

In future she'd stick to her own tried and true concoctions. She made up a flask as usual and thrust it into her shoulder-bag, ready to set off for work. It occurred to her as she did that her headache had gone. So Bodicote's tea had worked, after all!

She went outside and began the tedious ritual of checking the car. It gave some comfort to know she was at least doing as the police had suggested. She was by no means confident she'd be able to find a device if it had been fixed to the vehicle anywhere. Sally crouched to peer underneath the body, stretching out an old make-up mirror which she'd attached to a tennis racquet. By panning it to and fro she got a glimpse of various nooks not otherwise visible to the eye. She felt a fool doing it. Liam had been mocking of her home-made search device, but only until she'd caught him using it one day. After that he hadn't mentioned it again – but he still used it.

A strange dark lump was attached to the front axle. Oh, my God! But only a lump of mud. She sighed with relief. Open the bonnet and take a look at the engine next. No bits of wire she didn't recognise. But, let's face it, if the thing was wired to explode as she switched on the ignition, it would probably be done in such a way she wouldn't spot it. She hoped, if it happened, she'd be killed outright. To lose both legs, that would be worse, far worse. Or perhaps it wouldn't. It was a fine, disputatious point.

She slammed down the bonnet and stood back. It was a

wearisome job and she felt tired after completing it. Sleeping so badly last night, thinking about everything, that was the cause of that! She hadn't slept well at all for ages. Austin had noticed how tired she'd looked. Telling her not to come in so early. He didn't realise – or did he? – that she left home early because her heart lightened as she drove away from the cottage – and sank correspondingly as she approached it on her return. Austin. Austin and his plans. As if she hadn't enough on her mind.

She climbed into the driver's seat and switched on the engine without even thinking about it. It didn't blow up. She backed cautiously into the lane and turned the car towards Bamford.

Alan Markby walked into the regional headquarters building and made for his office. On the way, he passed the room which accommodated Prescott and two others. The door was open and he could see them gathered round something on a desk which they were studying. Pearce was with them, looking both embarrassed and glum.

Markby strolled in. 'What's all this? Mothers' Union meeting?'

Prescott looked up with a grin. 'Inspector's got his pic in the local rag, sir!'

'Oh, yes!' Markby remembered. 'Let's have a look, then!'

They passed it to him. Pearce, hovering dismally at the back of the group, said, 'It's nothing to make a fuss about.'

It wasn't. It was arguably the least controversial photograph of a police officer Markby had ever seen. Pearce and Tessa had been posed against their own front door. But for some reason, the picture had been chopped off so that only their heads were visible. That was to say, Tessa's head and Pearce's head and shoulders, he being the taller of the two. Tessa's expression was fixed and ferocious. Pearce was wearing a simple grin.

'She had her hair done for that,' said Pearce now in sepulchral tones. 'She's upset. I mean, look at it. I look like the ruddy village idiot! She wants me to phone the paper and complain. Can't see anything of the house – or the dog.'

'I've seen worse, Dave,' said Markby kindly. 'Newspaper pictures are chancy things. You don't look – look bad. Tell Tessa her hair looks very nice.'

It looked awful, he thought. She was a pretty girl, but the corkscrew curls and rigid topknot didn't suit her round face. It made her look like a cottage loaf.

He handed the newspaper to Pearce who gazed mistrustfully at the page bearing his image. 'My mother'll like it,' he said without sounding as if he drew much comfort from this thought.

As Sally drove along she felt undeniably altogether more relaxed. Still tired, but not irritable-tired. Just slowing-down.

At the thought, she did slow down, literally. It wasn't any good drifting off like this while driving! Concentrate! she ordered herself. She began to take extra notice of everything, as an exercise to keep herself awake, making a running commentary in her head.

It was quite a nice morning. What beautiful horses in that field, nicely protected with smart blankets. Thank goodness they'd seen the last of the frost for the time being. It was strange to think that before long Christmas would be here. That reminded her that she still hadn't bought any greetings cards. All the best ones would be gone if she didn't buy now. She hadn't made a list. She'd still got last year's list somewhere. Bump, bump. Must remember that pothole tonight on the way home.

Someone was ahead of her, a cyclist. Pulling out with elaborate care – it was so very difficult to concentrate – she overtook Yvonne Goodhusband, peddling briskly along on an antiquated bicycle with a wicker basket fixed to the handlebar. Yvonne was sensibly clad in tweeds, a headscarf tied on her hair. She saw who drove the overtaking car and signalled. Sally slowed, stopped and waited with engine idling for Yvonne to catch up.

Even so, she'd managed to leave Yvonne quite a way behind and it was a moment before she saw her in the mirror, peddling determinedly and with a certain abandon, rather in the manner of a cavalry charge. She liked Yvonne. It wouldn't do to say so to Liam. Though why not, for goodness sake? Was she required to tailor her every attitude to match his? As if to show that she didn't, Sally wound down the window and leaned out, shouting, 'Hi, there!'

The sharp wind which brushed her face was pleasant, reviving her. She must keep the window open as she drove.

Mrs Goodhusband had reached the car and halted, puffing, to rest one foot on the ground. 'Hullo, Sally dear! How's tricks?'

'I'm fine,' said Sally, interpreting this as an inquiry after her health.

Yvonne was taking time to repair damage by wind and exertion to her coiffure. She patted her hairline and tucked away errant curls before retying the headscarf.

'No more alarms and excursions?' She shook her head. 'I was so sorry to hear about Hector Bodicote. He was a village character. I know he used to wander about but we'd all got used to that. I found the news about all those books in his place rather sad. I'm sure he simply was immensely curious about everything, although that doesn't excuse any of it. I suppose he was quite ancient. Tristan was very upset.'

'Was he?' Sally was mildly surprised.

'Yes. Tristan's a very sensitive boy.'

Sally had seen Tristan about the village and he hadn't struck her as a boy. She'd assumed him to be about twenty-eight. But to a mother's eye . . .

'Was that right about the books?' Yvonne was asking. 'The old chap really pinched them?'

'So it seems.'

'Never can tell,' said Yvonne. 'I managed to catch one of those journalists and told him about our action group. He wrote it down but I didn't see it in any of the papers.' She prepared to cycle on. 'I'm just going down to the farm for some eggs. She keeps a few hens free-range. I don't buy from the supermarket. I hope you don't! Or if you do, make sure they're free-range! You pay a little more but it's the price of peace of mind, you know.'

'Yes, I will!' Sally promised hastily.

'We're marching the day after tomorrow, did you know about that?'

'I beg your pardon?'

'Day after tomorrow,' repeated Mrs Goodhusband helpfully. 'Our little committee and supporters. I told the reporter about it and rang our local rag, too. Invited anyone who'd like to join us to come along. The more the merrier!' She indicated the basket on her bicycle and Sally noticed, which she hadn't before, that it held several rolled papers.

'Just going to tack up a few more posters while I'm out and about! We're assembling in Castle Darcy at eleven a.m. and marching in orderly procession to the battery egg-production unit where we shall make our protest. I've informed the police as well. Everything's quite in order. Will you be able to join us?'

'Oh, gosh!' said Sally. 'I mean, I think I shall be at work at Bailey's the day after tomorrow.'

'Pity. However, if you're free, come along. And don't forget, I still want to talk to your husband!' Yvonne reminded her. 'I wrote and told him so but he hasn't been in touch. Tell him, whenever is convenient!' She waved and set off again, wobbling slightly.

It wasn't likely Liam was ever going to find a meeting with Yvonne convenient, thought Sally. But she'd let them sort that out.

Yvonne stuck out her arm, combining the traffic signal with a farewell wiggle of her hand, before she wheeled off to the right and disappeared down a muddy track. Sally drove on.

Despite telling Yvonne she was fine, she became aware that she didn't feel it. She frowned and peered through the windscreen. More than the sleepiness, a muzziness was setting in. She hoped she wasn't in for a dose of Meredith's 'flu.

Reaching Bamford she had a minor mishap at the roundabout.

It was such a silly thing and she'd never done anything like it before. She had looked and assumed it was clear for her to enter. She just hadn't seen the other car. It must have been there. It was very odd. It appeared, horn blaring, driver gesticulating rudely, and swept across her bows. It gave her such a start that she swerved and stalled. She was a careful driver and she didn't do that kind of thing.

She concentrated furiously after that and found she really needed to. Her mind was drifting. Figures wandered in and out in disjointed imagery. Yvonne on her bike, Bodicote with his goats, Austin with his yellow scarf flying in the breeze.

The auction rooms hove into view filling her with the kind of relief felt by travellers in the desert who'd sighted an oasis. She couldn't pretend that she was feeling other than distinctly strange as she parked. Her arms and legs seemed heavy and she moved – or felt she was moving – very slowly, like a swimmer negotiating a warm sea.

Still in the curious suspended state, she floated past Ronnie and Ted, bidding them good morning in a voice which seemed to come from a great distance. They, however, did not appear to notice anything amiss. Whatever was happening to her, and something was, it was taking place in her head.

'Morning, Mrs Caswell . . .' Their sturdy figures, Ronnie's baseball-capped, shimmered and faded into the brickwork behind them like a pair of djinns.

She proceeded to her tiny office and there made an effort to cast off the spell which enveloped her. It must be the 'flu. It had struck Meredith down and now it was going to attack her. What a nuisance. Perhaps she could get something from the chemist's on the way home.

She hung up her coat (not so easy because the hook moved about) and surveyed her desk. For some reason, she couldn't quite remember what it was she was supposed to do at it. She'd make a start in a minute.

'Hullo, Sal!' Austin's cheery voice broke into her reverie.

He bustled in. 'Someone's brought in a load of stuff to go in the next sale. We'll have to start listing it all up. It doesn't look up to much to me. Mixed china and glassware, none of it remarkable. There are some ghastly pictures. Highland cattle in a mist, that sort of thing. Not even in good shape. Frames aren't even worth anything. We'll put them altogether in one lot—'

Aware that his words were falling into unresponsive space, he broke off and peered at her. 'Sal? You all right?'

'I don't know.' She sat down heavily on her chair. 'I feel rather odd. I think I may be going down with flu.'

Austin cupped his hands around her face and tilted it so he could stare into her eyes. She stared back at him, wishing his face didn't shimmer in that odd way.

'Your eyes look a bit odd,' he said, concerned. 'Perhaps you ought to go home. Can you drive?'

'Don't know.'

'I'll take you.'

'No,' she protested. 'You've got work to do.'

She was aware, as she spoke, that another figure had joined them. She found it difficult to distinguish the face but the voice was Meredith's.

'Is something wrong? I came to see if Sally could make lunch today.'

Austin was explaining. 'She thinks it may be the flu. But I'm not sure. Take a look at her eyes.'

Meredith's face swam closer, concerned. 'I see what you mean. I'll take her home. OK, Sally? We'll stop by the medical centre. Ask nurse to take a look at you.'

That brought her out of the enveloping fog. 'No! There's no need for that. I'll go home and lie down. Then I'll be all right.'

'Sally?' Meredith's voice was filled with misgiving. 'Sal, have you taken anything this morning? I mean, pills or anything?'

'No. Don't take pills. Why?'

213

'Just that the pupils of your eyes are dilated. How do you feel?'

'Sleepy.'

'What are you going to do?' Austin asked impatiently.

Meredith reached for Sally's jacket on the hook behind them. 'Leave it to me, Austin. Come on, Sally, slip your jacket on. I'll take you now. And we will stop off at the medical centre and get some advice. It's on the way, for goodness sake. Is Liam at home?'

She shook her head. 'No, gone into Oxford, to the lab. Going to work there today.' She spoke the words carefully, pressing her tongue, which felt too large for her mouth, against her teeth.

She stumbled as they walked to Meredith's car. Meredith caught her and bundled her into the front seat. 'Take it easy.' She sounded worried but Sally was past noticing.

It was all a dream world. The car had stopped. Meredith hauled her out like a bundle of washing and propelled her, gripping her by the arm, towards a building which seemed familiar. They were at the medical centre. There were people everywhere, a busy morning. A faint smell of antiseptic. A nurse in a white uniform with a brisk Scots accent.

'Now, what is it, dear?'

Meredith's competent voice, explaining. 'She's drowsy. Her eyes look peculiar. I don't like it. It doesn't look like any kind of flu to me. I want someone to take a look at her.'

The nurse was speaking, something about surgery being full and none of the doctors free. If they waited until twelve—

'She can't wait until noon!' Meredith's voice, sharp with anger, broke into the fog around Sally. 'For pete's sake, take a look at her yourself! You can see something's badly wrong!'

The nurse's face swam nearer. 'I see what you mean. Just come round to my room for a second. 'I'll see if any of the doctors can take a few minutes between appointments. Who is the lady's own doctor?'

'Pringle . . .' Sally mumbled, feeling she really must take some part in all this.

'Just sit down, dear. Are you on any medication?'

Sally shook her head, collapsing on to the proffered chair. The effort of walking to the nurse's room had taken it out of her. Her heart was beating in a funny jumpy way and she began to take short, rapid breaths, trying to get air into her lungs.

The nurse moved away to address Meredith. 'You're a relative?'

'No, I'm a friend. I can get hold of her husband. Look, what's wrong with her?'

'Has she been like it before?'

'No, no! I've never seen her like it. What is it?'

The nurse lowered her voice. 'She's not taking anything?'

'Taking? What, pills? She told you she wasn't. She told me she hadn't. I don't *know* for sure, of course I don't. She wouldn't lie about it, why should she?'

'I feel sick!' Sally said loudly.

They jumped round. The nurse descended. 'All right, dear! Can you get over here?'

Sally was directed to a nearby sluice. She leaned over it, retching. The nurse was holding her head and calling out to a colleague to see if Dr Pringle was free.

A dribble of foaming brackish liquid dribbled down into the sluice. The nurse peered at it. Then she grabbed the nearest kidney dish and the next time Sally fetched up the liquid, the nurse neatly caught it.

Pringle had arrived. 'Hullo, Mrs Caswell? Under the weather? Let's have a look.'

A thermometer was shoved into her mouth, under her tongue. It hurt. Pringle was taking her pulse.

The thermometer was blessedly whipped away. 'Mmn . . . temperature's down a bit. Pulse irregular. Have you eaten this morning?'

'Breakfast . . .' Sally tried to remember. 'Toast . . . tea, *my* tea.'

'*Your* tea?'

Meredith broke in with, 'She brews up her own herbal teas.'

'Does she?' Pringle sounded startled.

The nurse said, 'She brought this up.' She produced the kidney tray.

Pringle frowned. 'Right! I think we'll get her over to the hospital. Better safe than sorry. I'll phone and make arrangements.' He made briskly for the door. 'Find out about that tea!' he ordered the nurse.

'The tea, dear?' Nurse was bending over her, voice firm. 'What is this tea you drink? Can you tell me exactly what's in it?'

'Always drink it,' Sally mumbled. 'Can't be my tea.'

'We need to *know* what you've been eating and drinking this morning, dear. Now, do try and remember.'

'What's wrong, for goodness sake?' Meredith hissed.

The nurse glanced up at her. 'We're trying to find out! She seems to be drugged.'

Sally murmured, 'It smelled rather nasty . . .'

'What's that, dear? Your tea?'

'No, not my tea, Mr Bod – Bodicote's tea. It smelled like – like mice.'

'Do you know what she means?' Nurse turned to Meredith again.

'Not a clue. Bodicote was an old chap who lived next door and his place might well have had mice.'

The name lodged obstinately in Sally's brain. There was something she wanted to tell them about Bodicote, she just remembered. Or rather, she'd just forgotten. She wished she could remember what it was. It might be important. Or it might not.

'I ought to tell you—' she informed them.

'What's that, Sally?' Meredith's face came closer, out of focus. 'What is it you want to tell us? About the herbal tea?'

'No. About what Yvonne said. Only I can't remember what she—'

'Watch out!' Meredith cried. 'She's going!'

They grabbed Sally just in time to prevent her pitching off the chair unconscious.

Chapter Thirteen

They took Sally by ambulance to hospital. Meredith travelled with her. At the hospital, all was organised bustle. She watched with concern as Sally was wheeled away. As the trolley squeaked out of sight, a well-groomed, middle-aged Chinese woman in a white coat descended on Meredith.

'Dr Chang.' The voice, against expectations, was a broad, reassuring North country one. 'We need to know what she's taken. I understand she may have drunk a home-brewed herbal tea. Have you any idea what it might be?'

Before Meredith could answer, hurrying footsteps tapped down the polished corridor and a dishevelled Austin Bailey appeared, clasping a vacuum flask. His bowtie had swivelled and instead of the bow going west-east, it now stood at north-west to south-east. The effect was to make it look as if someone had wound him up like a clock spring.

'I've left Ted in charge – what's going on? I called the medical centre and they said she'd been brought here! I managed to get hold of Pringle and he asked me about some tea. I told him Sally always brought in a flask and he said I should bring it to you!'

Austin held out the flask and Dr Chang seized it. 'Good! We'll get it analysed!'

'Hold on!' Meredith put out a hand as the doctor turned. 'She drank more than one kind. That's her office flask. But she may have something else at home she drank at breakfast. We could ask Liam, I suppose.' Doubt echoed in her voice. Liam probably wouldn't have taken heed of what his wife drank.

Austin took off his spectacles and waved them in the air. 'He's in Oxford. That is, he was at the laboratory. I rang him to tell him what happened and he was leaving immediately to come here.'

Dr Chang interrupted. 'Is there anyone at her home who could bring in any other canisters of herbal tea for us to analyse?'

Meredith and Austin looked at each other.

'It is urgent!' Dr Chang emphasised.

'Sally's keys must be in her handbag,' Meredith suggested. 'Let me have them and I'll go.'

Dr Chang hesitated. 'The patient's personal belongings – it's irregular. Really I ought to wait till the husband gets here. I suppose I could—?'

'I've got a spare key to their cottage!' Austin exclaimed. 'I'll go out and look for the tea!'

'You've got a business to run. Give me the key and I'll go,' Meredith urged. She turned to Dr Chang. 'Tell Liam – that's Dr Caswell – when he gets here that I've gone to fetch all the tea I can find at their cottage.'

Despite the urgency of her mission there was a necessary detour to the auction rooms to collect the spare key, which Austin produced from a drawer in his desk. It had a tattered luggage label tied to it, reading 'Sally's key'.

'I'll bring it back, Austin,' Meredith promised, grabbing it unceremoniously from his hand.

He took off his spectacles and blinked shortsightedly at her. 'I am really very worried. Sally is a dear person. Very dear to me. Besides, we've been discussing—'

There really wasn't time for this. 'Later, Austin, all right?'

She hurried from his office and drove at reckless pace to Castle Darcy.

The kitchen was neat and tidy and the pottery jars stood where they always had. Meredith glanced quickly inside each one.

Strange-looking dried leaves of various kinds, the teas. She looked around and saw a woven wicker shopping basket in the corner. She stacked the tea caddies in it and hesitated. Her impulse was to rush off back to the hospital with her booty, but it was important not to overlook any. She opened the kitchen cupboards but they revealed no more teas. She was about to leave when her eye fell on the waste bin.

There was a battered margarine tub in it, lying on its side, and spilling from it a crushed mixture of dried vegetation.

Meredith stooped and picked it out carefully. Most of what it had contained had spilled out into the bin. But there was enough left in the bottom of the tub for analysis. She sniffed.

'Phew!' she muttered. It wasn't like Sally to keep her tea in such a makeshift container nor did any other of the teas smell so fusty. But hadn't Sally mumbled something about Bodicote and a tea? Meredith picked the lid out of the garbage in the bin and fixed it carefully on the tub. Satisfied now that she'd found all there was to find, she hurried outside to her car.

Back at the hospital, Meredith handed over her collection of tubs and inquired anxiously after Sally.

'Mrs Caswell will be all right,' she was assured. 'Especially now we can hope to find out what she drank.'

Meredith retired to the waiting area and the public phones. After a hunt for a twenty-pence piece, she called Regional HQ.

'Alan? I'm at the hospital, not the Cottage, the Alice King. What? No, I'm fine! It's not me, it's Sally.' Interrupting another cry of alarm at the other end of the line, she went on hurriedly. 'They tell me she's going to be all right. She seems to have drunk some kind of herbal tea which made her ill. I thought you'd want to know. Liam's been informed, I understand.' As she spoke, her gaze caught a familiar figure.

'He's here,' she said. 'I'll see you later.' She hung up.

Liam had seen her and approached, looking bewildered and irritated in equal measure.

'They're pumping her out!' he said disbelievingly.

'They say she's going to be fine, don't worry, Liam,' Meredith consoled him.

'Why did she drink the wretched witch's brew? I told her time and time again about that stuff she makes up.' He rubbed a hand over his forehead. 'Now I've got to hang about here. What a place!' He cast a dismissive glance at his surroundings. 'I can't stick hospitals,' he added. 'Too many people.'

'Tough!' said Meredith unfeelingly, which made him blink. 'I dare say Sally's disliking them even more at the moment!'

'Right . . .' he mumbled.

When Meredith returned that evening, she found Liam crouched by his wife's bedside. Sally looked pale and drawn but, to Meredith's relief, appeared to have come out of the drugged haze.

'Bloody Bodicote!' said Liam briefly, glancing at Meredith but dispensing with any formal greeting. He clasped his hands and scowled.

'How are you feeling, Sally?' Meredith took a seat by the bed.

'I feel,' Sally whispered, 'as if I'd been put through one of those old-fashioned laundry mangles. But I'm all right now, so they tell me. I've you to thank, Meredith. You insisted we go to the medical centre on the way home. I didn't want to bother. I thought I was going down with flu, like you.'

'Yes, thanks,' Liam said awkwardly.

'It was Austin who first noticed you weren't well and drew my attention to it. Perhaps you ought to thank him, too, Liam?'

Liam was saved from replying by a nurse, who looked in and called, 'Patients' mealtime soon. Visitors, can you leave now?'

'I suppose they haven't had a chance to analyse all the teas yet? Or have they?' Meredith kept her gaze fixed on Liam, who looked very like a small boy being carpeted for a misdemeanour involving a catapult. She'd quelled more awkward opponents than Liam in her time and her motto was, once you've got 'em on the run, keep 'em running!

Liam muttered, 'That crazy old man, Bodicote, gave Sal some herbal brew or other and she was daft enough to drink it this morning after I left!'

So there! he might have added, but didn't.

'Don't keep on, Liam!' Sally protested weakly from the pillows. 'If it was Bodicote's, then it was a mistake. Bodicote must have picked something in error.'

Liam got to his feet. 'I've got to go back to the lab. I left in a rush and all my papers are there. I'll be back after dinner.'

He leaned forward and dabbed a kiss on his wife's forehead. Meredith noticed that as he did so, she turned her head aside, away from him.

When he'd gone Sally grimaced. 'Liam's cross because Bodicote gave me this tub of dried leaves, a tea. It was just before he died. I put it with my own pots of herbs and left it. I didn't have the heart to throw it out, not after what happened. This morning I had a bit of a headache, so I thought I'd try it. It smelled unpleasant and didn't taste too nice so I just drank the one mugful and binned the rest. But it seemed to work, too. The headache went. Unfortunately, everything else went too, after a bit.'

'I found it. Dr Chang has it now.'

Sally essayed a smile. 'Good job you're so thorough, Meredith.'

There was a movement at the door and someone else entered the room. They both looked up to see Alan Markby.

'Thought I'd call and see how you are, Sally.' His gaze held Meredith's briefly. He leaned his hands on the metal bar at the end of the bed, and smiled down at the patient. 'So? Feeling better?'

'Better-ish. Not so dopey, anyway. Still on the lethargic side.'

'That's better. Nasty experience for you. Take it easy, eh?'

'Can't do anything else, not in here. Thank you for coming in, both of you.' Sally lifted a limp hand and waved.

Meredith got up. 'The nurse will be back again in a minute to chase us out, so we'd better go. I'll come back again.'

Outside in the corridor, Alan asked, 'How's Liam?'

Meredith pulled a wry expression. 'Still grumbling. Blaming Bodicote. I think he's gone back to his lab. He'll be coming again to see her tonight. You'd think he'd forget about his wretched work for one day in the circumstances!' Her exasperation with Liam was obvious.

'Thank you for calling me, by the way.'

'Thought you'd want to know. I'd better go over to the auction rooms now and tell Austin she's all right. I'll give him back Sally's spare key. I promised I'd return it.'

Alan looked at her curiously. 'Austin has a spare key to the Caswell place?'

'For emergencies, I suppose. My next door neighbour has mine. You've also got mine, come to that! Have you spoken to the doctor here?'

'Not yet.' Markby glanced down the corridor. 'I believe she's waiting for me. I got in touch with her after you called me. Dr Chang, the hospital toxicologist.'

'You don't suspect this was anything other than a mistake? That Sally was poisoned?' Meredith's voice rose in horror.

'Keep your voice down. Poison is a loose term. Otherwise harmless substances taken in excess can be poisonous. In this case we know she took, probably accidentally, some harmful drug. By that token, yes, she was poisoned.'

A nurse was approaching. 'Are you Superintendent Markby? Dr Chang's waiting for you.'

Markby squeezed Meredith's arm. 'See you later.'

'Sure.' She watched him walk away in the wake of the nurse.

'Superintendent?' Dr Chang greeted him. 'Glad to see you. Incidentally, I'm glad someone thought to call the police.

Otherwise I'd have done so.' She pointed at a chair. 'Have a seat. Have you seen the patient?'

'Yes,' Markby took the seat indicated. 'She seems weak but fine.'

'She's lucky to be alive,' Dr Chang said without undue emotion.

'What was it?'

'*Conium maculatum*. Hemlock.'

He stared at her, astonished. 'What?'

'The stuff the Greeks gave Socrates to drink,' she explained helpfully.

But his silence had nothing to do with failing to identify the plant. Rather, it was due to an image which formed in his head. Frost-blackened *umbelliferae* growing around a clogged disused garden pond. One of them, he was almost ready to swear, had been hemlock. But if it grew in Yvonne's garden, the seeds had come in from the surrounding countryside. The stuff probably grew all over Castle Darcy.

Dr Chang was expounding. 'It's highly toxic even in a small dose. She was exhibiting all the classic symptoms, dilated pupils, poor coordination, temperature down, pulse jumpy. I've made a study of medicinal herbs. Hemlock *was* used as a medicine in the ancient world by the Arabs, Greeks, Romans . . . It's still occasionally used in some preparations. But it's a very dangerous thing and tricky. Best avoided. Fortunately, once we knew she'd drunk some form of herbal tea, we had little trouble. These toxic herbs are fairly easy to identify. As I say, I've had previous experience of them. I can't say I've had a hemlock poisoning for a while, though!'

She smiled cheerfully at him.

'It was in her flask?'

'Oh no, it was in a margarine tub, in a mix of dried herbs. Rather an unsavoury mix. I understand an elderly neighbour gave it to her. She was very unwise to sample it.'

'You've still got it? You haven't disposed of it? I'll need it!'

'I still have it and haven't quite finished with it. I need a botanist to look at it. As I said, I've some experience, but I need to be sure. It's not a pure mix.'

She went to a nearby shelf and returned with a battered margarine tub. She took the lid off and held it out to him where he sat.

A collection of crushed herbs lay in the bottom. 'Some of this is undoubtedly quite harmless,' Dr Chang observed. 'I think I recognise feverfew and sage. The quantity of hemlock may be quite small.'

Markby said slowly, 'Don't take me wrong on this, Dr Chang, but this needs to be kept secure.'

'It will be, never fear.' She replaced the lid. 'Look, Superintendent, I don't want to start a hare . . .'

Markby looked up at her. 'If there's anything else, I need to know.'

'Exactly. I've had a little chat with the patient. She tells me she's had spells of lethargy, dizziness and nausea before. She put it down to stress. The attacks, if one can call them that, stretch back about six months to last summer. She's worried now that it's been caused by her tea, that is to say, one of her own concoctions. We'll take a look at her tea, naturally, although the brew in the flask was perfectly harmless. I think we'll be able to confirm it was this present from a neighbour which has caused all the trouble.'

Dr Chang raised the margarine tub. 'It's not unusual for old country remedies to contain quite dangerous substances. People are interested these days in traditional medicines but, unfortunately, many haven't inherited the skills and knowledge to use them safely. Perhaps we, or you, can ask the old gentleman about this mix of his. Above all, warn him not to drink it himself!'

'Unfortunately,' said Markby, 'We can't.'

Chapter Fourteen

A crisp, diamond-bright morning, the sort which cleared the head and charged the batteries. Alan Markby walked into the building, whistling. Heads turned and expressive glances were exchanged.

'You're cheerful this morning,' observed Pearce.

He was disconcerted when the superintendent appeared to take that casual remark as a serious comment, considering it, turning it this way and that in his mind, before finally coming up with a reply.

'Not so much cheerful, Dave, as optimistic.'

'Right,' said Pearce doubtfully.

Markby clasped his hands on his desk and beamed at him. 'The hemlock, that was a mistake.'

'She drank it by mistake?'

'Brush the cobwebs away!' Markby reproached him. 'It was a mistake on the part of whoever has been conducting this campaign of violence against the Caswells. We've all been led up the garden path, that's what!'

'So what are we going to do?' The wary Pearce still wasn't quite sure he saw where Markby was headed.

'We're going to talk to everyone again. I do mean everyone! They are all of them sitting on information. There is something they are not telling us. Whatever it is, it's been making an unholy alliance of the most unlikely set of people. But they will all find that I don't take kindly to being messed around!' Markby jabbed the air to emphasise the point.

'Prescott can take Whelan. When he's finished there, he can go on into Bamford and chat to Austin Bailey. You can take the Goodhusbands, mother and son.'

Pearce groaned. 'And don't let Yvonne run rings round you. Someone can ring that Norwich laboratory and find out more about the research programme which has been going on down there in conjunction with the Oxford lab. And I,' Markby said, reaching for the telephone, 'will take Liam Caswell.'

A call to Castle Darcy went unanswered. Markby tried Liam's laboratory and was rewarded with a suspicious female voice asking what it could do for him. He asked for Dr Caswell.

'Dr Caswell is a very busy man. Besides, he doesn't come in every day. Who's asking for him?'

'Superintendent Markby, regional crime squad.' An audible intake of breath at the other end of the line. 'I know he's got a lot on his mind at the moment but I need to speak to him and he's not at home.'

'He'll be at the hospital!' The note of reproof in the voice was unmistakable. 'His wife had to be rushed in. But he did ring to let us know he'd be coming on here afterwards. I believe about eleven.'

'Fine, when he gets there, tell him I'll be along later to see him.'

Silence at the other end. Eventually, 'Come to the front office first.' The phone was put down on him.

'That's put the cat among the pigeons!' Markby muttered happily to himself. There was no pleasure like the pleasure of stirring up trouble for someone who'd been an irritation for some time. Small revenges are sweet.

The crisp early morning had developed into a day which was sunny and surprisingly mild. That was English weather for you. One moment it froze your toes and the next it tantalised with unseasonal springlike temperatures. Only imagine, it was nearly Christmas. A mere five weeks away. It didn't feel like it. Some of the shops had decorated windows with holly and images of Santa Claus. But there was a lack of seasonal feel. Markby wondered whether this was just because he was getting older. Christmas was a time for children, eagerly looked forward to and savoured. Now he just saw it as a time when he had to write all those cards.

When tourists came to visit Oxford's dreaming spires they didn't have in mind the sort of building which housed Liam's workplace. It lurked on a trading estate to the east of the city. Even beneath today's pale sun, the estate appeared windswept, uniform and workaday. Low-rise office blocks alternated with ugly prefabricated warehousing. The dull exteriors were enlivened with garish plaques each announcing the name of the business within. Before each unit, patches of turf which had been intended as a green break to the eye had been reduced by wear to trampled rectangles of dried mud dotted with clumps of coarse grass and weeds. The trees which had been planted at the same time as the turf laid, survived only as spindly sticks.

People, thought Markby, spent their entire working lives commuting to and from this place. Hard-working, ambitious, intelligent people, many of them. They started with enthusiasm and ideas and they slowly atrophied here, like the grass and trees.

At the estate's very furthest point from the main road lay the laboratories. They, too, were long, single-storey prefabricated buildings of post-war vintage. Markby's professional eye judged them to be difficult to render secure. Little wonder Michael Whelan and his companions had chosen to make a raid on them. Break a window, put your hand through, twiddle a catch and you were in. New-looking burglar alarms, little blue boxes, had been fitted. But they were tokens. By the time anyone answered their shrill call, any raider would be in and out again.

227

Oddly enough, the building facing Markby was a crumbling early Victorian house, obviously predating all the surrounding buildings. It had fallen on evil times. Unpainted, with cracks in the cornices and a suspicious droop to the lintel of the upper-storey left window, its downstairs windows were disguised by modern sunblinds. A plaque on the door announced this to contain the administration offices.

Markby entered and found himself facing the owner of the suspicious telephone voice.

It belonged to a middle-aged woman, very tall, very thin and ramrod straight. She was dressed in a khaki-coloured knitted suit and plainly tailored beige blouse relieved by a single string of pearls. Her hair was cut very short, greying and bristly. He suppressed an urge to salute her.

'Ah, Superintendent,' she said, disapproval in no way mitigated by the sight of him. 'Dr Caswell arrived a few minutes ago. I told him you were on your way. He's in Block A. Just go round this building and you'll see it, straight ahead.' Her hand dropped to the desk. 'You'll need this.'

She wore a wedding ring. Markby tried to imagine what manner of man might be married to this martinet. She handed him a small plastic envelope with a clip attached. Inside the envelope was a square of paper announcing, *Temporary Visitor*.

'Sign here in the book for it, would you? Put the date and the time of day, if you please.'

'Thank you,' said Markby. He complied with instructions, noting that he was the first person that day to be issued with such a visitor's badge. A quick glance at the facing page showed that only three had been issued the day before. He attached it to his jacket with some difficulty. The spring clip was awkward.

The guardsman watched his endeavours with a pained forbearance. 'You'll need to return that pass, Superintendent, when you leave. It is, as you see, numbered. We keep careful track of all passes.'

228

He promised to do so.

'We used not to have to bother with such things,' she said sadly. 'But since last year, when we had some unpleasantness, we've updated our security.'

A plastic envelope with a card in it wouldn't deter the likes of Whelan's cohorts. But such things, together with the shiny new burglar alarms, clearly made the woman feel safer. The insurers, too, he thought, would have insisted. The insurance cover on the building would be jeopardised if they couldn't show they'd at least tried.

'You were here, then, when the animal rights protesters broke in?'

'Not *here*,' she corrected. 'Not on the premises. They came at night. But I was an employee. I've worked here seventeen years. They did such a lot of damage. Broke windows and doorlocks, made such a mess over in the labs. I'm fond of animals myself but I couldn't condone such antics. I know vandals and hooligans when I see their handiwork.'

She sat down, dismissing him. He wheeled and marched out.

After acquiring his pass (numbered, signed for and to be returned), entering Block A was easy. He just opened the door. The updated security system had a long way to go. Facing him was a long corridor with a waxed floor. The internal partitions were flimsily constructed of plywood and glass and the murmur of voices, the rattle of receptacles and even the throaty hiss and roar of a Bunsen burner were all distinguishable.

Markby stood hesitantly by the door, wondering where to find Liam. His dilemma was solved when a young woman, working with her eye to a microscope in a cubicle to his right, looked up and spotted him through the glass partition. She immediately shot out and stood square in front of him, blocking any possible progress.

'Who are you?' she asked sharply and with a marked accent.

She was small but sturdily built. Her shoulder-length russet hair framed a heart-shaped face with an unblemished tawny skin. It was her eyes, however, which commanded admiration, green and dark-lashed, scrutinising Markby with scarcely veiled hostility. Her white coat was unbuttoned over a figure-hugging cream pullover, short scarlet leather skirt and black tights disappearing into snug black boots.

Some intricate piece of jewellery on a leather thong round her neck took his attention. In pattern it resembled a pre-Colombian carved panel, Aztec, Mayan, Incan. He couldn't distinguish between the arts of these ancient peoples. It was a maze of intertwining ropes or, Markby wasn't sure, snakes. The whole design led to its centre where a grotesque stylized bird's head with a gleaming ruby eye fixed the observer. Like its wearer it was striking but a little alarming.

'Yes, yes, you!' she repeated. 'Who are you? What do you want?'

Markby found himself taking refuge in indicating his Visitor's Pass. 'I'm looking for Dr Caswell.'

'Why do you wish to see him?'

It was time to tackle this firecracker head-on and establish some sort of authority. 'I'll discuss that with Dr Caswell. He is expecting me. Can you direct me to him?'

Her arched brows puckered, emphasising the extraordinary power of the green eyes. 'He's very busy. He has not told me he is expecting you. When have you made this appointment?' The disbelief in her voice was daunting.

'Look, er, Miss . . .' Markby, in his turn, leaned forward to study her plastic envelope, pinned to her white coat. It brought him closer to the jewel bird-snake and its cruel red eye. 'Marita Müller' read the pass.

'Miss Müller. I really can't stand here chatting to you, I'm afraid . . .'

'I am not chatting!' she said scornfully. 'I am busy. We are all

230

busy. Well, if you must see him, you must!'

She turned neatly on a booted heel and marched off down the waxed corridor. He followed meekly.

They fetched up before a door which she tapped and immediately opened. 'Liam? There is a policeman.' She hunched her shoulders in derision. Clearly civilian garb hadn't disguised his profession.

'Oh, right, thanks, Marita.' Liam appeared. 'Markby, I was expecting you. The front office phoned through. It's *all right*, Marita.' He ushered Miss Müller back into the corridor. There was a brief whispered exchange between them. Markby raised his eyebrows and seated himself in an available chair.

Liam's desk was cluttered with papers and the screen of his computer covered with script. A quick read told Markby nothing. He couldn't make head or tail of any of it.

Liam returned, closing the door. 'Marita's over-protective,' he explained. 'But everyone is warned to stop and question any unknown face. We've got security-conscious. It started after last year's raid and the explosive package I received has made everything worse, to say nothing of the abusive mail. It was a damn near thing, that package. Poor Sal hasn't got over it and the last thing she needed was what happened yesterday.'

'I went to the hospital last night, after Meredith rang me.' Markby hoped the tinge of reproof in his voice would be picked up by Liam, who ought to have done the informing. But Liam was impervious to delicate shades of criticism. 'How is Mrs Caswell today?'

'She said you'd been. She's a lot better, quite chipper. You do realise *now* we're dealing with a bunch of maniacs? Everyone here's very nervous in case the nutters, whoever they are, decide to strike at someone else on the staff next. They mean to get one of us. They'd have got me, if Sal hadn't opened the package.'

He paused. 'It was a fluke I didn't open it. If you don't get whoever's behind it soon, I can tell you, there are going to be a lot of complaints going to high places, and they won't all be from me!'

Being threatened with a higher authority didn't worry Markby, although he did resort, a little unworthily, to a dig of his own. 'Striking young lady, that.' He nodded towards the door. 'An overseas student?'

Liam blinked. 'One of our exchange post-graduate students,' he said tersely. 'We have quite a few. From the old eastern block, mostly. But I think I've told you about this before.' Thus Liam terminated what he evidently saw as social chit-chat. 'Look here,' he said aggressively, 'it's time you lot got things sorted out.'

'I agree!' Markby told him. 'Now, Dr Chang tells me that Sally drank some tea given to her by your neighbour.'

Liam snorted. 'Crazy old coot. He was, quite seriously, mad. Look at all those books they found in his place.'

Markby steered him back to the matter in hand. 'Let's stick to this tea business. It was in a margarine tub. Do you recall the occasion when he gave it to her?'

'Yes. She came from the garden with it. Recently, just before he died. She should have chucked it out. I warned her about trading with the enemy. He never forgave us that business with the turnips, you know. You heard about that? Sal gave some to his blasted goats. It didn't make them ill but made the milk taste funny. Who wants goat's milk anyway, I ask you? He raised the dickens of a hoo-hah, vindictive old sod. She didn't do it on *purpose*. We should have known he'd plot some lunatic revenge!'

'Just a minute,' Markby interrupted the other's irate flow. 'Are you saying that the late Hector Bodicote *intended* to administer a toxic substance to your wife by way of revenge for what he saw as an attack on his animals?'

'Of course he bloody did!'

'Isn't that unreasonable, Dr Caswell? It would be foolhardy. Such a substance would be traced immediately back to him.'

'And he'd say it was all a mistake. He was crafty. These old country people are. Cunning as foxes.'

'He wanted to *kill* her?' Markby persisted.

Liam hesitated. 'Probably not. No, not kill, just make her very ill – the way he thought she'd made his goats. Only they weren't ill. They enjoyed the turnips and suffered no ill-effects them-selves. It was only their milk affected and that only temporarily.'

'Drinking the tea might well have resulted in your wife's death had Meredith not taken Mrs Caswell to the medical centre and insisted she be examined. She could easily have crashed her car under its influence!' Markby insisted.

'Bodicote wouldn't think about that!' said Liam briefly.

Markby sighed. 'Well, Bodicote is dead and we can't ask him about it. It's still a very serious accusation, Dr Caswell. Can you substantiate it in any way, other than by conjecture?'

Liam exploded into words, waving his arms, his voice rising and no doubt audible all over the building.

'Typical! That's all I've got from you since this started! Nothing but sneers and scepticism! What need is there to substantiate a box of poisoned tea which exists? It'll be back at the cottage in the kitchen.'

'No,' Markby said sharply. 'It's at the hospital in the capable hands of Dr Chang, the toxicologist. As, indeed, are all the other canisters of herbal tea in the kitchen. All will be checked.'

Liam froze. 'It is? Good. Well, then. You've seen it for yourself! Yes, Dr Chang ought to check the lot. There's no knowing what Bodicote did.'

'Surely,' Markby asked curiously, 'you saw that all the tea canisters were missing from your kitchen? Meredith went out and collected them, right after taking Sally to the hospital. She borrowed a key kept at Bailey and Bailey's.'

'Yes, of course. Look, I've had other things on my mind!' Liam's irritability didn't disguise his momentary confusion.

'I rang your cottage this morning!' Markby said sharply. 'No one answered.'

'I went to the hospital.'

'It was early.'

Liam threw up his hands. 'All right! I didn't go home last night. I knew I had to go to the hospital this morning and I wanted to come on here afterwards. There seemed no point in trekking out to Castle Darcy. A colleague here kindly gave me a bed for the night in Oxford.'

'I don't know why, Dr Caswell, you are always so reluctant to provide the police with information of any nature,' Markby said wearily. 'It does make our task so much more difficult. You appear to take the attitude that we're prying into your private affairs.'

'You are!' said Liam shortly.

'Of course we are! It's an official investigation!' Markby's control finally snapped. Liam looked startled. Markby drew a deep breath and began again.

'I understand that, apart from the incident with the turnips, Mrs Caswell and Mr Bodicote got along reasonably well. The odd tiff doesn't make someone decide to plan a serious attack.'

Liam flung both arms in the air. 'You're so damn narrow-minded, you haven't an ounce of imagination! Call this an investigation? You coppers, you see everything in straight lines! It doesn't occur to you, I suppose, that Bodicote may have intended his poisonous brew for *me!*'

It certainly hadn't occurred to Markby. His puzzlement must have shown on his face because Liam went on,

'Thought so! If you ask me, that's just what it was! Sally's being taken ill was a – a by-product, if you like. He meant to make *me* ill!'

'How on earth,' Markby's temper was beginning to fray, 'could he think it would do that? You don't drink the herbal teas!'

Liam pushed his bearded face close. 'He didn't know that, though, did he?'

He straightened up and whirled round, snatching up a vacuum

flask from the desk behind them. 'See this? Sal makes up two of these, every morning before she leaves for Bailey's. Mine holds coffee and hers contains her herbal mishmash. But Bodicote didn't know that, did he? He looked into my study and saw a flask on the table and thought to himself that it contained the same tea as Sal put in hers. He did that, snoop. Peer through windows. I caught him several times. He always reckoned he'd come to fetch back one of the straying goats. If you ask me, he let the goats through deliberately so that he had an excuse to prowl round our cottage.'

'All the same—'

Markby wasn't allowed to finish. Liam had taken the bit between his teeth. 'I'll tell you something else, too! The old man snooped inside the cottage. You saw how he wandered in the night you came, after the explosion? When we first came to live there, he did that often. Just marched in when he felt like it. We had a few rows and I told him to stay out! But he still sneaked in when he thought I was busy in the study. Always an excuse if he was caught. You have no idea, Superintendent, of what I've suffered on account of that old man!'

Markby leaned back in his spindly plastic chair. 'Who else has access to your cottage, apart from yourself, Mrs Caswell and Austin Bailey, who keeps a spare key at his auction rooms? Why?'

'Sal felt someone ought to have a key. Austin's not a neighbour but when you look at the neighbours we've got out at Castle Darcy, you can see why we didn't leave a spare emergency key with any of them! Austin keeps one in case Sal loses hers while she's out of the place or we're away on holiday and someone needs to go in. During the day, provided one of us is at home, the rest of Castle Darcy's got access, if you like. The back door is an old-fashioned lock with an external handle. The big old Chubb key stays permanently in the lock on the inside. We open it in the morning and fasten it when we go to bed – unless we both go away from the village. It wouldn't be practical to keep turning it back and forth all day like a gaoler!' Liam snorted. 'Although, perhaps it would be prudent after this!'

'I'd like to refresh my memory of the layout of your kitchen myself. Its position *vis-à-vis* Bodicote's land. What can be seen from the window? What could Bodicote see from his hedge? That sort of thing. Would you object to my borrowing the key Austin Bailey holds? I believe Meredith has returned it to him. Or you could come with me to the cottage now, if you prefer to be there.'

Liam stared at him. 'Go and get the key off Austin, if you must.'

'Then perhaps you'd give him a call and authorise it.'

'Bureaucracy!' Liam put a hand to his forehead. 'This is a nightmare. Yes, I'll phone Austin. I'll phone him right away.'

Markby got to his feet. 'By the way, when you had the break-in here last year, the intruders wanted to release some beagles. Where are the animals in question now? I'd quite like to see them.'

Liam bared his teeth triumphantly. 'You can't, they've gone. There were only half a dozen of them. We moved them out after the raid. We'd about finished that programme anyway. Don't keep any animals here now.'

'Moved out where?' Markby was fairly sure the beagles would have been put down. But he wanted to see how Liam would react to being asked, and how he'd phrase his answer. Would Liam brazen it out or become surly and defensive? He'd offered no justification for their use, presumably because he believed he owed none, certainly not to a layman like Markby. But perversely Markby wanted to hear one, just the same.

As expected, Liam rightly read the question as a challenge and glowered. But a diversion saved him from the need to answer.

An imperious rap heralded Marita Müller. She fixed the intruder with snapping green eyes and a toss of the russet mane. 'Dr Caswell is needed on the telephone!'

Liam relaxed and allowed himself a faint smirk. He knew he'd cheated his visitor of an argument. He leaned back and allowed the centre of attention to move to the combative figure of his assistant.

'All right,' Markby told Marita, a trifle irritably. 'I'm going.'

You could hear nearly everything in this place, with its flimsy plywood and glass partitions, but he hadn't heard the ring of a telephone.

He took a final, frustrated, verbal swipe at Liam, before stomping out. 'You're well protected.'

'Need to be,' said Liam sarcastically. 'All kinds of cranks around.'

'Hullo, Markby,' Austin Bailey said nervously. 'One of your people has been over to see me. A bruiser of a young fellow, quite alarming.'

'Sergeant Prescott. I've come for Caswell's key. I understand Meredith returned it last night and Caswell should've phoned through and authorised my borrowing of it.'

Bailey rummaged in a desk drawer. 'Yes, he did. Here . . .' He produced the key.

Markby took it and read the crumpled label. 'This is always tied to it? Reading "Sally's key" like this?'

'Yes, why not? I've got a drawer full of keys. I need something to tell me what they all are.' In support of his words, Austin pulled the drawer right out and indicated a jumble of contents, including several keys, all with labels attached. Some were housekeys, others appeared to be furniture keys or security keys of some kind.

'What on earth do you do with all those?' Markby asked.

'Very handy,' Austin assured him. 'You'd be surprised how many old pieces of furniture, for example, turn up here locked and the key lost. Quite often I've found a key to fit. Or if I can make good a missing key to a little Victorian money-box, say, it just adds a touch of interest to it.' He pushed in the drawer. 'Look, what's going on? I couldn't tell that sergeant anything. To be frank, I wasn't going to discuss my business with him. It's hardly relevant!'

'Oh, you'd be surprised, Austin!' Markby told him cheerily. 'The oddest things can be relevant!'

Bailey flushed and pushed his spectacles up his nose with his index finger. 'Nothing I know has the slightest thing to do with all this! And look here,' he added doggedly. 'I really did object to the very personal line he took with his questions.'

Markby was still turning Sally's key in his fingers. 'How long have you held this here, Austin?'

'Oh, since last summer, I suppose.'

'And always kept it in that drawer?'

'Always.' Austin was growing uneasy. 'It's quite safe here.'

'Ever had cause to use it yourself?'

Austin's face turned a startling puce. 'That, if I may say so, is a damn insulting question!'

The Yale key turned easily in the front door. Markby pushed it open and stepped into the little hallway, closing the door carefully behind him.

Liam's study was to the left. He walked in and looked around it. The Caswells read the *Daily Telegraph*. There was a jettisoned copy in a wastepaper basket. So did a goodly proportion of the middle-class population. Markby went to the window which gave on to the back garden. There was a good view of the Caswells' own patch, but it was difficult to see over into Bodicote's. As Liam had rightly said, the goat-house, at the far end of Bodicote's paddock, was invisible from here.

The sitting room contained nothing of interest. In the kitchen, all was neat and tidy except for the waste bin which looked as if a large animal had rummaged in it. So it had, in a manner of speaking. Meredith seeking Bodicote's tub. The back door was fastened from the inside and the cumbersome key was in the lock, just as Liam had told him it would be. From this window, the view was similar to that from the study window: the Caswell garden and a closer view of the hedge dividing this plot from the next, Bodicote's. Markby could see the brass bedhead which had fallen to allow Jasper through on the fateful day. He turned the Chubb key anti-clockwise to open the back door and stepped outside.

A garden, any garden, always took his interest. Markby gazed a little wistfully down the length of this one, before walking to the hedge, where he paused by the bedhead and turned to look back. He could see into the Caswell kitchen, surprisingly well. To see into Caswell's study meant walking away from the hedge and up to the window. Markby, nose pressed against the pane, observed the computer, desk, phone, chair, a bookcase. This was what Bodicote himself had seen on the morning of the explosion, when he'd come to investigate in his cautious way.

Dr Chang would have wished to question Bodicote about the herbal tea. Markby himself would have liked to question Bodicote about a number of things.

As it was, the only being left who might be said to know Bodicote's mind was Jasper. And the best of lawyers couldn't cross-examine a goat.

He locked up the cottage and took the key back to Austin who made great show of putting it away, this time, in his safe.

Markby hoped it wasn't a case of locking the stable door.

Chapter Fifteen

'Your husband rang, Mrs Caswell.'

Sister stood by the entry to the ward, crisply efficient. 'He says he'll call by and take you home, if you wish.'

'This morning?' Sally was surprised. She had been for a bath and pulled her wrap tightly around her. It wasn't cold in the hospital corridor, but she wasn't used to standing around in a semi-public area, dressed in a nightgown and slippers, while equally informally clad strangers moved around her.

'Dr Chang says there's no reason why you shouldn't be discharged. How are you feeling? Did you eat any breakfast?' Sister had a nannyish way with her.

'I had some cereal and milk,' Sally lied. They had brought her a bowl of Weetabix on a tray, but when no one was looking, she'd scraped the mushed pulp into a plastic bag which she'd hidden in her sponge bag, to be disposed of when convenient. The very idea of eating made her want to throw up.

An elderly woman was wheeled past in a chair. The sight prompted Sally's conscience. 'I think,' she said, 'that I should like to leave. You've all been very kind, but I expect you need the bed.'

'We do,' Sister confessed. 'You won't be drinking any more of that herbal tea of yours, will you? Not for a while, anyway. Stick to milk or just water, is my advice, until your system has properly settled down. And don't ever drink any herbal mixture that isn't prepared by an expert or that you haven't made yourself from a source you're sure is safe! Accepting gifts when you don't know what's in them isn't a good idea.'

'Don't worry!' Sally promised. 'I've learned my lesson!'

She wondered whether Sister knew about the letter-bomb, or whether her last words had been uttered in unconscious irony.

In truth, Sally wasn't sorry to leave the hospital. She didn't like such places. She had slept badly and wanted to be at home. Liam arrived shortly after ten. They drove back to Castle Darcy in comparative silence. She'd been afraid he might start lecturing her about Bodicote, but he scrupulously avoided the subject. She wondered if either Dr Chang or Sister had told him to keep off it for fear of upsetting her.

The mild turn to the weather had brought numerous wildlife out into the open. There were rabbits on the roadside banks, unperturbed by the passing car as they nibbled dry tussocks of grass and the greener leaves of surviving hedgerow plants. Birds fluttered about the bare twigs above and hopped about on the ground, seeking any hidden bounty among the roots. Cattle and horses had again been turned out into the fields. They passed the two beautiful horses she'd seen before. One black and the other chestnut. They made her think of Black Beauty and the doomed Ginger in Anna Sewell's famous book.

The silence led to a strained atmosphere, nonetheless. Sally took a pocket mirror from her bag and peeped surreptitiously at her pale, tense reflection. Liam, observing her, was moved to try and lighten things.

'Lovely day. Can hardly think it's nearly Christmas.'

'How,' she asked, pushing the mirror back into the bag, 'can I be expected to think about Christmas? I can't think about anything. Life's just a nightmare.'

'You're still feeling iffy. When you get home, go to bed. I'll fix you up some lunch later.'

The new caring Liam was worse than the old grumbling one.

'I don't want lunch, thanks. I don't think I'll ever eat again. You don't have to stay home with me, Liam. I'll manage. It would be best if you went back to Oxford and got some work done.'

He was going to argue but a glance at her frozen profile changed his mind.

'Whatever you want,' he said.

Whatever I want, she thought. When have I ever had or done what I wanted? She'd been brought up to believe that one should not be selfish. Always be willing to accommodate the wishes of others. What that doesn't prepare you for, she thought bitterly, is the selfishness of others. But it was wrong, foolish, to blame her upbringing. She should have realised the flaws in its precepts years ago, ditched them all, and learned to fight for her own corner. Was it too late now?

They were at the outskirts of the village. Liam took the car round a bend and, with an exclamation of alarm followed by an oath, slammed on the brakes.

They squealed to a halt. Sally, propelled forward, was saved by her seatbelt, and by throwing out her hand to grasp the dashboard.

'Look at that!' Liam struck his hand on the steering wheel. 'What the devil is going on here now?'

The road ahead was filled with a motley band of people. Chief among these was Yvonne Goodhusband in slacks, Barbour and trilby hat. Across the Barbour was stretched a sash, in the manner of a beauty queen, only this read 'Organiser'.

Being organised by Yvonne were several followers recognisable as villagers and several who most definitely were not. These tended to be young and rather scruffy. There were a few young mums with bewildered tots in pushchairs. Tristan was there, holding one end of a banner emblazoned A BIRD IN THE OPEN IS WORTH TWO IN A CAGE. The other end of the banner was held in wavering fashion by a cadaverous man with long hair swept back from a receding forehead.

All of these were quite put in the shade by the chicken. It had a large, globular, bright yellow, foam body. Its head, a smaller ball, wobbled uncertainly atop the big yellow ball. Below, it was supported by legs in wrinkly yellow tights and yellow-painted tennis shoes. From the foam ball, through holes, protruded arms in yellow knitted sleeves and gloves which waved in jovial greeting at the car. There was a slit towards the top of the larger ball forming the body through which whoever was inside this curious monster could see where he, or she, was going.

'They've all taken leave of their senses!' gasped Liam.

'No, they haven't,' said Sally, remembering. 'It's the march to the battery unit. Yvonne told me about it.'

On cue, Mrs Goodhusband descended on the car and beamed through the windscreen at its occupants. 'Good morning!' she bawled.

Sally wound down the window. Yvonne came round to crouch by it and address them more moderately through the gap.

'Glad to see you back again, my dear. You do seem to be having a run of bad luck. Quite recovered, I trust? And hullo, there, Dr Caswell! We meet at last. A bit like Stanley and Livingstone, eh?'

'No,' said Liam discouragingly.

She was undeterred. 'We must have our little chat.'

'No,' said Liam again.

'Any time it's convenient. I told your wife!'

'Look here,' said Liam, leaning across his wife to speak to her. 'You're blocking the road. That's an offence.'

'Oh, the police are here, escorting us!' Yvonne indicated a white police car in which two hilarious young constables tried without much success to uphold the gravity of the law.

'Typical,' said Liam in sepulchral tones. 'Tell the police you're being bombed and poisoned and they're not interested. Send a bunch of batty women and unwashed dropouts on a march to a chicken farm, and they turn out in force! Not to protect the householder, mind you! But to protect these lunatics!'

'Don't be so rude, Liam!' Sally told him sharply. 'Anyway the police are going along to make sure the road isn't blocked and the law isn't broken at the chicken farm. That's right, isn't it, Yvonne?'

'Absolutely, my dear.'

'But the road *is* blocked!' howled Liam. 'And those idiot coppers over there in that car are sitting there doing sod all about it!'

'Never fear, Dr Caswell!' said Yvonne encouragingly. 'All will be well! We're moving off now.'

'Thank God!' he said.

Yvonne returned to place herself at the head of her troops. They formed up raggedly behind her, more or less keeping to one side of the road. The banner which had been drooping was raised aloft. Yvonne, the light of true faith in her eyes, and bearing a strong resemblance to the central figure in Delacroix's painting *Liberty Leading the People*, lifted a hand on high, turned and pointed across the fields.

'Wagons roll!' she cried.

'Wagons what?' demanded Liam. 'Don't tell me that woman isn't stark raving bonkers!'

The procession set off, despite Yvonne's heroic gesture, along the road, not across country. As it flowed past, Tristan, gripping one end of the banner, cast the car and its occupants a look of such singular spite that Sally felt a spurt of alarm. They wound their ragged way around a bend in the road and were lost from sight. The police car trailed in the wake, the young constables still in the grip of ill-concealed mirth.

At the cottage, Sally saw her own car in the drive. Someone had brought it back from Bailey's. She'd quite forgotten about it.

Indoors, she sat down in relief. Her legs felt quite wobbly. She supposed that was the aftermath of the hemlock. Liam continued to offer lunch, hot drinks, cold drinks, anything he could think of, and to mooch about unhappily when she refused them all. It occurred to her that their roles had been reversed. Whereas before it had been she who'd run round mothering Liam while he groused and snapped, now he hovered around her while she grew increasingly terse.

For the first time she wondered whether 'smother' had been what she'd done to Liam, rather than 'mother'. But even more than this, she realised that Liam, quite possibly, was frightened. She turned the idea over in her mind. She had, after all, almost died. Had the notion of life without her to run round and cosset him suddenly been presented to Liam in all its stark reality? Or could it be that he did love her, after all?

Much more kindly she said. 'I'm grateful, Liam, honestly. But there's really nothing I need right now. I am rather tired. I didn't sleep very well in the hospital bed. I think I'll go upstairs and have a nap now. Honestly, you might just as well go back to Oxford – or go and start some work here in your study.'

'I've left all my notes at the lab.' He looked less worried, relieved even. 'I'm glad you're going upstairs for a good rest. I'll come back early, try to be here around four, all right?'

She told him it would be fine. He still insisted on waiting until she'd gone upstairs, slipped off her outer clothes and got into bed. At long last, she heard him drive off.

Peace descended on the cottage at last. Sally sighed and relaxed on the pillows. She did feel exhausted. She drifted into sleep.

A little before two o'clock, Constable Barrett called in to Bamford station from the patrol car, parked in a lane just outside Castle Darcy.

'Sergeant? Barrett here.' He paused and snorted. 'Sorry, Sarge, bit of a frog in my throat. The demonstration's all over, broken up, gone home. No problems. That is to say—' He snorted again, quelling the laughter which rose in his throat. 'Except that we've a theft to report.'

The voice at the other end crackled.

'No, not from the chicken farm, sir. They never got on the premises. No, the theft has been reported by one of the demonstrators. A Mrs Beryl Linnacott, she lives in the village. She was on the march, dressed as a – as a –' Barrett struggled, failed, burst out laughing and apologised. 'Sorry, Sarge. But it did look bloody funny. She was dressed as a chicken. You know, sir, in a big foam suit? Well, it got a bit hot on the march, the weather being on the mild side today, and so when they got to the farm, she decided to take it off and—'

At this point, Barrett could manage no more. He thrust the mouthpiece at Constable McIntyre beside him. 'You go on, Mac. I can't!' He collapsed, sobbing with laughter.

McIntyre drew on the self-discipline of his Calvinist forebears. 'Hullo, Sergeant? Gary's got a coughing fit, must be a tickle in the throat.' (Aside, 'Shut up, Gaz, for God's sake!' Muffled wail from Barrett.) 'Hullo, Sarge, you still there?' McIntyre ploughed on determinedly. 'As Gary was saying, this Mrs Linnacott took off the chicken outfit. What? Oh yes, she had clothes on underneath! She wasn't left in her undies. It was because she had all her ordinary clothes on underneath that she got so hot—'

Barrett let out a muffled shriek. McIntyre put down the mouthpiece. 'If you can't keep quiet, Gaz, at least get out of the car!'

The voice crackled and McIntyre resumed his tale. 'She took off the chicken outfit behind a hedge and left it there, meaning to collect it when the demonstration was over. They were messing about outside the farm for about an hour. When they started off home, she went to get the chicken suit and it was gone. Well, I mean, seems clear to me some kids have pinched it for a joke. But she's very upset because she made the thing herself and she's proud of it. She's insisting we get it back. What? Yes, Sergeant.'

McIntyre turned to Barrett who'd regained some sort of sobriety.

'OK, Gary, my son. We're to keep a look-out for a giant chicken. You didn't think you'd be doing that when you joined the police force, did you?'

Barrett collapsed again, weeping with mirth.

Sally awoke at quarter past two, finding that against all expectations, she was now very hungry.

She got out of bed and dressed quickly in jeans and a sweater. The sun was still shining through the tiny bedroom window under the eaves, but with less power than earlier. Already the fine weather was waning, skies clouding over.

She went down to the kitchen to find she couldn't make any of her teas, because all the little pots of herbs had gone. She'd been advised to drink milk. There was milk in the fridge but she didn't fancy it. She opened a bottle of Evian water and drank some of that.

There was similarly little choice with regard to food. She might be hungry, but lacked the energy to prepare anything involving effort. Perhaps she ought to have let Liam stay. But no, it would be a waste of his day.

She slipped two pieces of bread into the toaster, and when they sprang up, spread them thinly with honey and took them into the living room and sat on the sofa to make the modest repast. She turned on the television and caught the three p.m. news update on Channel Two. The reports all seemed remote and of no interest. So what if the United Nations couldn't hold down the troublemakers in some problem corner of the world? The police couldn't find out who had caused her – and Liam – so much trouble in Castle Darcy!

The phone rang. She got up, glad of an excuse to turn off the television. She'd expected the caller to be Liam, but it was Meredith.

'How are you? I rang the hospital and was amazed to hear they'd let you go! Do you need anyone out there with you?' Meredith asked.

'They needed the bed and I didn't want to stay. I don't like hospitals. Thank you for the offer but Liam's coming home early, at four. And thank you again, Meredith, for everything you did the other day.'

They exchanged small talk and she put the phone down. Almost at once, it rang again.

'Sally, Austin here.'

'Oh, Austin!' She was glad of a chance to apologise for giving him such a fright.

'My dear girl, what are you saying? I'm just so very glad you were taken ill at the office and not in your car on some busy road! Are you sure you're all right now? Is Liam there with you?'

'No, but he's coming at four.'

'You're all on your own?' Austin sounded horrified.

'But it's all right, Austin, really.'

She put the phone down again, resumed her seat and finished the toast. Now she'd broken her forty-eight hour fast, she found she was ravenous. She went out to the kitchen, made more toast and opened a can of sliced peaches. It was a funny old meal, but anything would do.

The telephone rang again and this time it was Liam. She told him she was fine, had had a good sleep and eaten lunch. He repeated he'd be back at four.

She'd expected that to be the lot, but it rang again a mere five minutes later.

'Sally dear? Yvonne. I've just got back from our demonstration. I've stood down the troops! It was very successful, I think. Well, a minor hitch but the police are sorting that out. How are you, dear? All alone? Would you like me to jump on my bike and come down and sit with you?'

Sally declined this kind offer. 'You must be exhausted, Yvonne, after all your hard work this morning.'

She put the phone down. It was nice to think so many people

cared. But exhausting. She looked out of the window. A spot of fresh air was called for.

The phone shrilled. She picked it up. 'Hullo?' A click at the other end was the only response as the receiver was replaced. Wrong number, she supposed.

It was strange how much she missed the goats. Sally went to the hedge and looked over. The nannies' hut and Jasper's pen were a sad, deserted record of what once was.

She turned away and walked slowly down to the very bottom of their own long garden. In the spring, she thought, she really would tackle this neglected piece of the property. Last year, supervising the extension to the cottage and turning the barn into a garage had taken up all their time. But next year, in the spring, she'd dig over the ground down here. The fruit bushes were old and wouldn't fruit well, even if tidied up. She'd plant new ones.

Sally spent some minutes happily planning her new soft-fruit garden and then turned to walk back to the cottage.

Half way down the path, between her and the cottage, just by a gnarled old appletree, stood the chicken.

Sally was so startled she let out a short shriek, but then laughed. Yet another one who, returning from the demonstration, had come to see if she was all right. She walked towards the yellow monster.

'Hullo!' she called to it. 'Looking for me? Yvonne rang earlier and said the march went well!'

The chicken made no sound but began to pad down the path towards her. There was something unnerving about its silent approach. It was such a grotesque thing, all yellow like that. Yellow arms and gloves, yellow legs. Only its feet, clad in ubiquitous white trainer shoes, were not yellow.

Something clicked in Sally's brain. Her heart gave a painful lurch and, although she opened her mouth, her throat had closed up and she could make no sound.

The chicken in the procession had been entirely clad in yellow–yellow wrinkled tights thrust into yellow-painted shoes. Not white trainers, no. Yellow shoes. Sally could see them clearly in her mind's eye.

She managed to speak, asking huskily, 'Who are you? What do you want?'

It made no sound. She couldn't tell who was in there. She could see the slit and just make out, she thought, a pair of eyes. Unfriendly eyes. And now she could see that in one yellow-gloved hand, it held a knife.

Sally froze. This couldn't be happening. This must be some lingering effect of the hemlock. She was hallucinating. Drugs, poisons, they did that to you. The thing was monstrous, hideous, yet comical, something got loose from a cartoon book. It was so close now that she could make out the grubby fibres of its nylon fleece, and smell a curious odour emanating from it, compounded of sweat and the sweet, fetid miasma which rose from the depths of clogged ditches. It raised a yellow arm and the knife glinted in the sun. That, at least, was real.

The temporary paralysis which had held Sally motionless was broken. She leapt aside, dodged the forward lunge of the yellow arm and the knife and tried to run past the chicken.

It wheeled and struck out at her again, the tip of the knife actually catching in her sweater. She jerked free and the chicken wobbled uncertainly, bowing and swaying. The foam and nylon outfit was cumbersome. She had momentary advantage.

Sally plunged past it before it could recover, and raced towards the cottage. If she only could lock herself in and call the police. There was nothing else she could do. Bodicote had been her only neighbour and he was gone.

The chicken was lumbering after her at surprising speed. The costume, though awkward, couldn't be heavy. The grotesque pursuit ended at the kitchen door where the creature caught up with her. Sally whirled to face it and grabbed the yellow arm which brandished the knife. The owner of the arm was strong and Sally hadn't thrown off the weakness brought on by the hemlock. She couldn't make the hand release the weapon just by trying to shake it. Instead, she risked pulling the hand and weapon towards her.

Still gripping the wrist of her assailant, Sally doubled under their locked arms as if completing some movement in a country reel. The movement caused a downward thrust on the arm and to prevent losing its grip on the knife, the chicken had to bend – something which in its foam body was not really possible. It staggered wildly. Sally released the wrist and ran behind the creature.

The yellow globe rotated, bringing the wearer round to face her. The smaller ball of a head atop was nodding, loose on its stitching. It bore crudely sketched features, round eyes and smiling mouth. Its grin turned it into a halloween mask of unreasoning, malevolent glee.

But now Sally had the measure of it. Her one advantage was that the person inside the foam body had limited view. So long as she kept dodging behind it, the assailant's mental adjustment remained a fraction behind hers all the time, as the unknown being inside tried to relocate her and reposition itself accordingly. Whoever it was must be getting hot and tired in there. She finally managed to get right behind it as it stood uncertain which way to go. Sally gave it a mighty shove.

The chicken staggered again and, unable to right itself in the globular body, toppled over. The yellow-gloved hand dropped the knife.

Sally pounced on it and grabbed it.

She stood up. The chicken, after rolling in an undignified way on the ground seeking purchase, had managed to get to its feet. It stood a little distance away, watching. It made no move. The assailant could see the knife and knew the tables were turned.

Sally could, she supposed, try and force it to reveal its identity, but that would take time and anything might happen. There might be an accomplice somewhere, she couldn't be sure. All Sally did know for sure was that she had to get out of this village.

She backed away, watched by the silent creature in its yellow suit. The car was out front, but not the keys. The keys were in her shoulder-bag, on the sofa. She fumbled behind her for the latch of the kitchen door, managed to open it, edged backwards through the opening, slammed the door shut and turned the clumsy Chubb key.

For the moment she was safe. Front and back doors locked. All windows shut. Sally ran into the living room and rifled her bag. Her sweating fingers closed on the keys. She looked up as something moved outside the window. It was still out there, casting about. It was looking for another weapon and seeking entry.

Sally realised she was still grasping the knife. Keeping tight hold of it, she went through to Liam's study where the phone was, and dialled 999. Through the window she saw the chicken. It came up close to the glass, trying to see in. It could see her at the phone. For a moment she and the monster faced one another with only the thin glass between them.

Then it moved away. It – she could only think of the assailant as it – surely realised the police would be on their way soon.

Her garbled words into the phone must have made little sense but a reassuring voice at the other end of the line assured her someone would be there soon.

She put the receiver down. Now, where was the chicken? The choice was hers. Stay here or get out with the car keys and escape altogether? Would it be safer to remain inside? Barred in? Waiting for the police? Perhaps her assailant had fled?

Sally peered out of the front windows. Nothing. She went to the kitchen, at the back of the cottage, and peered out of the window there. The garden seemed empty.

She heard a faint click, followed by a creak of wood. Her blood froze in her veins. It wasn't possible. It just wasn't possible!

She turned slowly. The door from the narrow hallway into the kitchen swung open slowly. The chicken stood there – or rather, a frightening mutant creature did.

The enemy had removed the cumbersome body. Now whoever it was wore only the yellow knitted arms and gloves and the football-sized foam head pulled over the person's own head. Two holes had been ripped in the foam to allow the wearer to see in a grotesque sort of ski-mask. Otherwise the person wore jeans and a sweater, much as Sally did. As she'd feared, the unknown had spent the intervening minutes both in remedying the obstacle to its free movement and in searching for a new weapon. It had found one, a shiny new hammer from the garage.

The intruder leapt, swinging the hammer on high, gripped in both hands. It smashed into the kitchen door as Sally ducked. In return, she struck out blindly with the knife.

Chapter Sixteen

Sally was not conscious of having found her target. But she heard a gasp, followed by a low hiss of rage.

The creature staggered back, gripping one yellow knitted sleeve with a yellow-gloved hand. It had dropped the hammer.

Sally didn't wait to find out how severely she'd hurt it. She turned, unlocked the kitchen door and raced out to the car. She threw the knife on to the passenger seat, thrust the key into the ignition with trembling fingers and, lurching and crashing through the gears, drove away from Castle Darcy. Fortunately, she didn't pass through any speed checks on the way.

'I don't like her being out there alone,' Meredith said down the phone. 'She's only just come from the hospital. Honestly, Alan, I could wring Liam's neck. What's he thinking of, just pushing off back to his wretched lab? He's told her he'll be home at four.'

'She probably doesn't want him around,' Alan's voice replied. 'And who can blame her? Do you want me to call her?'

'Could you? I've already rung once and spoken to her and I don't want it to look as if I'm being a busybody.'

'Perish the thought!'

'She's survived two possibly lethal attacks, Alan!' Meredith snapped.

'*Pax*! I know it. I'll call her straight away. If I'm not satisfied, I'll go out there myself, *pronto*. All right?'

* * *

When he'd put down the phone, Markby frowned. He doodled for a moment or two on his notepad. When he realised what he was drawing he saw that it was a row of daisies in pots. Inappropriate, to say the least.

He picked up the phone and dialled Castle Darcy. No one answered. The ringing tone had a forlorn sound to it, as phones seem to have in empty houses. That might be misleading. She might be asleep or gone out for a walk. Yet he put the phone down, deeply dissatisfied.

After a moment he got up and unhooked his jacket. 'I'm going out for an hour, over to Castle Darcy, if anyone wants me!' he informed Pearce on his way out.

'Want me to come along, sir?'

'No.' Markby thought about it. 'Get on to Bamford. They're the local station for Castle Darcy. Ask them, if they've got a patrol car in the area, to go to the Caswells' cottage. It won't do any harm.'

Pearce was picking up the phone as he went out of the room. There was some unwritten law which meant he never got from his office to the main door of the building without being stopped at least twice on the way. This time was no exception. Markby dealt with both delays as quickly as he decently could, and finally ran down the stairs and out into the car park. His sense of urgency heightened by the hold-ups, he drove off without more ado. He did not, therefore, see Pearce, who'd sprinted after him, signalling wildly that he should wait.

What Pearce had wanted to tell him was that, having phoned Bamford as requested, he'd been informed that a patrol car had already been dispatched to Castle Darcy in response to a 999 call.

As it was, Markby discovered this for himself when he arrived at the cottage and found a police car outside. Two uniformed men were searching the area of the garage in desultory fashion.

256

Markby called out to them and introduced himself. 'What's going on?' he demanded.

McIntyre took it upon himself to explain. 'The lady called 999, sir. She was nearly hysterical, by all accounts. The operator wasn't sure she wasn't just drunk or high. She reported being attacked by a chicken. The operator asked her if she really didn't want the RSPCA? Then she said it was a person dressed as a chicken. That's when the operator thought she had a nutter on the line. Anyway, fortunately the operator passed it on to us. We knew straight away it wasn't a joke because the chicken costume was reported stolen earlier. From a Mrs Linnacott.'

Beryl Linnacott, grandma of twins. 'The animal rights group?'

'Yessir. They held a protest march to the chicken farm this morning.'

Markby swore beneath his breath. He looked at the cottage. 'No sign of her?'

'None, sir. We've been right through the house. And down the garden. Both front and back doors were unlocked. There's no car here so she might have driven off somewhere. There is one thing . . . Got that hammer, Gary?'

Barrett produced a hammer wrapped in a sheet of newspaper.

'This was on the kitchen floor. We thought perhaps forensics might look at it. Neither of us can see any blood on it, not with the naked eye. There's damage to the back door. Not outside though, as if someone tried to force a way in. It's inside, as if someone tried to break out. Doesn't seem to make much sense. I mean, the door being unlocked anyway.'

'What about Dr Caswell? Her husband?'

They glanced at one another. 'No sign of anyone else, sir. He should be informed, you mean?'

'Yes. Hang on. I've got his workplace number on me.' Markby hunted through his notebook. 'Here, let him know the bare facts. You were called out. She wasn't here when you got here. Don't mention that – yet.' He indicated the hammer. 'And find the

257

chicken outfit. Whoever wore it couldn't leave the village in it. It has to be discarded somewhere.'

'Not on the property, sir.'

Markby looked towards Bodicote's empty cottage. 'Try next door, in the garden and paddock. There's an empty goat-house.'

While they went to look, he went back to his car and radioed Pearce with the information. 'We have to find her. Try the hospital again and Bailey's auction rooms. She may have gone – or be trying to get – to Meredith. I'll go there.'

'If she's alive,' said Pearce discouragingly.

'We've no body and as yet no evidence of one. No bloodstains, just, so I'm told, a hole on the inside of the back door which I'm about to take a look at.'

It wasn't a hole so much as a sizable dent. The door was unlocked, the key, the same old-fashioned Chubb, was inside. The front door, on the other hand, had a Yale lock. That too, according to the two constables, had been open when they arrived.

There was a shout from the direction of Bodicote's cottage. Barrett was coming towards him, beckoning.

'In the goat-house, just like you said, sir. The body and the feet, that's to say, the yellow shoes which made up the feet. The rest of it, the head and sleeves and gloves are chucked behind a hedge at the bottom of the paddock.'

'Get them all over to forensics,' Markby ordered. 'And tell Inspector Winter, I said so.'

Winter wouldn't like his men being commandeered, but Winter could lump it.

The ring at the door came as Meredith was rinsing out her few lunch dishes. One plate, one mug and a knife, to be precise. She left them on the draining board, wiped her hands on a towel, and went to see who it was.

The door had a frosted glass panel. Through it she could see the outline of a head and shoulders. The head was bulky, as with longish hair. The whole upper-body shape was swaying to and fro in a curious manner and it seemed to her that she could hear, through the glass, laboured breathing. The whole thing was alarming enough to stop her in her tracks.

As she stood irresolutely in the hall, a fist struck the door several times. 'Meredith!' cried a voice, familiar despite being distorted.

Meredith darted to the door and jerked it open. A dishevelled Sally Caswell stood on the step. Her face was streaked with sweat and grime. Strands of wet hair clung to forehead and cheeks. She opened her mouth, but seemed unable to explain her distress. Instead, she raised a hand holding a sharp kitchen knife.

Actions speak louder than words and Meredith's instinct was to slam the door. Sally must have read the message in her face.

She exhibited increased distress, imploring, 'No . . . Meredith! Please, let me in!'

'Put the knife down, Sal,' Meredith did her best to sound reasonable despite the hideous possibilities of what her friend might have done. 'Just drop it on the ground. You don't need it.'

'Knife?' Sally's eyes stared at her in bewilderment. Then she looked down at her own hand and gave a little cry of dismay. 'I didn't realise . . . It's all right . . . I don't know what to do with it.'

'Give it to me, then?' Meredith stretched out a cautious hand. 'Here, I'll take it, like this, fine.'

She detached the knife from Sally's hand easily and stood aside to allow the visitor to enter.

Sally stumbled into the hall and tried to push back her hair. 'I'm sorry . . . I didn't mean. Meredith – someone tried to kill me.'

It took a little while and a glass of brandy to get the story.

'I'll call the police,' Meredith said.

'No!' Sally stretched out a hand to prevent her. 'I've already called them. I called 999. They said they were on their way. But I didn't wait.'

'Then all the more reason for calling them now! If they turned up and found the place deserted like the *Marie Céleste*, they won't know what to make of it.' A thought struck Meredith. 'What about Liam? Should I call him too?'

'Liam?' Sally appeared to find it hard to concentrate on the name. 'Oh, yes, Liam. He said he'd be home at four. I don't want to frighten him.' She spoke the last sentence automatically.

The sensitivity of Liam's feelings wasn't something worrying Meredith. She glanced at her wristwatch.

'I'll call the lab,' she said firmly. 'If he arrives home and you're not there, Sal, he'll worry. It's best I call him first.'

But at the lab, they said Dr Caswell had been in and had left. He was, Meredith supposed, somewhere between Oxford and Castle Darcy. She tried Regional HQ and was told Superintendent Markby wasn't available. She asked for Pearce and told her story to him.

'He's called in,' said Pearce. 'He's been out at the cottage. They're looking for Mrs Caswell. I'll let him know. Keep her there with you, can you, Miss Mitchell?'

That wasn't difficult. Sally clearly had no intention of leaving. She was slumped in the corner of Meredith's sofa, shaking and crying quietly.

'I'll make some tea.' Meredith would have liked to call Dr Pringle. But a suggestion that she did had already been vigorously rejected by Sally.

'They'll take me back to the hospital, and I don't want that! I'm not sick! I was attacked! I can't stand much more of this. I don't know what's out there, Meredith. I only know it hates me!'

To Meredith's relief, Alan arrived some twenty minutes later. Sally was calmer and persuaded to retell her story in a fairly coherent way.

Alan, for his part, supplied what he knew, that the chicken suit had been reported stolen earlier and that remains of it had been found in Bodicote's goat-house. He also had some questions which he put as gently as possible.

'You ran out of the cottage via the back door, the kitchen door, Sally?'

'It was in the kitchen!' Sally's eyes filled with tears. 'I couldn't get past it!'

'Alan . . .' Meredith began anxiously.

He signalled to her to be patient a moment. 'Sally, I don't want to upset you, but there's something I've got to clear up. The front door of the cottage was open when the police car got there. Did you leave it open?'

She shook her head.

'How do you think the person in the chicken suit got into the cottage?'

She leaned forward. 'But that's just it, Alan! It couldn't – but it did! I'd locked the back door. The windows were all shut. The front door was shut on the Yale lock.'

'It must have—' Meredith began, met Alan's eye, and didn't finish what she'd been about to say.

'What about Liam?' Sally mumbled. 'He must have got back to the cottage by now. He won't know what's happened.'

'Police officers are still there. They rang the lab to let him know but it seems he had just left to return home. I expect he's reached Castle Darcy by now. In any event, the officers will wait until he turns up.' Alan studied Sally. 'What do *you* want to do, Mrs Caswell?'

'Stay here,' Sally whispered. 'If Meredith will let me.'

'Of course!' Meredith assured her.

Alan nodded. 'That sounds like a good idea to me.'

'I don't want to go back to Castle Darcy.'

'I don't think you should, not just at the moment.' Alan looked at Meredith. 'Can she stay with you for a while, a few days? I don't know about Liam Caswell.'

The idea of Liam beneath her roof didn't appeal much, but Meredith was prepared to make an heroic effort in the circumstances. It proved not to be necessary.

'I don't want Liam here,' Sally said unexpectedly. 'I can't cope, not with all this and Liam too. I don't want to see him, not just yet.'

Alan caught Meredith's eye and they retired to the hall.

'We'll hope to get a fingerprint from the knife, but if the attacker wore gloves, any prints will probably turn out to be those of Sally herself or yours!' Alan said quietly. 'Clearly it's dangerous out at the cottage and neither of the Caswells ought to be staying out there. Liam may wish to go to a hotel, although that would mean leaving his computer and all his work which he couldn't conveniently move, I suppose. He might not wish to do that. In any case, I'd like her to stay here. She needs the company and support of a friend. Needless to say, I'd appreciate it if you kept a close eye on her and didn't let anyone into the house you might have any doubts about.'

'Does that include Liam?' she asked.

Alan avoided her eye. 'I don't think you can keep him out, if he calls, and she's agreeable. But it's up to her whether she wants to see him. If she doesn't, shut the door in his face. It won't do him any harm.' He hesitated. 'He might make a fuss, I realise that. Think you can manage?'

'Of course I can manage!' she snapped. 'Liam Caswell? One hand tied behind my back! I've been storing up the things I'd like to say to Liam for years!'

Alan had to laugh despite the circumstances. 'Just don't annihilate the poor fellow!'

'Alan?' She lowered her voice. 'Whoever attacked her must have opened the front door. The chicken – I mean, the person in the suit – it had a key. It must have had a key!'

'I had a key yesterday,' Alan said. 'The one Austin keeps. I took it back to Bailey's in the late afternoon. Austin made great show of putting it away in his safe. But previously he kept it in an unlocked drawer. Anyone who walked in his office could have borrowed it for a few hours and got a copy cut in minutes by a shop with the appropriate machinery. Austin wouldn't have missed it. The drawer's full of keys.'

'You think that's what happened?'

He shrugged. 'I don't know. But whatever you do, don't let her out of your sight!'

When he'd left, a rattle of tea-things directed Meredith to the kitchen where she found Sally washing the dishes. Her hands were still trembling, and the crockery was in imminent danger, but the household task seemed to be helping her regain some control.

'I heard,' she said. A cup chinked noisily against its neighbour in the bowl.

Oh well, Meredith thought. It wasn't expensive crockery.

Aloud she asked, 'What Alan and I said in the hall? Alan's right. It's up to you if you want to see Liam or not. It's my house and he can't barge in.'

'I don't want to make any trouble for you.' Sally straightened up, reaching for the tea-towel. Her eyes mirrored her misery. 'But I can't see Liam, not just yet.'

'If you heard what I said to Alan, you'll know I'm spoiling for a fight with Liam.' Meredith grimaced. 'I suppose he is your husband and I oughtn't to say that to you.'

Sally turned her head away. After a moment she said, 'I keep thinking there's something I ought to have told Alan. Not about the chicken. About something else. It is something which happened the day I was rushed off to the hospital. Earlier, as I was driving into Bamford.'

'When you were taken ill,' Meredith reminded her, 'and while we were at the medical centre, you mumbled something about Yvonne and Bodicote. Something Yvonne had said?'

'I've forgotten!' Sally admitted. 'It might come back. Yvonne said how sorry she was about Bodicote. Then something more about all of them being used to that.'

'To what?'

'That's what I can't remember. Oh, by the way, I let your cat in.'

'Cat?'

'Yes, a striped one. It was sitting outside the kitchen door in the yard, mewing very pitifully. I think he ran into the living room.'

Meredith went back to the sitting room. The cat sat before the electric fire, bolt upright with his tail curled round his front paws. He surveyed her with wary yellow eyes.

'Hullo, Tiger, where have you been?' she asked. 'I've been wondering about you.'

He closed his eyes slowly and reopened them.

'All right,' she said. 'You can stay. I'm not going to throw you out.'

He responded with a chirrup and lowered himself stiffly to a crouching position.

Sally came back. 'He is yours, then, is he? I wasn't sure because you've never said you had a cat. Is he all right? I mean, don't take this wrongly, but he's a bit thin.'

'It's all right,' Meredith told her. 'I've got a cupboard full of catfood.'

Liam arrived not much later. Meredith opened the door to find him on the threshold, red in the face and furious.

'What the hell's going on?' He stepped forward as if he expected her to usher him indoors. Finding that instead, she blocked his route, he stopped, momentarily disconcerted. 'Where's my wife? They said she's here!'

'Yes, she is here. She's resting.' Meredith remained blocking the door.

Liam glared at her. 'Well, let me in then!'

'No, sorry, Liam.' Meredith smiled at him serenely. 'It is my house, you know. She's quite all right but she's had a very bad experience.'

'I know that!' Liam yelled. 'The police were at the cottage when I got there! I couldn't make head or tale of their story. Something about a chicken! Turned out they meant that foam creature on the protesters' march! I saw it myself, earlier. I always knew those people were dangerous! Have they arrested her? That barmy woman Goodhusband?'

'Another marcher, a Mrs Linnacott, reported it missing after the demonstration, so it doesn't have to be one of the protesters. We don't know who was wearing it, Liam—' Meredith braced herself for the outburst which must surely follow. 'Sally doesn't want to see you right now.'

'Rubbish!' The shouted word echoed across the street. Liam, as if aware that he could attract unwelcome attention, lowered his voice and went on gruffly, 'She's my wife and I don't know what your game is! All I know is, I want to see her and I don't believe she doesn't want to see me!'

'I'll call you later, Liam, when she's better able to decide what she wants.'

He stared at her, baffled. 'What have you put into her head?' he demanded hoarsely. 'What the devil have you been saying to her? You were always a bad influence on her, from the moment she first met you!'

'What?' It was a turn in the conversation for which Meredith hadn't been prepared. 'What does that mean?' she demanded indignantly.

'What I say. You liberated professional women and your bloody independence! She was perfectly happy as my wife. But every time she'd been hobnobbing with you, she came back behaving as if she'd been at some wretched women's lib meeting!'

'Actually,' Meredith snapped. 'The impression I got was that she was miserable as your wife!'

'What do you know about it?' Liam made as if to push past her, but she was as tall as he was and the resolute look in her eye made him hesitate.

Nevertheless, he'd succeeded in rattling her composure. The question was one she couldn't answer. No outsider, however close, understands exactly all the little nuances of the relationship between husband and wife.

Meredith took refuge in, 'She's told me she doesn't want to see you right now, Liam. I think you ought to respect that.'

'I'm not like your police boyfriend, you know,' Liam retorted. 'Picked up and dropped, picked up and dropped again. I don't play those kind of games. And you can tell her that, from me!'

'And you,' Meredith took up his earlier question, 'know nothing of the relationship between Alan and me!'

'For the last time,' Liam drew in a deep breath. 'Are you going to allow me to see my wife?'

'And for the last time, no. Not just now. She's had a very nasty fright. For goodness sake, Liam!' Meredith burst out in exasperation, 'Can't you understand that? Haven't you got any sympathy for her point of view?'

'What about me?' Liam yelled. 'I've had a number of frights! People have been trying to kill me!'

She gazed at him in wonderment. 'No, they haven't. They've been trying to kill Sally! The person in the chicken suit, the poison in the herbal tea – for all I know, even the parcel bomb was meant for her!'

'I was there, too!' Liam shouted.

'But you didn't open it, did you?' Meredith heard herself say. 'Even though you were there when it arrived. You took very good care not to open the thing! Poor Sal did that!'

There was an ominous silence. Liam's faced had paled to a waxy white. 'Are you saying—' His voice croaked. 'Are you saying that I, in some way for some reason God only knows, tried to harm my wife?'

'Did you?'

She had thought Liam might attack her physically at that point, but instead he put a hand to his beard and rubbed his fingers across it, keeping his gaze fixed on her face.

'You're crazy,' he said at last in a flat voice. 'It's probably your hormones. You single career women are all the same, neurotic as hell.'

'Get lost, Liam!' Meredith abandoned finesse. She slammed the door in his face.

When she went back into the house, she found a stricken Sally standing in the kitchen doorway.

'I'm sorry, Meredith. I shouldn't have put you through that. It's not fair to expect others to fight my battles for me. I should have seen Liam and told him to leave.'

'No, you shouldn't!' Meredith retorted, still in battle mode. 'I'm better equipped, as of this moment in time, to deal with him.' She reflected on the episode. 'Although, I suppose I finished up saying things to him I shouldn't have said.'

'You can say what you like to him,' Sally's voice was more resolute than Meredith had heard in a long time. 'I meant what I said to Alan. I don't want to go back to Castle Darcy while Liam is there. In fact, I don't want to be anywhere Liam is. I don't want to see him today, tomorrow, ever again. We're finished.'

There was a silence. 'I'm glad,' Meredith said at last. 'That's another thing I oughtn't to say. But I'd be lying if I said I didn't think you were doing the right thing.' She shrugged. 'I've never been married and it's a bit rich, urging someone else to quit their marriage. But for crying out loud, Sal, I don't know what Liam needs, but it isn't a wife. A keeper, perhaps.'

Sally walked past her into the sitting room where she sat down again, smoothing her skirt over her knees. 'I'm not walking out on Liam in pique. I'm not just doing it because of what happened today. I could have gone long ago, but I didn't. I hung on, trying to make things work. You see, Aunt Emily brought me up to believe marriage was for ever.'

'Was Auntie Em married herself?' Meredith asked, leaning on the doorframe, arms folded.

'No.' Sally allowed herself a small smile. 'But she had strong ideas about the state of matrimony. I go along with them in essence. I mean, I would stick it out, if I thought things would get better. But they won't. I irritate Liam. I smother him. And sexually, I bore him.'

'He's said so?' Meredith bounced off the doorjamb in indignation.

'No! Calm down, Meredith! But he doesn't have to say so. He's been having affairs for years. That means he's bored with me, right? I think he's had every overseas student at the lab. He thinks I don't know.' Sally grimaced. 'I sometimes think I'm a bit slow on the uptake, but I'm not that daft. I do realise – have realised it for some time. The latest one gave him a really grisly present, a tie-pin like a snake. He's got it hidden in a drawer and thinks I don't know. You should see the horrid thing!' Sally essayed a weak grin.

'For a while I told myself it was only to be expected. It isn't all his fault. After all, Liam is a very attractive man. Of course, those girls, they – they chase after him. I've had to expect that. It's very hard for him to resist all the time.'

Meredith could have disputed this interpretation of things. It was, she suspected, rooted in another of Aunt Emily's articles of faith: namely that Liam Caswell had been a 'catch' and Sally lucky to have captured him. Emily had told her niece this and impressionable, unworldly, nineteen-year-old Sally had believed it. She'd continued to believe it though Liam had proved a faithless husband and a self-centred bully. He remained a distinguished man in his chosen field, good-looking and, though desired by other women, he was her husband. It had consoled her for his infidelities. Even now, she still clung to it like a child who cannot face the dark without a particular soft toy, even though that toy may have long been reduced to a bundle of rags.

Sally was gearing herself up to further revelations. 'I'm going to go into partnership with Austin.'

'What!' That came as a shock. But perhaps it shouldn't. Sally had gone from Aunt Emily's house to a husband's bed. She'd never faced the world alone and couldn't envisage it, even now. She needed an alternative safety-net.

'I mean a business partnership,' Sally urged. 'Not any other kind. That is, Austin would like another sort of partnership as well. But I'm not ready for that. It's going to take me a while to get over Liam. I couldn't commit myself to another close physical relationship yet. But the business, yes. I've gone through all the figures with Austin. It's a good investment. And I'm interested in it. I like the work. I'll be there full-time and learn more about the whole thing. It's a whole new future for me and I'm looking forward to it.'

'Does – Have you told Liam about this, going into business with Austin?' Meredith asked the question slowly.

Sally's confident manner faltered. 'No. He doesn't know. I didn't want to say anything till I was sure. He won't like it. But now, it doesn't matter if he likes it or not.' She regained her confidence and smiled brightly at Meredith. 'Does it?'

Chapter Seventeen

Markby stepped out of Meredith's house into the street and found himself beneath the fitful glimmer of the lamplight. The inky blue dusk which had been the backdrop to his arrival was fast deepening into night, a winter evening well set in. Even so, it was only – he glanced at his wristwatch – twenty past four.

He went first to Bamford police station. Winter greeted him with a certain amount of embarrassment.

'To think those two numbskulls went through that cottage and saw all those books and just didn't bother to report it! They thought the old man might have been a bit odd!' Winter snarled.

'No denying he was odd,' Markby pointed out.

Winter fidgeted about and said. 'About his death. I've gone through it all again with a toothcomb, all the evidence we presented to the coroner, the autopsy report, the lot. There was nothing which could allow us to argue for suspicious circumstances.' He paused. 'If it was rigged, it was bloody well rigged.'

'Yes, it was. I haven't come to talk about Bodicote. I've come to ask a favour. This knife . . .' Markby produced the article in a paper bag borrowed from Meredith. 'It's important evidence in an attack on Mrs Caswell. I need it sent over to forensics at once. I'm not going back to regional HQ at the moment. I've – I've got another call to pay. Could you take care of it?'

Winter brightened, glad of a chance to restore confidence in his organisation. 'I'll send a car over with it at once. Got anything to send with it?'

'I've scribbled a few notes.' Markby proffered torn-out sheets from his notebook.

The knife in safe hands, Markby drove out of town. At the junction where he had to turn left if he wanted to go to Oxford, he hesitated. There was no car behind him. He sat for a moment in thought, until a flash of yellow light from the mirror dazzled him. Headlights were coming up behind him and forced a decision. He turned the car towards Oxford.

He headed for the laboratories and made it just in time. In the reception building, the guardsman was putting together her belongings prior to departure for the day. She wasn't best pleased to see him.

'Dr Caswell has left.' Her manner indicated that Liam, persecuted beyond endurance, had sought sanctuary elsewhere. Emigrated, even.

'I know. I really want to see Miss Müller, one of the post-graduate students, if possible and she hasn't gone home yet.'

'No.'

'Not gone home yet?'

'No, you can't see her. It's not possible.' She swept up a jumble of papers and thrust them into a steel filing-cabinet drawer which she shut with unnecessary vigour and locked. 'Miss Müller didn't come in today.'

'Oh, why is that?'

The woman receptionist delivered what she no doubt hoped was a definite rebuff. 'I believe she's feeling unwell. She phoned in first thing. She will have had one of her heads, poor child.'

'Which head might that be?' Markby asked politely.

'I can assure you, Superintendent, that migraine is no laughing matter!' She bristled and glared at him.

'Believe me, I wasn't laughing. Migraine, I know, is very distressing. Can I have her home address?'

She was deeply shocked. 'Most certainly not! I would never give out the address of one of our single women – to a man!'

Markby smiled at her. 'Most commendable. But I am a policeman, and that's a little different. My wish to see Miss Müller is in connection with an inquiry.'

She was the type of defender who is killed at his or her post. 'You can't visit her now. She's ill with the migraine. I've just told you. You surely don't intend to bother the poor young woman when she's on her sickbed?'

'Look, Mrs—' Markby consulted the nameplate perched on her desk. 'Mrs Worral, that's for me to decide. All I want from you is her address. Now, please.'

She conceded defeat with a last swipe. 'I don't like this. I shall report it in the morning to Dr Caswell. It's highly irregular.' She waited to see if this last-ditch threat might sway him. It didn't. She sighed again, re-opened one of the filing-cabinet drawers and took out a folder. After a quick search through it, she found what she needed and scribbled an address on a notepad.

'Here you are.' She tore it off with a flourish and handed it over. 'But if, despite all I've told you, you're intending to call on her tonight, it's rather *late*, isn't it? Even for police work?' There was a definite nasty note in the last question. She had him down as one of Those Men who preyed on young women.

'A police officer,' said Markby, 'can never be sure he'll pack up at the end of the day when the clock reaches five.'

Despite herself, she glanced at the clock, and flushed.

'Well, it's nice to know,' she said primly, 'that our police force is always on watch!'

'Like Cerberus,' he said, 'the force has many heads and one of them is always awake. Oh, by the way, you won't go phoning Miss Müller and warning her I'm on my way, will you? I'd rather you didn't. That's an official request, by the way.'

The look she gave him was indescribable.

* * *

The house was another of Oxford's many red-brick Victorian villas. Like numerous others, far too large for a modern family, it had been converted to multiple occupancy. Markby, standing outside beneath the streetlight, checked the address and looked up at the bay-windowed frontage. He'd parked around the corner and approached on foot to avoid announcing his arrival. He couldn't, in any case, have parked before the building. All kerb space was taken up by other cars, including a venerable lime-green Mini. The windows in the front of the house were lit, including the basement's. Those were uncurtained and he could see a young man lying on a divan. Earphones were clamped to his head, his eyes were shut and he was clicking his fingers.

Hopefully, Marita Müller was also alone. A row of bells by the front door was matched by a row of namecards.

Markby pressed 'Müller'.

For a while nothing happened and then a window was pushed up above his head. He stepped back, out of the porch and looked up.

Marita Müller's mane of russet hair appeared over the ledge. She peered down suspiciously at him.

'Good evening, Miss Müller!' he called.

'The police,' she returned, investing the words with total scorn. 'You were the one who came to the laboratory. What do you want?'

'Five minutes. Just a talk with you. Can I come in?'

'I am in my bath.'

'No, you're not,' said Markby reasonably. 'You're leaning out of the window.'

'Pig!' she retorted and slammed down the window.

Shortly afterwards, feet pattered towards the door which was inched open. Her voice issued through the crack. 'You can talk to me here.'

'Fine!' Markby said loudly. 'It's about Dr Liam Caswell!'

The door flew open and revealed Marita clad in an emerald

274

green kimono which enhanced the colour of her eyes. He wondered whether the old green Mini also belonged to her.

'You can come in,' she said discouragingly. 'But five minutes only. You said five minutes. I am getting ready to go out.'

He followed her up the stair to the first floor. On the way he noticed that whoever had converted the house into flats had been free with muddy-hued linoleum and brown paint.

Marita's flat provided instant contrast to this dull entry. It blazed with colour. The furniture was mostly elderly. But soft furnishings had been draped with bright Indian print shawls and wooden furniture had been painted white. Scarlet, green and orange cushions were scattered everywhere. Across one wall stretched a mural, an abstract, in the same brilliant colours. A gas-fire burned pale flames. The combined effect hurt his eyes. He blinked.

'What do you want to say about Dr Caswell?'

He brought his gaze back to the defiant figure in the green robe which stood in the middle of the colourful room, arms folded. She put him in mind of an exotic bird in a tropical garden.

'Mrs Worral, the receptionist at the laboratory, told me you'd phoned in sick with a migraine. You say you're getting ready to go out?'

'It is better. Migraine is like that. It comes and it goes.' She shrugged. The wide kimono sleeve slipped revealing the edge of a bandage.

'And you've hurt your arm, too! My, you are having a run of bad luck,' Markby consoled her.

'You said you wanted to talk about Liam.'

'Liam now, is it? Not Dr Caswell? But you must know him fairly well, after all, working with him. He's had some bad luck recently too. So has his wife. She's had another bad experience today but you'll be glad to know she's all right and staying with a friend.'

Marita hunched her shoulders. 'So? They're staying with

friends! I'm really not interested. Should I be?'

'No, not both of them. Only Mrs Caswell. Dr Caswell is still at Castle Darcy, on his own. How did you hurt your arm?'

She hissed at him. 'It's not your business! I cut it – in the lab. I dropped some glass slides.'

'Really? Difficult to cut your arm like that, I should have thought. Cut your hand, perhaps. Not upper forearm.'

The green eyes glittered. 'What is it you want? You said five minutes. Already two minutes are gone. Now you have three.'

Markby seated himself uninvited on one of the white painted chairs, ignoring her signs of increased annoyance.

'I understand you're one of the post-graduate students taking part in a regular exchange scheme? What is your home university?'

She set her mouth in a straight line, squeezing out the name, 'Jena!'

'Oh? Really? In the former DDR?'

She gave him a pitying look. 'Times have changed, you know. Germany is one Germany again, now.'

'So Jena, that's not your home town, then?'

She shifted her stance and tugged at the kimono sleeve. 'I don't have what you'd call a home town.'

Markby smiled at her. 'To be without real roots is a pity. Are both your parents German? This room—' He indicated the décor around them. 'It makes me think of a hot climate, bright colours, Latin rhythms.'

She thought before she decided to answer. 'My mother was from Cuba, a singer. She studied in the DDR.' Although Markby had pronounced these letters in the English fashion, she pronounced them *day-day-air*. 'She met my father there and married him.'

'Really? And did she never go home again, to Cuba?'

'Yes, she went back to Cuba. We all moved there when I was a small child. My father was an agricultural chemist. He worked in

Cuba until my mother died and then he brought me back to Europe again.'

'How old were you then?'

'I was seven.' She was growing restive. 'My life isn't interesting to you.'

'But it is. Did you know, I wonder, that Dr Caswell's wife is a very wealthy woman?'

She blinked, disconcerted by the jump in the conversation and frowned. Obligingly, he repeated the sentence.

'Yes, I understand!' she snapped. 'But it still has nothing to do with me. I suppose she's lucky to be rich. I don't know.'

'Some people might say Dr Caswell was lucky. When he was an impecunious young doctor, he married a wealthy young woman. Now, some years later, just at a time when, possibly, much of her original fortune has been spent, she's inherited a second fortune from an elderly aunt.'

The green eyes narrowed. 'This is not important to me. Why do you insist on telling me these things?'

'I think it's very important to you, Marita,' he said.

She studied him, then without warning, smiled serenely. 'I know what you mean to say by all this. But you're wrong. I respect Dr Caswell. He is a famous man, you know, in his own special field. I like him, too, very much. I think he likes me. It's not a crime, I think, not even in England. But I'm not some silly romantic kid. I don't expect him to leave his wife for me.'

'Indeed, you're not. You're a highly intelligent and, I imagine, hard-headed young woman. It must be quite a culture shock to someone brought up under the old East German regime, suddenly to be in a Western consumer society. A little like Ali Baba when he found himself in the robbers' cave. Do you know that old story?'

'I know it.' Her voice was filled with scorn. 'It's a story for children.'

'Not only for children. Those old tales are about human nature.

277

Ali Baba found himself surrounded by riches and felt he was entitled to help himself, arguing, no doubt, that the goods were ill-gotten anyway. But there was a snag. In his case, forty of them. Do you remember the end of the story, Marita? The faithful Morgana killed all the thieves with boiling oil. When I was a kid, it puzzled me that no one tried to return the thieves' booty to its original owners. Wasn't Ali Baba also a thief? Now I know why. The human conscience is highly adaptable to circumstance.'

As he spoke, a succession of reactions had gleamed in her eyes: anger, suspicion, dislike, caution. Now the eyes were cold, the extraordinary green iris glittering like the frost of recent early mornings.

She caught at the edge of the kimono sleeve and tugged it well down over her bandaged arm. 'I know this much about England and how you do things here. I don't have to let you stay here in my flat, Policeman, and I don't have to talk to you or listen to your tales of the Arabian Nights. You have your five minutes all finished. Goodbye.'

He rose to his feet. 'Thank you for the five minutes, Marita. I'm sure it's been interesting for us both.'

He got out while the going was good.

He went back to his car around the corner and sat reviewing matters in his head. He was jerked from his reverie by the rattle of an elderly engine. The lime-green Mini shot out of the street, across his bows, turned left and buzzed away like a demented maybug.

Markby reached for the radio, praying Pearce was still at regional headquarters. He was.

'Dave? I think I've startled a hare. The girl, Marita. She's just driven off like a bat out of hell. I think she'll be making for Castle Darcy. I kindly let her know Liam is there alone. I'm following. Get hold of Prescott if he's still there and meet me out at the village.'

278

* * *

The minor road out to Castle Darcy was little used at this time of the evening. Markby's headlights swept through the darkness and picked up the place name. A moment later, another set of headlights was switched on, flashed once, and darkened again. They pinpointed a stationary car on the other side of the road, parked on to the grass beneath some trees. Markby pulled over to join it and got out.

Pearce and Prescott emerged from the other car and came to meet him. Prescott produced a torch.

'The girl's just arrived,' Pearce said. 'We only just got here in time. She scooted up in the Mini and let herself into the cottage. Front door. Caswell must've given her a key. Bit daft of him. I'd have expected a brainy bloke like that to have more common sense!'

'Not the same thing, Dave.'

Guided by Prescott's torch the three police officers walked along the dark country road until they reached the pair of cottages. Bodicote's was abandoned to the night, but lights gleamed behind the downstairs windows of the Caswell cottage. The Mini was parked just past the cottage in the gateway to a field.

'Right, time to disturb the lovebirds. I'll go to the front and you keep a watch at the back. She may make a run for it.'

Markby walked up the path and knocked at the cottage door. A curtain twitched at a window. There was a delay and Markby thought he caught the mutter of voices. Then Caswell's voice called out, 'Who is it?'

'Superintendent Markby!' As if you don't know! thought Markby. 'Like to talk to you, Dr Caswell.'

'Just a moment!'

There was some movement behind the door and a rustle. Liam opened the door fractionally and peered through. 'Oh, it is you. Well, come in then.'

He stood back to allow Markby to squeeze past. At the same moment there was a female shriek from outside the cottage and the sound of some vigorous disturbance.

'What—?' Liam started forward.

Pearce and Prescott appeared round the side of the cottage, bearing the struggling Marita between them.

'Making a run for it, like you said, sir.'

'Ah, Miss Müller,' said Markby genially. 'Join us, won't you?'

He didn't understand the words, but was fairly sure she was swearing at him.

It was a curious party. Liam and Marita sat rigidly side by side on the sofa, careful to avoid touching. Markby sat at apparent ease in an armchair. Pearce sat thumbing through his notebook and Prescott lounged bulkily by the door.

'This is a high-handed intrusion into my home!' Liam announced. 'And I shall want an explanation for it! You don't have a warrant I'm sure!'

'Don't need one, Dr Caswell. You invited me in!'

'I can throw you out again, too! Even though you've stationed your thug there blocking the door.'

Prescott looked mildly offended.

'You can certainly request us to leave and return when we have a warrant, but I don't advise it, Dr Caswell. Best to get the air cleared now, don't you think?'

The girl said, 'You are Fascist pigs!' She rubbed her arms. 'You have hurt me. I shall complain!'

'Sorry, dear,' said the amiable Prescott from the door. 'Didn't realise you had a bandaged arm.'

She scowled.

'Keep quiet, Marita, and leave it to me!' Liam instructed her. 'Now then, Superintendent. As it happens, I agree with you. It's best to clear the air now. I understand you went to see Miss Müller here and frightened her. She's from that part of Germany which was formerly the German Democratic Republic. A visit from a policeman is more alarming to her than you might realise. Old memories die hard. She is alone in this country and didn't know where to turn for advice. So she came to me, the person in charge of her department at the laboratories. Quite understandable in the circumstances, I think?'

'Letting herself in with her own key,' Pearce said.

'Ah—' Liam fell silent, chewing his lip. 'I gave her a key a while ago so that she could come and fetch some papers for me, one day in the laboratory when I was busy. I forgot she hadn't returned it.' He turned to her. 'That's right, isn't it, Marita?'

'Yes!' she said woodenly.

'A great pity,' Markby observed, 'that you didn't remember about it when I specifically asked you who had access to your cottage. When I requested a key so that I could come out here and check the layout, I was directed to Austin Bailey. Why didn't you think of Marita's key then?'

'I've told you what happened,' Liam said. 'Being a copper, you'll try and twist it, no doubt. But that's what happened.'

'If we're going to tell fairy stories,' said Markby. 'Why don't I tell one? Miss Müller knows I'm interested in old tales. It might make good listening.'

'I doubt it,' Liam told him.

Marita raised her hand and made a circular motion by her temple. 'His story will be as crazy as he is!'

Markby smiled cheerfully. 'All the same, let's see how it goes – or I think it goes. A handsome and successful research scientist and a beautiful young student begin an affair. It's not a criminal offence so we won't argue about it. I doubt very much that when it began, however, the scientist quite realised what a redoubtable young woman she was.' Markby turned his gaze to meet Marita's fierce green eyes. She stared back with disdain and made another circular movement of her forefinger.

'The scientist is famous but his work has not been financially well rewarded. He is dependent on the money brought to the marriage by his wife, who had inherited a considerable estate from her father. But he has tired of his wife. The money's almost all spent and he has begun to think that perhaps he can now leave her and set up with his new love. But then, his wife inherits a second fortune. No question now of leaving her and forfeiting a share in the money and the comfortable lifestyle it would provide! Nor does his new love fancy domestic bliss in a small flat. She has had a glimpse of better things. So he and his girlfriend hatch a plan. A callous plan which will remove the wife – but leave him in possession of her fortune. I gather there are no other surviving members of Mrs Caswell's family? You and she have made mutually beneficial wills?'

Liam, his voice trembling, said, 'This is outrageous!'

'I agree. It gets more so. They get an idea. A year ago animal rights extremists targeted the lab. Why not, then, use this to cover any attack now on the wife? What's more, the young woman announces she can rig up an explosive package! I don't know about your father being engaged on agricultural projects in Cuba, Miss Müller. I fancy he may have been in weapons research! However . . .

'The package is posted to arrive while the scientist is away in Norwich. Only, due to an unforeseen cancellation of plans, he doesn't go to Norwich and is here when it arrives. He's able, however, to make sure his wife opens it. Incidentally, it's addressed simply to "Caswell", just in case the postwoman remembers.

'But the wife isn't killed. The scientist realises he's been very foolish and put himself in a dangerous situation – and in the hands of a very dangerous partner.' Markby nodded at Marita.

'But he's got the tiger by the tail, as the saying goes. He can't cut loose. Their original plan has failed. But they haven't given up, or at least, the young woman hasn't given up and the scientist, having let the djinn out of the bottle, can't do much about it.

'One or other of them has been tampering with the herbal teas drunk by the wife for some time, experimentally. So far, all they've done is make her feel off-colour. Incidentally, they must have collected the flowers, leaves and seedheads back in the summer, which shows premeditation.

'When the old man next door dies, they have a new opportunity. The chance to tamper seriously with some tea given to the wife by him. After all, he's dead and can't deny the charge. Sooner or later the wife will drink the tea and, with luck, have some kind of accident whilst drugged, perhaps in her car. The plan fails because the wife's friend takes her immediately to a medical centre. The conspirators are getting desperate. The scientist is possibly too frightened by now to act, but the mistress is made of sterner stuff and not afraid to take a risk. He has told her that his wife has returned to the cottage and is there alone. The mistress realises she has a not-to-be repeated opportunity. She arms herself with a knife and sets out for Castle Darcy.

'By the time she gets there she's realised that she needs to formulate some plan in case she's seen. But luck is with her. She arrives in the village to find a demonstration taking place just outside it, at a battery chicken farm. People are taking part in it who don't look like villagers and she will be just one more stranger if she associates herself with it. She lurks about the fringes of it and sees the grotesque chicken figure retire behind a hedge and divest itself of its costume. The mistress slips behind the hedge and makes off with the disguise. She may have intended to use her key to gain entry to the cottage, but in the event, it's not necessary because the wife emerges and begins to stroll down the long, secluded garden. It couldn't be better and the disguised mistress attacks.'

Markby shook his head. 'But she fails again. The wife escapes and in her hand, she's holding the knife which the attacker wielded but was forced to drop. The attacker was careful to wear gloves and probably thinks there won't be any fingerprints.

However, Mrs Caswell remembers striking out with it at her assailant. She doesn't know whether she inflicted any damage. However, if the assailant was wounded by that knife . . .'

Marita's fingers strayed towards her bandaged arm and were snatched back.

'Then quite possibly there will be traces of blood on the blade. Perhaps sufficient to give a DNA fingerprint which will tell us the identity of the person struck.'

The room was quiet. Liam sat expressionless. Marita said in a high, uncertain voice, 'I don't believe you.'

'I've just arranged for the knife to be sent over for forensic examination. We may require a blood sample of you, Miss Müller.'

'I shall refuse.'

'Why should you do that?'

Before Marita could reply, Liam said, 'Be quiet, Marita. You shouldn't answer questions without a lawyer present.' To Markby he added, 'Miss Müller is a student on my exchange programme. I'm responsible for her. I cannot allow you to question her in such a way that she may say something which could be misunderstood. This whole thing is a tissue of fantastic speculation. You are trying to use Miss Müller to give it some credibility.'

'All right,' Markby told him. 'Let's turn to the husband's actions. Following the attack, the thing the husband fears most happens. His wife has fled to her friend's house and declines to return to their home. She may seek a divorce. He isn't sure how much she knows about his adulterous affairs over the years. But any competent inquiry agent could get the information for her. Moreover his general treatment of her has been intolerable, as several people have witnessed. He has little hope of emerging from the divorce with anything but a couple of suitcases. He will have to move heaven and earth to get her back or the money will slip out of his hands for ever. And it is the money which matters, isn't it? If necessary, the scientist is more than willing to dump his mistress. The world's full of pretty girls, but few of them bring a fortune with them.'

Marita's manner had changed. The anger had faded in her green eyes, to be replaced by a more thoughtful look. She leaned her head against the sofa cushions, but the air of relaxation was deceptive, Markby was sure.

'This – every word of it – is absolute nonsense!' Liam was breathing heavily. 'Of course, the danger to me and to my wife comes from extremists! I received anonymous threatening mail!'

'So you said. But you didn't report it and your wife didn't see it. You didn't even mention it to her until after the explosive package.'

'But I received others, a crazy letter from Yvonne Good-husband and another cut-and-paste letter which was anonymous, you saw it yourself!'

'Oh, yes. I think you made the cut-and-paste one yourself, Dr Caswell, and got Marita to post it in London.'

Liam rose slowly to his feet, almost unable to speak with emotion. 'You cannot prove a word of this preposterous tale. You certainly can't prove that I had any part in it!'

He clutched his head. 'All right, I know I've been stupid! I admit it – I flirted with Miss Müller and she may have misunderstood my attachment to her. But I certainly never plotted with her or anyone else to harm my wife. I wouldn't ever do such a thing. I *love* my wife, Superintendent. I realise that your girlfriend has persuaded her to leave me temporarily, but I assure you, I shall leave no stone unturned until I get Sally back!'

Marita turned her head to look up at him.

'As for Miss Müller,' Liam hurried on. 'I know very little about her background. It's possible – as you have described – that she took it into her head to try and kill my wife, believing that if Sally were dead, I would enter into some kind of permanent relation-ship with her. But I assure you, that was never my intention and I never suggested to her—'

285

'You bastard!' Marita snatched a small bronze ornament from a table by the sofa end, and leaped at him.

It took three of them to pull her off, by which time she'd succeeded in inflicting considerable if superficial injury to Liam, scratching his face, and gashing his brow with the bronze horse.

'I think,' Markby said, panting, to Pearce, 'that you'd better take the young lady with you, Inspector!'

Still putting up vigorous resistance and swearing in several languages, Marita was escorted away by Pearce and Prescott.

Liam who'd sought remedy for his injury in the bathroom, returned, holding a facecloth to his damaged forehead. A thin trail of blood had run down one side of his nose and into his beard.

'The girl's crazy!' He seemed genuinely shocked. 'She's mentally ill! You saw how she went for me! What more proof do you want?' He glared at Markby beneath the impromptu dressing.

'Proof of what?' Markby asked him.

Liam blinked. 'Of what you were saying, that she tried to kill Sally! You were telling the truth, were you, about that knife? There could be Marita's blood on it?'

'Examination of it will tell. I'm hopeful.'

Liam ran his tongue over his lower lip, his face a picture of fear. 'For God's sake, I didn't know what she was up to! I thought it was all the animal rights people! They sent me abusive mail! I know I didn't report it but you can't prove I didn't get it! As for the one I gave you, you're mad if you think I pasted it up myself! I bloody didn't! It just turned up in the post, promising to "get me". A grubby, illiterate little threat from some grubby and illiterate hooligan!'

There was a ring of true grievance in his voice.

It was enough to cause a flicker of doubt in Markby's mind. 'I'll get my proof. At the very least, I think you realised what Marita was up to, as soon as that explosive package arrived! And you went along with her plans. Although, for my money, you were in on it from the start!'

286

The fear had faded from Liam's face. 'You—' he jabbed a finger at Markby, 'are as crazy as that Müller female! I'm phoning my lawyer, right now! Gerald Plowright. He's in London. Stay there! The phone's in my study!'

He burst out. Markby followed to the door and stood listening from the hall as Liam engaged in agitated conversation on the telephone. In due course, Liam reappeared, still clasping his brow with the blood-stained facecloth, but otherwise in control.

'Gerald, my solicitor, advises that I should say nothing until he gets here, which won't be until tomorrow. He'd like a word with you, Superintendent.'

Markby walked past him and picked up the phone. 'Superintendent Markby.'

'Gerald Plowright here,' said a smoothly efficient voice at the other end. 'My client has given me a résumé of what's occurred. I have advised Dr Caswell to say nothing more to the police until I arrive. Unfortunately that can't now be before tomorrow morning. In the meantime, should you have any idea of taking Dr Caswell into custody, I must strongly object. You cannot question him now until I arrive, and you certainly cannot claim that he is likely to abscond. He is a distinguished scientist with an international reputation and not a petty criminal. He is, he assures me, entirely innocent of any misdoing and most anxious to clear his name. And, of course, to restore the harmony of his marriage.'

'We have detained his mistress,' Markby said. 'I think she'll talk.'

Plowright uttered a sound of worldly dismissal. 'Pah! Come, come, Superintendent. The fantasies of an hysterical young woman?' He paused to lend weight to his next words. 'A *foreign* young woman, at that? Hardly grounds for holding Dr Caswell in detention overnight.'

Markby managed to keep his voice even. 'You'll appreciate, Mr Plowright, that we're talking of a serious crime, attempted murder.'

287

Plowright pounced, verbally at least. 'It is serious, I agree! Dr Caswell is reeling – reeling, Superintendent – from the knowledge that this young woman tried to kill his wife! What's more, she attacked him, I understand? In the presence of the police! Clearly, she's unhinged. Have you other evidence against my client, aside from the demented ramblings of this girl?' Into Plowright's oiled tones crept a hint of the hand of steel within the velvet glove. 'I hope I shan't have to apply for a writ of *habeas corpus*?'

'I have no clear evidence at the moment,' Markby admitted.

'Then I suggest I meet you with my client at your office at, let us say, eleven tomorrow morning?'

Markby set down the receiver. Liam was waiting in the hallway. He took the facecloth from the gash and inspected it in a mirror. 'This will leave a scar. She's mad. You want to get a psychiatrist to her!'

'I will see you tomorrow at eleven, together with Mr Plowright, in my office!' Markby growled.

Liam quitted the mirror and went to the front door. 'Right! Gerald will sort this out, you'll see! Goodnight, Superintendent!'

Markby walked down the path reflecting, not for the first time in his career, that those who could afford expensive legal advice stood an excellent chance of manipulating the system to their advantage.

'But they are not,' he muttered, 'going to run rings round me!'

Stopping them doing so, however, might be difficult.

Chapter Eighteen

Markby stepped from the light of the Caswell cottage into the blackness of a country night. Not that Castle Darcy was completely without street-lighting. But such as it was, it was a quarter of a mile along the road where the main collection of buildings was sited.

This fact reminded him that Castle Darcy had a pub, The Traveller's Rest, which had a good reputation. During the summer months it was the focus of a popular evening excursion from Bamford. Pearce and Prescott had already departed with Marita. He felt, after all that had taken place, in need of a pint. Instead of following in their wake, he turned his footsteps towards the village.

He soon began to wonder, as he picked his way over the verge and along the unlit country road, whether he wouldn't have done better to have used the car. A twisted ankle would just about round off this day. The walk wasn't lonely. At night, in the country, one is never alone. There is another world all around which only comes to life as the sun goes down. Ahead he could see a dull glimmer of light which hovered over the village and the pub to which he cautiously wended his way. Far across the fields to his left he could make out pinpricks of light which were probably the battery egg-layer units, source of so much concern to Yvonne Goodhusband and her friends.

In such circumstances, one's own senses become sharpened. Hearing is more acute, so that when something fell or jumped into the water at the bottom of a wayside ditch, the tiny splash was magnified on the night air and Markby nearly jumped out of his skin. His nostrils, no longer stifled by traffic fumes, caught a whiff of disturbed stagnant ooze, a powerful rottenness.

His feet crunched on the road surface as if he walked in seven-league boots. Once, pausing to look across at the chicken farm, he thought he heard an echoing crunch and turned his head. Something moved in the gloom beneath the trees but all around was other movement. Odd rustlings in the hedgerows accompanied him and the chill wind rattled the bare branches of the trees above. Despite himself, he quickened his pace, hurrying instinctively towards the comfort of the glow of light ahead, heedless now of the danger of tripping.

The pub appeared out of the darkness like a brightly lit liner out at sea, full of life and noise. He pushed his way through the door into the warm interior, a place of low, blackened oak beams and uneven plaster. There were few people in the bar tonight. It was early, he realised. The place had only just opened up for business. He bought his pint and leaned on the bar to talk to the landlord, a burly man with heavy shoulder muscle turning to fat. A bell rang in Markby's memory.

'Expect to be busy later on?' He wondered if the same stirring of memory troubled the other man.

'Might be.' Mine host wiped down the bar in slow motion. His hands, extremely hairy on the backs, were like shovels. Markby glanced up at the licence pinned above the bar. It informed him that Moses Lee was permitted to sell beers and spirits. There was another notice informing the customers that the pub was part of a network which kept its members informed of trouble-makers' identities. Banned from one pub, you were banned from them all. It was unlikely that Mr Lee got much trouble in his pub. Not with forearms like that.

'Provided it don't turn frosty again,' pronounced that gentleman. 'Summertime we get a load of visitors. In winter, the road puts people off. They think it'll be dangerous driving back to town, no lights and the surface tricky. Council never does any gritting on our road.'

Markby picked up on this grievance. 'They probably don't realise how many drivers use it.'

The landlord agreed. A raddled blonde in a skin-tight dress unsuited to her figure and years appeared at the other end of the bar. Her eyes, ice-sharp, raked Markby and he knew he might as well have the word 'police' hanging above his head in neon letters, rather as Moses Lee had his licence to trade hanging above his.

'Give the gent another on the house, Moses!' she ordered huskily.

Mr Lee was built like a baron of beef, but clearly his fair helpmeet ran the pub.

'Please,' said Markby. 'I appreciate it, but another time, if I may. I'm driving.' He turned his attention back to Moses. 'Village has grown in size, I expect, over the last few years.'

The landlord agreed again, but with a new access of caution. It had grown somewhat but they'd been spared any new housing estates. 'We don't want to happen to us what happened to Cherton. You can't see the old village there now. Just surrounded by the new houses. Terrible.'

'A lot of people are looking for homes in a village like Castle Darcy, unspoilt,' Markby went on. 'A friend of a friend of mine brought a place out here somewhere. Name of Caswell.'

The expression on the landlord's battered features became increasingly wary. 'That'll be out of the village, back on the road to Bamford. Coupla cottages standing by themselves. They bought one of them.'

'You know the Caswells, then?'

'I know about *him*.' The landlord chuckled but choked the laugh off mid-way. 'I know his wife to exchange the time of day. Seen her down the village shop. Nice-looking woman and very pleasant.'

'I've often thought I'd like to buy a place somewhere like this. No other cottages for sale that you know of?'

The landlord leaned on the wooden bar, which creaked beneath his weight, and surveyed Markby as if judging his suitability to be a resident of Castle Darcy. 'Old feller died recently, right next door to the Caswells, Old Hector Bodicote. He was a village character. His place might go on the market. Mind you, you'd need to spend a small fortune on it, doing it up. Old Hector never did anything to it. I'm not saying the family will sell. Maybe one of them might come and live in it. His niece farms over Westerfield way, but I heard her son's thinking of getting married. He might take the place on.'

More people came into the bar and the man abandoned Markby, who drained the last of his pint and pushed his way out of the warm interior into the chill of the night again. He retraced his steps.

As before, he was aware of leaving light and company behind him and venturing forth into a more primitive world. And as before, he hadn't gone far when he fancied his ear caught the rattle of footsteps dogging his own.

'This,' he told himself, 'is pure imagination!' He began to whistle softly to himself and strode out, resolutely blocking his ears to any faint scrape and scuffle behind him.

He passed Liam's cottage and wondered what he was doing now. Back on the phone to Gerald Plowright, probably, hatching up tomorrow's strategy.

Markby almost walked into own car, barely able to make it out where he'd left it. He unlocked the door and slid into the seat with undeniable feelings of relief. Inside the car was warm, slightly stuffy, and reassuring. As he reached for the ignition, however, he got the fright of the night.

A hand tapped on the window, right by his ear.

Markby let out a muffled curse, nearly dropped the key, and raised a startled gaze. What he saw caused him to swear more loudly and struggle with an alarm rooted less in surprise than in something much older and atavistic.

A face peered in, surrounded by long, tangled hair, its expression urgent. It was hard not to believe for a moment he hadn't been approached by some nocturnal woodland deity. However, Markby realised, after the first initial jolt, that it was human. A tramp? No, there was something familiar about it. The hand rose again from the gloom outside and rapped on the window more loudly. The being's mouth formed, 'Hullo!' and he faintly heard the word through the glass. It was Tristan Goodhusband.

Markby let down the window. 'What do you want?' he snapped. It was bad enough to have been given a fright. After the frustrating interview with Liam and suffering the bland but determined words of Gerald Plowright, Markby felt that just now, the last person he could be bothered with, was Tristan.

'To talk. Sorry if I made you jump.' Tristan, in apologetic mode, was probably as rare an apparition as any Green Man. He appeared uncharacteristically unsure.

'Did you follow me down to the pub and back?' Markby demanded.

'Yes. I wanted to see where you were going,' Tristan was frank about it, at least. Even more frankly, he went on, 'When you went into the pub, I didn't go in after you because I didn't want to be seen hobnobbing with the police. Besides, I steer clear of Moses and his old lady. Private matter. I didn't know what you wanted in there. I reckoned you were making inquiries. Then you started off back again and I thought I wouldn't get a better opportunity to talk to you on your own, without letting everyone know about it. Fact is—' he hesitated. 'Perhaps I should have had a word with you before this.'

Markby sighed and leaned across the front passenger seat to unlock the far door. Tristan walked round the car and got in beside him.

'All right,' Markby said. 'What's it all about?'

Now he was in the car, Tristan seemed more certain of himself. 'I was walking by the cottage earlier this evening. I saw Caswell's tart drive up and later on, your men. So I hung about and then you came. They took her away!' Tristan grinned. 'She put up a hell of a fight. It took the two of them to get her into the car! She kicked one of them in the crotch, the big burly chap.'

Markby wasted no time on sympathy for the luckless Prescott.

'You call her Caswell's tart, so I presume you know of an affair between them?' His dislike of Tristan was increasing. But he'd long suspected the young man knew more than he cared to tell. If this was the moment he'd decided to impart some of his knowledge, Markby would listen, especially if it was about Liam.

'Whole village knows about it,' said Tristan. 'As soon as Mrs Caswell drives out of one end of Castle Darcy to go to work, the girl drives in the other end and they're at it all day until just before Mrs Caswell gets back. The girl always leaves in time. Once or twice, mind you, Mrs Caswell nearly caught them. People in Castle Darcy like Mrs Caswell, so no one's ever mentioned it. Not wanting to upset her, you see.'

Little wonder, thought Markby, that Liam's book had been making slow progress! He grunted. It was always the way that people knew more than they let on. For whatever reason, in this case a mistaken sense of decency and kindness, they'd kept knowledge of Liam's extra-marital affair to themselves. If just one person had spoken of it to the police when inquiries had begun into the explosive package, they'd have got on to Marita at once.

'Will you get him?' Tristan asked.

'Caswell? Get him for what?'

'I don't know. For sending that dodgy package, maybe.'

'What do you know about that?' Markby snapped.

'I know it wasn't sent by any animal rights group. I'd have heard about it on the grapevine. Everyone in any branch of the movement has been talking about it. No one knows a thing about who sent it. It's upset a lot of people, our more respectable sympathisers especially, which is bad for us. We don't operate in that way, but mud sticks. We've been getting the blame for something we haven't done. Word has it, even the extremists are miffed. Not that they've any objection to letter-bombs. But they're usually quick enough to brag about any stunt they pull off. Now someone's stolen their thunder.'

Tristan shrugged. 'So, if none of us sent it, it has to be someone else. If his wife hadn't been the one to open it, I might have thought she'd done it. Found out about the girlfriend, perhaps, and decided to send him a farewell present in every sense of the word! But as she was the one who got caught in the blast of the thing going off, it had to have been him or the foreign bird.'

'You could,' Markby said with barely concealed anger, 'have told me this before! To have been assured it hadn't originated in the animal rights movement would have saved us a lot of wasted time on inquiries.'

'Sure I could have told you. And you'd have believed me?' Tristan laughed. 'Course you wouldn't! As soon as it happened, your heavies were round to Mick Whelan's, leaning on him. I didn't like that.' Tristan's humour evaporated. 'Mick's a sick man. If I'd had any ideas about helping you, I forgot them once I saw you were leaning on Mick.'

'No one leaned on him. Inspector Pearce is actually quite concerned about the man's health. But go on.' Markby tapped his hand on the steering wheel.

'Keep your hair on!' advised Tristan. 'Listen, I want you to understand why I – I took the line I did.'

'By line,' growled Markby. 'I take it you mean withholding information pertaining to a crime?'

Tristan grew angry. 'I'm trying to tell you, all right? But if you're going to take that attitude, stuff it! I don't feel kindly towards the police. Why should I? I've been grabbed by the boys in blue any number of times and slung in a van, duffed up on the quiet – and don't say no copper ever does that sort of thing, I've had the bruises! I've been charged with public order offences, all that kind of crap. Why should I help the police? No reason at all. Don't give me any good citizen bilge. I make up my own mind what's right for me. The animal rights movement is right for me. I'm still not quite sure I want to help you now.'

Markby asked suddenly, 'Did you send a cut-and-paste threatening letter to Dr Caswell? It arrived the same morning as a letter from your mother.'

Tristan hesitated. 'All right, yes I did. Only the once! I didn't send him any others. It was more a joke, really. Mum was writing him one of her oh-so-reasonable invitations to talk through his problem with her! I thought, what the hell. Let's give the guy a bit of a fright. So I made up my own letter, glued up bits of newsprint. I've been travelling around the country, from demo to demo. I was passing through London, so I stuck it in a postbox there, just to confuse the trail.' Tristan looked surprised. 'That's funny?'

'No,' Markby suppressed a moment of wry humour. So Liam, after falsely claiming to have received threatening mail had actually received such an anonymous letter! No wonder Markby had sensed the fear in Liam when Caswell had brought both letters to him! Matters had been slipping more and more out of Liam's control.

Tristan had interpreted the stifled chuckle. 'You don't like him, either, do you? You'd really like to get Caswell, if you could. Am I right?'

Markby didn't reply. His silence was taken for assent.

'Thought so.' Tristan's belligerence had faded. 'My mother's out at a meeting tonight. Over at Beryl Linnacott's. Thank God someone stole that chicken suit. Old Beryl looked a complete nutter in it. Made people laugh at us and I kept telling her so. It might get us publicity and pictures in the papers, but who wants that sort of publicity? Like we'd all escaped from the local asylum? Anyway, there's no one at home. I've got something I'd like you to see. I can't really explain it. I can only show you.'

The Tithe Barn stood dark and deserted. The cats were grey shadows prowling through the dark undergrowth. One emerged to twine itself round Markby's legs as Tristan hunted for his key. Markby's heart gave another hop. He'd finish a nervous wreck at this rate.

Tristan let them both in and led the way upstairs to a self-contained flat.

'My place. My mother, she's a good sort, but she's over-powering. If I'm to live at home, I have to have my own space.'

Markby looked around. Basically, the flat was a large bed-sitting room with an ensuite bathroom and a small kitchen unit in one corner. As a rent-free dwelling, it was very comfortable.

'I don't cook or anything,' Tristan had noticed Markby's appraisal of the facilities. 'I eat with my mother. But I make coffee and so on. Want a cup?'

'No, thank you.' Markby sat down. 'I haven't time to waste, Mr Goodhusband. Whatever it is, just show me or tell me or whatever it is you want to do.'

'Right.' Tristan went to a cupboard and returned holding a camcorder. 'Just watch the TV screen over there.' He busied himself setting up the camcorder to run the film.

'I took this early one morning. I was on my way back over the fields. I'd – I'd been over to the egg-units, trying to get some film of the interior of the chickenhouses. I didn't, as it happens, the alarm system went off. So don't think you can dream up some charge of breaking and entering.'

Tristan paused. 'There's a right of way over the fields, it runs behind the pair of cottages where Caswell lives and old Bodicote lived. I rather liked old Bodicote with all his faults. He was nuts, of course, definitely a weirdo, in fact a D.O.M. But it was all genuine, not faked. A real eccentric.'

'D.O.M?' Markby was slow on the uptake.

'Dirty Old Man. Our local Peeping Tom. Didn't anyone tell you that? Suppose they wouldn't. The villagers are clannish. Them against the outside world. He was well known was old Hector, for creeping up and peering through your windows or snooping on courting couples. In fact, I had a bone to pick with him myself. I think he was spying on me and – and a girl the other evening. She spotted him in the bushes and let out a squawk. He scarpered pretty quick so I didn't catch him. But I thought, if I ran into him in the village, I'd let him know I was on to him.

'Anyhow, I was on the other side of the hedge to the goat-house that morning when I heard the nannies kicking up a dickens of a fuss. That made me curious and as I wanted a word with the old chap anyway, as I told you, I parted the hedge and peered through. I saw—' He stopped.

Markby leaned forward, 'Go on. What did you see?'

'I saw something I'll never forget.' The bluster had gone from Tristan. 'And I filmed it. Watch.'

The camcorder whirred softly into action. On the TV screen appeared a jumble of images, resolving into a spray of hedgerow. It was followed by a shot of the corner of the goat-house and then—

Markby drew a sharp breath as Bodicote's sprawled body appeared on the screen, but lying on its back, not – as Meredith had found it – on its stomach. A figure appeared to the left of the screen and stooped over Bodicote. Liam Caswell. Liam caught at the old man's shoulders and heaved the body over. With a sick feeling in his stomach, Markby realised that he was watching the final stages of a murder.

Liam arranged his lifeless victim with painstaking care, taking his time. The calm orderliness of the way he treated the body, as if it had been no more than a first-aid dummy, was more chilling to see than any act of violence itself. Only once did Liam seem to suspect any other presence and it called up the single moment of emotion. He lifted his head and looked up briefly towards the hedge, suspicion in every line of his tensed frame.

'Nearly caught me then,' said Tristan. 'I ducked down and held my breath. I've often thought, since then, that if he'd caught me, he'd have killed me, no doubt about it. It was a close shave.'

Liam, satisfied he was still unobserved, relaxed and continued to pose the body as he wished it. He pushed the lump of rubble with his foot until Bodicote's wounded head rested against it. Then he stood up, surveyed his handiwork and gave a little nod. He turned and went out of the frame. The film continued to focus on Bodicote for a few minutes and then abruptly ended.

In the ensuing silence, Tristan sat, with the camcorder on his knees, watching Markby.

'You – had – this—' Markby said very quietly. 'And you said nothing about it? You deliberately suppressed evidence of the most serious crime which can be committed against the person?' His voice had been rising in volume as he spoke.

'No!' Tristan defended himself. 'I didn't suppress it. Haven't suppressed it, you've just seen it, haven't you? I didn't make any decision about it. I wasn't in any state to! For Chrissake, I was in shock! It's not the sort of thing you expect to stumble on during an early morning walk in the country. I didn't know what to do with the film.'

'You didn't—?' Words almost failed Markby. 'There was no question what you should do with it! You should have brought it to the police at once!'

'The old man was dead!' Tristan shouted. 'After Caswell had left the scene, I nipped through the hedge and took a look for myself. He wasn't breathing! I couldn't bring him back to life! You couldn't expect me to make up my mind there and then. I brought the camcorder back home here and ran the film several times. Each time made me realise more what a weapon it was. I wanted to make the best use of it. I had Caswell in the palm of my hand with it! I'd never get another chance like this one.'

'Blackmail? You intended blackmail?' Markby half rose from his chair.

'No! Not in the way you mean! I wasn't after money! I worked out that, if I kept it, and if in the future Caswell's laboratories started up their foul animal experiments again, I could use it to make Caswell stop. If I gave it to the police, they'd arrest Caswell, but someone else would take on his work! I wanted to be able to stop Caswell's animal research projects! Maybe that isn't what seems most important to you, but it was what seemed most important to me!'

A married woman grabs at her baby; an unmarried one reaches for her jewel-box. The quotation had been Markby's own response when Bodicote had referred to a question of priorities. It wasn't so simple. The line between altruism and selfishness, thought Markby now wryly, was thinner than might be supposed.

'What matters to me,' he told Tristan, 'is justice for an old man.'

Tristan was silent.

'What changed your mind about showing me this?' Markby nodded at the blank TV screen. 'Since you seem to have decided to keep it and use it for your own purposes, something must have caused you to do a U-turn.'

Looking down, Tristan mumbled. 'When Mrs Caswell was taken to hospital and Caswell started telling everyone Bodicote had tried to poison her, I realised that he meant to kill her, too, to kill his wife. I put two and two together, the letter-bomb and the poisoned tea. The man was a killer and I was crazy to keep the evidence to myself. I knew then I had to show you the film. But I'd put myself in a bit of a fix, not showing it to you at once, I knew how you'd react. So I dithered a while, if you like. But I've shown it to you now.'

Tristan looked up. 'So you can get him, can't you? That is, it won't show he was trying to kill his wife. I don't know what evidence you've got on that. But he killed old Bodicote, didn't he? He's not going to talk himself out of that one, is he?'

'No,' Markby said. 'And neither are you going to talk yourself out of your extraordinary behaviour in withholding evidence which would have solved all this from the outset. You knew that no one in the animal rights movement was claiming responsibility for the letter-bomb. You knew that Caswell's mistress regularly visited the cottage. You knew that Bodicote was a Peeping Tom and probably spied on Caswell and the girl. Finally, you filmed this—' He indicated the screen. 'From start to finish, you knew. You might even, had you come forward earlier, have saved the old man's life.'

'Bloody ingratitude!' Tristan seemed more resigned than angry. 'But it's what I expected. You can't oppose the coppers and you can't help them. No wonder the police have got an image problem.'

He tossed back his long hair and fixed Markby with a sententious gaze.

He had succeeded, for the moment at least, in reducing the superintendent to silence.

Chapter Nineteen

'My client,' said Gerald Plowright, 'would like to amend his earlier statement.'

It was two in the afternoon and a great deal had happened since Liam had arrived with Mr Plowright, as arranged, at eleven.

Faced with the camcorder film, Liam had been frightened but defiant. 'So? I lost my nerve! I mean, I found him like it. I thought I'd get the blame, so I – I arranged him a bit. He was dead!'

'Found him like what, Dr Caswell?'

'Lying on the ground. He'd fallen, bashed his head.'

'So there was no need to rearrange him.'

'I just improved a bit. I know it's not the done thing. Like improving the lay in golf.'

'Improving,' said Markby with open disgust, 'is what you're doing now to your story.'

'Look here!' began Liam but was summarily ordered to silence by Mr Plowright.

Plowright's attitude towards his client had perceptibly altered during the day, as had his own manner. The film had rattled the solicitor. From smug and confident, he'd become terse and tetchy. From time to time, he darted impatient glares at Caswell. Liam had, to use a popular phrase, 'dropped Gerald in it'.

Hence, thought Markby, the announcement of a revised statement.

'A complete statement this time?' he asked.

'Yes!' yelled Liam. 'I didn't know about the letter-bomb. I didn't know Marita had made the thing. It was all her doing! I would never have tinkered with anything so damn dangerous! When it arrived, that morning, and went off, I thought, I really believed, it had been sent by extremists, probably the same ones who had broken into the lab last year! After all, I'd been receiving abusive letters—'

Markby stared at him. Even now, after all this, Liam was still insisting he had received the phantom hate mail. That niggle of doubt which had assailed Markby throughout made itself felt again.

'You destroyed them, you say. You said nothing of them to anyone. Dr Caswell, I have only your word for it that you received any.'

Liam leaned forward, his jaw thrust out pugnaciously. 'I got 'em! I tore them up in disgust! They were vile – said things about my book! I wasn't going to show the things to anyone!'

'About the tampering with your wife's herbal teas,' Markby switched tack.

'Don't know—'

'I should tell you that the girl is talking her head off.'

'Unreliable witness!' interpolated Mr Plowright.

Markby was irresistibly reminded of a television courtroom drama, an early Perry Mason, perhaps. 'Objection!' 'Sustained!'

'She couldn't have done it without your help and connivance, Dr Caswell.'

'I was influenced,' said Liam baldly, staring at the opposite wall. 'I was completely under her spell.' His gaze lowered and met Markby's. 'She's that sort of girl, Marita. She's hypnotic, like a snake. She's got a thing about snakes, too. She gave me some jewellery, a pin, and she'd got a matching necklace herself. It gave me the creeps. Made me think of human sacrifice.'

'Made you think of murder?'

'I was only talking of Marita's taste in trinkets!'

'My client,' resumed Plowright, his protuberant eyes moist with candour, 'is a scientist, a practical man. He was defenceless against the wiles of Miss Müller. Putty in her hands, Superintendent. She subjected him to the most astute emotional blackmail.'

'Marita did it all!' mumbled Liam. 'I don't know about these things! You can't expect me to have controlled someone like Marita. You can't blame me. I didn't make a bomb! I didn't dress up as a chicken—' He groaned and clasped his head. 'I didn't know what she was going to do next! But I couldn't stop her!'

Markby had his man and knew it. 'To get back to the teas,' he began remorselessly. 'Who collected the hemlock and where? I notice it grows profusely around Castle Darcy.'

Mr Plowright settled in his chair. This was going to be a very long day.

'So that's it,' said Sally. 'Funny sort of feeling, knowing that your husband and his latest fancy bit have been trying to bump you off.'

'You must try and put it all behind you, Sal,' advised Meredith, replenishing the gin and tonics.

For one who had been such a modest tippler, Sally was taking to the odd dram with alarming ease. Meredith resolved to keep an eye on this development. For the moment, however, Sally needed a stiffener or two. Now that Liam had started talking, the revelations coming from both him and his mistress promised to keep the tabloids happy for weeks when the matter came to trial.

'Enough for several blockbuster novels,' Alan had said. 'From Marita alone. All about her affair with Liam, about plotting to send the package – still saying Liam knew about it, by the way – tampering with Sally's own tea and with Bodicote's herbal blend. Dressing up in the chicken suit. Hell hath no fury like a woman scorned! Or left to carry the blame, whichever it may be.'

'Just you remember that!' Meredith had advised him. 'Was there blood on that knife?'

'A little, probably not enough for our purposes. Fortunately there were more stains outside the cottage and we found the chicken mask and gloves, hidden on Bodicote's land. They were both blood-stained. Marita must have bled quite a bit, giving us good samples. She folded in the face of the DNA evidence. A research scientist herself, she knew what it meant.'

'Of course you must have Aunt Emily's chairs and cupboard,' Sally urged. 'I'm really very grateful, Meredith, for your support right through this. Rushing me off to the medical centre when I was poisoned and taking me in as you did after that horrible business of the chicken. I still have nightmares about that thing.'

'Glad to help, Sal. But you must let me pay for the chairs. I don't think, sadly, that after all, I've room for the cupboard too. This is a very small house.'

There was a pause while they both glanced critically around Meredith's tiny sitting room.

'I certainly shan't let you pay for them!' Sally declared. 'It'll be nice to know they have a new home where they're appreciated. I remember auntie dusting and wax-polishing them. To have watched them go through Austin's salerooms would have been much harder to bear.'

'Well, thanks again. I will look after them, I promise, although any polish in this house is sprayed from a can. How is Austin, by the way?'

'Being very sweet. We're definitely going into business, but I've had to explain that marriage is out for the moment. Austin says he'll wait. He's inclined to be old-fashioned in romantic matters. Not that I mind.' Sally gazed meditatively into her gin. 'I suppose I have to carry my share of the blame for everything that happened. I should have divorced Liam years ago. I knew in my heart he was no good. Couldn't bring myself to admit it aloud.'

'Sal!' Meredith yelped. 'You can't excuse what he did on the grounds you didn't leave the man!'

Sally looked up, her frank features unusually guilty. 'Meredith? I did do something really nasty.'

'You? Find it hard to believe.'

'I find it difficult to credit that I did it. It wasn't the sort of thing I'd ever done before. I can only put it down to being under a lot of stress! Well, I know now they were tampering with my tea, but even so, I'd really had it, up to here!' Sally gestured with her hand held flat to indicate the limit of her tolerance.

'And?' Meredith was curious and a little apprehensive.

'I just focused on Liam's book. It seemed to represent everything which was wrong with our marriage. His work, his obsession with the research, all those affairs which were with nubile lab assistants, so tied in, do you see? I – I made up some cut-and-paste letters, saying awful things about his book. A couple of mornings when Liam thought I'd gone to Bailey and Bailey's, I'd hopped on the London train and posted the things so they'd have a London frank. I just wanted to tell him how I felt. But I couldn't. So I did it in the letters, anonymously.'

Sally bit her lower lip. 'He never said a word about them. I knew he'd had them. I saw them come in the post. Until the morning of the letter-bomb, then he told me about them. So I had to mention them to Alan. I mean, I had to say Liam had told me about them. But do you think, now all this has turned out the way it has, I ought to tell Alan the truth? That I sent Liam the poison pen letters? Not the one which came the same time as Yvonne's letter. But the other, earlier ones?'

'Yes,' said Meredith faintly. 'I think you ought to tell him.'

'It floored me,' Meredith said.

'You? It knocked the wind completely out of my sails! I was so sure the fellow had invented the letters!'

All around them, the buzz of voices, laughter and the chink of glassware and cutlery on china indicated a busy Saturday night at The Old Coaching Inn. Its particular ambiance of chintziness and Olde Englishery was unchanged. However, its former manager, Simon French, had departed to even greater glories, it was said, in the Surrey stockbroker belt. Meredith rather missed his brash presence. But if French hadn't left, there was no way Alan would have been persuaded to come here tonight.

'Compared with everything else, it was harmless enough,' Meredith defended her friend. 'And she was suffering both emotional stress and herbal poisoning.'

'No one's going to charge her with anything. There's no evidence, anyway. Liam destroyed the letters. But it was a dangerous thing to do and it wasn't without effect! It gave Liam and Marita the idea to send a letter-bomb! After all, one bit of abusive mail can lead to another! Liam's shifted his ground, by the way. His story about finding Bodicote dead has changed. He now says Bodicote was blackmailing him. There was a quarrel and he thought Bodicote was going to attack him. He, Liam, picked up the rock to defend himself. Bodicote came at him and he lashed out.'

'Liam must be barmy,' she said. 'If he thinks a jury will buy that.'

The Hungarian-style chicken was very good and she had got her appetite back. The flu was now a distant memory. Monday would see her back on Bamford station at the crack of dawn waiting with all the other glum commuters. Rush-hour on the London underground. A new week in the office and a brimming in-tray. Back to work. Back to life. Marvellous.

'Not clinically,' Alan objected. 'He won't pull any diminished responsibility plea!'

'I mean barmy to think he could get away with it, with all of it. All those affairs with leggy students. His wife had to twig sooner or later. Dicing with fate in the shape of the supercharged Marita. As for murdering poor old Bodicote—' Meredith picked up her wine glass. 'That was a foul, cowardly thing to do. Can he prove he paid Bodicote money?'

'No, that's a weak point in his present defence. But Plowright is working on it.'

'So why did Liam kill him? What harm could he have done?'

'From Liam's point of view, he could have done a lot. "Poor old Bodicote", as you call him, was actually rather an unpleasant old man. He was a book thief on a grand scale. He was a voyeur. A Peeping Tom. It's a nasty little habit whatever the circumstances. In Bodicote's case, it also proved fatal.'

Into Alan's voice crept a resigned despair. 'And they all knew! The whole damn village! He crept up on couples snogging in cars or doing what comes naturally under the hedgerows of a summer evening. He peeped in cottage windows and lurked about while young women pinned their undies to the washing line. He was an absolute and thoroughgoing pest. But would one of them mention it to Gwyneth Jones when she was making inquiries about him, after his death? Oh, no. They talked about his family, about their distant schoolday memories of him, about his expert knowledge of goat-care. But about his sneaky little habits? Not a word. Because he was, when all was said and done, a local. One of themselves. The nearest anyone came to it was when Yvonne mentioned to Sally that Bodicote wandered about but that they "had all got used to it". Poor Sally, drugged, realised nevertheless that whatever it was the village had got used to, the police might like to know of it. But in her confusion, she lost it, and only really remembered the other day.'

'Speak no ill of the dead,' Meredith suggested. 'That still holds good in old-fashioned societies.'

Alan swallowed a mouthful of steak and reached for the wine bottle to top up their glasses. 'You know what bugs me most? The old chap more or less confessed it to me! During our conversation that night, after the explosive package had arrived at the Caswells', I asked what he'd done on hearing the explosion. He told me that first of all, he ran down to check on Jasper. The next thing he did was go through into the Caswell's garden, approach their cottage from the rear, listen to Liam and Sally arguing in the kitchen and then go and peer through Liam's study window. I should have realised the old man had done that sort of thing many times. Liam himself even complained to us that the old man snooped. Or take the way Bodicote described Liam's computer to me. *That machine of his was switched on, with writing all over it, like a telly . . .* That's not the description of a computer-literate man. But it *is* the description of a man who'd seen Liam's computer before and could describe it. Bodicote had surely never been invited into Liam's study. No, he'd seen it through the window.'

'And through one of the windows, I suppose,' Meredith mused, 'he also saw Liam and Marita?'

Markby chuckled. 'And how! "At it!" in the apt phrase of Tristan Goodhusband! Completely carried away, with a gawping Bodicote, nose pressed to the windowpane, as spectator. Marita tells us they caught him several times. They chased him off.

'Bodicote knew, as the whole village knew, about Marita. Bodicote, like the other villagers, liked Sally and didn't want to upset her so had said nothing. In addition, of course, he was coy of calling attention to his own activities, spying on Liam and his mistress. But Bodicote, unlike the other villagers, had another, private, battle with Liam – over the goats. On one of the occasions when Liam and Marita had caught him ogling them, there was an exchange of abuse. Bodicote shouted words which were a threat – or construed by Marita and Liam as a threat – to tell Sally what was going on. Liam, knowing that Bodicote dearly wanted the Caswells to quit the cottage, was afraid he'd do just what he threatened. Marita now claims Liam told her not to worry about Bodicote tipping off Sally. He'd take care of it. Take care of it, he did.'

Markby's face and voice had grown sombre. 'I had a gut feeling that set-up was all wrong. The old fellow laid out like it.

The cap turned downwards, his head pointing towards the goat-house.'

'There was another thing, too,' Meredith said. 'When I took Jasper back through the gap in the hedge, the old bedhead blocking it had fallen on to Bodicote's land. But if Jasper had pushed at it from Bodicote's side, surely it would have fallen on to the Caswell's side? Liam must have propped it back on returning home, but at the wrong angle and not very securely. It fell down on its own.'

Alan sighed, crumbling a piece of bread into a heap of crumbs. 'I did see that and I can confess to you now, it put me wrong. I was too clever for my own good. The bedhead having fallen down on Bodicote's side seemed just too obvious. I thought, if anyone had killed Bodicote, then perhaps that person had tried to throw suspicion on Liam by making it look as if someone had come through from the Caswell side. Liam's continual rows with Bodicote must have been well known, making him a near-perfect fallguy. But it was as you say. Liam jammed it hastily back into place after going through the gap. Pushing it into the hedge from his side, it leaned towards Bodicote's ground. It's a heavy thing. It just toppled under its own weight and a little later, Jasper wandered through.'

'By the way,' Meredith asked him. 'What's happened to Jasper? Bodicote was very fond of him.'

'Mrs Sutton's got him. She farms and has plenty of grazing. She didn't want to keep the nannies and has sold them on, but she's kept Jasper for old time's sake.'

'I'm glad,' Meredith told him. 'I've been a bit worried about Jasper.'

The waiter came to take their plates, promising prompt arrival of that moment of truth – the dessert trolley.

'You know,' Alan said. 'In that conversation with Bodicote, the old fellow also told me something which, later, ought to have suggested how he died. Every morning, first thing, he went down

311

and let out the goats. But Jasper was let out first because Jasper kicked up merry hell until he was freed from his overnight pen. Bodicote told Libby, the postwoman, about it. Everyone knew. When Bodicote heard the explosion, the first thing he did was run down to check on Jasper. Because, as you say, Jasper was a friend and if you think a friend might be in trouble, you drop everything and run.'

Across the room, Meredith could see the dessert trolley wending its way towards them, groaning with cholesterol. She fought her own inclination to run.

'Liam knew it, too. On the morning of his death, Bodicote got up as always and went down to the goats. He let out Jasper. Then he went into the nannies' house. Liam was lurking nearby. He caught Jasper – which actually wasn't necessarily difficult. Jasper was curious by nature and could be tempted to approach. Liam picked up the rock Bodicote used to prop open the door – he'd pinched that from Liam, so Liam probably thought it sweet revenge! Then Liam did something to make Jasper bleat out in distress.

'Bodicote wouldn't have thought twice. He'd have abandoned the nannies and come running out of their house without a moment's hesitation. Liam was waiting. Afterwards he tried to be clever by making it look as if Bodicote had been walking towards the goat-house when he stumbled and fell – or was butted by Jasper.'

The trolley had arrived but Meredith was silent. 'Madam?' asked the waiter.

'Could you come back?' she asked. 'In a couple of minutes?'

'Life goes on,' Alan prompted gently. 'Don't let this put you off your food.'

'I'm not put off. Wish I was in a way!' She grimaced. 'I lost a few pounds with the flu but I'm putting it all back on again.'

'You look just fine!' he told her loyally.

'Thank you, kind sir! It's just that, thinking about that arrogant blighter, Liam, ties my stomach in knots.'

'He is arrogant. You described it to me. His brilliance, the nature of his research work, the adoration of all those female students, all contrived to encourage him to think there was nothing, but nothing, he wasn't entitled to do if he saw fit. The idea he might go to gaol, even now, doesn't register with him. He is, as he sees it, too important. A man not like others! He still thinks he's going to get off, with a little help from Mr Plowright.'

Alan snorted. 'Not if I have anything to do with it! The old Greeks had a word for it, *hubris*. The gods up on Olympus kept an eye open for any mortal who got ideas that he could do as he wished with impunity. That was the prerogative of the gods themselves and any human who tried it, got reminded in no uncertain way he was only mortal! A touch of mortality is what Liam's personality lacks.'

'And Tristan? Will he be charged with anything?'

'Oh, him,' said Markby. 'He's been let off with a lecture. He did come across with the vital evidence. Still, no harm in giving him a fright.'

'He's had a few frights,' Meredith observed. 'Bodicote spying on him and his girl in the bushes. Finding Liam crouched over the body.'

'Oh yes, the girl. It seems she's the daughter of the local pub landlord and he's rumbled what's going on. Tristan is currently terrified of leaving home. Serve him right! Any man who presumes to take advantage of Moses Lee's daughter must need his head examined. He used to be a prize fighter, you know.'

'Mr Lee? Isn't that illegal?'

'Course it's illegal. That's how I know about it. We busted up a secret "mill" when I was at Bamford, years ago. Moses was the star turn. Big money changing hands. Blood everywhere. Moses has reformed since, with age. But still, not a man to annoy.'

'Poor Tristan! Got to feel a bit sorry for him.'

'You know,' Alan reflected, 'Tristan said to me that "it wasn't

313

the sort of thing you expect to stumble on during an early morning walk in the country!" But Bodicote would have had the answer to that.'

Alan leaned back in his chair and quoted, 'It is my belief, Watson, founded upon my experience, that the lowest and vilest alleys of London do not present a more dreadful record of sin than does the smiling and beautiful countryside.'

'*Copper Beeches*,' said Meredith.

'Ah! Another Sherlockian!'

She rested her chin in her hands. 'We don't need dessert, do we? Shall we have coffee back at my place?'